The Descent

Kara Reiter

WARNING:

This book contains mature scenes not suitable for all audiences.
Reader discretion is advised.

AUTHOR'S NOTE:

If you are a member of my family—and I say this with grave importance—read no further.

This book is one of many historical accounts on the New World's creation, forged by the Ancient Library and transcribed by the god of Wisdom in 1 D.A.

PROLOGUE

Hellano, the god of Afterlife, was not just a lover. He was a friend.

Our opposites have attracted us since we were given our titles eons ago. Myself, the goddess of Beginnings. We stepped and swayed together in a hypnotizing dance. I gave life, he ended it. We were the rise and fall. Push and pull. The yin and the yang.

Until the scales that balanced us shifted.

Hellano had never been offered such a deal. He had never pulled focus from me, from us, until Kysi. The god of Mortals and Bargaining offered him something unheard of: independence. The ability to remain in balance on his own, without the need for another half. Without the weight of another's sway against his ... Without me.

He had barely taken the time to think about it.

The deal was struck, and their faces stared down at me as I fell. A force unlike gravity pulled me impetuously, snapping the locket from my neck—the one *he* had given me—as well as the beating mass behind my chest. I plummeted farther and farther, the feathers from my wings falling away and turning to embers that danced in the air.

As I descended, the thought of where I was going did not occur. I could not be concerned with what would become of me when a much more pressing question weighed on my soul.

Why?

My love, who ignites my purpose, betrayed me for power in the Heavens. Centuries of intertwinement, of loyalty and love, met with a duplicitous bargain that has cracked my soul and left me powerless. What do I have now if not the motivation to return, the tenacity to obtain revenge and reclaim my dignity? I'll find my way back ...

Even if it means striking a deal with Kysi myself.

I had only spoken to him once. It began as an issue related to our divine duties, but quickly advanced into a more casual, friendly conversation. Aside from Hellano, who I was always able to speak to effortlessly, this occurrence was rare for me. I was not exactly a ray of sunshine, but for some reason my rough exterior relaxed in the presence of his warm aura.

Only for a bit, though.

"Anewla? What kind of name is Anewla?" he had asked, leaning against the table with a teasing smirk.

"Why are you the god of Mortals *and* Bargaining?" I replied. Technically, if I had spent enough time searching, I could have found a book with the answer. But the Ancient Library is far too vast for anyone to waste their time looking for information on such things of little importance.

Kysi had shrugged his shoulders at this question. "Mortals are always bargaining. If I couldn't bargain with them, none would worship me, or worship who they think I am. Plus, making deals makes my job much less boring," he had said, giving a sly wink before taking one of my grapes and popping it into his mouth. "Now"—he clasped his hands together— "about that name. I can change it for you. For a small fee, of course."

It was impossible to hide my grin. "You strike me a fool. Be careful, I can make the birth rate of humans decline drastically."

I remember Kysi's expression hesitating in response to my baseless threat, as if it had struck a chord. But just as quickly as it came, it went. The look he replaced it with was like one that I had seen many times before.

At first, it reminded me of the way Hellano would often peer at me. Fueled by an endless love, he would drown me in the honey hue of his gaze. But Kysi was not driven by the same adoration—could not be, for he hardly knew me.

He had leaned closer then, the smell of his natural scent surrounding the air and imprinting on my memory like a brand. "I admire you," he had said while allowing his eyes to drift down at my figure. "I've always admired powerful women."

My friendliness dried and flaked away, leaving behind a burning anger in my chest. The bravery he had to disrespect the god of Afterlife so casually, to disrespect ME.

Before he had a chance to react, I snatched his face in my hands and fixed his glare to mine. "Know your place," I had spat, "or I will render all of your men sterile and women barren."

I will admit it was a bit malicious to use a joke that obviously affected him and turn it into a serious warning, but at the time I had wanted to make myself crystal clear.

His eyes grew cold as I continued, "I will create no more humans. Within a century your title will be worthless, leaving you destined for what lies beyond our realm, fated for the permanent ending."

In the Heavens, the goddess of Beginnings and the god of Afterlife are the foundations to all that exist. We create life and end it, and all other deities rule over smaller aspects of the world. Like bargaining for example, Kysi's intolerable profession.

When a deity's purpose has been served, they pass on to the eternal resting place—the Shadowlands.

Looking back, I know the position I held above the other gods had gone to my head. If met with my younger self, I would not want to be my friend either.

I still believe being condemned to Earth and forced to live under Kysi's thumb was a bit dramatic on his part, though.

Except it does not *feel* like I am under his thumb. Since my arrival, nothing has happened. I assumed he would torture me from above, but so far, the closest thing to hell I have endured is how much elbow grease it's taking to scrub the soap scum off this bathtub.

For the last three months, all I have been able to think about is that day. Despite the crowd that had gathered around me when I fell onto the hood of that Honda Civic, only one person witnessed me fall from the sky. To this day, Mona does not fully believe what she saw, which is fine by me. I do not know how I would go about explaining the fact that her live-in maid was once the most powerful goddess in the Heavens.

My predicament has been a humbling experience to say the least. After rolling off the car in pain—which is still a sensation I am getting used to, by the way—Mona followed me through the street, along with everyone else, to witness my tantrum.

They murmured to each other with concern as I screamed obscenities to the sky, knowing that Kysi and Hellano could hear every bit of it. Hell, all of the deities could.

Although the lower ranking gods cannot do much to help me in this situation, I have a feeling none of them have even tried.

If that does not speak on how much of a frigid bitch I used to be, I'm not sure what does.

When my outburst was over, Mona came to me sobbing in the street. It is a bit embarrassing to look back on, but maybe that is what influenced her to take pity on me, because she kindly offered me her home in exchange for cleaning services. To be met with a bargain so quickly upon arriving felt like salt was being rubbed in my wound. However, I accepted. There was nowhere else for me to go.

And so, the days turned into weeks, the weeks into months, and here I remain. I have tried countless times to get Kysi's attention. At times I even begged Hellano to strike me down. Each day I am met with nothing. By now, anger has washed away only to leave behind a layer of confusion. Why Kysi would put me here just to do nothing is beyond me.

"How long you gonna' keep this up?" Mona leans onto the door-frame of the bathroom.

Wiping sweat from my brow, I reply, "Until it's clean."

"You *know* that's not what I mean," she says. I drop the brush and sit on the floor, leaning my elbows on the edge of the tub while she continues her weekly lecture. "Listen, I don't mind you staying here, but it's been *three* months"—she holds the fingers up to give me a visual— "do you have any intention of doing anything other than being my maid and eating my food?"

Hunger is another thing I am still managing to get used to. Although we eat regularly in the Heavens, it was done more for enjoyment than necessity.

"You should really consider applying for some jobs, then you can buy your own Cheerios," she says, giving me an excited, motivational look that is undoubtedly rooted in sarcasm.

I lean my head back and release a disgruntled moan, "Ugh, my gods, I smash the hood of your car and you give me a place to stay. I finish a box of cereal and you crucify me. Make it make sense."

She clicks her tongue. "I've been working since I was fourteen in my mother's—"

"—your mother's café, yes, I know. Please." I pinch the bridge of my nose. I have heard this story enough to know it by heart, because she says it exactly the same way every time. I don't just know that story, I know damn near all of hers. This woman has shared every detail of her life with me. Sometimes I think she does it in hopes I will tell her a little about mine, but most of the time I think it is just so she can fill the silence. By this point, I know enough about Mona to remember what I did to create her, when she will die, and what of.

My brows lift to my hairline as an idea forms.

Hellano may have taken my position when he struck the deal, and Kysi may have forced me to live in the human world, but neither of them can take away my knowledge of the Heavens; more specifically, my knowledge of how the god of Afterlife operates. I know the recipe for death just as I do life, and I know the Law that binds them.

"What, what is it?" she questions, leaning off the doorframe.

I struggle to contain my smile. "You're right." I stand up from the tile. "I know exactly what I'm going to do." Why had I not thought of it sooner? It is perfect. Motivation takes root as I begin my first order of business. "Mona," I say, looking directly at her, "in eight years, on the eve of Valentine's Day, don't forget to lock your doors."

Her brows furrow with bewilderment as I exit the bathroom. Before I turn the corner in the hall, I hear her scoff something about how I would make a great candidate for Haldol. Whatever that means.

Part One

THE PERFECT DEAL

Chapter i

Eight years later.

In the Heavens, any god or goddess has access to knowledge regarding the Law. However, most of them only know the Law that affects their area of expertise.

Not me.

Call me a romantic because I was infatuated with Hellano. His sun-kissed hair was the dawn and dusk of my day-less life. His lips the perfect hue of a dusty rose. I wanted to know everything there was to learn about him.

My naivety paid off because through my studies, I cultivated the knowledge of what forges human death.

To simplify, it is a complex algorithm made up of elements and figures no human would recognize. That is what all the gods' purposes are, just various kinds of equations.

I click my pen before scribbling more notes in a patient's chart. Reaching for another, I open it to reveal Heather, age twenty-four, dealing with prenatal anxiety and fleeing from an abusive boyfriend.

This one makes no sense to me. I spend all day listening to people's problems, gathering information on them that I can add to my formula—my equation for death—so I can figure out when they will die and intercept it. I have not had enough time to figure anyone's out yet, except for Heather's.

On one end, my calculations predict she will die in three months. Something like strangulation, probably by her boyfriend. Normally this would be good for me. I want to save someone with little time left, that way Kysi and Hellano will notice something is off and pay me a visit sooner rather than later. On the other end, I am finding her death will not happen for another fourteen years. It does not add up.

A knock diverts my attention from the file. I am met with a familiar smirk, one that makes the smile lines near his eyes deepen ever so slightly.

"Thought I told you"—I close Heather's chart and fold my hands over the desk— "I don't date patients."

"But I'm not your patient." Ivan strides to the opposite side of my workstation and sits in the chair across from me, comfortably draping his ankle over his knee. "Not anymore."

I raise a brow. "And you came here to break the news in person?"

"Yes." His jade eyes linger over the waves in my hair. "I'm sorry to break your heart like this, but I'm seeing someone else." There is a mischievous shadow in his grin.

"So, I wasn't good enough for you." I lean back, swiveling my chair from side to side.

"On the contrary," he contests, "you were too good. And too ..."—his gaze leaves my hair and meets mine— "distracting."

"How can a therapist be too good?"

"I didn't like how quickly you were helping me solve my problems." I tilt my head, waiting for him to continue. "Because that meant soon, I'd have no reason to come see you."

As an ER Nurse, Ivan seeks therapy for stress management. He is definitely one of my less complicated patients. Or, was.

"Isn't that the goal?"

"Not mine," he says without hesitation. He is aware that I know exactly what he is getting at. "One date."

"Ivan—" Although this man has only asked me out once or twice before, his demeanor has given the impression that he has longed to do it again during each session we have together.

"—One."

I let out a defeated sigh. I would be lying if I said I was not attracted to him. We look roughly the same age. I appear somewhere around twenty-three in human years, but not so many twenty-three-year-olds have doctoral degrees, so I had to bump up that number. I settled on thirty-two.

I try to think of a response while spinning my pen between my fingers. "I typically don't go out with younger guys," I tease.

"Oh, come on. You look younger than I do."

"You do know how to flatter them." I chuckle, meeting his warm gaze. His eyes remind me of dew-covered grass sparkling under the morning sun. "Fine. You can pick me up at seven."

My other earring is stuck somewhere in the depths of my boudoir drawer. I am already a little behind, and it does not help that my nervous fingers keep fumbling each time they wrap around the sterling silver. Finally, I pull it out and secure it safely to my other lobe.

Out of all the years I have lived on Earth, never once have I been on a date. First it was studying at the university that kept me busy, now it is work. Dating is something I have never felt like I had the time for. Plus, committing to a relationship with the intention of leaving them and returning to the Heavens does not seem like the nicest way to break up with a person. I have to admit though, it does get lonely sometimes. Especially when being with someone is all you know.

Hellano and I had been together since the dawn of my existence. Being with him did not feel like dating at all. It was like we were fated for each other.

Enough about him.

I do a double take in the mirror to go over my outfit one more time. The cashmere dress hugs my figure, almost meeting where the thigh-high boots rise up my leg. Their black velvet is a nice accent to the rest of my delicate ash-colored outfit. It is sophisticated and classy. My hair cascades over the fabric in waves of onyx, falling around my waist.

When I hear him knocking, goosebumps line my arms. Rubbing them away, I grab my purse.

Ivan matches my color scheme, with black bottoms and a gray sweater that rests over his defined shoulders.

"How did you—" I eye his attire.

He appears just as surprised. The short laugh he lets out is smooth, so much so that I am left wishing it lasted longer.

"I knew we were made for each other." He winks before extending a hand for me to take.

A short drive leads us to the outskirts of town, where the road meets shallow woods. He pulls into an alcove with a walking trail stemming from it. Ahead, I can see water trickling from rocks.

"Everything is already set up." He reaches over and unbuckles my seatbelt. "Don't get out just yet."

Already this is such a stark contrast to my last relationship. Although Hellano and I were often passionate, it always felt as though distance was between us. It would take some getting used to, especially since I haven't had any sort of intimacy—emotionally or physically—in eight years.

I watch Ivan in the rear view grabbing a basket from the trunk. He then comes around to open my door. I step onto the gravel, taking in the clean air. He takes my hand in his and leads us toward the trail.

"You know, if I didn't already know your deepest, darkest secrets, I would be worried about a man luring me into the woods on a first date," I say.

A piece of chocolate hair falls over his forehead. "You don't know my deepest darkest secret." I think there's a glint of truth behind his otherwise joking behavior, but I cannot say for sure. "That's for the second date."

"You said one," I remind him.

He squeezes my hand. "I have until the end of this one to change your mind."

As the waterfall comes into view, I am also met with a tree adorned in fairy lights. A table rests beneath it with a bouquet at its center, the roses perfectly hugging sunflower petals.

A second date does not sound too bad.

"It's beautiful," I admit.

All of this, the extravagant décor, the waterfall—is it normal? Why would anyone go this far, especially for someone they do not exactly know?

Ivan sits the basket on the table and begins taking out an assortment of fruits and cheeses. "Here's a secret," he says, "during all of our sessions, I hated not being able to ask you questions instead."

Oh, gods.

I really hope he doesn't pry too much. If lying is a craft, my hands are all thumbs. For now, I will humor him for the sake of acting natural. If he asks something I cannot answer, my only option is to dodge. "Questions like what?"

I watch as his hands sort grapes. "How do you like your coffee in the morning?" he asks without missing a beat.

Heat rushes to my face. Hopefully it is not as noticeable as it feels. Now these questions, I can answer.

Perhaps it is the wine talking, but I would consider myself officially wooed. Despite wanting to ask him to come in, I am not brave enough to spill the question. Unfortunately, he is a gentleman and does not ask.

Ivan pulls me into him, placing a hand on my cheek before pressing his lips to mine. They are soft and sweet, the taste of wine lingering on our mouths.

The euphoria stays with me long after he leaves. As I lounge in my pajamas, the sectional feels especially lonely after such a nice date. I bask in the details of the night, soaking in the blissful memory.

"Tell me," a sunken voice echoes from the shadow leading to my kitchen, "did it hurt when you fell from heaven?"

I go to scream, but nothing comes of it. Like a deer in the headlights, I remain still on the couch, staring into the abyss through the doorway. As adrenaline floods, without a warning I grasp my glass of lemon water and hurl it through the entryway to the kitchen.

A hand extends from the shadows and catches the glass. It hangs motionless—a tableau of suspense as light gleams off droplets of water speckled on its surface. A halo of darkness surrounds ivory skin as he steps into the light. Obsidian hair, identical to the darkness behind it, drapes lazily over a matching brow.

Kysi.

CHAPTER 2

"You." I stand. Years worth of anger builds rapidly as I stride forward. Swinging the back of my hand, it lands on his defined cheekbone.

He reaches up, palming the area I struck. "Okay." He rubs his jaw. "I deserved that."

"That's not all you deserve you motherf—" I start swinging, but he does not let me land another blow. Instead, he grabs my arms, holding me steady as I fight against him.

"So feisty," he says, "you realize I'm a god, right?"

I stop and meet his gaze. Hatred coils in my stomach in response to his degrading words. "I am a *goddess*," I spit, "one more powerful than you." I shrug his arms off of me.

"Angel, you know just as well as I that you're basically mortal here."

"Fuck you." I turn and trudge back to the couch. If he has come here to bully me, I am no longer interested in the conversation.

Like a black cat, he slinks fully into the living room and makes his way to the other side of the couch, draping an arm over the back.

"What do you want?" I have to repress the urge to strike him again upon seeing his pristine dress shoes hiked up on my coffee table.

"I want to know why you"—he points a ringed index finger at me— "prevented the death of your old roommate."

It takes a moment to connect the dots. Finally, a laugh erupts from my throat at the realization. That was eight years ago? Time flies when you are orchestrating revenge.

His eyes gleam with something I cannot quite place—irritation? Fascination?

"I need to check my phone." I reach for the cord and pull it from the side table on the opposite end of the sofa. Kysi amusingly watches my cell slide across his lap as I drag it by the charger towards me.

Mona has called six times, left two voicemails, and thirteen texts. My grin widens. "How's Hell-no handling this up there?"

Kysi wipes invisible dust from his pants. "I don't think he noticed."

I pause. Didn't notice? Excuse me? "How can the god of Beginnings and Endings not notice when someone has basically overruled their decision?"

Kysi looks directly at me. "That's why I'm here." For the first time since arriving, his expression becomes serious. "Your former consort has no idea what the fuck he's doing."

A disturbed satisfaction undulates through me. Either Hellano never took the time to properly learn the algorithm, or he is struggling with double the work. Life and death were always meant to be separate but equal. They have never existed in one being before.

"Well, well, well." I cross my arms behind my head and lean back, kicking my feet up beside Kysi's. "Isn't that karma for you?"

He rubs his forehead. "I don't think you understand the magnitude of the situation, angel."

"Enlighten me, oh powerful one." I want more details just so I can revel in their mistake of sending me here.

"I was supposed to meet you shortly after you arrived to discuss the logistics of your newfound situation, but Hellano's negligence has kept me very busy." He stretches his neck as if he has just left from a long day of work. "It's gotten to the point now that, without intervention, it will affect more than Earth."

Oh, shit.

"It's *that* bad?" I ask. One mistake here, an accidental death there, it wouldn't make much of a difference. Over time however, the more he fumbles with his new responsibility, the bigger it snowballs.

If the world falls into chaos because of him, it would affect everything in existence. If extinction were to occur, Kysi would not have mortals to rule over. Thus, his title and duty would no longer be needed, and he would pass on to the Shadowlands. It would not be just him that would die, but other deities as well. If nothing exists to experience pain or pleasure, then the god and goddess responsible for those would also cease to exist, along with countless others over the course of the downfall of the universe. For deities, our purpose fuels our existence like a beating heart.

Mistakes rarely happened while I was in charge of creating life. It gives a whole new meaning to the term "unwanted pregnancy." In short, I impregnated an elderly woman.

Okay, it sounds weird when I put it like that. I just forgot to cross my t's and dot my i's, next thing I know Kysi is storming up to me in the Ancient Library, the same day I threatened him.

I was in the middle of reading the Law of All Gods when he flipped it closed, interrupting me. "You put an immaculate conception on Earth and didn't think the god of Mortals and Bargaining should be made aware?"

"I beg your pardon," I said, slowly placing my fingertips on the table and standing, "are you aware of who you are speaking to?"

"Goddess of Beginnings. Your soul is one of the oldest among us," he said with confidence. "Your predecessor is probably rolling in her grave, if they even have those in the Land of Shadows." His eyes were bright, almost glowing like bioluminescent algae in a shimmering lagoon. They were handsome and striking as they stared back at me with amusement.

"I'm sure my predecessor would not have tolerated being spoken to in such a way," I responded.

He met me with a smirk then. "Let's sit," he suggested, gesturing toward the table, "we got off on the wrong foot."

I kept my eyes on him as we both sunk into opposing chairs. After plucking one of my grapes from a bowl, Kysi said, "That poor old lady thought she was the new mother of God. Everyone else just

21

assumed her menopause was late, as she had a bit of a reputation in the retirement home."

A slight chuckle escaped me then, but I stifled the end of it. There was something about his nonchalant, playful features that made my muscles slacken.

"That's neither here nor there." He waved a hand. "I took care of it. What are you reading over here anyway?"

Kysi then proceeded to chat so effortlessly, like his dialogue was rehearsed and perfected. He asked questions without prying, leaning into all my responses—no matter how bland they may have been.

Cue him trying to flirt with me, me rejecting him, and getting cursed to Earth. Now here we are.

"There's still time to fix it, but everything *will* cease to exist unless action is taken." I do not respond, unsure of how someone "nearly mortal" has anything to do with it. "What are you thinking?" he asks from the other side of the couch. It seems as if gravity has brought us a bit closer.

My couch has a dip in the middle.

"I'm thinking about what you expect me to do about all of this."

He reaches forward and gently swipes a stray hair from my face. It shocks me. I almost flinch, but my adrenaline has died down, so I just freeze in place. A nuance of tenderness shows behind his eyes, then he clears his throat. "Why don't I come back tomorrow, we can sort through more details." He stands and hesitates, hovering over me for a moment. "You have every right to hate me. I hope to change that soon, angel."

I'm extremely confused. "You can start by not calling me angel."

A grin appears before he disappears through the shadow of the kitchen. I step into the space he left and turn on the light. The glass I threw at him rests on the counter.

It is difficult for me to sleep tonight. So many questions press on my mind. How did he even manage to send me to Earth in the first place? How does he expect to fix this? Should I even help him? It seems I don't have much of a choice unless I want everything to turn into nothing.

A thought dawns on me. I always forget the god of Mortals and Bargaining is not limited to bargaining with mortals. He undoubtedly made a deal with someone in order to gain the power it must have taken to send me here. But who?

I collapse into my chair. One coffee was not enough. Thank gods it is just an office day and I am not seeing clients. I instinctively flip open the nearest file. Why am I doing this again? There is no point in figuring out when they will die now that I know it won't affect anything. I stare at the patient's name while the gears begin to turn.

That is why I could not figure out when Heather was going to die! It's one of Hellano's mistakes. He must have put two death dates on her.

Three knocks on the door are followed by it swiftly opening to reveal the handsome, brown-haired man I saw the day before. In his hands is another bouquet, one of lilies and freesias. "Happy Valentine's Day." He closes the space between us to hand me the flowers and plants a kiss on the side of my face.

"Thank you." I gently rub a silky petal between my fingers.

"Does it earn me a second date?" he croons.

"Hmm," I sarcastically think aloud, "maybe."

He grins and responds, "Are you busy?"

Well, Fridays used to be for calculating death days, but I guess it's kind of useless now. I shake my head.

Ivan pushes off the desk and strides to the door. Being desperate for intimacy, the fear of him leaving takes root, but it does not have a chance to grow. Instead, he closes the door to my office. The newfound privacy fills the air with sexual tension.

"If I asked to come inside last night, what would you have said?" he asks with a coquettish tilt to his voice.

I would've said yes.

"Hadn't thought about it," I lie.

He turns his head in disbelief. "Really?" My cheeks warm as he steps forward. "Well," he says, closing in on me until I am flush with the desk, "now that you're thinking about it. What would you have said?"

Ivan looms above me, fiddling with a lock of my hair. I do not want to admit, embarrassed to actually, that after just one day I was pretty desperate for him. And equally disappointed when I had not sensed that same desperation from him.

I sense it now, though. "I would've said yes."

Before, his eyes were yearning, like trying to catch prey. Now, they peer down at me as if I have finally been caught in their snare. His hand lets go of my hair and cups the side of my face. He steps in, closing what little space there is between us.

His lips clash with mine. They dance together like flames in an inferno. The palm on my cheek reaches back to a handful of hair, while the other slips to my lower back and pulls me harder into him.

I have never seen this side of Ivan. He has always been soft, funny, flirty. This is primal and instinctive. The kiss becomes more aggressive, deeper, as if it seeks to devour me. He pushes against me, hoisting me onto the desk on top of my papers. Out of instinct, my legs wrap around his waist as a warmth erupts from my center.

It has been so long since I have felt intimacy. I drink it in as though I was dying of thirst, running my fingers through his soft hair. With a torturous sense of impatience, I pull him closer with my calves.

Ivan parts the kiss, slightly out of breath as he rests his forehead against mine.

"What? What is it?" For the love of all that is holy, why did he stop?

"We shouldn't." There's a twitch in his brow that gives me the impression he thinks he made a mistake. Pushing him away, I pat down my disheveled hair. Despite only being inches apart, I put a distance between us.

"Believe me, I want to." His hand rubs where it remains at my back as a silent testimony to his truth. "I just don't want to move too fast."

It is oddly sweet and painfully boring at the same time. But, fine. I can handle lengthy foreplay.

"Why don't I come over tonight." He tucks hair behind my ear. "I can cook for you."

There is earthiness and pine in his musk, which doesn't help me as I try to come down from the spiraling arousal. "Fine," I say, "but next time, follow through." Pushing him away, I step to the floor and wipe the wrinkles from my blouse.

"With pleasure." He winks. "Lots and lots of pleasure." And with that, he leaves me to collect myself.

CHAPTER 3

Years ago, when I was still living with Mona, we were celebrating my completion of another semester at the university. She had a few more drinks than I did that night, and it was safe to say she was hammered. Given the fact that I undoubtedly had one too many margaritas myself, I told her the truth about me.

"Anewla Delphine," she had said, using the last name I had chosen for myself, "you are about two plums short of a fruit pie." Her laugh was so contagious that I could not help but follow her lead. I knew she would not believe it, figured she would not even remember it, until now.

"It's a lot easier for me to believe that this is a coincidence than it is for me to believe you're a fallen goddess," she says through the phone.

"Then it's a coincidence." Maybe she will let it go.

"But it's not," she rebuts.

Or maybe she won't. "You're right, it's not," I admit.

I trust Mona. She is probably the closest friend I have ever had. Come to think of it, she is the only friend I have ever had. Over the years, I prayed to all the gods I knew to get me out of this situation, knowing that none of them would listen—because I never gave them a reason to.

I was not exactly popular in the Heavens.

"I'll accept the fact that you miraculously fell from the sky and totaled my car, I'll even accept the fact that you knew my house was going to be broken into *eight years* in advance, but I cannot bring myself to believe you're a deity responsible for creating everyone I know, including me," she says, clearly in denial.

"How are you justifying those?" I ask solely out of curiosity.

She takes a moment to think about it. "You fell out of a plane and you're psychic."

Whatever she needs to tell herself in order to sleep at night.

"*If* what you claim is true," she says, "and hypothetically, you are some powerful goddess, what can you do? Grant wishes, cast spells, fly?"

"No, no, and I used to. Once upon a time." Gods, I miss my wings.

"Well, what can you do?" she sounds almost dissatisfied with my answers.

"Sorry to disappoint," I say, "but I'm basically human now."

A familiar three knocks break our conversation. "Mona, I'll have to call you back."

"Anewla Delphine, don't you dare—"

I will apologize for hanging up on her later.

After fluffing up my hair, I swing the door open. Kysi leans against the doorframe, one foot crossed over the other.

Son of a bitch. I forgot he was coming. Wait, why did he knock?

"Didn't want to break and enter this time?" I say, not inviting him inside.

"Didn't break anything, angel. Just entered. In fact, I did the opposite of break. I saved your drinking glass." He looks at me expecting an invitation.

"You have to go," I admit, "rain check."

Kysi's brows raise, as if he cannot believe I'm prioritizing anything over saving the universe. He said last night we had time to fix it, anyway. Obviously, there is not that much of a rush or he would appear much more concerned. "Rain check?" Annoyance lingers in his tone.

"I have a thing."

He brushes past me, waltzing into the threshold. "You have a date."

"Breaking and entering." I follow him. "And how would you know?"

"Just entering." He leads me to the kitchen, opening my fridge. "Which is called trespassing, by the way."

"Answer my question. Have you been spying on me?"

He pops his head out from behind the refrigerator door, string cheese laying lazily between his lips. He bites down, casually snacking on my food. "I'm the god of this place, I spy on everyone. Speaking of, it's time to retire those granny panties, sweetheart."

I am a kettle that's whistling with anger. He has been watching me for eight and a half years, peeping in on me in my underwear? "You sick fuck—"

His head falls back in a laugh, accentuating the tightness of his jawline. "I was kidding, angel," he teases, "I keep an eye on you, sure, but I've never invaded your privacy like that. I respect you."

Respect for me? This man's attitude is night and day.

"Despite how badly I want to." He closes the fridge and takes another bite of cheese.

After everything Kysi has put me through, his words are about as reliable as a sieve for holding water. "What are you even doing? Why are you rummaging through my food like a dirty raccoon?"

He shrugs and turns toward me. "Is there any way you could hate me more?"

The question is so arbitrary. Then again, so is snooping through my cabinets. What could be worse than taking away your abilities, your lover, and everything you knew and loved? "No," I respond, "I don't think so."

A conflicted look crosses Kysi's face. He seems torn, holding a ringed hand up to his chin as he mulls over whatever issue he is having. After a moment, he brings the hand up and runs it through his hair. The darkness of it turns a shade of blue when the light hits it exactly right.

"I haven't been honest with you," his voice is raspy. He says the words like they are poison. I look at him, waiting for him to continue. Kysi glances at his watch, which I have a feeling is on his wrist more for fashion than functionality. The god of Mortals and Bargaining does not sound like a title in need of a clock, it is obvious this was done as a nervous tick. "It's almost time for your date. I'll come back after." Kysi goes to leave, but I grab his arm to stop him. The touch excites my dark side, wanting to feel if the other bicep matches this one.

I shut down that part of myself quickly. "You'll come back right after," my words come out as more of a threat, "and you'll tell me *everything* I want to know."

He pauses, then nods.

Not five minutes after Kysi leaves, Ivan arrives. He swings in, greeting me with a kiss that tells me he had been waiting to do that since leaving my office this morning. I eagerly kiss him back, and when it ends, I am left longing for more, just like before. He makes himself at home in the kitchen, sitting down a couple of grocery bags he brought in. "Frutti di Mare," he says as he turns on the stove. "I think you'll like it."

Ivan cooks with rolled up sleeves that expose the ripples of muscle along his forearms. He is a confident chef; obviously this is a hobby of his. I lustfully observe, taking in the delicious view and fragrant mixture of spices. Every now and then, he catches me staring and grins or gives a wink. It only makes it that much harder to take my eyes off him.

He serves me at the table just before pouring Pinot Grigio in a glass and pushing it towards my plate. The food looks incredible; a seafood pasta garnished in parsley and a lemon wedge.

Once he is situated across from me, he glares expectantly in my direction. So, I take the first bite.

It is the best fucking dish I have *ever* tasted.

The sauce is infused with garlic and white wine, enhancing the flavor of tender shrimps and scallops. I have to suppress the urge to crawl across the table and throw myself at him. Seriously, he is hot, *and* he can cook? A moan of approval escapes me, and he grins in response.

I am halfway through my plate when I notice that he's barely touched his. Instead, he watches me. I embarrassingly slurp the rest of a noodle into my mouth. "What?" I look down at my shirt, half expecting it to be stained.

"I never want my time with you to end," he says.

After last night, this morning, and now, screw lengthy foreplay.

"Why does it have to?" Finishing off the wine in one swig, I swallow the last of my liquid courage. Stepping up from my seat, I walk to the other end of the table without tearing my gaze from his. He looks up at me as I swing my leg over, straddling his lap. The hungry side of Ivan I saw in my office this morning peeks out, but I can tell he's trying to suppress it.

I don't want that.

After planting a kiss along his jaw, I move to his neck and slowly begin working at the buttons on his shirt. When I move my hips over him, a groan erupts from the depth of his throat. I can feel Ivan hardening beneath me as his hands grip my hips, guiding me back and forth. One slips back, gripping my ass with authority.

His shirt is unbuttoned three-quarters of the way, which is good enough for me. I let my hands explore the mounds of his chest. It's structured, but not too hard. Moving my mouth to his, I rub the length of his torso and feel each ridge between his stomach muscles.

"We shouldn't," he says, not stopping.

"I disagree." I start to work on the buttons of his pants. He gives a groan before kissing me harder.

"You have no idea how badly I want to," he says, his breathing erratic and heavy. I manage to undo his button, but just as I finish unzipping, he grabs my hand.

I stare at him, flushed and confused. These feelings are building up into frustration as my patience has now officially worn out. "Okay what is your problem?"

"I have to tell you something." He is still trying to catch his breath. "I want to fuck you, gods I do, but I can't without being honest with you first."

"What the hell is it—"

Hold on. He said gods. Plural. Polytheism is rare where I live, and according to his patient chart, Ivan is an atheist.

"No." I stare into those emerald eyes as understanding sweeps across my face. Disappointment shadows his features as the hair atop his head begins to darken before my eyes. His irises brighten into a lighter green that almost glows ... like algae in a shimmering lagoon. The next thing I know, Ivan is gone.

I am left straddling my enemy.

CHAPTER 4

I freeze over Kysi. He appears frozen as well, but finally speaks up, "Told you I was saving my deepest darkest secret for the second date."

Earlier, when I told him that I could not hate him more, I was wrong. I can. I do. Fueled by anger, I swing my leg off of him and reach for the vase in the corner.

"How." He catches it when I send it flying in his direction and stands. "Dare." I grab the wine glass and throw it too. "You." The bottle goes next.

Kysi doesn't even flinch as they hit his torso. It infuriates me even more to see him unaffected, catching the objects before they hit the floor and placing them on the table. The wine that was just served to me drips down his chest; the same one I just had my hands all over.

"You said you respected me," I spit.

"I do—"

"—All this," I interrupt, spreading my arms out, "just because I rejected you?"

He holds up a hand in an attempt to silence me. "What? You think that's why I did all of this? Gods, Anewla so I'm just a glorified stalker to you?"

Is he kidding? "You just had another face on?! And how would I know any different anyway? You haven't told me anything! You put me here and left for nearly a decade!"

He pauses, grabbing a napkin to wipe the wine off his chest. "I'm sorry," he says, and there is so much that comes through in those words: regret, sadness, defeat. He starts working on the buttons of his shirt. "You're right," he says, looking back at me. I can still see the hint of Ivan in his eyes, a residue of what could have been. "You don't know the story. You have every right to be angry. Hell, you'll still have every right after I explain it to you."

I can feel my chest getting blotchy with frustration as I pull out the dining chair, letting it skid across the hard floor and echo through the room. Plopping down in it, I cross my arms over the table and fix my seething glare on him. "I'm all ears."

As Kysi stands, thinking about where to begin, all I can think about is Ivan. The first time I allow myself to date and it ends up being the one that cursed me. Considering I was betrayed in my only previous relationship, I think it is safe to say I have horrible taste in men.

"It's just that," he trips over his words, "this isn't how I wanted it to happen."

I look at him and shrug my shoulders, silently pushing him to continue.

35

But he just looks at me and sighs, having made up his mind not to say anything.

"Get out," I intone threateningly. The last thing I want is to be around him, and if he will not give me answers, then I see no more reason to be.

With a sympathetic glance, Kysi tries to reach for me, but I lean away before he can get too close. "I said get out." All he does is nod, and when I blink, he is gone.

After minutes of sitting in silence at the table, I eventually drag my feet to the bedroom. Part of me does not want to take off the clothes from dinner. I was wearing them around Ivan, before I knew who he really was. That same part wants to leave them on and pretend the night went differently.

My heart is opened twice, and it gets burned twice. Fool me once, I guess.

As the clothes hit the floor, I leave them behind with the memories of a fake man.

I am taking a leave of absence from work. I am incapable of providing care to my clients in my current state. How can I solve their problems when I sparsely have my own in order?

My bed is my primary habitat for the next three days. I am plagued with confusion. After going so long without intimacy, getting a taste of it has me eager for more. I yearn for Ivan, and I can only assume that because Kysi was him, that's the reason I somehow yearn for him too.

It is infuriating, like an itch that cannot be scratched by anyone but him. The fact that I still crave that connection after what happened, rather than be repulsed by it, sickens me. My mind and body feel as though they are at war with one another.

There is a pounding at my front door, with a muffled voice on the other side. Mona?

For the first time in days, I leave my bed for a reason other than to grab snacks or take a piss.

I unlock the door—not that locking it would keep Kysi out anyway, but I still did it just in case he was watching from the Heavens, as a subtle message to keep out.

"You look like shit." Mona squeezes past me and drops her bags by the couch.

"What are you doing here?"

"Visiting, I'm past due for one. Now, what's wrong with you?" She follows me into the bedroom as I sink back into my nest to rot.

"Remember Kysi?" I mumble through the pillow.

I see Mona in my peripheral thinking back to the drunken night we had. "Not your ex, but the other one?"

"Yeah," I say, even though now I'm not sure if Kysi is my "ex" too or not. I'm going to go with no, and pretend it never happened ... right after I finish telling my best friend. "I made out with him."

Her eyes widen. "You did not!"

I groan in disappointment and bury my face in the pillow.

She shakes my shoulder. "You slut! When?"

I cannot help but laugh as I pull myself from the darkness of the sheets. "A couple days ago." I begin telling her about Kysi putting on the face of Ivan, and how I had been giving him therapy for months, never knowing. As I tell her the details, she acts like she needs popcorn for the show.

"Kysi sounds hot," she says once I finish.

Expelling a sigh of disbelief, I give her a shove. "That's your response to all this? It's creepy, not sexy!" I have never been to a teenage slumber party, but this feels similar to how I imagine it would be.

"I'm just saying"—she puts her hands up in defense— "if there was a guy going through all that effort for me, I'd put out." Her teasing grin meets my rolling eyes. "But in all seriousness," she continues, "it's pretty fucked up. I hope you get your goddess powers back and smite him."

Me too, girl.

"So, how was your almost death day? Was it everything I said it was going to be?" I question.

"You were right." She seems unsurprised. That drunken night, I had warned her again.

"I'm always right."

It is her that rolls her eyes now. "I'm gonna take the guest room. I'd stay and pet your hair until you feel better, but in all honesty, you stink sis. Take a shower." She hops off the bed and saunters out of the room.

After bathing, I flop onto the bed. It is only when I feel my hair has started soaking the sheets that I realize I did a horrible job at drying it. But the towel is all the way in the bathroom, and my blankets will dry eventually.

"Angel," a sinister voice cascades from a shadow in the corner of my room.

No, no, no. I point to the voice. "Trespasser."

"Guilty," it responds.

"Get." I grab the nearest pillow and throw it into the abyss. "Out." I hear him catch it, then watch as he makes his appearance into the light.

"You have a habit of throwing things." Kysi places the pillow against my headboard.

I snap at him, "Only at you." When he plops beside me on the bed, I immediately slide over to the opposite side.

"I know you're mad. I would be too, but we have work to do."

He is here on business, I get it. Fine. I will do what I need to do, comply in order to save ... well, everything, then I will convince Hellano to send me into the Shadowlands. I am tired of being under Kysi's thumb.

"Hellano and I made the deal long before we sent you here. I had read in the Ancient Library that the gods from before, the ones in the Land of Shadows, still exist."

I finally meet his eyes. "What?"

"They're alive," he continues, "our past lives are all there." When I give him a quizzical look, he goes on. "Our souls exist in numerous bodies. Only one is allowed to reign at a time."

This is incredible knowledge. I must admit, I have spent countless hours in the library but most of the subject material I studied was centered around the logistics of my own work, Hellano's, or basic Law. From what I have read on the Shadowlands, it is a place where gods go to rest after they are replaced. The Law of Reincarnation states that all gods and goddesses must pass on in order for a new mind to take their place and avoid being corrupted.

Additionally, there is also a law that protects the minds of knowledge seekers. Learning is a right; all gods have access to an almost infinite amount of information, and what they learn must never be taken from them against their will. Unfortunately, the library stays mostly empty. I even took it for granted by not studying a wider range of subjects.

"So, there's just a bunch of me's in the next realm?" I ask.

He shakes his head. "Not exactly. Think of it more like your family. They look different, think differently, the only thing you all share is a soul. I was able to send you to Earth with the knowledge I gained from your predecessor," he says without missing a beat.

"You went to the Shadowlands?" My scream is a whisper. I do not want to wake Mona. If she saw him here, she would not be throwing anything but her hands.

Before I have a chance to ask, he explains, "I convinced Hellano to send me there. Then, I had to rely on my bargaining skills to get me back—"

"Who sent you back? Who'd you make a deal with?" I interrupt.

Striking green eyes stare back at me. "Your Soul Mothers."

One of my previous incarnations, I assume. But why would I—or they, make him this deal?

"It took some convincing." By now he is an inch closer to me. I had not even realized that I was leaning into the conversation. "But like a mother-daughter bond, your past lives care about you."

"If they care, then why did they do this to me?" I intone bitterly.

"Maybe because they thought it was in your best interest?"

A sarcastic crow escapes. He must find my soul to be so foolish.

Kysi ignores my chuckle. "I have to go back, and I need you with me. You can convince them to strike me another deal. If anyone knows how to reverse it, it's them."

"You're the god of Bargaining and you need *me* to convince them?" Kysi has the ability to bend the will of others, mainly humans. But just because it is harder for him to glamour gods does not make it impossible.

"These aren't mortals, Anewla. I can only do so much."

A trip to the Shadowlands was not exactly a New Year's Resolution of mine. The thought of meeting my past selves, my Soul Mothers? I do not know what to make of it. I have never entertained the thought of having a mother. I was not born, merely blinked into existence.

No one is exempt from the Law of Reincarnation. In order for a new goddess of Beginnings to be created, the original must create their replacement at the same time the god of Afterlife is sending them to the next realm. By the time I arrived, my mother was already gone.

It is the same idea with the god of Afterlife. He sends himself to the Shadowlands and I create the replacement.

We do the same for other gods, Hellano and I simultaneously agree to send them on and make a new one—though I have only done it once myself. The Law states that there must always be a beginning and an end, meaning the goddess of Beginnings and the god of Afterlife must exist forever in order to make this so. As long as mine and Hellano's soul exist, we form the foundations of all life and death.

Now it is just Hellano.

"You idiot." I rub my temples. "Do you even understand the power you've given him?" Kysi basically gave a loaded gun to an impulsive dimwit, and our survival has rested upon the hope that Hellano does not figure out how to use it.

"Rest assured, angel." He crosses his hands behind his head and settles comfortably into my bed. "Hellano does not even know he has that kind of power. I doubt any of the gods do. But, just as a precautionary measure, I hid the book with that info in the library. It would take him centuries to find it."

It would appear unwise to hide a book in the most obvious place, but Kysi had no choice. It is strictly forbidden to take a book from the Ancient Library.

"Additionally, Hellano can barely manage your job on top of his. You think someone itching to be sole ruler of the universe would be putting said universe at risk?"

He has a point. I relax my head on the pillow I threw at him earlier and massage my aching scalp. I cannot believe how much he has royally fucked everything. Talk about going above my head in the chain of command. Why did he choose Hellano to have both powers, why not me?

"*This* is what you get for striking the deal with *him*," I jibe.

"You'd have wanted both roles? You'd have said yes?" He scoffs, "Please. Don't get me wrong, loyalty is important, but your dedication to that professional killer was infuriating."

My silence is a testimony to his truth. I would never have hurt Hellano the way he did me. He was my everything.

Releasing a sigh of defeat, I drape my forearm across my eyes and block out the dim lamplight, block out Kysi too.

"Angel?" he calls from beside me.

"What?" Wait, did I actually just respond to that?

"Your hair has soiled your shirt."

"I know."

"Your shirt is white."

I immediately jerk my head down. This flimsy T-shirt does not leave anything to the imagination. It certainly does not help that it is cold in here.

Once again, I use him for target practice. He groans as the pillow hits him in the face. There is the hint of a smile spread across his cheeks when he pulls it off of him.

"You wanna know something?" He turns, propping himself up with his elbow.

"No," I say, not even trying to mask the attitude as I flip over to face the wall. The air near my ear gets warm as he leans in. A pine scent fills the air around me, a sullen reminder that the Ivan I was just with, never truly existed.

"I wasn't exactly pretending to be someone else." The sarcasm has left his voice. His words are soft and fragile, as if they might break if he says the wrong thing. "I was me."

Chapter 5

Kysi must have some skewed version of love if his idea of it is ripping the woman he fancies away from everything she knows, stripping her of her title, and cursing her to his world.

Oh, and I can't forget the part where he tricked me into being romantic with him.

Why did he show up as Ivan months ago? He mentioned before that he was supposed to meet me here shortly after the deal was made, but Hellano's ignorance had kept him busy. I am sure a god that holds the lives of your people in their hands without knowing what they are doing would definitely increase a person's workload. Had he planned to show up as Ivan then, or himself?

Kysi leans back behind me, returning to the position he was previously in. I keep trying to think of how to ask. Maybe it is best I don't. Considering the disappointment I feel having only dated Ivan for two days, I would prefer not to know if there was a chance I could have been with him longer.

I am about to tell Kysi that it is time to go when I shift to see that he has gone limp beside me. With a hand draped over his chest and the other resting on the back of his head. His closed lashes sweep over relaxed features. The ebony hair that usually throws a piece here and there along his brow, lay back with the rest on the pillow, enjoying the same sleep as Kysi. His succulent lips are slightly parted, blushing against creamy skin.

My heart stutters in response to such a handsome man.

I have to wave the image of wine dripping down his chest from my mind. It is normal to have unwanted needs, especially after such a long stretch of celibacy. I still do not appreciate them, though.

If I wake Kysi to leave, he will probably just keep talking instead. So, I roll back to the other side and pull the covers over me.

The sound of laughter pulls me from sleep, along with the smell of pancakes. Feeling through the blankets, I realize I am alone in bed. Without any aesthetic maintenance, I pad over to the door and make my way to the source of the smell.

Breakfast. That is what I need right now.

As I enter the kitchen, my eyes meet with Mona's. She wiggles her eyebrows at me before turning back to Kysi, who has made himself at home over the stove.

He looks at me next and gives a sheepish grin, followed by a wink. I try to ignore the sweep it sends through my stomach.

"Do you know who this is?" I turn to Mona, picking up her orange juice and taking a swig.

She nods. "I was dumbfounded when I saw him come out of your bedroom this morning. I was right last night. You really are a slut."

The shock of her words nearly makes me inhale the drink.

A chuckle comes from both of them. I can't believe Mona has not ripped his head off. I suppose being the god of Bargaining can make a person incredibly convincing. I wonder what he told her ...

Kysi lays a plate in front of me. The pancakes are adorned with raspberries and bits of chocolate, just how I like it.

That little spy.

It smells too good to pass up. I eagerly grab a fork and take a bite. It is annoyingly delicious. He proudly notices the satisfaction I attempt to hide.

I eat as they chat. Kysi talks about the most beautiful sights to see on Earth. Mona listens like she still cannot believe she's sitting in front of a god. I find myself eyeing the chair at the end of the table, the one Ivan—no, Kysi and I were on the other night before everything went south.

He softens when he notices my glances.

Mona wipes her hands. "Well," she says, clearly taking the hint, "I've got errands to run."

"I thought you were on vacation?" I sarcastically call her out.

"Shut up. I'm leaving." She stands. "Be back later. Try not to throw anything else, okay?"

I shoot Kysi a dirty look as the door closes behind her. There is an awkward stillness as I poke at the food in front of me. He clears his throat.

"Thanks for breakfast," is the only thing I can think of to say to break the silence.

When I look up from the food, I see that he is not nervous at all. I watch as his eyes roam over my hair before they meet mine. It's not the easiest to ignore the way his bicep tenses when he runs a hand through his wavy hair. It is usually straighter, so I guess that means he slept good last night. He nods and begins picking up the mess he made from cooking.

He cleans, too? Well, fuck me good.

Shame he's a snake.

"When would you like to start?" he asks, turning the sink on.

I know he is referring to our trip to the Shadowlands. Part of me is eager to return to the Heavens so we can convince Hellano to send us into the next realm, but at the same time, it feels embarrassing to return after suffering such a gruesome fate.

"Give me an hour? I'd like to mentally prepare myself a bit ... and brush my teeth."

A smile peeks through. "Sure thing, angel."

I have grown accustomed to my life on Earth. Content with it, actually. It is only now that I'm on the cusp of returning to the Heavens that I am realizing it.

I would prefer not to do any of this. It's apparent that I have no choice—because of course the fate of the universe rests in *my* hands.

Had the decision been mine, I would stay. Not just to continue in my career, but to work for something greater: a husband and maybe a few kids. No more than a distant dream, as Hellano would never allow me to conceive.

Still, if I had it my way, that's how it would be. With vacations twice a year, and every Sunday spent in loungewear on the couch, watching TV with my family.

Perhaps being sent here was not a bad thing. Maybe the *real* curse is having to leave.

I have spent eight years running on the fumes of my betrayal. It has been my distraction and my motivation in this life. I never took the time to look around and be content with it.

Now ... it is too late.

As I run the brush through my hair, Kysi appears out of nowhere behind me. "Gods!" I flinch. "Why didn't you just walk in?" I am beginning to understand why teleporters are often referred to as invasive.

"It's quicker this way." He opens his palm. "Allow me."

I look him over cautiously before placing the brush in his hand. "Are you rushing me?"

"Maybe." He begins gently running it through my darkened curls. "Maybe not."

As he glides it through my hair, I find myself relaxing for the first time in days, despite being in bed the whole time. Closing my eyes, I bask in this simple act of being cared for.

"You look tense," he says, sitting the brush by the sink.

"Yeah." I let out a breath. "That's what holding grudges will do to you."

Kysi places both hands on my shoulders. It is the first time we've touched since Ivan, and those incessant, desperate urges flicker in my stomach at the warmth of his skin on mine. I lift my lashes to see him peering at me through the mirror with the same hungry eyes I saw in a different face.

Ever so slowly, he dips his head below my ear and plants a soft kiss on my neck. "I can help you relax." Then, he moves to the opposite side and presses his lips there as well. His every movement transfixes me, as if he is a captivating piece of living art.

For the life of me, I can't understand *why* I want to give in. To let him touch me in the way I was begging Ivan too. How can I desire someone I loathe? Am I that weak, that deprived of attention?

No, I am stronger than this. The same way that I do not need his half-hearted apologies—which probably were given so I would be more inclined to help him—I do not need him to satiate my self-sabotaging urges.

Turning away from the mirror, I face him, our noses inches apart. His eyes are a burning forest, alive with an intense, untamed energy. When I run my hands up the length of his chest, his own smoothly trek down my sides before settling on my hips. I trail my fingers over the soft fabric of his shirt before wrapping them around his neck, and then grasp at the base of Kysi's skull, taking in a fistful of hair and jerking it back.

The grip on my waist tightens at the sudden assault as I speak with a calm anger. "I can't tell if you're brave or stupid. The universe is dying because of *you*, and I have to clean up the mess. So, if you want my help, I suggest keeping your hands to yourself."

As I release his midnight strands, his head lowers to reveal a coy smirk that only serves to piss me off more. He clicks his tongue. "We all need a little physical therapy every now and then, right?"

When I threaten him with my eyes, he lets it go. "Fine, I'll be here when you change your mind. For now, I'll settle for a hug."

Before I can protest his arms tighten around me, and everything goes black. Only for a second, but that brief moment felt like being sucked into a vacuum. The pressure builds quickly, popping my ears before we land in the entryway of an immaculate estate. Looking around, I see windows from floor to ceiling that peer over an endless forest. A fire crackles to the side, serving as the focal point of the room. The chimney it rests under is comprised of various gemstones, with assorted colors and shapes. Sunlight beams through the window, reflecting off the stones and casting a pool of spiraling color across the living room.

It is breathtaking.

Before I can comment on the architecture or ask where we are, I feel a sudden weight emerge on my back that nearly makes us both tumble. After appearing, they flap and twitch momentarily before settling.

My wings.

Gods, I have missed my wings.

To stretch them out feels like taking off heels after a long day. Kysi stares in awe as if he has never seen them before.

The feathers are primarily an ashen gray. Their uniqueness rests in the way they adjust to light in each room I walk through. Not drastically, but just subtle enough to make the transition apparent.

There are downsides to them as well, like the fact that they double as a giant mood ring that cannot be taken off. Luckily, they only respond to anger by darkening their feathers.

Now, as they bask under the reflection of jewels, they are unable to figure out which hue to focus on. I have never seen them under lighting like this.

Wherever we are, it is my new favorite place.

It is rejuvenating to have them back; my only wish is that the rest of my old self came with them. Their presence is a reminder of the power I once held that I no longer have. The disappointment is dizzying.

"You may not have the title anymore, but you certainly still look like a goddess." Kysi breaks my train of thought.

When I look at him and see the colors of my wings reflecting off the glowing emerald of his eyes, he holds my stare for a moment before we break away from each other.

"Welcome to my home."

Given the landscape, I would not have guessed we were in the Heavens. Now that I think about it, I suppose it makes sense that the god of Mortals and Bargaining would have a giant cabin in the woods.

When a brand-new god is created, the Heavens builds them a home. The structure is a representation of their duty, their livelihood, and their purpose. Hellano's had more of a macabre essence to it, while mine was decorated in greenery, with vines that stretched from the floor to the ceiling like veins to a beating heart. The thought of it makes my chest hollow.

That is another thing I miss. Home.

Once again, I feel faint.

"Why are we here?" I ask, blinking away the clouds behind my eyes. Are we not supposed to be, I don't know, somewhere more productive? Why aren't we at Hellano's trying to strike a deal?

"I wanted to see something first, in case we don't get the chance to later," he says.

When he does not continue, I give him an expecting look. "What did you want to see?"

His heavy lashes sweep the floor, the window, and then me. "This." He motions to the wings. "I've always wanted to see them here." Striding over to the fireplace, he runs a hand over the glimmering chimney. "Every time I saw you, it was like they were a color I'd never seen before. Somehow, they'd always accent your features." He turns back to me. "You go with anything."

I'm uncertain how to respond to that.

"I'd always wondered what they'd look like in lighting like this," Kysi says.

It takes me a moment to understand, but when I do, my cheeks flush like rubies reflecting in the sun.

It is rare for a deity to make changes to the home the Heavens built for them. Remodeling would be considered rude to those that reigned before you, as well as those after. However, it is tradition for gods to leave their mark before they are reincarnated. The way they do that varies with each soul. It is usually something small, like notches in wood.

"You remodeled your house to compliment my wings?"

This time he smiles. Not a smirk, a real smile. It is more handsome than I care to admit. "I would've," he says, "if it hadn't already been like this."

The weight of his words settles around us like a dense fog, obscuring everything but the palpable tension of the moment. He is saying that his home, which was made by the Heavens, intentionally accents me. Maybe I am getting ahead of myself, misunderstanding him. This sort of thing simply does not happen. A house has never been made for any god other than the one residing in it.

Kysi notices my confusion. "This was built to represent me, to reflect Earth and people"—he gestures to a painting of a landscape, then another of two figures dancing— "and you."

I look up at him as he strides back to me, trying to remain patient while he gets to the point.

"Breathe in," he says, taking a breath. "What do you smell?"

I inhale and recognize his natural scent first, the smell of a lush forest. Through it, something else lingers. "It's you, woodsy, but also …" I think aloud, closing my eyes to focus more, "like a freshness? Like spring."

"That's you," he points out.

As soon as he says it, I know it to be true. My house smells like the dawn of spring. So do my clothes. And my hair.

"Why?" I ask.

There is a heavy silence between us while he takes a minute to respond. With an eager yet hesitant expression, I am given the impression that he has been waiting to answer this question for a lifetime.

"Because my soul is in love with yours."

When the wooziness returns a third time, it is hard for me to believe that it is due to the weight of his words, despite them being a hard pill to swallow.

We are soul bound.

I have read of gods that held ties with others while skimming through books, but always assumed it just meant they shared a strong connection, like friends or lovers.

For hundreds of years, I believed Hellano was tied to me in the same sense.

But what he is saying implies we hold a bond that transcends lifetimes; one we cannot control.

Is that the pull I keep feeling towards him?

"Why did you do it?"

The reminder of his deal fills his eyes with disappointment. "You were never meant to be with Hellano. I bargained to get you away from him."

Excuse me? He doesn't get to make those decisions for me. Soul bound or not, I am my own person who gets to choose the path I take in this life.

"I think your Soul Mothers agreed because they hate Hellano's spirit just as I do. That's how it's meant to be. He was corrupting you."

I scoff in disbelief. "How would you know? You'd only spoken to me once before."

"You were doing too much," he abrasively expresses, "creating too much life. You were overpopulating Earth with everything. People, animals, plants, all of it. In order to keep the balance, it meant Hellano had to end more lives. But it didn't keep the balance, not really. My people became miserable. They were calling to me more than ever and I couldn't do anything for them."

Kysi has much influence over people's lives on Earth, but the one thing he cannot do is create or destroy the life on it. I am the beginning, he is the middle, Hellano is the end.

I had lost sight of that.

He steps away and begins pacing, actively becoming more worked up as he tells the story. "I tried to adapt, help them as much as I could. It didn't matter. The more life you created, the happier you were. The more death Hellano caused, the happier he was. The difference is that you did it subconsciously because you loved him. He only loved you because you gave him more things to kill."

"That's not true—" I defend myself, blinking back the thickening fog in my skull. It almost begins to hurt, but that cannot be right. There is no pain in the Heavens.

"Oh, it's not?" he interrupts. "Did you ever stop to notice how much he winked and whispered sweet nothings into your ear every time there was a baby boom? Or when you'd create forests so thick they smothered everything beneath them?" He continues pacing, running a hand through his hair. Right now, Kysi does not just look hurt, he looks heartbroken.

"Stop—" I wince at his words. I wouldn't do that. At least, I don't think I would. It's hard to think at all when there's a pressure building under my scalp that threatens to bring me to my knees.

"You can hate me all you want." His hands meet the air in frustration. "But imagine everything you care about being tossed around for enjoyment by the one you love, all while seeing them in the arms of another that only seeks to devour them."

I collapse under the pressure of an invisible vise. Hitting the floor, a crushing weight compresses against my bones and threatens to cave my chest in. My body is merely a vessel at the mercy of a monstrous abyss. Each muscle and joint suffocate under the agonizing burden as it feels like the walls of my soul are attempting to expand. As if the deep, icy darkness of the ocean floor wrapped itself around me with the intent of flattening me completely.

Kysi rushes to kneel beside me. Red clouds my vision as I strain to open my eyes, and it is not the reflection of rubies in the sun.

It is blood. My blood.

When he speaks, his troubled voice is no more than a muffled hum. Just as I'm gradually losing my eyesight, my sense of sound goes with it.

What is he saying? I sense his hands on either side of my head as he pulls me to look at him. For a moment it is a brief reprieve, another sensation to focus on. Through the crimson streams, Kysi is utterly panicked, terrified at the sight of me. From what I can tell by reading his lips, he is wondering "what the fuck is happening."

At this point, I think my head might implode. I use what strength I have to blink away the thickening redness, but it only serves to blur my vision more. When Kysi finally takes his hand away, it's smeared with a thick maroon.

My eyes are bleeding.

Then, he leaves. Just disappears before me.

Leaving me to die alone.

CHAPTER 6

I do not think it is the Shadowlands that awaits me. Instead, it feels like I am headed to nowhere. Into nothing. Just before I go completely blind, I see two figures appear in an embrace. They rush to me with muffled voices. Though my hearing is clouded, I can tell the two are yelling. They argue back and forth as they kneel next to me. One puts their palms over my ears, the other holds my hand, squeezing it and pressing the back to their mouth.

At last, the pressure begins to subside. In its place comes a warmth that spreads through my body.

A moment passes of complete silence, and I think I might be dead. My arms limply hit the floor as hands brush over my face. At first, I see two of everything, but with each swipe Kysi sends over my eyes to clear the blood, everything starts to come back together.

"Thank gods," he says, out of breath.

"What—" I choke on warm liquid in the back of my throat, tasting copper on my tongue.

He helps me roll to my side as blood streams from my mouth. With a shaking hand, I reach up to touch my ear, then my nose, both slick with the remnants of my draining insides.

I'm still trying to catch my breath when I see Kysi glance at the other person. I follow his gaze to find Meena, the goddess of Pleasure, at the other side of me.

"I don't know what just happened," she says, "but you better figure it out soon. I have a feeling it won't stay gone."

The god of Mortals and Bargaining is seething. "This is Luther's doing," he says with a clenched jaw.

"Hold on, you don't know that." Her wintery eyes give him a warning. "Kysi, you better not do anything irrational, or I won't come help you"—she nods in my direction— "or her again."

Meena is not my biggest fan. To be honest, none of the gods are—I can hardly blame them. I like to think of my experience being mortal as humbling, if not anything else.

Kysi visibly tenses. "My soulmate was just a blood fountain, and you don't think Luther has anything to do with it?" he growls.

"I don't know, and neither do you," she snaps. "Stop looking for someone to blame other than yourself. I mean, why did you even bring her here? She's practically fucking human!"

"Look at her!" He gestures to a wing. "Does this look human to you?"

My head spins as they bicker back and forth. I can still just barely feel the dull ache beneath the warmth of Meena's power.

I do not think the god of Agony had anything to do with it. The timing is too off. If he wanted me to suffer, why did he not do it while I was on Earth? He has no knowledge of my return to the Heavens. Plus, I doubt he has any personal grudges against me. I barely talked to the guy.

It felt like I was dying a true death. That's something not even Hellano can do, now that I know our past lives still live on in the Shadowlands.

Unless ... somehow having both my title and his gives him the power to create an eternal death.

"Ky." I squeeze the hand holding mine to get his attention. He immediately stops arguing and turns to me. "What exactly was the deal you made with Hellano?"

Although it would have been nice letting Kysi bathe me, given how exhausted I am from escaping death, I am not entirely on board with him seeing me naked. When he offered to help with the bath, I could tell it came from a place of care rather than attraction—which is the only reason I did not also get his blood on me today.

I stand awkwardly in a towel, watching him pull clothes from his dresser to give me.

"Why don't you just take me home?" I suggest.

"At this point, I'm scared to take you anywhere. As much as I hate that what happened might be my fault, I think jumping from Earth might have been too traumatic on your body." He grips the back of a shirt.

Riiipp! Riipp!

What a waste of perfectly good fabric, but if I must wear his clothes, my wings need to fit through somewhere.

Not all gods have them. Those that do not, learn to teleport—or phase, as many call it—in order to give themselves similar advantages to those with wings. It is more than similar in my opinion. Phasers can jump anywhere, as long as they know where they are going. Meanwhile, other gods have to travel by air. Although any deity can learn to teleport, it is an incredibly difficult skill.

If he cannot take me back to Earth, then phasing to my home here is out of the question as well. I would prefer not to travel without clothes, or ones I do not own, and possibly be seen.

When I make my public return, I want to be back on top.

He turns while I change. Afterward, I listen to the call of the bed and pull myself under the covers. There I sit, patiently waiting for Kysi to explain himself.

Coming around, he sits on the edge beside me, clearly unprepared to spill the details of his mistake. "Let me just start by saying, I wouldn't have made the deal if I knew it would hurt you."

I give him a look, remembering how Mona's hood became crushed under my impact.

"Not *that* kind of hurt," he says, reading my expression, "but I am sorry for that, too."

Leaning back, I cross my arms and give him my undivided attention.

"All it was, was your title in exchange to send you to Earth. He had to agree not to kill you unless I told him otherwise," he explains.

Unless he told him otherwise.

I do not know if I am being irrational or responsible in not trusting him. Additionally, Hellano can't just 'agree' not to kill someone. It is his *soul duty*, none of us can escape that. From what I gather, the outcome of the deal had to have given him the ability to exempt me from the fate of death, just as it gave him the power to send me to Earth instead of the Shadowlands.

Regret filters through him. "I should have just done nothing," he says, "never made that godsforsaken deal. At least then you'd be whole, and I could continue loving you from afar."

It is my own fault that I never learned about the Law surrounding soul bonds. To be honest, it never seemed important enough to spend my time on. Nothing did, really. Unless it was about Hellano.

But given the fact that Kysi is technically older than me, even though my soul is older than his, I can only imagine the avidity he held when I was created. A mate just for him, ready to spend millennia together.

Only for the god of Afterlife to snatch me up.

"Why didn't you just try to break us apart here? Why did you go to the Shadowlands, risk not being able to come back, and send me to Earth?" I ask.

A sad smile lifts across his cheeks, as if he wished it were that easy. "Soul bonds aren't always lovers; I'd just hoped we would be. I spent a few hundred years with your predecessor, who was mated with my Soul Father. She was my best friend. Although it was difficult to say goodbye to her, I was eager to meet who could be the love of my life."

Through the lingering anger in my chest, a spark of pity seeps through.

He continues, "When you clung to Hellano, it was a shock to not just me, but the other deities as well. None of us had ever heard of the goddess of Beginnings and the god of Afterlife falling in love. It just doesn't happen."

Now I understand why. What he said earlier, about the misery endured by those on Earth, is the product of the unnatural alliance of life and death.

"I thought surely it wouldn't last and things would go back to how they were always meant to be. So I satiated my need to be around you by visiting the Ancient Library, waiting for you to pick up any other book than a damnable fairytale of that bones-for-brains."

I shift with embarrassment. There are no 'fairytales' of Hellano ... if there were I would have read them.

"When you put the immaculate conception on Earth, I saw it as an opportunity to break the silence between us. Try my hand at connecting with you. When the conversation ended the way it did, I knew he had to be corrupting you in some way. Just as it's unnatural for souls of life and death to come together in love, it is for the bonded not to get along. That's when I became concerned about our connection. I couldn't find anything in the library on soul bound enemies. Then the thought of our tie possibly breaking came to mind, and I couldn't bear the thought of losing a rare and beautiful connection before having the chance to experience it."

That is why he chose to send me to Earth. When he arrived in my kitchen that day and spoke to me on the couch, he mentioned how he was originally supposed to meet with me after the deal was struck.

He planned to live a life with me.

From his perspective, it was a win-win. Without the relationship between me and Hellano, things were supposed to go back to normal for humans. Being the god of Mortals, Kysi could fulfill his duties on Earth just as he would in the Heavens. With me away from the god of Afterlife, the possibility of our bond being broken would no longer be an issue, and he could begin working on a relationship with me.

I lean slightly forward. "You could've just told me."

Kysi raises one brow, as if to say, *"You're kidding, right?"*

It takes a moment for me to understand, but after taking a second to sort through all of this information, it makes a little more sense why he did not.

If it is true I was somehow being corrupted and our connection was weakening, it would not have mattered what Kysi said. At that point I was loyal to Hellano, and the tie between us had not been strong enough to influence me to leave him.

"After you fell from the Heavens, Hellano struggled to maintain both titles. All my energy went to absorbing the impact of his actions, to spare my people as much suffering as possible." He does not look at me now, but at the floor as he thinks back on the last eight years.

This is the burden other gods carry. My actions, Hellano's actions, affect them. As Hellano struggled with his newfound responsibilities, it caused even more hardships on Earth that Kysi had to deal with. From every accidental death, unplanned pregnancy, every forest fire to disease outbreak, the god of Mortals had to be there. Whether to ensure aid be brought to people in disaster, or simply shift luck in the favor of someone who was dealt an unfair hand by Hellano, Kysi could not escape the pressing responsibilities of his soul duty and that is why it took him so long to meet me.

"After time had passed and Hellano still hadn't adjusted to the outcomes of our deal, I knew he was never going to. I'm not powerful enough to calm all the waves he makes, and I knew if things continued, eventually the chaos would consume Earth, and the Heavens with it.

"But all of this couldn't be for nothing," he says, looking back at me, "I still hadn't even gotten a *taste* of you. So, I put on the face of Ivan, just so I could experience what it might have been like if the deal had worked."

Part of me still clings to the idea that I would have helped, would have fixed everything if I had known, but I can't continue to be as naïve as I was back then, not when the state of our realms is at risk.

"And when this is all over," he says, "if you still don't want to be with me, I'll know it's not because I didn't try."

Damn.

After all that, I am finding it hard, and illogical, to stay mad at him. And what a fool I was, to have been with the wrong person for hundreds of years, while the other gods knew we were not supposed to be together and said nothing.

Because I never let them.

Not only were they weathering the storm of our actions just as Kysi was, but I was also like Velcro to Hellano, not leaving his side unless it was to visit the Ancient Library. I never quite opened my schedule for others. Seeing myself in a different light, a darker one, feels like dry swallowing a pill.

I was so entitled and vicious.

Kysi gazes at me with a familiar look. It is the same one he gave me at the library the first time we met. I thought it looked like love then, but having not known about our connection, settled on it being a product of his lust and became offended. Now, I know my initial impression was correct.

It *was* love.

The only way a person could love who I used to be, is if they are my soulmate.

There's no denying he is telling the truth about our bond. I feel it in my urge to reach for him, to gather him in an embrace and apologize.

So, that is what I do.

Leaning forward, I wrap my arms around his neck. It comes as a shock to him at first, but he quickly sinks into the hug like he has waited hundreds of years to experience it.

Because technically, he has.

Kysi is warm to the touch, a stark contrast to the chill that always seemed to radiate from Hellano. With my arms crossed around his neck, I rest my hands atop his broad shoulders and breathe in his woodsy aroma. He squeezes me back, as if letting go would be the end of a perfect dream, one he is not sure would ever return.

Although my attraction to him is a growing flame, I would rather just focus on getting to know him better for now. If we can't find time amidst the journey of saving our realms, then I'd like to make the effort to once this is all over.

"Would you still settle on being a friend?" I ask.

His grip never wavers as he responds, "I'll be whatever you need me to be."

When we finally part, his gaze catches on something behind me. I follow them to the feathers at my back.

They are ... different.

Like the sun reflecting off oil, the gray of my wings shimmer with iridescence.

In his living room, they were simply reflecting off the colors of the gemstone fireplace. Now, they are doing it all on their own. The only time they change by themselves is due to an emotion, but they have only ever darkened in response to anger.

I have no idea why they are changing now.

"That's ... new." Kysi holds a feather between his fingers, running his thumb over the blooming hues. Given the fact that I was bleeding from my orifices earlier, I do not take this as a good sign. It may be beautiful, but so are vipers. Death often strikes with the same resolve.

I wait frozen in fear for something to happen. For the pressure to return, the bleeding to come back, anything. Then all at once, they stop. The last bit of color moves out as the original shade settles into place.

"That was amazing." He runs a hand across the span of them. "Do you know what it means?"

I shake my head in response. I was hoping that because Kysi was incarnated before I was, he might have wisdom on the matter, maybe from my Soul Mother. But it appears we are both at a loss.

He releases a wing and glances to the sheets I'm under. "Well," he says with a sheepish grin, "since I have to settle on being a friend, I'll take the guest bed."

I awaken under the forest green canopy that drapes from his towering bedframe. A note rests on the pillow beside mine.

Good Morning Angel
Breakfast is ready for you in the kitchen.
I'll be back before you have time to finish it. Sit tight.

69

With lifetimes of love,

Ky

.

Stretching my legs through the plum satin sheets, I am pleasantly surprised at how well I slept. I had every expectation of tossing and turning all night considering the recent events that have unfolded, on top of the uncertainty of the future. There must be something in this bedding, because as soon as I laid down, I went out at the same time the lights did.

Kysi's floors are cold on my bare feet. I lazily trudge through the hallway, resisting the urge to go snooping through the other rooms. I noticed what I can only assume to be the entrance to the kitchen yesterday upon my arrival. As I pass the swimming lights in the living room, I enter an alcove that borders the windows.

My assumption was correct, but I would have never guessed to see such intricate architecture. The ceiling is dressed in elaborate artwork that trails down the walls and under the cabinets, doubling as a backsplash. The paintings taper off from the workstation, leaving the rest of the space with an untouched cream background. More windows bring in natural light through the recess a bench is built into. On the table in front of me rests a bouquet of lavender and white peonies, with greenery surrounding their colors.

I wonder if Kysi did that on purpose, or if it is just his love for admiring nature that brought them here.

There is not any food on the table or the counters, but I find what I think is my breakfast upon opening the fridge.

I should've known it would be something extravagant.

The first thing I notice are the oranges. They're somewhat peeled and halfway open. Their skin curls off them in strips, creating the illusion of a flower. Bites of kiwi rest under them to look like leaves on a stem. Grapes are then cut into quarters, surrounding the main attraction with smaller, more petite blossoms.

Now he's just showing off.

I take it over to the bench and force myself to ruin this master-piece. Why would someone create something so beautiful just for another to destroy it?

Wait ... I did that. I created life just for it to be torn apart. All for Hellano.

And just like that, I'm full.

Now would be a great time for Kysi to return, it would make a good distraction from my self-loathing. I think about the note left, and how it said he would be back by the time I had finished eating.

"Liar," I mutter under my breath.

"Did you say something?"

The voice catches me off guard. I hadn't heard anyone come in.

Meena eyes me from under the archway that leads back into the living room. Her knee-length hair drapes around her figure in some form of worship. I never noticed how bright it shined until now. The glow from the glass panes behind me soak it in, reminding me of winter under the full moon. Her dark skin is a perfect contrast to the striking white of her hair.

She is a sight to behold.

"Just thinking out loud," I finally respond. "When did you arrive?"

As she strides over, her hair flows like a veil behind her. "Hours ago, when Kysi left." She sits across from me and looks over the flowers. "Well, aren't you special."

So he did get them for me.

I lower my gaze. "You're kidding, right? He sent you to come babysit me?"

She scoffs, "Before you get your granny panties in a twist, remember how you turned his perfectly waxed hard wood floors into a red carpet."

Granny panties? Who the fuck is this woman? Why is Kysi telling her details about my personal wardrobe?

Okay, I'll admit. I might have one or two pairs ... but I only wear them on laundry day.

"Even if you did know how to teleport," she continues, "I don't think anyone could do it in that condition, not even Kysi. And because I don't know how to either, he thought it would be best not to leave you alone and come back to find you liquidized on his mattress."

The detailed picture she just painted sends a chill down my spine. "Fair enough." I wipe my hands. "But I'm awake now. Where's Ky? I'd like to go home and put on clothes that don't have rips in the back."

"About that," she says, "there's not going to be enough time for you to go strolling down memory lane, so I brought you some of my clothes." When she stands to leave the kitchen, I see her wings for the first time.

They are almost completely see-through. The only reason I noticed them was because their outline reflected in the sun when she turned around. I never knew she had them.

Back to the issue at hand, I haven't been home in nearly a decade. Who are they to tell me I cannot go? Especially when Kysi has been gone for hours and I have done nothing but sleep and eat in that time? I could have done all that at my house.

I trail behind her. "I don't think it's up to either of you." The annoyance is clear in my tone. "Now where is Kysi?"

She stops in front of the loveseat, grabbing an outfit from the chair. "Good gods," she groans, tossing me the clothes, "I could honestly care less about what you do. I'm doing this for him. So, no. You can't go home. And no, I can't tell you where he is."

So, what? I'm just a prisoner here? Fuck that.

"Listen I don't know what your deal is with him, but Kysi does not control me." I pull down his boxers and step out of them as they hit the floor, replacing them with the leggings she threw. It's taking everything in me not to throw something back. "And you don't either. Now, I'm leaving. You can either send me Kysi's way or I'll find my way home. Your choice."

Meena pauses, I can see her weighing out the options. Finally, she rolls her eyes when I start unbuttoning his shirt. "Fine." She waves her arms up in defeat. "He's at the Ancient Library, but you cannot let anyone see you. Nobody knows you're back yet." She turns and mumbles something about doing too much for him as she plops on the couch.

Her bronze hoodie falls just above my hips. It's a tight fit around the wings, but other than that it works fine. I'm about to leave, but then I remember something.

"I know you mentioned that you're only doing this for him ... but thanks anyway. For saving me."

"I know how you can repay me," she says, "don't break Kysi's heart ... again."

CHAPTER 7

The library is more extensive than I remembered, but everything else remains the same. It still holds the same ancient smell, and when I say ancient, I mean *old*. Similar to the natural musk of a retired cat lady. The ceiling is high reaching, with shelves that rise up the walls. Moreover, smaller cases create aisles down the middle. Not all areas are parallel. I have found rooms filled with cases that curve and create wavy pathways. From an aerial view, it has always reminded me of the inside of a cell. Every so often I will spot a hallway that leads into another section that holds its own set of uniqueness, despite feeling exactly the same.

I have no idea how I will find Kysi in the seemingly endless rows of books. They stack high, the shelves holding an ongoing string of sconces that cast a dimly lit glow over their spines.

It wasn't all that hard getting here unnoticed. I have said before, the gods do not really take advantage of the library. The list of things I can think of that they would rather be doing is almost as vast as this place. The main hurdle was convincing Meena to tell me which way to go once I left.

I pass row after row, not seeing a soul. After a while, my legs begin to tire. I must have been wandering for over an hour by now.

Screw this.

I flex my shoulder blades back, lengthening my wingspan before taking flight. I'm a little out of practice but manage to balance myself out in no time.

Gods, it feels good to fly. As I glide over the bookcases, I almost forget to look for him. I'm too distracted by the gusts of wind that hug my face with each whip of my feathers. I'm stuck in the euphoria of it when I hear a muffled call from below.

Kysi glares up at me, clearly unimpressed.

My landing is not exactly graceful. I practically barrel into him. He catches me with a grunt, saving me from hitting the floor.

"Anewla." When he says my real name, especially in that tone, it is obvious he's not very pleased with me. "Please tell me why you're flying around the library, sticking out like a severed thumb."

"Um." I balance myself off him. "I think the saying is sore thumb."

His jaw twitches as he waits for me to explain myself.

"You said you'd be back soon," I protest, "yet here you are hours later. And nobody is around anyway. This place is a wasteland."

"I'm sorry for my tardiness." I can tell he is struggling to move on from the fact I was just a blimp in the library. "But that's no excuse to put yourself at risk like you did. If Hellano finds out you're here before I can speak with him, who knows what would happen. Until we're confident that he's not the one behind what happened to you yesterday, we must keep your presence here a secret."

"What, you think he might have gone back on the deal? I thought you said he couldn't hurt me?"

"Technically, he can't. Someone else might be doing his bidding," he suggests.

It really would be nice if he could update me on these things, rather than leave me in the dark and enclose me in his house like a zoo animal. He even sent a zookeeper. "Why didn't you tell me?" I ask what presses on my mind.

"Because you would've insisted upon accompanying me, and I didn't want to risk you being seen." A twinge of annoyance clouds his tone as he motions to my wings, frustrated that his effort was pointless.

"You could've at least let me wait for you in my own home," I mumble, knowing it still would not have changed the fact that I would insist upon accompanying him.

Kysi sighs and rubs his forehead. "I'll make sure you get to go home before our work is done." He gives me a promising look and then takes my hand to lead me through the shelves, as if he is worried that I will fly away and get myself seen.

I am not trying to be difficult. I am here because I want to play an active role in finding my own answers. I do not want to sit somewhere, wasting space while someone figures it out for me. Hellano was the reason I failed consistently in my duties as goddess. He was the reason I abandoned my moral compass and constructed another with a broken needle that always pointed toward him. I let a man corrupt me and I want to rebuild myself.

"What are we looking for?" I ask.

"You really want to know?" He pulls his attention away from the shelves and waits for me to nod. "We're looking for a book on eternal death."

Well, that's grim.

He must be concerned that what happened last night was a precursor to the real ending, which sends a shiver down my spine ... because that is exactly what it had felt like.

I do not respond. Anxiety creeps into my chest as I begin to look over the tomes. Part of me hopes we do not find the book we are looking for. Ignorance is bliss and I wish that I could be naïve in whether or not I am dying.

Another hour goes by, and we still have not found a book to help us.

"I'll be back before you have time to finish," I mimic his tone before I exaggerate running a hand through my hair, "sit tight."

A laugh escapes him. "In my defense, I thought I knew exactly where it would be."

I look at him, then ahead to the endless rows, then back to him.

"Don't worry," he says, tightening his hold on my hand. "I think we're getting close." He glances behind me, pulling on my hand once more. "Your wings are doing that thing again."

Looking back, it appears he is right. Once again, they have turned iridescent. An idea comes to him in the form of a spread smile.

"What is it?" I ask.

"Oh, nothing." He slides his finger adorned with obsidian over the spine of a book. "Just that I think I know why your wings have been acting up."

I am curious to know his theories. It could be anything really. Not having them for eight years, my near-death experience, losing my title, it is tough to say for sure. The day I fell to Earth, they burned in the atmosphere, so maybe these new ones just grew in differently.

It is comforting to know the Heavens still views me as a goddess. "What's your theory?"

"You know how they darken when you're mad?" My senses heighten at the feel of his thumb idly running back and forth over mine.

"Yeah?"

He winks at me. "I think they get colorful when you experience another big emotion."

We both halt in unison as soon as we round a corner. Ahead, a man sits in the floor, leaning against the bookcase. His knees are hugging his chest, head buried in a book in front of them. There are other opened ones scattered around him.

"Oh, uh. Hello," Kysi says.

"Hello." The man doesn't look up to greet us. All I can see of him is the sandy hair that flows down his shoulders. I glance at Kysi to see that he is visibly confused.

"Are you new?" he asks to the man on the floor. I had not thought of the possibility that Hellano may have already begun making new gods.

A chuckle comes out of the man so quietly, I almost thought I did not hear it. "No."

"I don't recognize you," Kysi responds as we start walking closer to him, "and I've met all of the gods."

The man is silent.

"Who are you?" I ask.

"My name is Cato," he says into the book, "I am the god of Wisdom."

The god of Wisdom? We do not have a god of Wisdom? Kysi must be thinking the same thing; he looks at me and shakes his head. By the time we reach this god of Wisdom, I can see one hand holding the book while the other points into it, his thin finger following the words as he reads them.

"Why have we never met before?" Kysi asks.

"I stay here," Cato answers without missing a beat.

"I've spent over half of a millennium in this library. I've never seen you," he says.

"It's a big library."

Kysi's jaw twitches at the sarcastic remark. When I still lived here in the Heavens, I had a log of all the current gods. He was not on it.

"When was the last time you … saw anyone?" I question.

"It's been a while."

"Can you put the book down?" Kysi is getting actively annoyed.

"Yes," Cato responds.

We both stand there waiting for him to do it. A minute ticks by, and I can feel the heat coming from Kysi's ears.

"Listen—" Just as Kysi is about to go off on him, he reaches a stopping point and places a thin string between the pages before gently closing it.

"How can I help you?" Cato asks from the floor. I finally get to see his face when he looks up. He appears youthful, yet full of age. His hair does not just reach his shoulders like I originally thought, instead it travels down the length of his back. The light blonde almost takes away from his eyes.

Almost.

As I look into the mysterious god's irises, it feels like I might fall into them. Despite being as white as the ground on Christmas morning, they remind me of a black hole. They are as endless as the archives around us. As he looks back at me, I think he might try to engulf me in them. But he just stares.

I guess it makes sense for him to be an awkward individual. I probably would be too if I had not talked to anyone for "a while." After glancing at Kysi with a sympathetic look, I lower to sit by Cato. A short moment passes before he follows my lead and meets us on the floor.

"Cato, who made you?" Maybe once we figure that out, I can gauge how old he might be.

"Lilliana was my creator," he says.

Lilliana. The first.

Kysi's eyes go wide. There is no way that is possible. How has he not been reincarnated? There is no bypassing the Law.

Additionally, he would have gone mad by now. How is his mind not corrupted?

"Are you aware of the laws that govern the Heavens?" Surely, he has to know this is a peculiar situation.

"I am."

"So, how is it that you've avoided them?"

Cato twiddles his fingers over his knees, as if he is unsure what to do with them now that they are empty. "I haven't avoided them."'

Just as I'm about to ask him to explain, he starts talking. "The Law was written by Lilliana and Drayxi. I was her first creation, made for the purpose of retaining information and answering questions. The Heavens made this my home. It grew as Lilliana began creating the foundation for everything we know to exist."

The pieces start to fall together.

"She made you with the intention of never reincarnating you, in order for you to serve as a fountain of knowledge?"

"Indeed," Cato confirms, "not everyone has since the beginning of time to study all of this." He lifts a hand to the shelves. "Even I haven't caught up."

Kysi interjects, "How is that possible, being as old as you are? And how has your mind avoided corruption?"

When Cato meets his eyes, it looks like he holds the same concern of being swallowed whole inside them. "You gained the power to strike a deal so powerful to send the goddess of Beginnings to

Earth, my ability to avoid reincarnation and the perish of my mind most likely comes from the same source you gained your power. To answer your other question, the Ancient Library documents the events in time. Time is forever, so it is a collection that will always be expanding."

My stomach feels like it is in freefall. Cato mentioned how he has not caught up with the library's continual additions of information, which means he does not know what is happening now. He is not aware that everything existing in time is at risk of being erased. Additionally, Kysi doesn't know *how* my Soul Mothers were able to give him the power. It all relies on us going to the Shadowlands and hoping they can reverse it.

"Please excuse my manners and allow me to introduce myself, my name is Anewla—"

"Anewla Delphine?" He snaps his attention back to me.

Hearing a deity use my chosen last name in this realm takes me a bit off guard. "Um, yes—"

"You're the Fallen Goddess."

I've never been referred to as that before ... I do not know how to feel about it. "How would you know if you haven't caught up with the library?"

Cato reaches for a book to his side and waves it at me. "I jump around a lot. I'll say, what happened to you was a plot twist I never expected." He chuckles quietly to himself.

It is hard to keep a lid on my annoyance. Looking at it from his perspective, once you have read a million books, I suppose nothing seems to surprise you anymore. I can see why he would be giddy over a plot twist, but I still have to stifle my anger.

"If you're Anewla, then that makes you just who I suspected." He points a boney finger at Kysi. "God of Mortals and Bargaining."

Kysi cocks his head to the side in confusion.

"Figures," Cato says, "Soul bound lovers can never stay away forever."

I look over at my "soul bound lover" and he shrugs his shoulders as if to say, *"What? Can't beat fate."*

"Speaking of soul ties," Kysi says, "is it possible that Anewla's relationship with Hellano weakened our connection?"

With books in hand, Cato swiftly rises. He hovers in the air for a moment before landing on his feet. I look up to see blue-green wings that produced the levitation. They curl into his back again.

"It's possible," he utters while walking away. Kysi and I both stand to follow him. "But there's no evidence to support that claim. No soul bonds have ever been weakened. However, one has been broken due to a permanent ending."

A wave of anxiety falls over Kysi.

As Cato strides through the aisles, he slips hardcovers into slots on the shelves. His wings reach to the side and push them neatly into place. It's like he has an extra set of arms. I have never seen anything like it, nor had any idea such flexible appendages could exist. They move with a purpose all their own—individually, but also a part of him. It is as if sections of his personality reside within each membrane. One is more rigid and stoic, while the other aloof and pompous.

"Can you tell us about permanent endings?" Kysi asks after swallowing a gulp.

"Why do you need to know about that?" Cato asks, taken back a bit. Part of me is surprised he doesn't know, that even the god of Wisdom is fallible in his expertise.

"Something's happened to Anewla, and we need to cancel it out as a possibility. Can you help us?"

Cato turns suddenly. "I have something that may be of service to you." Then, he disappears in front of us, the rows of tomes that were hidden behind him becoming clear.

He is a teleporter. A phaser with wings. That's rare.

"Up here," he calls down to us. I look up to see his figure between a recess in the shelves that almost touch the ceiling. I wonder how many of those there are that we never noticed. With a flick of my feathers, I jump to catch myself in the air. I can feel Kysi's glowing green eyes on my wings. When I reach Cato, he's already standing behind him.

They walk to the back of the annex, where a pile of pillows and blankets meet a wide hammock. Lights hang independently overhead. This must be his home inside his home.

Cato positions himself on the floor near the cushions. He begins sifting through books that lie arbitrarily about. Kysi and I stare in awe and curiosity as his wings help sort them out. "Ah," he says,

opening a rusty colored one. I can see from here that the title reads
The Law of Permanent Endings.

It sends a chill through me.

Kysi must have noticed, because he strides over to rest a palm on
the dip of my back for comfort.

"I've been meaning to finish this one." His hollow eyes fill with
curiosity. "What do you need to know?"

We recite to him the course of events that had taken place over
the last few days. He listens intently, like he enjoys being told stories
just as much as reading them. Every now and then, the god will look
down and flip through the book, then bring his attention back to us.
When Kysi finishes, Cato silently turns page after page, searching for
an answer.

"I'm not seeing anything about blood loss—" He cuts himself off
and goes silent.

"What? What is it?" I step forward.

His eyes roam the page, no doubt absorbing the words in them
the same way I was worried they would absorb me. Finally, he looks
up and recites the passage. "The frailty of hierarchical gods is that of
any. A god's title and soul are intertwined, without one there cannot
be another. It is for this reason that taking the title away from a
hierarchal god is forbidden."

The hand on my back shifts with unease.

We already knew that a god's title and soul are connected, and
when a deity's job becomes useless, they move on to the Shadowlands. But the difference between that situation and mine, is that

those gods did not have their title taken from them. It went with them into the next realm, as it wasn't being used.

Mine was stolen.

"So, what? My soul is dying?" I ask.

Cato humphs, perplexed. "It should already be dead."

CHAPTER 8

Blood drains from Kysi's pale face. This is a different fear than when I had bled in his living room. All at once, he snaps out of his daze and begins to move.

"We have to go back." He quickly wraps his arms around me.

"Wait." Cato holds up a finger. "This has happened before."

"With all due respect I really don't care about a history lesson right now." His arms tense, but I push out of them before he has the chance to send me anywhere. Under his lashes, eyes darken. "Anewla," his voice has turned cold, demanding.

It pisses me off.

"You don't get to make the decisions when it's my life that's at stake here," I snap at him.

"Your life is at stake because of me!" He pleads, "Being out of the Heavens has to be what's kept you alive. Please, let me take you back."

"No deal," I say to the bargainer.

His eyelids close as he takes in a deep breath before running a hand through his hair, tousling it. When I sit down next to Cato, he begins pacing back and forth.

The god of Wisdom eyes us before continuing, "As you probably know, all gods except the goddess of Beginnings and the god of Afterlife can be sent into the Shadowlands without a replacement being made. This is different from stripping the title from them. Their soul lingers in our afterlife, just as ours do. A reincarnation of them can be made at any time."

"Yes," I confirm, "it's like they're put on hold. Or paused."

"Precisely," Cato concurs. His right wing flips a page for him. "But when a god loses their title, their soul dies along with all of the lives that it has lived in. This has occurred a handful of times in deities of a lower status. If one soul is rotten, meaning if all of the reincarnates are malicious, they will receive the permanent ending. Unfortunately, there is no information on how or why this occurs. It does say that it is against the Law to strip a high-ranking god of their title, because the Heavens and Earth rely on the balance. It does not specify what defines a hierarchal god, either. Technically, you and Hellano are at the top of the food chain so to speak. Then it's Kysi and all other gods trickling down from there." The tip of his wing sways under his chin as he enters deep thought. "Surely Kysi is considered high-ranking ..."

"Where are you on this food chain?" I ask.

Cato grins. "I'm not on the food chain, just the one who tells people about it."

Kysi can't seem to stay still ahead of us. He motions at Cato to get to the point.

A skinny index finger points to the letters as he reads, "In the beginning, three gods reigned: the goddess of Beginnings, the god of Time, and the god of Afterlife. The god of Time's duty was to protect the existence of us all. If Life and Death were to be threatened, the god of Time would reverse the course of events to manipulate the outcome. But the god of Time, named Kairos, did not want to follow the Law of Reincarnation. He used his abilities to avoid passing on to the Shadowlands." Cato flips a page. "Ah, yes, this is where I was," he says before continuing. "Kairos would have been successful if it weren't for the soul bond between him and the god of Afterlife."

Silence fills the air in thick waves. The god of Afterlife and the god of Time were lovers? Not just any lovers, but soul bound. Their bond was the first to ever exist. I wonder if the two gods created soul ties as a way to share their love across lifetimes, or to allow other deities to experience what they had. Maybe it wasn't them at all, maybe it was just the cards they were dealt. I have never known the Heavens to be coincidental. Then again, there is a lot I do not know that is all coming to light now.

Looking back on my life with Hellano, it pulls so many things together. There was always this emptiness in him I could feel when we would lie together, when we would laugh together, it was always there. I thought I could fill it. Now I understand why I never did.

"Kairos loved Death," Cato continues, "but nothing compared to the connection that he had with Prosenth, the third reincarnation of the god of Afterlife. During a night together, Kairos admitted that he had avoided the rule of reincarnation. Prosenth was torn between his duty to the afterlife and his love for Kairos. In an effort to save his soul tie, Prosenth called to the Heavens to strip Kairos of his title. The Heavens granted the wish, resulting in the first permanent ending. Despite the eternal death of Kairos, the soul bond remained. Cursing the god of Afterlife to long for a love that will never be. Due to the unfathomable anguish in Prosenth, he created a law that forbids calling upon the Heavens to relinquish a title from a hierarchal god."

All Prosenth wanted to do was save his love, so he did not have to send him to the Land of Shadows. In return, the Heavens killed him.

Everything I knew prior to today was wrong. The knowledge that the Law can be broken is devastating. The only thing keeping gods from disrespecting the system that governs us is their belief that it results in a never-ending rest in the Shadowlands.

This must mean that my past lives know about the ability to call upon the Heavens, and that must be what they did in order to give Kysi the power to make the deal. Which would mean Cato's assumption for the reason why his mentality hasn't crumbled after this long would be correct; these abilities had to have come from the same power source.

Kysi kneels above me and takes my hand in his. "Angel," he says softly, pressing the back of my palm to his mouth, "you've heard the story. Now, can we go to Earth? Please?"

His irises remind me of the reflecting emeralds of his living room; utterly captivating. Unlike Cato's, I wish I could swim in these. I would be content if they swallowed me whole. When he talks to me like that, it is hard to say no.

Cato clicks his tongue. "Your love for her may ultimately be what drives her away." His voice causes me to break eye contact with Kysi.

All of a sudden, the pull to agree with him vanishes. When I look back, he is staring daggers into the god of Wisdom.

The moment it hits me, I pull my hand away. "You were trying to glamour me?!" My wings twitch and deepen their shade to a black almost as abysmal as his hair. Where is the nearest hardcover? It does not take me long to find it on the other side of Cato. When I reach across him, he leans out of my way, happily granting me access.

To my annoyance, Kysi catches the book I throw at him. Grabbing more, I keep sending them his way. "Don't EVER"—Cato saves one from my grasp, quickly replacing it with another he doesn't mind me throwing— "manipulate me like that again!"

Kysi lifts his arms to dodge the flying atlases and encyclopedias. He knew that my connection to him, the trust I was building with him, was a weakness for compulsion.

My eyes water with betrayal. My naivety is beginning to amaze me.

Once the books around me end up at Kysi's feet, a hush comes over us. I look toward him, but not at him; I cannot look at him. Tears of frustration are about to fall, despite my efforts to hold them back. I have already made myself vulnerable enough by expressing such anger, I don't want to let them see my sadness too.

In a few steps, the annex is behind me, and the endless rows of cases are below. Kysi's voice calls out from Cato's room. It only makes me soar quicker through the labyrinth. His voice jumps, and I look down to see that he is phasing, trying to keep up.

He cannot teleport to me if he doesn't know where I am.

I dip down into one of the aisles. The tears do not have a chance to dampen my cheeks before wind from my feathers rolls them away. I twist through the rows until I can no longer hear him.

Finally landing on my feet, I balance myself on a shelf instead of him this time.

It feels as though everything has caught up to me at once. I spent eight long years alone, only to open up to someone that never truly existed, to forgive the one that used a mask to pry open my heart and squeeze it until it popped. All that fighting to get back into the Heavens, only to be met with bleeding eyes and the threat of a permanent death.

I loved Hellano, too. How could I be so ignorant? Loving a god who only praised me when I gave him sacrifices to devour. That's not pro-life. That's pro-torture. I tortured the life that came from me. What I have done is in direct contrast to my soul's purpose, and I can feel the crushing weight of my actions.

It is unnatural for the goddess of Beginnings to care so little about her creations.

I deserve this. Hell, I deserve a lot more than this.

I deserve the permanent ending.

A hand presses on my upper arm. When I lift my head, I'm relieved to see it's not Kysi that found me, but the god of Wisdom

I sniffle. "How'd you know where I was?"

It is obvious Cato doesn't know how to comfort people, as he awkwardly pats my shoulder. That is okay, though. Just the effort is comforting in itself.

"I know my way around."

Rather than telling me why he is here, he simply expresses it in a hug.

The embrace catches me off guard. I definitely was not expecting this to come from a recluse like him, but considering the fact he may have never experienced the companionship of another, I give into it. I need this too ...

His sandy hair falls over us. It's warm, like him. His shirt catches my tears as we squeeze each other like long lost friends.

"He is scared for you," he states.

"Yeah," my response comes out as barely a whisper, "it's still not an excuse, though."

His bargaining power is one of the things that sets him apart from others. Each god has their own abilities. Being the god of Mortals, he can take on the appearance of any human. But Kysi is also the god of Bargaining, which gives him the ability to glamour. It's not supposed to work very well on other deities, unless they have their guard completely down.

Which is what I was beginning to do with him.

"It's not," Cato agrees, releasing me from his embrace.

I wipe my eyes. "None of this makes sense anyway. I'm still here, why am I still here?"

The god of Wisdom doesn't like not knowing the answer to things. He disappointedly shrugs, but I sense a hint of determination behind his expression.

We sit in the silence of the library together. After a while, I pull him to stand with me. "Would you mind getting me out of here? I think I'm a bit lost."

He grasps my hand and I pull him up. "Of course," he says. When his arms wrap around me, it's not just to teleport. It's another hug.

A hug goodbye.

We hit the ground on the back of the property. Thick clouds spiral around us, only parting to exhibit the sparkling bridges that connect Cato's house to other parts of the Heavens. He takes in the scenery, breathing in outside's sweet, luminous fragrance.

It is a special sight to see, someone this caliber of introverted experiencing the outside world for the first time in gods know how long. His gaze never lingers from the crystalline overpass as he asks, "Where are you going?"

With a sigh, I decide how to answer. I do not think it would make much of a difference to be honest.

"I'm going to find Hellano," I admit. We need him to send us to the Shadowlands, so we can set everything back to how it was before. Kysi stated in the past that he needs me to go into the next realm and convince them to help us. Technically, that would mean I can just handle it myself.

I don't need Kysi.

I can fix his mistake on my own.

The god of Wisdom stares for a second, then lets a grin spread across his cheeks. "Rise from this a victor," he encourages as we part. "I do love a happy ending."

There is no point in walking to Hellano's, not now that I'm headed straight into the lion's den.

I glide over the staircase that protrudes from a cliffside, taking in the way it glitters with black and purple, as if the entire structure is one enormous geode.

Reaching the summit, an unfamiliar estate greets me. It is definitely the same building, but has changed drastically since my last visit.

What used to be decaying vines that wrapped around pillars at the front, have been replaced with dark blossoms. The trees that line the side of the deep, crimson brick hold identical flowers, although their branches appear to have long been void of life. The dead grass is moist with dew from a lazy fog that encompasses my ankles.

Here, life comes from death and death comes from life at the same time. They are no longer separate and equal but intertwined in a power struggle.

It is completely unnatural.

As I stride through the stone portico, nausea swims in my gut. My fingers turn slick, as if the atmosphere is whispering a warning that I cannot yet hear.

Ahead, the door lay ajar.

"Hello?" I call from the outside. The stillness of everything, even the fog, creates a panic-induced migraine.

I force myself through the threshold and take in its surroundings.

The interior mirrors outside in the sense that life and death are undergoing a battle to overcome one another. Dry dirt spreads throughout the once beautiful marble flooring, housing larva that just barely moves. The walls bleed painful tears of sap. As I move forward, a bitter chill brushes my skin like a ghost. When I take another step, it is replaced with a searing heat.

This house feels sick.

"You," a grave voice calls from above.

Looking toward the balcony overhead, I'm taken back—absolutely appalled at the sight of him.

Hellano's face is entirely sunk in, and dark circles hug his eyes with a dreadful embrace. Hair that once mimicked the sunrise has now rusted and dulled. The god of Afterlife is thin, weak.

I've spent lifetimes with this man, and I barely recognize him.

"Me," I say, pushing away the ache in my temple.

"You're doing this?" He grips the railing with compromised strength. "Did you finally come for me?"

Slowly inching my way to the crippling staircase, I begin to ascend the balcony. "I haven't done anything, 'Lano."

The use of his nickname causes a twinge of emotion to prick his features, as if it was painful to hear.

There's so much I want to say, so many questions I need answers to. Why did you do it? Was any of it real? Did you ever love me?

It is neither the time nor place for that conversation, so I trudge forward and try to stay on topic.

"Everything has been fine until yesterday. Me, the house, it was all normal." He inches farther away, almost frightened by my presence. "It has to be because you're here, because you're back," he concludes.

I reach for him as he stumbles, but don't make contact. Our proximity is a catalyst to the eruption of pressure that pushes on the sides of my skull. I cover my ears, bending down to withstand the force. My insides feel too big for my skin to hold, as if they are trying to escape. Hellano doubles over as well beside me.

Chaos engulfs the home. The floor cracks to separate the two of us, flowers bloom rapidly and then die over the mangled vines that entangle the railing. My sense of sound begins to fade, muffling Hellano's agonizing wail.

Straining to peer at him, I find his mouth agape, body contorting as he pries at his own skin as if something is trying to force its way inside.

A maroon fills the corners of my eyes. With each passing second, I see less. It does not matter how much I try to blink it away; it is blinding me.

The pressure is unbearable. The moment I think it can't get any worse, liquid bubbles up from the pit of my throat. It takes a moment for me to realize that the foreign pain on my neck is actually my own nails, clawing against my esophagus in a desperate attempt for air.

I am drowning in my own blood.

Just let me die already, is all I can think of, over and over again. This is an agony so all-consuming that I welcome the embrace of a permanent ending.

Anything to stop this.

A weight falls against my wings before the pressure intensifies.

This is it. This is death.

As hot, thick blood streams from my mouth, I feel a reprieve in the depth of my throat. I am choking and coughing, gasping for oxygen. It is not enough. The more I take in, the more I need. The pain that is relieved from my temple moves to my spine as a stinging, violent fire erupts in my back. My thighs take a hit, but from what I could not say. Then, a force barrels into my side. The agony between my shoulder blades does not allow me to focus on what strikes me, or the pain that it induces.

Is this the permanent ending, just getting beat to shit for all eternity?

Apparently, it does not last forever, because one more blow to the temple makes everything go away.

CHAPTER 9

Faint whispers pull me from a deep slumber. I focus on them, attempting to make out what they are saying.

"What if she doesn't come back from this?"

A slow pause hangs in the still air.

"She will," the other finally responds, "she has to."

Through the shivers of my skin, I am conscious of every vein that trails to my chest. They transport slow, icy blood to a frozen block that rests behind my ribcage. It is heavy yet hollow; a hole of nothing that threatens to spread until it swallows me whole, an unbearable blizzard in a deep, endless void.

Unaware of what death is like, I imagine this is the closest I have been to it.

My eyelids are as heavy as the pressure that previously weighed against my skull, but somehow, I managed to lift them.

In the mortal realm, my bedroom greets me. Before my memory fills in completely, I assume it's just another day. One where I go to work, plot my revenge, come home, and watch tv.

Then, I see him.

He stands in the corner, accompanied by a familiar face. It appears he hasn't slept in days, his hair lacking vitality along with the glow that usually illuminates his eyes.

That is, until they meet mine.

Kysi does not hesitate to stride toward me. I fight the instinctive urge to open up to his comfort, still angry over what he did in the Ancient Library. All I can manage to let out is a raspy, "No," that stops him in his tracks.

He does not get to be the hero now, does not get to swoop in when I am vulnerable and use it as an opportunity to gain my trust back, just so he can carry it as a weapon against me.

"Out," I rasp, lifting a shaking hand to the door.

His mouth opens in protest, but I do not give him the chance to.

"Out," I repeat, straining to put more effort into my tone. Taking notice of that, he wisely decides not to push it any further and takes his leave.

Mona sits beside me on the bed, propping herself up with an arm on the other side of my legs. "Your wings are pretty rad." A sad smile twitches upward. "From what I saw of them anyway."

"What happened," I say in a dry swallow.

Her glossy eyes think back to the memory. "I thought you were possessed or something when I came in ... those alien appendages of yours were going crazy, like the air was suffocating them; throwing you around like a rag doll before they shriveled into your back." She shivers at the thought. "Your entire face was bathed in blood, fresh blood, and it was draining down your neck and coating your clothes. Kysi and I cleaned you the best we could, he's been changing the bandage on your leg every few hours or so. The man has barely spoken to me since you both arrived. I haven't seen him eat or sleep, if that's even something your ... *kind* does."

I do not have the strength to express that yes, we do sleep and no, we don't need to eat.

She sighs. "Now you're all caught up. When you're feeling better, I expect to be caught up as well." She stands to leave. "Oh," she says, turning at the door, "and I expect free therapy from this indefinitely."

A hyperthermic slush swirls in my diaphragm like a deadly fever. All I can do is shake against the internal ice storm and grip my blankets until my hands threaten to cramp. Just when I think I might—*might*—be on the verge of sleep, having caught it after a long chase, three raps pull it from my reach.

Kysi enters holding a tray. I turn my head in the opposite direction.

Crimson streaks my wall like a morbid slaughterhouse.

With a groan, I decide that maybe keeping my eyes closed would be best instead. He says nothing as he rounds the bed and lifts the blanket from my leg.

The cold air bites my skin like a dozen starving leeches, jerking me forward to grab the comforter. I have spent hours collecting what little body heat I've been able to muster under the tent of my sheets, and he releases it all in two seconds.

A somber expression, one with hints of concern and a silent yearning, burden his features like a cloudy day does starving wildflowers. His face speaks words that never part from his lips, because they don't need to.

I'm sorry, they say. *Please let me help.*

I love you.

With hesitation, I release the blankets my body so desperately wants to wrap itself in. Slowly, he begins to clean my wound. I lean back to rest my head against the same pillow that I used against him only days ago.

Typically, injuries thump with a heated pulse as they heal. Not this one. At least, not that I can feel. My original thought is that my decrease in body temperature has created a numbing cold, preventing me from experiencing whatever pain my thigh would endure normally. However, when I peer from under my lashes, I find that the abrasion is not nearly as serious as the bandage made it out to be.

Clean cuts brush over my skin like a meteor shower. Although one is rather large, none appears to be a genuine cause for concern. Before annoyance can arise due to the realization that he interrupted my near sleep for *this*, I am stung with a searing pain. Inhaling sharply, I clench the covers that I hold to my chin.

"Sorry, that's it. I'm all done," he says, replacing the bandage along with the bedspread that kept in my wasted snowball of warmth. "I need you to sit up for me please."

"No," I say through clacking teeth. I will never listen to another word he says again.

With a sigh, he tries again. "Please, I made you soup."

The sound of a hot meal is all I need to comply. I remind myself as I push up to lean on the headboard that I am doing this because I want to and not because he asked me.

Placing the tray over me, he goes for the spoon. The glare I give him is one sharp enough to cut through stone.

He clears his throat, backing away to quietly sit in my desk chair.

With shaking hands, I lift the contents to my lips, but most fall out before they reach my tongue.

"I can—"

"No," I cut him off, embarrassed by my inability to stay still enough to eat.

With a frustrated exhale, Kysi rests his chin over clasped hands. Just as I am about to tell him to leave, that I do not want him just sitting there watching me struggle, I manage to swallow half a spoon full.

It tastes amazing, but I'm not looking for taste. I'm looking for warmth.

"Did you not heat this?" Disappointment washes over me. Tears threaten to swell in my eyes, but I blink them away, not wanting to cry over such a silly thing. I was just really hoping to bring the color back to my lilac gray fingertips.

Kysi tilts his head. "What?"

"I was just expecting it to be hot is all."

"It is," he says, motioning to the bowl, "I mean look, there's steam coming off of it."

He is right.

I run my hands over the bowl, feeling nothing from it. As I hold them there, I realize that it makes the cold lessen, but not go away. My sense of warmth is gone, smothered out by the chilling void that sucks what hope I had left into its black hole.

This is a special kind of torture.

A tear falls before I can catch it. Kysi leans forward.

"Thanks for the soup," I say, turning away from him to place it on the side table. Eager to get back to my cocoon of blankets in an attempt to raise my body temperature, I lay facing away from him, pulling the sheets to my chin.

I flinch when a *thud* hits the floor at the end of the bed. Kysi lets go of Meena upon landing, who confusingly takes in her surroundings.

"Damn it Kysi, stop kidnapping me," she growls, tugging the hem of her shirt down. "It's so rude ... where the hell even am I?"

Under the plume of bedding, I speak up. "Sorry for the mess." I greet her, eyeing the crimson streaks that flake over my wallpaper. They follow my gaze to the blood-stained design. "Ky didn't mention he was bringing guests."

As the god of Mortals, Kysi has the ultimate say on if and when deities can enter this realm, thus granting him the ability to bring anyone to Earth from the Heavens that he pleases.

Ignoring me, he gets straight to the point. "Can you help her?"

Meena makes a poor attempt to hide her annoyance as her snowy eyes drift to mine. "She doesn't look to be in pain now," she grumbles. Even in animosity, her features are captivating. It makes one wonder why she had not been named the goddess of Beauty instead.

If it was not for the soul bond, I have no doubt that Kysi would be with her. It is obvious she cares for him through her surface-level anger. Perhaps it is not merely on the surface, but deeply rooted, and I am the cause of it.

Because he loves me.

"Your energy is warm," he explains. "Please. She won't eat."

Meena's gaze lingers on him. She scoffs in defeat, striding over to my bedside while pushing up her sleeves. My desk chair skids across the floor before she plops down in it.

"Thank you."

"I'm not doing it for you," she remarks, "but you're welcome."

As her palms spread over my ears, the blizzard inside slows but its chill remains. No heat emanates from her. While she does not contribute to the cold, she does not lessen it either.

After releasing me she asks, "Well?"

The knowledge that she is only doing this to be useful to Kysi almost makes me pity her. I do not have the heart to say no, so I simply nod my head and thank her again.

He stands near my feet at the end of the bed, visibly relieved to have found a solution for me. When I ask him to give us a moment alone, it is clear that he wants to object, to stay with me, but doesn't argue.

"Why do you help him?" I ask once the door closes.

Her brows furrow, taken back by my bluntness. It's apparent that answering the question isn't all that appealing to her, however, she does anyway. "He is my friend."

"That's not all, though. Is it?" I pry.

Looking to the spot where they just stood together, she swallows hard. "No. No, that's not all." After tucking a strand of ivory hair behind her ear, she continues. "We were lovers for a while, but ... he always kept going back to the Ancient Library. Later, I realized it's because he was searching for you. Every day he'd go, hoping to find the goddess of Beginnings. How could I compete with a higher power?" She says it like I am the greater catch, like I am the one who was not hateful to everyone and ignorant to my own fallacies.

What a tangled web. She loved him. He loved me. I loved Hellano. He loves someone that does not exist.

It is difficult to keep my teeth from chattering but somehow, I manage. "He told you this?"

Staring down at her feet she says, "It was after we split. We remained friends because, well, I cared about him. Still do in my own way."

Is it possible to have a soul tie with someone who possesses one for another? I ache at the possibility. It would not be her fault, but the thought of her, in all her beauty, wanting Kysi ...

It makes me illogically jealous.

Must be the connection, because I have no other reason to feel this way.

At the same time, I also empathize with her. To remain loyal to Kysi, to help the one he loves, the one that ultimately took him away from her, makes it impossible not to have some respect for her.

"I'm sorry," I admit.

By her bewildered expression, that was the last thing she expected to hear from me. A soft smile tugs at the corners of her mouth. She leans back, releasing tension for the first time that I have seen. It is short-lived, her eyes widening into saucers as she reaches an arm back. "Where the fuck are my wings?"

"Don't worry," I assure her, "they'll come back when you leave. Be thankful that you can't feel pain, by the way." Once again, my eyes catch on the massacre of my room.

"Gods," she mumbles, as if truly taking it in now. "I need a drink. Where's your liquor?"

"I'm not sure how well human whiskey will work for you but there should be some in the dining room."

Kysi must have been waiting in the hallway, because before the door can close shut, he slips through. With a washcloth in hand, he heads straight for the mess. I can only imagine how exhausted he must be. Yet, here he is, cleaning blood from behind my dresser because I hinted that it was bothering me.

I want to tell him to stop, tell him he doesn't have to do that, but I know he is just using the excuse to stay near me.

At some point, I must have fallen asleep. Dreams of the crumbling house linger as I stir in bed. Its threat to engulf me under the walls—ones that bleed just as I do—works to plant a thick sense of doom right where the freezing mass piles in my chest.

All of a sudden, I feel it.

Warmth.

It is gentle and soft. Just its simple touch reminds me of endless different things. Coffee on a Sunday morning. Windswept hair in the summer. A smile directed at you from someone you love. Spring. Life. Beginnings.

I want more. Need more. More. More. More. Reaching for it in the depth of my fading nightmare, I pull it towards me in desperation.

"Hey, hey," the voice is just as cozy as the touch. I can feel it coaxing me from my daze, one that I have no desire to escape from in fear that when I do, this precious heat will leave with it.

I fail to fight waking, fluttering my eyes open to take in Kysi's frame under the dim lamplight. It casts shadows over his features, contouring his face in a way you would only see in a painting.

He is halfway over me, arms tense under my palms.

And warm.

"You were having a bad dream—" Cutting him off, I pull him closer.

All is forgiven the moment he complies.

Leaning up, I press my mouth to his. Each kiss heats my lips like beating rays over a field of sunflowers. Like them, I chase warmth.

The flames of his tongue ignite another in the pit of my stomach. I bask in every kiss, willing myself to leave it only for a moment, just long enough to tug my bottoms down.

Perplexity falls over him, but he does not let it interrupt my advances. I take hold of him again and pivot, swinging a leg over to trap him under me. Gripping the hem of his shirt, I create one less barrier between us by pulling it over his head.

His defined chest feels like a stone left under the blistering sun. Its cozy embrace expands past my palms, trailing up the length of my arms. The sensation is dizzying. I peck at his skin in a frenzy, nipping at it with my teeth as I give in to the craze.

"Angel, baby," his heavy voice cascades beneath me like thick honey, "not that I don't fucking love what you're doing right now, but what are you doing right now?"

I silence him with another kiss, reaching my hands down to the button of his pants. His length springs free, solid and inviting.

If my libido could sing it would be a simmering rhapsody, each chord an auditory testament to my desperate desires.

Impatiently I line myself over him, lowering to emerge in the sauna of his touch.

Kysi exhales a moan, firmly placing his hands on each side of me, attempting to guide and do the work himself from below. Surely, because he is concerned that I should be resting, but too enveloped in the intimacy to turn it down. After all, he has been waiting hundreds of years.

I do not allow him to take over, though. All I can do is focus on melting the cold mass and closing the void in my chest as much as possible.

Uncovering his mouth, my fingers trail over his shoulders and pull them towards me. He sits up, leaning in to press his mouth to mine just before he swiftly rids me of my shirt, tossing it to the side to meet his on the floor.

I press my bare chest to his, escaping the blizzard that once consumed me with each roll of my hips. As I throw myself down on him, the knot in my stomach grows tighter, until it's him that has to cover my mouth.

An arm wraps the span of my back, holding me as I give in to the pulsing bursts of euphoric heat. "That's it," he says with a grasp over my jaw, "good girl."

It's only after I come down that I allow him to take over. He lifts me by the hips to pump into me from below, stimulating the lingering waves of pleasure that continue to fade. When he begins to tense, I know he's almost there.

"Fill me up," I say in a ragged breath, embracing what more he has to offer. Pressing deep, he releases in throbbing waves. I grip the ropes of muscle over his shoulders and press my lips to his as he falls into his own intoxicating climax.

It's rejuvenating to be enveloped in warmth, surrounded by it again. I don't want this to end, don't want the cold to creep back through.

Long after we've caught up with our breathing, I remain over him. As he trails his hands up and down the length of my back, I finally break the silence.

"You're warm."

His fingers hesitate before continuing their path. "When Meena touched you, she wasn't warm?" I shake my head in his neck, and he hums in confusion. "Maybe it's a soul tie thing."

Lifting my head, I peer into eyes brighter than I have ever seen him wear. They cast a green glow over his cheekbones. With the onyx strand that rests over his brow, their colors remind me of Halloween. Or a black cat.

Bad luck? Possibly.

But I think I'll take my chances.

"Can one god have a soul tie with two?" I question.

"No," he replies in a low tone, one coated in utter relaxation and fatigue.

Thank gods. That means Meena is not cursed like I thought she was. My jealousy has a bit of a reprieve now.

Only a bit, though.

While it seems that the sex has brought me back from the pits of an icy hell, I still can't help but think that having a soulmate would feel different.

There is a natural pull, one that grows stronger with each moment spent together, but I assumed it would be more of like an awe inspiring, all consuming, magical love filter or something.

"I'm sorry about the first time we met," I admit.

"I'll make you a deal," he says, trailing kisses along my shoulder, "I'll forgive you if you forgive me."

Over half of a millennium of loving the wrong person, manipulating Earth and his people, and throwing various items at his head, all erased if I return the favor and forgive him for glamouring me because he was worried about my safety?

"I'll take that deal."

He lays back, pulling me with him. The rhythm of his heart thumps steadily near mine and I swear they beat in unison. When I feel his muscles relax against me, I know he's drifted off.

When I rise, Kysi remains asleep beside me. Mona was not kidding when she said that he has not gotten any rest, because he hasn't moved from this position in hours. The ripple of his back is the first thing I notice as he lays on his stomach with arms under the pillow to support his head.

It makes sense that he is a god. Even in sleep, with ruffled hair and pursed lips, he looks like one. The body heat he so graciously shared with me lasted for most of the night. However, a storm brews in my chest.

I cannot help but wonder if Hellano is having the same problem right now.

My attempts to slip out of bed undetected yield pointless, as he stirs the moment I inch away.

"Hm?" he groans as if to ask where I'm going.

"Just a quick shower, five minutes," I respond.

With a sharp inhale he runs a hand over his face to rid himself of the will to fall back asleep. Before I move any further, he pops out of sight, leaving the sheets to fall through where he just laid.

A light flicks on, and the sound of running water emerges from the bathroom. The door swiftly opens to reveal his frame, beckoning me to come.

"I don't need help, you know." My smirk is contagious, pulling one up from the corners of his lips as well.

He winks from behind the frame, lifting a hand to test the temperature. "I know."

Once I enter the bathroom, he turns to hoist me onto the counter. While he takes the bandage off, I see the damage to my thigh under full lighting for the first time.

It is not that bad, despite its appearance suggesting otherwise. Bruises overcast jagged cuts, most of which are both narrow and shallow. Only one appears deeper than the rest, where the brunt of the force was.

"How did this even happen?"

He stays focused on the task. "You didn't notice? The mirror on your desk is broken. You flew into it when I brought you back. Don't worry, I cleaned up the glass."

Damn, I loved that boudoir.

"Thanks," I say as he turns to check the water temperature once more. As I step off the counter, I feel the coldness in my diaphragm expand. Instinctively, I reach for him but catch sight of my reflection above the sink.

A deep welt takes up a portion of my forehead. Its purplish tint reminds me of the rock staircase that leads to Hellano's estate. Not only that, but my skin has paled too. I have drastically lost weight, which I am sure doesn't help with the frozen block swelling behind my ribs. When I awoke feeling half dead, I do not think that assumption was far from the truth.

Because I look half dead.

My altered, compromised form is a nightmarish reminder of the trauma I've recently endured. It is proof that what I have gone through is, in fact, affecting my body.

If it is affecting my body, then the gaping hole in my chest—the one that cannot be seen or felt by anyone but me—must be the product of my damaged soul. It feels as though a piece is missing, gone somewhere to a place no one can travel.

Lost.

Kysi notices my condemnatory stare. He walks over, wrapping his arms around me and pressing his chest to my back. The warmth immediately distracts me from my ghostly figure.

"You, my angel, look beautiful in everything." He observes my reflection. "You don't just carry it in your hair, your lips, or your eyes." He slides his thumb gently across my mouth. "You carry power. Strength. Endurance. You carry the nature of a Queen of gods."

I sit under the weight of a heated blanket—which doesn't do much, but it is something—as I wait for Kysi's return.

Mona and Meena left a while ago, but they should be arriving soon as well. They magnetized upon first glance, giggling like schoolgirls and whispering in each other's ears. Out of all the peculiar occurrences I have witnessed and experienced, this has been the most surprising by far.

Meena with a mortal ...

A meeting is in order, one where we can put our collective brains together in order to search for an answer as to what is going on.

The main goal is to get into the Shadowlands, but not only did my proximity with Hellano spark what could have been a catastrophic event, we now know that what happened was not a one-time occurrence. What if going to the Shadowlands initiates another bleeding spell, one that takes me out for good?

So many unanswered questions. I can only hope that Cato will have more information to bring to the table once the meeting commences. I keep thinking back to what Kysi said.

You carry the nature of a Queen of gods.

How can he think that? I have never done anything powerful. I had a soul duty to create life and I did not even do that properly. My peers despised me, my title was taken from me, and then I fell here where I became weak and humanly.

Realistically, I was always weak.

Weak to Hellano's influence, my own selfish desires, the power I allowed to go to my head. Everything I once believed gave me strength, made me who I am, was actually keeping me from my true self.

How much do my Soul Mothers know? What would they think of me if they learned that our collective lives are at stake, that our end stems from the negligence and naivety of their successor? To take it further, how would they react upon learning that it is not just us threatened with the permanent ending, but everything. Earth is just the beginning of a war for survival. When disaster rains down on mortals, the gods and goddesses responsible for managing the outcomes created by the hierarchy will lose their grasp on their soul-bound duties. Life and Death are the foundations for their existence. That which affects the foundation, affects everything that rests upon it.

The only one remaining would be Hellano.

Again, having both my title and his would technically mean that if everything was wiped away, he could simply start rebuilding.

But his mind would deteriorate from a prolonged existence, leaving him unable to start anew—even if he could find the balance of Life and Death inside him.

His outcome would turn into an eternal struggle, filled with imbalance and madness.

To me, that is worse than simply not existing at all.

"*Come out of this a victor,*" Cato had said.

All the knowledge that he has consumed since the very beginning serves as a motivation for me.

The god of Wisdom is in my corner.

For someone of such intellect to believe in me, the Fallen Goddess, makes me trust that it must have been an informed decision of his. Which means that there may actually be a way out of this.

I pull from that possibility, visualizing the determination of victory in the form of the frigid cold that branches throughout my body. If the blizzard is meant to break me, I will turn it into my own storm. With each beat of my heart circulating the ice, I will let it be a reminder of my new duty.

I will restore balance to the Heavens and Earth, and ensure that they will never be threatened with extinction again.

As if appearing from my thoughts, Cato materializes near the coffee table. His sudden entrance startles me—I jump under the blanket.

Gods, I hate when they do that.

I look upon him, noticing something has changed. What used to trail down his back now rests at his shoulders.

"Did you cut your hair?" I squint.

Cato awkwardly shifts his weight. "I did."

There's a sense of nervousness in him aside from his usual gawkiness. It is challenging to stifle the grin that threatens to spread across my cheeks, but I manage.

This being his first public outing, Cato wanted to look presentable.

"Looks nice." I pat the spot beside me on the couch. "Learn anything new?"

"Actually, yes." He takes the seat beside me. "I'll save it for when the others arrive. How are you feeling?"

"As good as I can be, I guess."

The scenery catches his attention. Everything from the plants around my entertainment center to the engraved wood on the coffee table gets taken in. When he finally notices my personal collection of books on the shelf to the side, he instinctively goes for them but stops himself.

"May I?" he asks in a mannerly fashion.

His enhanced formality to this social interaction tells me that he has done a fair share of studying etiquette before arriving.

I motion to the books. "Have at it."

Although I am sure the science of the mind for our otherworldly selves differs vastly from the human psychology I studied, it is just as intriguing to attempt to compare the two as I examine him investigating the spines.

From ants, to humans, to deities, isolation affects us all. That is the beauty of life. At the core of every being, we are all the same.

If only I did not have to lose my title in order to figure this out … it would have prevented the torture I put my creations through, which served as the catalyst for Kysi to make the deal. If I had learned sooner and avoided being a recluse that only spent time with my exact opposite, none of this would be happening.

The selfish silver lining to the downfall of everything is in the woodsy air that surrounds me in an embrace. It is the eyes of verdant fields to my spring.

It is him.

Kysi.

As Cato sifts through the pages, I realize he holds one of the more maturely rated books in the assembly. He pauses on a certain page, raising an eyebrow.

Gods, of course he had to pick up that one. "Where's Ky?" I ask.

Startling him, Cato snaps the pages shut and replaces the book in its sleeve on the shelf.

"He said that he had one more thing to do." Grabbing another book with a more appropriate theme, he skims the pages. "Should be back soon."

I wonder what else Kysi needed to do? He had planned to come back with Cato.

The door opens to the crinkling of to-go bags and fading laughter.

"Where's Kysi?" Meena asks while Mona parts into the kitchen with their leftovers.

Before either of us have a chance to answer, the empty area of carpet between the coffee table and television fills with two figures, one hunching over the other.

A wailing sounds from the figure under Kysi, but it fades as soon as they land, along with the wings at their back. Everyone impulsively takes a step back to assess the situation.

A hush falls over the space upon the realization of who is accompanying Kysi.

Hellano's eyes dart around the room in panicked streaks.

CHAPTER 10

The god of Afterlife works to slow his breathing, as if it was painful to do so before. "Where am I?"

He has not seen me yet, but I have a feeling that he will go back to screaming the second he does.

"Earth." Kysi is quick to respond. "I found you doubled over, shrieking in pain. How do you feel now?"

Sweat beads over his pores, dampening his rusty hair. "I'm on fire," he says, "but better."

"Anewla is here," Kysi says. Just as my name is spoken aloud, Hellano visibly tenses. Thinking back to his betrayal, I relish the thought of scaring him. Kysi cuts my fantasy off short when he finishes saying, "She isn't the one doing this to you."

Hellano's eyes dart toward me when I say, "I wish I could take the credit." But right now Kysi holds more of my focus. "Are you crazy? Why would you bring this leech into my home? Especially after what happened the last time we were within five feet of one another?"

Kysi looks to me as if he was cornered, having no choice but to teleport him. "I went to question him. When I arrived, he was in the exact same state of agony as before, from when I came to save you. It had to be because the Heavens was stuck shoving what soul it took from you into him."

"What?" Hellano questions from the floor, face flushed with redness.

From what we know about a title and soul being intertwined, Kysi and I theorize that my soul did not absorb into Hellano's when I fell to Earth because I was in a different realm than him. Perhaps due to some unknown reason, the Heavens cannot transfer souls if they do not reside in the same world. This would mean that Hellano had my power, but not my spirit. This may also be the reason why he was never able to master the responsibility of both roles on his own. When I came back to the Heavens, we think my energy was recognized and there was an attempt to complete the process. If our theory is correct, two questions remain.

Why did the Heavens not finish the job the moment I returned to it? How and why did I survive its first attack on me?

"So, you risked bringing him here and causing my eyes to bleed?" Irritation burns in my voice. Carelessness is not an attractive quality. Having us both in the same realm again could have put me at great risk.

"You don't bleed immediately," he defends. "First, it's pressure or dizziness, then it's blood. I would've put him right back the moment I noticed any discomfort on your face. This way, we get to test the limits of soul transference and possibly gain the advantage of having him here for questioning."

I suppose he does not consider anger a feature of discomfort.

"What questioning?" Meena cuts in. "How do you expect any help from him? Need I remind you that he wants the opposite of what you do?"

Hellano may want both titles, but I think if he is threatened with returning to an insufferable limbo, he might give us something.

"We've already learned one thing." Kysi wipes his shirt as he steps away from Hellano. "He said he was on fire, meanwhile I can practically hear Anewla shivering from here." He glides over, lifting the heavy blanket and meeting me under it. "Come here, baby."

Meena is plainly mixed up at the sight of my reaction to Kysi's touch. "Okay," she says, perplexed. She continues while taking a spot on the love seat, "So, they're opposites. It makes sense they'd be hot and cold."

"Actually," Cato chimes in, causing everyone's head to turn. "It doesn't have anything to do with their divergence, but everything to do with what Kysi mentioned earlier. Soul transference."

"I'm sorry." Meena points a painted nail at the stranger. "Who are you?"

"My name is Cato, the god of Wisdom."

If she was not puzzled before, she certainly is now. Before she has the opportunity to ask, Kysi answers her.

"Found him in the library, nobody knew of him, now you're caught up." He looks back to Cato. "What did you find?"

The goddess of Pleasure is clearly disgruntled at being left out of the loop until now.

125

With his hand spread over his chest, Hellano sits up on the floor and works to steady his breathing.

"I found a—"

"Wait," I say, holding up a finger. "Before we start, I'd like to know how Ky knew where I was."

Did Cato tell him right after our conversation outside the library? Right after he comforted me and acted like my friend? Despite being thankful that Kysi did save me, I need to know for certain whether or not Cato can be trusted.

Their eyes meet one another from across the room. I notice a layer of respect and thankfulness in Kysi, which leads me to believe that Cato had a moment with him in the library just as he did with me.

"After you left," the god of Wisdom begins, "I went back to the annex. I always try to keep books on current events nearby for easy access. As I sorted through them, I found the book about you I was reading. Because you mentioned meeting with Hellano, I decided to follow you while the book logged it in real time. When I saw that things weren't going well, I teleported to Kysi, who was still searching for you. He must have sensed your danger, because he was desperate to find you, he just didn't know where you were."

The air leaves my chest. Cato had been watching out for me.

"I owe you my life," I say.

"Mine as well, apparently." Hellano rasps from the carpet. Our eyes meet, and I hope my gaze will pierce right through him. Kysi senses my rising tension and runs a hand through my hair.

"I told you that I liked happy endings," Cato says with the twinge of a smile. It works to keep my attention off the traitor on my carpet as I mirror it in response. "Back to the issue at hand," he continues, stepping away from the bookshelf to pace around the room. As he speaks, he continues to take in his surroundings. Gently, he touches the frame of a painting and the leaves of my plants as he passes them by. "I found a book named Matters of the Spirit. It explained that soul ties hold a small piece of their partner's spirit within them. When someone's soulmate has a permanent ending, the portion of their spirit that resided in them dies as well." Cato pulls his gaze from the décor, landing on Hellano. "You didn't agree to Kysi's deal just for power, now did you?"

The god of Afterlife sits perplexed at these words, having no knowledge of a soul bond that died towards the beginning. Hellano has always been cold-blooded—in the literal sense—why is it now that he burns up, sweats profusely?

"I don't know," Hellano speaks, "I just ... thought that maybe the power of life would fulfill me, take away the empty space that anchors in my chest. Except now, it is gone, now it feels nothing like an empty space. Instead, I'm *too* full. There isn't enough room inside me." His gaze reaches mine. "History says that malice and aversion are natural behaviors for the goddess of Beginnings and the god of Afterlife to have, but that wasn't the case for us. You loved me completely."

My chest caves in at the sound of him acknowledging it. Kysi twitches, tightening his hold on me.

"Before you were created, I assumed the coldness thrived in me due to the innate relationship our spirits share. So when you came along, I tried to switch the narrative." Now Hellano's twinge of guilt becomes something more outright, he carries it all through the glossy haze that falls over his eyes. "I convinced you that we were fated for each other, and it worked. You fell in love with me."

There is a different kind of chill in me now, one rooted in spite. From the moment I blinked into existence, he was there ready to use and manipulate me. It was planned.

"However, the feeling never went away," he continues, "I remained cold. By then, you were already so committed to me. So loyal. If you couldn't take away the infinite ache in my heart, I figured that I could at least use you to give me something else I wanted."

Death.

Perhaps spending over half of a millennium with him really did leave a scar on my spirit, because the goddess of Beginnings is not typically known to crave violence. Then again, I have done many things my past lives would probably never think to do, like loving the enemy and rejecting the man our soul is bound to.

And the list continues to grow.

I break away from Kysi and lunge across the room. I have had days to recover from what happened at his estate. Right now, I am stronger than him, and it is my intention to make sure I remain that way.

Hellano lifts his hands to dodge my blows, doubling over as I sling a foot into his side. With how much I am seeing red, it would not surprise me if my eyes were bleeding again. The pain in my thigh is nothing but a dull ache, pulsing with the rhythm of my swinging leg. Each impact has a purpose, a meaning. I strike him for the countless hours spent in tangled bedding. Then again, for the way he would use my laughter as music and twirl me through his estate.

My whole life, just a puppet. A toy. Something to be used, played with, and inevitably broken.

He was my *everything*.

Cato taps his foot as he waits for the brawl to end. Meena leans forward to get closer to the action. Kysi gives me a second to get a few hits in before I feel his forearm wrapping around my center to hoist me off of him.

"I'm not finished," I spit, kicking and squirming against him, "let me go!"

Meena disappointedly slouches back in the love seat. If she had the ability to sense how much pleasure I just received from finally letting out eight years' worth of pent-up anger, she would have a heyday.

"Not that I don't love to see you get feisty," he grunts against my swinging limbs, "but we can't get more out of him if you knock him unconscious."

We fall back to the couch, and I reluctantly stay put, not objecting when Kysi holds my back to his chest. It may have felt nice to give back some of the pain that Hellano branded on my heart, but the warmth of Kysi's touch brings inescapable comfort.

It's rewarding to see Hellano wipe blood from his nose. This is why I love Earth. I get to make him bleed.

He exhales sharply before drawing in another breath, voice intense with emotion. "It wasn't all a lie. I loved you too. In my own way."

"Now, *I'm* about to go at him," Kysi announces from behind me.

"Can we please continue?" Cato interjects, clearly impatient to get back to a more productive conversation.

Hellano's hazel eyes never fall away from me. "I made the deal to fix that godsforsaken bullet hole in my chest. You never complained about being empty inside. I thought if you couldn't fill the void, maybe your power could."

I lean back into Kysi. "Why didn't your past lives ever do anything like this?"

Cato pokes at my aloe. "Because they never lived long enough to really experience it. Which was another reason why you took the deal too, huh? Another reason to get Anewla to love you. You didn't want to be replaced."

What Cato is suggesting is that Hellano's pain wasn't always present. It grew over time. Because he is due to be reincarnated sooner than everyone else, that means our unlikely union was not just an attempt to fill the void, nor was it for the purpose of providing him with more life to kill. Another ulterior motive that Hellano had for seducing me was the intention of making me so madly in love with him that I would never think of creating his successor.

Much like Kairos, the god of Time, did when he tried to escape the Law of Reincarnation.

Hellano's face tires in defeat. "Yeah. That too." His shoulders relax slightly. "But Kysi made the perfect deal. I get to melt the growing ice in my chest, and you get to make a happy life for yourself on Earth. He said he'd look out for you."

Our eye contact is like a thick chain being tugged at both ends. Neither of us let go, and through the rusty metal of my lividity sparks a ray of pity.

There is no way Hellano was experiencing the same intensity of the bitter chill that I am now, but the idea of having even just the smallest amount always nested behind my ribs ... it would be like the sound of water infinitely dripping right in my ear; perpetual, maddening, chronically hopeless as it grows with time.

A nightmare.

And through it all, each desperate attempt to save himself from the growing torture ... he still fed what flames were left of our love and tried to make sure I would be taken care of after the deal was struck.

"You were wrong, Hellano." Cato turns to face the room. "You must have been pretty desperate to bargain on a hunch. The aversion both of your souls shared was not the cause of the hole in your heart. It was Time."

"Time?" Hellano and Meena question simultaneously. Kysi and I relive the forgotten history of Kairos through the god of Wisdom's didactic memory as he quotes the Law of Permanent Endings with keen precision. Hellano never wavers upon hearing the news of his lost soulmate. He looks to his hands as Cato finishes the retelling, processing all that was said with a level of newfound understanding.

"Now we can get to the important part, the more time sensitive information," Cato continues. "Prosenth asked the Heavens to take Kairos's title, not transfer it. Which must be why Anewla didn't immediately die upon returning." He turns to me. "Tell me, what happened the first time you bled?"

As I recall the events, Cato rubs his thumb over his chin in deep thought.

He looks just past me. "You were next to her when she came to? Were you holding her?"

Kysi nods to answer.

An expression of satisfaction emerges, as if he just solved the case. "There you have it. It wasn't Meena that saved her, it was you."

"But I just helped her earlier?" Eyes as wintry as the chill in my core look to me.

I give a sentimental glace in Meena's direction. "I didn't want to offend you ..."

She looks offended now.

"This is all an educated guess, of course." Cato tries his best to stay on topic. "But I believe that when the Heavens targeted you, Kysi's soul was fighting back, refusing to give the remnant of you that resides in him. That's what makes soulmates extraordinary; they hold a fragment of their lover in their heart. Literally."

Before this moment, the thought of Kysi having a piece of my spirit would have made me angry or uncomfortable. Now, as the strength of our connection sinks in, I am wholly grateful. A rare bond saved me in a rare moment. Kysi saved me.

Why did Prosenth let go of the remnant of Kairos in him, the one that created the space in his chest to nest in for all of eternity? Perhaps he was putting his faith in the Heavens out of desperation, naively trusting it not to burn him.

But it did, leaving a permanent scar.

"You speak of the Heavens as if it is conscious," I say, "which would mean that the souls of Life and Death are not at the top of the food chain; it is."

"Well, just me now sweetheart," Hellano comments. I shoot him a threatening look. Of course he would push his luck with me.

He hasn't changed a bit.

"In a way," Cato responds, pulling out the daggers I stare into my natural opposite. "I theorize that the Heavens operates less like a being with a conscience and more like a machine with a job to do. I called to it myself to test this theory, asked for something minute that wouldn't make a difference, but I didn't receive a response. This leads me to believe that gaining its attention requires more than just 'calling out' to it." He uses air quotes. "Or it only intervenes on important matters."

"How would a machine classify what's important?" Meena questions.

Cato responds, "I didn't say it was a machine, I said it may operate *like* one." His heightened intelligence serves to make him more impatient at the fact we are struggling to keep up. She raises her hands in defense, giving a silent, sarcastic apology.

Metal clatters in the kitchen. Mona peeks her head out into the living room. "Sorry. Knocked over the utensils. I'm not here."

I think we had all forgotten she was.

Hellano looks to all of us like we have lost our minds. "A *mortal* is here?"

"Not here." She shakes her head.

My gaze darts toward him. "She has more of a right to be here than you, it's my house." I cross my arms.

Mona snorts, quickly clearing her throat and going back to being invisible.

"As we now know," Kysi speaks up, "Earth works as a hideaway for the both of you. The Heavens can't move spirits if it can't find them," he says to validate our previous theory. "Since this world is technically ours, it will serve as a safe haven until we figure out where to go from here." His finger trails the length of my arm in a lazy graze. The obsidian band reflects off the sunlight from the window with each stroke.

Things are beginning to make much more sense now that we've had this conversation. The ice in my ribs is due to the partial absence of my soul, which has forced itself into Hellano. This also explains why he feels as if there's not enough room inside of him now, and why he is dripping sweat on my floor.

"Where do we go from here?" Meena asks, forcing her gaze away from Kysi's hand.

"My original plan was to speak with the god of Afterlife," he begins, clearly resentful enough not to say his name, "convince him to send us to the Shadowlands and talk with her Soul Mother about how to fix this."

Meena scoffs, whipping hair over her shoulder. I would be offended too if my closest friend excluded me from so much of their life. Maybe he refrained from mentioning it to her because he knew that she would not support him essentially committing suicide. After all, there was a serious chance that Kysi would not have returned.

Considering the way Meena's face resonates with disagreement, it is clear that her opinion is also in conflict with Kysi's idea of going back. However, she remains silent, speechless against her scorn.

"That should be fine," Cato says, slowly making his way back to the bookshelf. It appears that his relationship to books is like a soul bond; he gravitates towards them. "As long as the god of Afterlife remains in this realm, you should be safe to travel the others."

"Not so fast," Hellano speaks up. "Why would I help you? I don't want to go back to that never-ending gap in my chest and I *don't* want to be reincarnated."

Classic Hellano, making everything more difficult. If he does not have anything to gain, it is not important enough for him.

Cato humphs and looks to Kysi. "Sounds like you have to make another deal, Bargainer."

CHAPTER 11

Steam seeps from the bathroom door as I sift through files from work on the bed. Although it has not been long since I left therapy, nostalgia blankets me as if these notes were taken lifetimes ago. The lingering doom encompassing our universe has me wishing I could jump into these files and pick up where I left off, as if that would take me back in time.

Back before these problems existed.

Kysi popped Meena back into the Heavens once Cato took his leave. Mona generously offered my guest room to Hellano and took the couch for herself. Her stay here was not meant to last this long, but she extended her getaway. Can't say I blame her. If there was this much drama at her place, I would still be shacked up there. When Kysi and I departed for the night, she was basically playing Twenty Questions with Hellano against his will.

I hope it is making him miserable.

Light filters through the room as Kysi swings the bathroom door open, breaking my train of thought. My frustration with Hellano is quickly forgotten as I set my gaze on a sight to behold.

I did not think his hair could get any darker. The dampness gives more length to his midnight strands as they dangle over his cheekbone instead of eyebrow. Droplets speckle across his chest and travel down his toned stomach, ending where a towel begins.

"Like what you see?" He catches me looking him over and winks, lifting his arms up to lean against the top of the doorframe.

Aaaand the floodgates are open.

My reasons to pursue him are irrelevant. Consider it his warmth, the bond, whatever excuse sounds tangible enough to justify, but all I can think about is being wrapped up with him. Only us, tangled together as the world ends.

"Hm," I say while sliding off the bed, "let me get a closer look."

The corners of his lips perk upward in a handsome grin. As I stride closer, the atmosphere thickens like sweet, molten sugar. Similar to the way teleporting pulls me into a void, the mounds of his biceps call to my hands with their tantalizing contrast of hardness and heat.

"Yup, these look good." I tease him while dragging my palms over his arms. They trail over his torso next, acting without a conscious thought as if they were meant to explore him. "These check out."

His smile broadens, which makes it impossible for my eyes to follow my fingers as they skim over each ripple of muscle along his abdomen.

"I don't even have to look at these," I remark, finally tearing away my gaze, "but I will anyway." With a sarcastic gasp, I point to where the towel is tucked into his waist. "What's this?"

His face turns satirically surprised, puzzled as if he also does not know the answer.

I tsks. "How can I answer such an enrapturing question if I can't see everything?"

With a tug, the towel hits the floor. He springs out, ready just as before.

"Hm," I mutter, "I should be thorough."

Kysi peers at me with ravenous green eyes as I lower myself before him. The moment I tear away from his hungry glare, I am met with the glimmer of a pearlescent bead. His package is smooth and inviting. I explore it with my hands, leaning in to flick my tongue in random patterns over the skin. His breathing quickens above me, body working solely on its own as he moves back and forth through the doorway into my hands. The way he tenses implies that he is struggling to control himself.

In one motion, I run my tongue from the base of his shaft to the drop of white at his tip.

"Gods," he groans, gripping the frame still.

A heavy exhale escapes him when I take the head between my lips. With each pull from my mouth I take him deeper until there's no more space to fill.

A hand runs through my hair, settling on the side of my face. He wants to guide me but refrains, like a gentleman.

What will it take to break him? I want to see him give in to the impulses, the urges to take over. Picking up speed, I bob more violently onto him.

A low rumble bubbles from above. "Angel," Kysi growls, "I'm about to cum."

How nice of him to warn me.

I keep my pace.

"I'm gonna—" A drawn out moan fills the room as I drink him up. The hand over my hair tightens as he takes in a fistful, steadying my head while he instinctively drives himself into my throat in bursts. The second his high lets up, I'm released.

Kysi lifts me from the floor, meeting his lips with mine in a hard, intoxicating kiss. It's not just articles of clothing that he greedily pulls off, but the protective layers around my heart. Each touch peels back another until I'm wholly exposed; body and soul.

His hands glide over me like a sculptor's, my form responding to their every impression and command. He deepens our kiss with a push, one that guides us closer to the bed.

Our lips part, but our bodies never hesitate in their intimate dance. As he hovers over me with brightening emerald eyes, I bask in the way they roam over my every pore like he is committing me to memory. But when he runs a hand down the length of my frame, reaching the most sensitive area, those eyes lock on mine. They close briefly at the feel of my wetness, a zealous anticipation forming over his features. I notice his tongue just barely grazes across his lips before he dips down, planting damp kisses along my neck. The wind of each breath he takes on his way down my body sends chills through me.

Kysi hesitates just over my center. I'm aching to feel him, desperate under the spell of a soulmate's connection.

His eyes flick up to me, craving to witness my reaction to his touch. Slowly, his head lowers.

Pinpricks of pleasure erupt with each swipe of his tongue. "Mm," he hums with affinity, the vibration sending my back into an arch. He extends an arm, snaking it over my stomach to where his palm rests on my chest to hold me down.

Each ambitious stroke hits my bundle of nerves, creating involuntary moans that only seem to make him hungrier for more. He slips two fingers through my entrance, slightly curling them in and out. My core tightens as they pick up speed, pumping into me with fervor.

I wrap my hands around the arm that pins me as I near a quaking orgasm. My hips roll upwards of their own accord, itching to show him affection against my rising desire.

As a rolling climax barrels through me, I grip his arm to steady myself. It lifts upwards to cover my mouth, stifling my cries of ecstasy. He maintains his pace while I ride through it, my muffled noises filling the space around us.

Kysi doesn't stop right away. Instead, he continues to run his tongue through me, taking in the product of his labor. He rises after having his fill, lying beside me over the sheets to wipe hair from my face. I respond by burying my head into the covers, away from the light of the room. He smirks before reaching across me to turn off the lamp.

The house smells like a diner. It might as well be with the amount of food Kysi is making. Just when I think he is almost finished, he finds something else to throw in the pan. I watch as he anxiously pokes at a crackling egg.

This behavior has persisted all morning.

We discussed the plan in bed. In order to convince Hellano to send us to the Land of Shadows, we will offer to protest that he be given a new soul bond. If the Heavens can move spirits, surely it can replace what that spirit is attached to. Additionally, we will ask that he receive an additional five-hundred years to live before he is required to be reincarnated.

The catch is that we will not be specific about *who's* bond his soul will be tied with. Our idea is that by connecting him to a dead god—not permanently dead, just one that has not been reincarnated—the hole inside him, the one I was unable to fill, will remain once the change occurs. This way, he will feel an urge to move on to the Shadowlands and avoid breaking the Law of Reincarnation. If he chooses not to go, he still gets half of a millennium. However, it is unlikely that he would last much longer being incomplete due to the lengths he has already gone to fill the void in him. It is entirely possible that bonding him with a dead god could fix his issue, even if he's not present with them in the Shadowlands.

I try not to think about that, though. I have never seen a deity's mind become corrupted due to age and prefer to never see such a thing. Especially if it is someone that I have cared so deeply about.

However, if this goes according to plan, Hellano would get a life in the Shadowlands with his new mate, I would get my title back and create his successor, balance would return to the realms, and bing bang—everyone's happy.

Unbeknownst to Kysi, I have my own plan. Because I am unaware of how things operate in the Shadowlands, I have decided to keep my goal a secret, just in case I am unable to fulfill it.

Humans do not go to the Heavens after they die. Truth be told, I am unaware of where they go.

My time on Earth has connected me to them, and being a therapist has given me insight into the horrific hand some of these mortals have been dealt.

It is not fair that this is their only option.

Whether it is gripping cross necklaces or building alters, almost everyone I have met shares the same hope for a second chance.

I want to give them one.

After I speak to my Soul Mothers, I am hoping to have a better idea of their power and limitations in regard to how they "call to the Heavens." When we arrive, I will gauge their behavior in order to determine whether or not they might agree with my plan to reconstruct the Heavens to fit humans in it as well. If they give me even the slightest impression of disagreement, I simply will not tell them. At that point, I can only hope to gain enough information from them to give me the ability to beseech the Heavens with this request myself.

In truth, being the true goddess of Beginnings gives me a moral imperative to protect the universe from devastation. If the sake of our realms is at risk simply because of a request to the Heavens that spiraled out of control, then no one should wield the power to do such a thing anymore. That way, the threat of extinction could never return. However, I have no way of knowing if gaining this independence would be possible until we arrive in the Shadowlands.

I watch as Kysi fidgets, flipping the egg every couple of seconds. Because I have given him no impression that I am hiding something, I can only assume it is presenting Hellano with the deal that has him shaken.

"It'll work," I reassure him.

He flips the egg again. At this point, it is taking twice as long to cook. His eyes skim over the ingredients, the stove, the cabinets—everything but me. "Yeah, that's not all I'm worried about."

Before I have the time to ask, Hellano interrupts us. He strides in through the kitchen, snatching a piece of bacon before sitting in a dining chair.

The dining chair.

Gods, having him here is so weird.

"So, watcha got for me, lovebirds?" Hellano asks with a full mouth.

Kysi turns off the stove and pulls a hand towel off his shoulder. Shortly after I sit across from Hellano, my breakfast is laid in front of me. He eyes my plate before shooting Kysi an expectant look.

"Go get it yourself before I turn the heat on," Kysi barks at him, sitting in the seat next to mine. He places a warm hand on my knee while I giddily take bites of his meal.

I love eating his food. He loves watching how much I love eating his food. It's a good dynamic we have.

Hellano rolls his eyes and trudges back into the kitchen.

Kysi leans in, stealing my attention away from the fluffy pancakes. "Listen—"

"I hope you've got something good for him." Cato rounds the corner, pulling out a chair on the opposite side of me. "You know, something that doesn't engulf the universe in chaos and kill us all."

Bewilderment filters through Kysi. "How'd you get here? I didn't invite you?"

Cato throws him a questioning glance. "You never revoked the invitation?" he says, clearly surprised that the god of Mortals and Bargaining has been so negligent to a key aspect of his job.

Kysi lifts his chin as he remembers. "Right." He waves a hand. "Sorry, been a little preoccupied."

"You're always welcome on Earth," I say to Cato. "That's the perk of being soul tied to the god of this place." I circle my fork in the air. "I get to tell him who doesn't need an invitation. Right, Ky?"

"Right, angel." He pecks my cheek before returning to the kitchen.

"That's the perk of being friends with someone who's soul tied to the god of this place." Cato mimics my fork wave with his finger.

The sound of faint whispers comes through our collective chuckle, quietening us both. I rise perplexedly, following the noise to where Kysi and Hellano stand in the kitchen. It is not the fact that they were discussing something in secret that takes me back, but the closeness of their faces. Hellano meets a heated green glare with determination.

In a trice, Kysi lunges at Hellano, taking the collar of his shirt in unbreakable fists and slamming him into the fridge. Magnets go flying, and the sound of containers topple inside. The attack comes as no surprise to Hellano, who works to steady his form and gain the advantage.

"What the fuck?" I reach forward hesitantly to avoid getting caught in any crossfire. Hellano may have been able to take Kysi before, but not now.

Kysi draws back and lands a blow on his cheek, the impact staggering them to the floor.

"Stop it!" I demand, but neither of them pays attention. "You're going to break my house!"

It is as though I'm not even here.

I personally think that I have done a great job tolerating the excess masculine energy lately, but now, it is entirely too overstimulating.

With Kysi essentially being the god of Earth, I decide to trust my gut when it tells me he is exempt from feeling pain here. I reach across the stove, gripping the handle of my cast iron. Egg flies over the blood on the floor when I swing it at his temple.

He goes limp, falling beside Hellano who looks at me with a puffy, darkening eye.

I point the frying pan at him. "Unless you want what he got, I suggest you tell me *exactly* what the hell you two were just talking about."

Long ago, my spirit created the god of Mortals and Bargaining to watch over her creations. One that would keep the others at bay, lock the door to Earth so they could only operate from the Heavens. Due to the nature of our roles, our spirits have always worked in close proximity. Over the course of countless past lives, a layer of trust was built between our souls.

Kysi broke that trust.

Little did I know, no thanks to him, he *lied* to my past lives to make the original deal. According to them, my successor has already been made and I simply went to Earth instead of the Shadowlands in order for Kysi—who graciously got me away from the god of Afterlife—to swoop in and start a life with me.

"But like a mother-daughter bond, your past lives care about you," Kysi had said.

My Soul Mothers wanted to give me the chance to lead the life I was supposed to live, so it probably didn't take much convincing on Kysi's part.

But Hellano claims that he was not willing to run the risk of being denied ...

So, he glamoured them.

Additionally, Hellano would not send him to the Shadowlands to begin with unless he had something to gain. Kysi told my previous lives that the god of Afterlife agreed to send him to the next realm if he protested against his reincarnation.

As we know, the real agreement was my title. My Soul Mothers believe that my power went to Kysi, so that he could create the new goddess of Beginnings to take my place. Upon her arrival, the title would then transfer to her. She would hate Hellano like the rest of them, he would be replaced, balance would return, and Kysi gets to live a long life with me on Earth.

My knuckles whiten around the handle of the cast iron as I sit in the dining chair and listen to Hellano tell the story in a puddle of sweat, egg, and plasma.

"If I'm going to be helping him again, I want something specific," he says.

"Why wouldn't you just do it? Do you want our worlds to end—want to be left alone with our spirits battling within you?"

"Who's to say this is permanent?" He slings sweat off of his arm, holding up a saturated palm. "It could be a side effect of soul transference. My theory is that once it's complete, things should level out. In that case, I'd just start over—build a new universe from the ground up, as I'll be the sole foundation to existence."

It's hard to believe I once loved this bastard. "Why don't you? As the god of Afterlife, I'm sure you'd love to watch the world burn."

"I'd still be empty," he states flatly.

Damn.

His only goal is to fill the void and keep living. A seemingly simple motivation that he has fought centuries to achieve—to live and be happy.

There is a bitter understanding in my tone, "What do you want?"

At the base of my contentment rests a lingering devotion. A mere dying ember, but it remains. Even as the years passed and the hatred grew, it never fully extinguished. My entire life, all I wanted to do was please him. I loathe how the chains of that desire still hold me hostage.

"See," he begins, "I'm aware of how sly Kysi is with deals. If he isn't specific enough, the bargain can be entirely different from what the recipient intended. If he says that he'll deliver you boat loads of cash on Wednesday, one might agree in exchange for whatever it is that he wants in return. But the god of Bargaining doesn't plan to deliver until a Wednesday over a thousand years from when the agreement was made."

"I'm well aware." I wave the skillet at him. "Get to the point."

"When your little boyfriend entered the kitchen, I asked what the deal was going to be. He mentioned getting me another five hundred years tacked on to my lifespan, which will have to be renegotiated.

He also mentioned fixing my soul tie—transferring it like he did your title. I'll accept that, but I want to decide who it will go to."

I lean back. "Fine. Who's soul?"

Hellano's honeyed eyes pierce through mine. "Yours."

CHAPTER 12

Kysi lays limp on the tile next to Hellano. Glancing down at the cast iron still tight in my grasp, a twinge of guilt surges through me.

I am angry at the secret he had been keeping, but now I see why he had been acting so nervous all morning.

He was going to tell me.

Kysi has gone through great lengths to experience what it is like to have a soul bond. I understand the rage that would ensue upon hearing someone was trying to steal it—especially a sworn enemy.

I drop the skillet on the table and carefully bypass puddles of Hellano's bodily fluid. "Cato, little help?" I motion for him to assist me with Kysi.

His dead weight nearly cripples the two of us as we carry him to the sofa. Once he is situated, I wet a kitchen towel and begin wiping the blood from his hands and arms. Hellano weakly stumbles in and falls to the floor, sprawling out under the fan that spins lazily overhead.

"Why the hell do you want a soul tie with me?" I scrub Kysi's obsidian band. "Gods, I swear—if I wasn't so guilty for hitting Ky with the very cast iron he used to serve me breakfast, I would be giving you the closest thing to a permanent ending I could think of."

Imagine taking away someone who was destined for another, only to try again the moment they finally had them.

What an asshole.

"You haven't even let me explain before moving to threats." He humphs, "You've always been the type to ask for forgiveness rather than permission."

"Just answer my question."

"Think about what Cato said. The god of Time was created to protect us. Now, you're threatened with the true death just like he had, and although I hope everything would balance out if the transference completes, I can't say for sure that it will. Cato said it's probably the soul tie that saved you," he says, "Kysi wouldn't give up the piece of your soul that he carries. If we had that, we could basically do Kairos's job—well, the most important part of it, anyway. Our spirits would be protected in each other."

I hate to admit that it makes sense—almost like insurance for our souls.

"What about you?" I ask. "You don't want my power at all?"

Hellano shakes his head. "I only took it because I didn't want to feel broken anymore, nor did I want to be reincarnated."

Cato chimes in, "You only feel this way because you've lived long enough to feel the weight of it. The pain lingers in your soul, emerging after however many years. If you would just obey the Law of Reincarnation, the ice in your heart would let up."

"My time may be up," Hellano says, "but I never lived ... never truly loved."

An anchor sinks into my gut.

Ouch.

"It wouldn't change the fact that you and Kysi have feelings for each other—wouldn't change much of anything for either of you. Plus ..." Hellano hesitates, his next words a weighty crutch, "you are the only thing I've cared for. If I can't have all of you and be whole, I'll settle for just a piece."

Kysi twitches. "Over my dead body," he snarls, removing his hand from mine as he sits up. "What happened? I know *you* didn't render me unconscious." He rubs tired eyes.

"Um," my voice cracks, "so first I'd like to say sorry."

"For what?"

A cackle emerges from Hellano. "She rocked your shit with her frying pan." His laughter deepens, then I hear Cato's bubble out.

Jerking my head to the side, I shoot the god of Wisdom a scornful glare. He clears his throat and finds quiet.

"It's not funny," I bark at the two of them.

I turn to find the glow of Kysi's eyes, a grin forming beneath them. "You what?" he says in a breath. "Hit me with a skillet?" He chuckles then, tilting his head back to give in to the laugh. "Color me impressed that you incapacitated the most powerful god in this room with one swing."

The most powerful god? Now I'm just offended.

"If I can knock you out, wouldn't that make me the most powerful god? I can do it again if you don't believe me."

He smirks, the glint of arousal behind his bright green eyes. "So feisty," he mumbles, leaning forward to press his lips to mine.

Although the warmth is intoxicating, I am the first to pull away. "How are we going to fix the mess you made with my Soul Mothers?"

Kysi throws a sideways glance at Hellano. "For someone so hell-bent on staying alive, you certainly act with a death wish."

Hellano raises his hands in defense. "You had plenty of time to tell her yourself."

After releasing a sigh and ripping his glare away from the enemy, his features soften the moment he looks at me. "I should've told you against my will to remain on your good side. Forgive me."

Although I almost cracked his skull open, I do not need that to make us even. Being the sole focus of those verdant eyes is enough to make my knees buckle. I cannot stay mad at him.

"I want another thousand years and the soul tie," Hellano interrupts, pulling our gaze away from each other.

Kysi hardens at the sight of him. "Six hundred years and you can tie yourself to anyone but her—or anything. Perhaps a noose?"

"Eight hundred," he counters.

"Seven."

"Done, but I still want that bond."

I will not sit here and be talked about as if I am for sale. "Quiet," I demand, tone sunken and riddled with impatience. They become still, waiting for me to continue. "Six hundred and I'll do the soul bond."

"What?" Kysi asks, panged by my statement.

"Trust me." Hopefully, my tone is enough to relay that my loyalties lie with him. "It won't change anything."

He looks me over, shaking his head. "Don't make me do this."

My entire existence has been manipulated by these men. I care about Kysi, but it is time for me to choose my own path. "I'm done being a puppet to the both of you. Make the deal."

His lashes hang low as a heavy breath of defeat flows out of him, the exhale murmuring resignation. Betrayal shadows his features, similar to what I held for Hellano.

It breaks my heart.

"God of Afterlife, do you agree to send Anewla and myself to the Shadowlands in exchange for a prolonged lifespan of six hundred years?" With a set jaw, he grinds his teeth at the next part. "And do you agree to return Anewla's title, in exchange for a soul bond with her?"

Hellano mulls over his proposition, dissecting it for any potential loophole. "I agree."

With a shaky voice Kysi says, "Then we have a deal."

The following day is spent preparing for our departure. We could have left immediately, but Kysi claimed he had some things to tend to first.

I think he's just avoiding the inevitable.

He was gone for a while after I convinced Mona to take Hellano sightseeing. We do not have much as far as tourist attractions go, but there is a lovely cemetery I am sure he would enjoy.

Despite the urge to stick to Kysi like the honey he adds to the orange chicken, I give him space to cook. He does not say a word. The silence is eerie.

After he brings me dinner, he immediately takes the seat across from me—*the* seat—and begins eating. He does not look up to witness the expression of approval that always falls over me when I take the first bite, which is a statement his dismay.

I clear my throat. "Thank you for dinner."

"You're welcome."

No eye contact, no "angel," nothing. I would prefer not to spend our last day connected like this. He finally looks up when I push the dinner away.

"You're upset." I pull my hair from its loose braid and let it fall over my shoulders. It cascades down the length of my arms, snagging his attention like moonlight trapped in a midnight tide. His eyes illuminate—perhaps against his will. He is fuming inside, but unable to hold a grudge the same way that I could not yesterday. "You think it will change what we have—drive me away from you." I pull myself to stand, lifting my knee on the table. If his eyes were a compass, I would be true north. They lock on me like a fortress gate, unmoving and impenetrable as I crawl toward him. "Let me show you that it won't."

Kysi's hesitation is clouded by desire. The tether between us enters a battle of tug of war with each closing inch. When I reach him, he gives in to the impulse.

He shoves dinner to the side before reaching up to kiss my needy lips, greedily pulling me from the table and onto his lap. He is rougher with me now, struggling to hold back the lingering anger and overwhelming desire. I am engulfed in hard, sloppy kisses as he fists the back of my hair. But each action feels cut short, as if he's not completely following through with them.

Now's not the time to hold back, Kysi.

I'm not so nice to the buttons on his shirt this time around. They go flying—hitting the wine glass, the wall, the floor. I lift the fabric from the bondage of his belt before exploring the hills of his chest.

This was how we were supposed to begin. Not with a false persona to hide behind or mountains of lies yet to be revealed, but with everything in the open. Our past, our pains, ourselves.

Because to desire another with that knowledge on the surface, is a truly beautiful thing.

I am not sure if he tugs off my clothes with vexation or avidity, but it is arousing nonetheless. With each article that falls to the floor—both mine and his—he grips me everywhere; my hips, my back, my breasts, like it is his right. He pecks, licks, nips at my skin in a possessive frenzy. Each heartbeat is a thunderous echo between our tangled breaths.

"I love you."

The words hang in our atmosphere. Through the reflection of his eyes, I find myself. In a fleeting moment, I realize the confession did not come from him.

My track record with relationships has made me doubt my idea of love, but there is no denying this. It is different from what I had with Hellano. My love for him was constantly trying to be loved back. It was against my character and utterly selfish for me and others, yet wholly altruistic for him.

There are no requirements in this love, no conditions. Just us.

He hesitates. My vulnerability is just as naked as I, without reluctance. "Love me. Please."

It is a plea to give me what I have spent centuries looking for in the wrong place. But I am here now, willing and ready to take all that he has to offer.

The primal part of him always caged, rattling the bars of its prison, and itching to be set free—to fall into the web of a lover's bond and devour it like flames to a parched forest—escapes.

With shameless desperation, he stands. His hand coils to the back of my head as we crash into the wall, taking the blow that causes a painting to fall. When I feel him line up to my entrance, I grip his shoulders with anticipation. The way I respond to his touch causes a rumble to emerge from the pit of his throat. When he pushes in, a gasp interrupts my breath. It does not take us long to adjust to each other before our synchronized whimpers and moans reverberate through the dining room. He fucks vigorously, feasting upon my very essence.

"Say it again." His husky voice drips with a dark allure, each syllable fanning the flame in my stomach.

My heavy declaration wavers against the pounding of his hips. "I love you, Ky."

From the wall and back to the table, Kysi drops me on the edge of where we just ate. At first his hands are tight around my waist as he drills deeper into me with each angry stroke. Then, I become trapped between his arms as he grips the edge of the table behind me.

I'm entirely full—of him, desire, love. The fluff of onyx hair hits my chin as he bows his head to fuck me harder. Just when I feel the edge nearing, the rising ecstasy halts.

Before annoyance becomes the forefront of my emotions, he gives an order. "Turn around."

Apparently, I'm not quick enough, because the moment I move he does the rest of the work for me and shoves my hips over. When he reenters, I feel something else go in somewhere else.

He leans over me, his breath teasing my earlobe. "Safe word is honeydew," he warns while pushing in further, his thumb doing the same. I lean into him as he snakes another hand to my front, circling over my pulsing clit. As I find my own pace against him, I notice that it doesn't matter how I move; he responds to it all the same, like

KARA REITER

simply having me is enough to make him finish. I'm climbing and climbing and climbing with each press against him.

"You want to cum?" The hand over my nub, along with the one above his cock, slows. "Ask."

"Excuse me?" I push back, but he's quick to keep them away. One leaves completely, landing a blow on my cheek.

"Ask me for permission."

My stubbornness wants to override my need for release, but inevitably fails. "May I cum?"

"Hm," he hums, mulling it over. "How should I let you? This way?" He drags a finger over my clit, sending an electric pulse through me. "This way?" He sinks into me, the head of his cock hitting a wall. "Or this way?" Shivers wash over me like drizzling rain to thirsty earth as his thumb circles in another sensitive area.

"All of them—any of them—just don't stop." My desperation inflates with each passing second.

"So greedy," he tortures me with the words. "If you want it badly enough, I could be persuaded."

At this point, I'll beg like a damn dog if it means getting a reprieve from this demented edging. "Please," I plead, "please let me cum." When I squirm against him, he gives me more, but not all of it. "Watch me come. Please. I want you to watch." That strikes a chord, prompting him to drag me from the table.

Kysi pulls me through the hall and into the guest bathroom. The mirror is wider here than the one attached to my room, casting a reflection over the entire space. My midnight hair fills the sink as he bends me over the counter, picking up where we left off.

"Say it." He pulls my hair back, forcing my gaze to meet his through the mirror.

"I love you."

Deeper he goes, the confession reeling him to a climax. "Again."

"I love you." The glass before me catches my breath.

"Don't stop."

As I say it over and over, "I love you. I love you. I love you," his head falls back. It's not just the sex that he indulges in, but the weight of my words.

"May I cum?"

Illuminated eyes open slightly as he tilts his head forward, just enough to refocus on my needy expression.

"Yes, my angel. Look at me and cum."

It is difficult to keep my eyes from rolling back when the waves come forth. This feeling is entirely foreign. Through my overwhelmed senses rests a conjuration, a wish to never experience what it would be like to be without this again. It is a mutual love, one that competes in the most romantic of games—a battle to prove which one is more devoted, more passionate.

Nothing will take this away from us, I will make sure of it.

Kysi keeps the pace until I come down. When I do, he quickens behind me. The fact that it does not take him long to finish tells me that he has mastered control. "I love you too baby." A pulse throbs in me. "With all of my soul."

As Kysi picks up the mess we made, the reminder that our departure is drawing near eats at me. He did not mention the details of his journey there. All I know is that my past lives agreed to help him under false pretenses. By using vague and misleading language topped with the cherry of glamour, he tricked them into a deal they never would have agreed to without being manipulated. Giving my power to the god of Afterlife is the last thing they would want. I am anxious to see how they will react upon hearing the truth of what happened.

Thinking back, the Law of Reincarnation has been an issue for deities on multiple occasions. Hellano shares the same will that Kairos had. What is it that makes gods crave to remain in power, even at the expense of their minds? Perhaps the mania seeps in earlier for some, willing them to fight against their fate.

Even Lilliana, the first goddess of Beginnings, bypassed the Law for Cato. If she could call to the Heavens and grant the wish that his mind never falters due to age, why could she not do it for the rest of them?

I understand Lilliana's reason for making the god of Wisdom truly immortal. In a dire situation that calls for knowledge, no one wants to be hindered by the endless rows of the Ancient Library. Giving it a guardian, a soul to roam its aisles and assist those in need, is a necessary solution.

I am not sure if she intended for Cato to become the recluse he is today, given the fact that none of the other reigning deities have ever seen him, or knew of his existence. However, because he has made several trips outside of the library since meeting us, I get the feeling that he is indulging in the action, placing himself inside the story rather than reading it. The natural pull he has toward anything in written form tells me that he is too passionate to stay away from books, though. It is his duty, after all—none of us can escape that.

Thinking of him reminds me of what he said about traveling realms. If Hellano remains on Earth, I can go to the Shadowlands unharmed. With that being the case, I could also go back to the Heavens.

I need to visit home. My real home.

Not only are their furry faces that I would like to see, but if I am going to make an appearance in the Shadowlands and meet my Soul Mothers, along with countless other past lives I am sure, I would prefer not to arrive as the Fallen Goddess. They need to see me as the answer to this problem—the savior of the universe—the one that will end the impending chaos and bring forth a new Heavens.

A New World.

One where I rise again not just as the goddess of Beginnings ...

But the Queen of it all.

CHAPTER 13

I mention to Kysi that he needs to take me home as I secure the fallen painting back on the wall. He turns to me with kind eyes before pulling me into him. Ever since I told him that I loved him, he has been extra touchy. Not that I am complaining.

"I'll take you anywhere you want to go," he promises, "but you may not be happy with the state of your place."

As soon as he says it, I curse myself for not connecting the dots sooner. Now I understand why he avoided taking me before.

Hellano's estate was a wreck, so it makes sense that mine would be too. None of his furniture was missing though, so maybe I can still wear my old clothes. The thought of that is all too nostalgic, and not in the best way either. Putting on the clothes that I used to wear sounds like slipping into the body of my past self. The cruel, cold, bitch of a person that I used to be. It is a painful memory that makes me wince, but I suppose the only way to cleanse the stain is to break my new self in.

"I can handle it," I tell Kysi. With a nod of concurrence, he tightens his hold around me.

A wave overtakes us like a hungering vortex. My ears pop, the pressure a macabre reminder of my near-death experience. It sparks fear, only to dissipate the moment we land on uneven ground. My wings are quick to return, flapping as if they had missed their time in the sun.

"I'll never get used to seeing them." Kysi looks them over as if it is the first time.

Stretching them out, I inspect my surroundings. After a couple breaths, I recognize this as my old bedroom. The bed hangs low from the ceiling, which was once lined with deep brown branches that stemmed from trees in the corners of the room. They no longer hold thick, lush leaves.

Where are they? Anxiety surges through my chest as I squint, searching among the decaying tendrils of wood. The smallest, most dull lights twinkle throughout the dying branches like fading stars in a hopeless abyss.

Thank gods they are alive, although just barely. I have missed my fireflies.

I pull from Kysi, welcoming the room as I once did every morning. "Honeys," I call to them, "I've returned."

A faint buzz filters through the air. A knot forms in my throat at their weak greeting, knowing they used what little strength they have to do so.

They missed me too.

That is what I love about my creations; they are so forgiving. I disappeared for years, yet they are still happy to see me even on the fence of death. When their buzzing fades, I can sense their plea for help.

They think that because I am here now, I can save them. Return everything back to the way it was. But I must leave them like this.

A tear falls despite my efforts to contain it. "I can't stay." Breaking the news to them feels like a crack in my spirit. "I will be back. When I return, I'll never abandon you again."

My promise to the lightning bugs can't end with them. I have other animals here, just beyond that door. If I were to step out, creatures that once frolicked about would be too busy fighting to stay alive. But as their mother, how could I simply ignore them?

I rip my gaze from the dimming lights on the ceiling to find Kysi behind me, attempting a stoic expression. His face is blank, carrying no frown, but behind glossy eyes he holds immense guilt. If it weren't for the faint drip—one that I almost did not notice—fall from the side of his face, I wouldn't know the extent of how much it pains him to bear witness to this. The only thing I can gather through the silence is his—our—sorrow.

I take a breath, preparing myself to open the bedroom door.

The site of them makes my knees buckle. I hit the floor, and it just barely stirs them awake.

All of them balance on the fence of death. My birds no longer fly, their absent melodies filling the space with an eerie silence. Lana, the snow leopard, lay limp by the bleeding oak in the center of the room. Behind her, I see Bane's leathery tail poke out from behind the tree.

He's one of the oldest animals to reside here—an albino alligator created by an ancient Soul Mother of mine.

Nothing moves now. Every creature, from the antelope jackrabbit to the giant brown bear, is pinned to the floor against their will. Their eyes hang low, sluggishly opening and closing to keep death at bay.

I lied earlier; this is too much. The gaping hole in my chest is nothing compared to this. My hand clasps over my mouth to stifle a sob. I have to get it together, swallow the insufferable misery. Because mothers cannot give in to despair; not when their sole responsibility is to make sure their children never do.

"I'm home only for a moment," my broken tone hits the glass ceiling, reaching past them all, "bringing nothing but a promise. Let fear be a coward at the gate of your minds, for if as much as a bee passes on from this realm, I will reign hell over the Heavens. Take my words and do not slip from here. I command it."

A rumble stirs the branches of the oak as they respond with obedience. Kysi awaits me by the door in a respectful silence, stepping aside as I pass through with a creeping resolution.

For everything to be on the brink of extinction all because of a rotten deal ... it puts into perspective just how fragile the Heavens really is.

I am determined to make sure history doesn't repeat itself, by not allowing it to have the option to.

Yet another symbol of this macabre nightmare stares back at me from my closet. Most of my clothes are fabricated from plant life, which once held vibrant hues of forest greens and an array of flowering accents like foxglove and baby's breath. Each piece was unique, but now they all look the same—dead.

To my surprise, the dress I grasp does not crumble under my touch. It is dry, but the decaying vines remain knotted together as if they too are clutching a lifeline.

It seems as though I have no choice but to arrive as I am. Human clothes or shriveled dresses, I won't be able to disguise myself from reality.

And maybe that is not a bad thing.

This garment is more than what meets the eye. It's a tribute to my pain, my rage, my heart, my withering character—no, not withering ... changing. It serves as a message: despite my betrayal and descent, I will not neglect my roots just because they are broken. To betray me is to betray life.

May my will constrict the Heavens like a python does its prey, engulfing it within me to digest and give me strength.

Slipping it on feels like stepping into a ghost, its melancholy tendrils hugging me like a second skin. What used to trail down the length of my legs in lattice-like vines, now stops in the middle of my thigh. Pieces fall from their woven spots, leaving random strands that dangle no further than my knee. The braided plant is looser in certain areas, creating more volume and depth to the dress.

At first, I think one of my fireflies has fallen from the ceiling, but when I look down, I see the vines slowly wrapping over my body in a loving embrace. Through silence they exclaim their intention: to make me appear as the liberator I am meant to be ... even if it means using the last of their energy.

I do not want that. I would rather wear rags. They know it too, and that is what makes their sacrifice all the more purposeful.

I witness a weary tendril wrap around my arm, feeling another mirror it on the opposite side. A few more move up from my chest, circling my neck before trailing up behind my ears and pushing my hair back. They form a band over my head, smaller vines stemming from it ever so slightly. All at once, tiny flowers bloom from them in one final breath.

Kysi peers at me in awe, lips parted and unblinking. The only movement from him is the strand that falls to his brow, as if to get a better view for itself.

"Captivating." His eyes are glued to my waves of hair that caresses the dress, hugging it the way it does my figure.

I walk toward him and wrap my arms around his neck. He responds by holding me close. "Ready?"

"Ready."

From there I leave behind my disturbed home, taking with me the promises made.

A bashful breeze welcomes me in an unknown forest. A timberland of hope surrounds us from all angles, the only indication of compromised life resting in the shallow detritus below.

As I stand within the breathing woods, the melancholy that clings to me lets go, drifting away just as the rustle of leaves do at my feet. I wait for pain, anticipating for my wings to pass through my shoulder blades, but it never comes.

Kysi takes notice of my quizzical expression, leaning to the side to reveal his chateau in the distance. We are still in the Heavens, but the life here makes it seem like beautiful Earth.

I part from him, turning to inhale the sweet aroma of pine. Hints of moss tease my senses, along with the scent of scattered wildflowers. The ground is firm yet yielding. It is solid, but offers enough cushion to make me feel lighter, inside and out. A twig snaps under my feet, releasing a pleasant crack through the quiet serenity.

The risk of losing this magical place only makes me appreciate it more. My pace quickens as I near a sprint, letting the crisp air slide over me like silk across moisturized skin. I glide through the endless forest, each trunk of bark that I pass is a whisper of love, of acceptance.

I have always wondered if all flora and fauna recognize me as their mother just as those in my estate do. Every now and then on Earth, it seemed as though they would occasionally pause to take notice of my presence. Except now, the forest is not merely saying hello.

With heavy breaths I come to a halt, taking notice of the way each branch above and blade below curl toward where I stand; almost as if offering me an embrace.

In silent acceptance I meet the ground, sprawling out on the forest floor. Monarch and morpho butterflies emerge, offering a performance just for me. The air around them rustles delicately with each beat of their wings, offering flashes of electric blue, orange, and black.

It is not just nature's kindness that mends my sorrow, but the fact that it recognizes me as its goddess. My physical presence has not been enough of a reminder that I am still me—that my soul is not wholly lost—but this is.

At the same time I notice Kysi nearing, so does the forest. Its behavior shifts, as if offended at the interruption. However, I know he is loved all the same by the way it softens, the butterflies migrating over to greet him as well.

"I've never seen it act quite like this." His eyes roam to take in the scenery. "Nature isn't just alive. It lives," he says it as if he too needed the reminder. "It loves."

A handsome smile spreads across his cheeks in response to mine. I lift my hand for him to take, and instead of rising to meet him, I pull him down with me in the grass. Together we stare up at the swaying leaves and the soft flicker of butterfly wings. The weight of today's problems float away like tiny parachutes off dandelions.

I am not sure how much time passes, but I only avert my gaze from the veiny branches above when I sense Kysi looking over at me.

His expression is difficult to read, one of patience and harmony that sit under thick, unblinking lashes, with a speck of something I cannot place. I search for what it is he expects me to notice, roaming over the firmness of his jaw. I trail my vision downward toward a raised bicep, following it past his forearm.

In the palm of his hand rests a velvet, heart-shaped box. It is the color of dark rosewood, with gold outlining its frame.

It lays open.

A teardrop of moss agate sits upon a gold band. It radiates elegance and class while absorbing all aspects of my personality. Through it is a statement to my divine role—and an oath to the man I was supposed to be with all along. It is breathtaking ... and a little nerve-wracking.

"I ... said I love you, like, three hours ago?" My bewilderment cannot be expunged, like the chuckle that falls out of him.

"It's not because of that." His gaze remains on me, while mine is tethered to the ring. "If I can't be bonded to you from the Heavens, I ask to be tied to you on Earth. Let's make Heaven not a place, but a feeling that outlasts the confines of time and follows us where we walk together. Will you take this gift and declare yourself mine, from now until a permanent end?"

Marriage is not a tradition in the Heavens, however, lovers often give one another a token. Something small, symbolic. Adopting a mortal custom is a fitting gift, considering the nature of our titles.

Kysi is asking for the ultimate promise, one that's bigger than having a connection we are unable to control. This is his attempt to create something more than what I'm scheduled to share with Hellano, yet it is built with such a fragile foundation. Even humans make this oath legally binding, and all he wants is my word.

"Yes." I accept his proposal, because what does it hurt? We're about to lose our bond on my accord, so if wearing a ring makes him feel better about that, I'm happy to ease his conscience. "It's a vow."

That relieves tension in his shoulders. "Then I offer the same vow." He plucks the ring from where it nestles in the box, taking my hand to slide it over my finger in a perfect fit. "I promise to love you through vicious waters, keeping you mine and never letting go."

"Then we have a deal."

The anguish is less severe this time around, but it still hurts like hell. Kysi's grip tightens around me as my wings force their way into my shoulder blades, submerging themselves into every nook and cranny of my spine. Every digit is a cry for reprieve. I wince against him, fisting the fabric of his shirt.

"Almost over baby," he comforts.

I take a breath as the torment subsides, noticing how the particles in the air hold more weight. There's a tension—a knotted coil twisting the atmosphere. It is hard to explain—something just feels … *off*.

Parting from Kysi, I look through my bedroom in search of something, lacking the slightest idea what. My gaze quickly falls to him, who stands disturbed; lips parted, and brows furrowed. Seemingly prompted by an unknown source, he moves to the door.

"Ky?" My steps replace his as I follow him through the hall, the frame of his shoulders a hardened display of angst. As we round the corner to the living room, he abruptly halts, nearly knocking me into him.

Cocking my head to the side, I observe everyone seated. A televised glow illuminates the otherwise lightless room. Meena holds Mona's hand, whose frozen gaze is transfixed on the screen, glazed by the veil of horror and woe. We follow her focus to the broadcast.

"They lost audio about ten minutes ago," Cato breaks the silence from where he leans against the arm of the couch. "Now it's just footage."

An anchor lands in my gut at the display of chaos. Videos from all corners of the world filter through the screen like a devastating prophecy fulfilled. Twisters spiraling in mountain lands, deserts drowning beneath cloudless skies, oddities that counter the logic of science and leave the world in a state of panic.

How could this happen in such a short amount of time? It's as if the snowball of my descent has been building in place, finally strong enough to break through Kysi's barriers and wreak havoc upon the human realm. He appears just as stunned as I, and between us lies heavy guilt.

The television cuts to airborne footage, zooming in on a crumpled city. It surveys the area, scanning over those that have survived as they limp through the carnage in search of family or aid. One man pulls at a slab of concrete, struggling with a bent leg unwilling to cooperate with him. At last, he manages to heave it over, revealing what lies motionless beneath.

Under the wreckage is a woman painted in ash—so much so that she nearly blends in with the debris around her. The man falls to his knees, pulling at her arms and what they hold within them.

An infant.

Mona mumbles profanities before burying her face in her knees. A muffled sob follows.

Hellano stands, fanning his shirt as he nears the curtains. He pulls them back in one swift motion. A dooming cherry hue filters my house. Nausea swims in my stomach as the crimson sun mocks me, like it is staining the world with the blood of those that have died thus far.

"Whenever you're ready," Hellano urges from where he stands.

"Do it," Kysi responds without hesitation, reaching for me.

The god of Afterlife opens his hands, releasing shadows from his palms. Some glide across the floor while others swim through the air towards us, almost as if each tendril has its own personality.

"See you when things feel right between us, flower." Hellano peers at me while his abysmal fog encases my legs.

Flower.

The word falls from his lips just as it did eight years ago, back when it was more of a name to me than my given one. I was his little flower, the only beam of life he had no desire to snuff out—or so he said.

Then he plucked it.

Kysi lifts my hand. "You may be waiting a while," he bites in response while exposing my gift.

Hellano's eyes search for a moment before landing on the mark. His jaw twitches just before my vision darkens behind his smothering power. I am swallowed by a sea of black, having nothing but Kysi's hand to grasp in the void of floating nothingness.

Then, it slips away.

CHAPTER 14

In a desolate space, weightlessness carries me to no destination. I'm suspended by a lack of gravity, uncertainty coiling in my gut the longer I drift. Alone.

Is this where humans go when they die? If not the Shadowlands, then where? This limbo between realms may harbor more souls than my own, like a landfill of dumped consciousnesses—doomed for madness against the insufferable *nothing*; doomed to be collectively isolated.

Without notice, a grunt echoes in the void.

"Kysi?" I call into it, hoping to get a response so I can gauge the distance between us. A cold surface hits my tailbone before my wings have time to return. I groan at the unexpected bump.

"Right here, angel. Follow my voice."

A long-held breath breaks free, dissolving the tight concern in my chest. Kysi has been through this once before, so there is no need to panic—although my instincts say otherwise.

How terrifying must it have been for him the first time around. To be alone in the unknown, risking your life in an effort to help your people escape from endless torture and save your true love—who barely even knew who you were—from corruption.

My wings lift me from the ground. His voice is an auditory lighthouse, a beacon of expired loneliness that this limbo attempted to suffocate me in just moments ago.

I barrel into him hard, having not realized the speed I gained. With a *humph*, my hands land on either side of his head. The surface beneath us feels as though it has not touched the warmth of sunlight in ages. I pat him down, just to ensure that he is still whole after such a terrifying travel.

"Where are we?" I ask. "Can't see a thing."

Perhaps it is our closeness that lifts the mood, because when he speaks there is a teasing glint behind his otherwise sullen tone. "Me? Oh, I'm totally fine. Thanks for asking," he grunts from under me.

I playfully swat at his chest, which invokes a chuckle between the two of us. The soulful melody reverberates through the pitch-black chamber. The sound does not just tug at my heartstrings, but plays them in long, elegant chords.

I will never get used to the way he can turn my mood around so effortlessly. In the midst of a universal collapse, in a place where gods go and never return, I'm laughing.

If this abyss is anything like the permanent ending, I would thankfully fall in.

The pang of cranking gears jerks our attention away. Light seeps through a widening slit above, illuminating the pit in which we lay.

Kysi's head tilts, looking behind me at the source. I blink away stars and follow his gaze.

Many silhouettes peer through the brightness, their heads downcast to observe us new arrivals. Whispers of concern murmur through them.

"What in the Heavens has brought you back here, god of Mortals?" one speaks into the pit.

"And Bargaining," another corrects them.

Kysi shifts below me, prompting us to rise. I slide off of him and we stand together, eyes heavenward at the onlookers. Because his reputation in the Shadowlands is about to become tenuous at best, I think it would be wise for me to do the talking.

"My name is Anewla." I introduce myself to the figures, mindful to project power in my tone. All of their heads shift toward me at once. Against the corona of light surrounding their silhouettes, I can see that each individual is cloaked in a hood. It is no easy feat to conceal how creeped out I am by their synchronized movements, but I manage by suppressing the shiver that rolls through me. "I am the youngest goddess of Beginnings, demanding presence with your leader."

Chaotic whispers erupt once more.

Time is of the essence; each tick of the clock's long hand is another mortal soul lost to the chaos of Earth. After a moment passes with no response, I take that as my cue to come forth from the pit. The muscles in my back tense against my mental command—wings catching me after I jump.

Simple yet marvelous architecture opens up to me as I ascend from the ground. The slate gray walls push focus to detailed illustrations of artful history. Where paintings lack, divots in the stone peek through—carvings of all things beautiful and macabre; from flowers and skulls to busts of screaming faces neighbored by ones of delight, it is as though each deity has placed their mark here—designing it to be an awestriking balance of our purposes and abilities. Each piece is breathtaking, yet none asks for attention. The room exudes an aura that both a philistine and a connoisseur of art would be comfortable in. The most noteworthy quality, however, is the glassless windows. Light gives way to nihility, as if the Land of Shadows hovers within an orb.

It is me who looks down on them now—a few dozen, maybe—but only for a brief moment. Friction sounds as my feet scuff stone, gently hissing while they slide across the smooth floor. In a blink, Kysi is beside me.

The hooded deities stare back at us like cultists—or ghosts.

The first one to speak is a woman with pore-less, almond skin. Although visibly confused, she stands with humble confidence. Under the shadows of her hood, gold bands glimmer around intricate dreads. "Youngest?" she queries. "Where is Brair?"

I assume that was who they named to replace me. Because these people seem to know of my descent, I tell them, "Yet to be conceived."

Panic fills the room. Despite the windows lacking panes, their worried tones bounce off the walls. They stir like a swarm of agitated bees.

"Silence."

The echo of their distress fades. A robed figure, no different than the others, comes forward. The *tap tap tapping* of elegant shoes click across the slab of ground. When the oncoming figure stops at the forefront of the crowd, nothing but an enthralling quiet is left behind.

Manicured hands reach for the hood, lowering it over locks of butterscotch hair—strands that frame hardened features. I do not know this woman, but something about her feels familiar.

"Then how is it that you're *here*, Anewla?" Her voice cascades like a slithering serpent, filled with the venom of her speculative contempt towards the man beside me.

Droves of impaling eyes await my answer. How many details do I give to these strangers? After the trust Kysi broke, I am hesitant to give mine to them freely.

"Please state your name." I dodge the question.

The woman tenses with agitation, clearly displeased by my lack of response. "I am your eldest Soul Mother." She leads with this, I note, to emphasize her position of authority. "My name is Lilliana, the first incarnate of life and the head of the Council of Shadows." Her arms extend to the room as a silent introduction to the cloaked figures.

I'm not sure why, but for some reason I assumed she would look older. I would say she appears somewhere in her mid-thirties. It leaves me wondering if she has always had this appearance, or if we all really do age, just so slowly that it is barely noticeable.

How odd is it that a council runs the Shadowlands? What more do they have to delegate, apart from issues such as Kysi's deal, which has only come just the once?

"You wish for me to speak freely to the council?" I ask in an attempt to convey that a private conversation may be more suitable. It would be unwise to spill sensitive information—especially involving a universal collapse—to a group of visibly anxious people.

Lilliana hesitates before tilting her head to the side. "Gather the Nine," she utters to the woman who spoke up previously. "Leave us," she then orders the Council of Shadows. They obey immediately, disbanding in unison. "Come, daughter. Relay what you know to the elders."

It is certainly bizarre being referred to as 'daughter' by a person I just met three minutes ago. What's even more unusual is the knowledge that I technically have numerous Soul Mothers, all of which will probably refer to me as the same.

Cranking sounds once more as the gaping hole I flew out of closes. When it shudders into place, I realize that it doubles as a wide, round table. We follow Lilliana as she strides over to it.

"The eldest deities, I presume?" Glancing at her, I notice the subtle undertones of indignation in her features. She is holding a grudge against Kysi, straining to convince otherwise.

"Some, yes. Others hold the position due to their impact on your realm."

As if spoken into existence, the Nine step in from the hallway in single file. They bring with them a sense of rigid professionalism; less like individuals and more like machines with a job to do. Could these ancient gods somehow hold the power to manipulate the Heavens?

I watch as they circle the pit, taking seats upon what I originally thought were merely pieces of decorum—busts carved into cylinders of stone that stem from the floor. Not all stools hold faces, but those that do match the person's that sits upon them. Due to this assigned seating, Kysi and I are forced to sit on either side of Lilliana.

"Why do you call yourselves the Nine?" I am the first to break the silence. "There's only eight of you." Irritability settles over my skin like poison ivy, and it takes an immense effort not to scratch the itch to display my discomfort, especially when they all lower their hoods in unison.

"In memory of someone," a man with auburn hair and a down-turned gaze speaks from the right. I cannot make out whether his expression is that of anger, misery, or boredom—thick curls hang over the cliff of his forehead and shadow his appearance. The only distinction I have to go off of is his jawline, which hardly exudes joy.

There is only one way that a god could pass from this realm or avoid it entirely, and that is if their soul received the permanent ending, which leads me to believe this 'someone' is Kairos, the god of Time. They must feel as though he was meant to be an active part of this council—they have all mourned the loss.

Negative energy radiates from the Nine, so pungent that I can almost hear it crack like static in the atmosphere. All of it is directed at Kysi, as if he were a lightning rod for their collective animosity. They do not need an explanation to know that he has betrayed them, our presence here is proof enough.

"Allow me to describe the way it feels to have your soul ripped from your body." Their heads turn to me, all except for the auburn-haired man, whose eyes remain at his feet. "Pressure builds inside, growing and growing until you're not just writhing for release, but astonished that your brain hasn't caved into it yet. But it won't—it can't. Everything will sound fuzzy, like there is cotton stuck deep within your ears. That's how you'll know the bleeding has begun. But if you don't notice—if the force in your bones doesn't allow you to—you'll see it next. Your vision will turn red as the compression forces blood into your tears. A burning will erupt in your chest as your lungs begin to drown and every crevice of your insides flood." My gaze is sharp, flicking to each of their hovering eyes. Kysi stares blankly at the table, picturing the traumatic memory of what happened that day in his living room.

A heavy coat of unease lay upon each of them now. "Why are you telling us this?" the woman with gold bands around her braids asks.

"To avert your attention," I explain. Kysi's fist lay over the stone, tense. "Vengeance, justice—whatever you'd like to call it—has no place here now. Because if you all don't listen to me, what I just described will come for you as well. What's done is done. So, I ask that you aid us in restoring balance to the realms and avoid wasting your energy on revenge."

I am met with deadpan expressions, struggling to read through their body language and into their psychology.

What are they thinking? I can't lose Kysi—*won't* lose Kysi. They would be wise to heed my warning, but not just because the fate of the universe is at stake and time is of the essence ... but also because if they do not, if they hurt him, they would not live to witness our realms burn.

Since the beginning, deities have remained submissive under the threat of a permanent ending. For the most part, they never broke the Law; they fulfilled their duties and moved to the Shadowlands when it was their time. Our lack of immortality has kept us in check. I am not comfortable with the knowledge that it exists within the Shadowlands, especially the place where deities have the power to alter realms.

If I can find out how they call upon the Heavens, it will not just be my realm that changes.

"You may begin." Lilliana pulls me from the daydream, urging me to fill them in on what happened since Kysi's previous visit.

They listen with intent as I recall these last eight years. I have to be careful not to reveal too much of my plan; I know for certain they wouldn't agree with it all. The less people I have against me, the easier it will be to reach my goal.

"The first thing I need is my title back," I tell them. "And due to the threat of extinction, I ask to be placed as reigning monarch of the Heavens. As goddess of Beginnings, my duty will be to protect the New World and kingdom within, ensuring that its integrity is never jeopardized by those who reside there. Additionally, I ask to be granted access to enter the Shadowlands at will, bringing with me the members of my council and court to work alongside the Council of Shadows—whom I hope will provide wisdom to ensure my rule be just and righteous. A New World, fit for all beings—humans included."

To my left, the woman with gold bands moves with effortless grace. Her comportment demands attention without giving a verbal command. "My name is Verina," she introduces, "third incarnate of life. Please, tell us, why bring humans to the Heavens?" She gestures with a delicate flick of her wrist.

If I tell them that it is really based off my personal connection with them, they would be much less likely to take my proposal into consideration. However, I can think of other reasons why their presence would be beneficial. "They drive our purpose, why shouldn't we understand them at a deeper level? By applying the opportunity to have interpersonal relationships between deities and mortals, it will bring our lives new meaning—lives in which none seek to make realm-altering bargains and desperate attempts to avoid death."

Verina nods in understanding. "And what is it that the god of Afterlife wants in return?"

"Hellano demands that his spirit be linked with mine in a soul bond, along with an additional six-hundred years added to his lifespan."

The auburn-haired man lifts his head then, revealing his face at last. There's a natural tightness to his features, as if he lives in continual suffering—perhaps not physically, but emotionally. His almond eyes tell of an agony that reaches through the depths of his being. "Take it," he pleas.

Lilliana raises a gentle hand. "Prosenth—"

"What makes you so eager?" Kysi interrupts. Where curiosity lacks in his tone, hostility resides.

Prosenth peers at me from across the space. Behind his eyes is an appreciation for the deal we made with Hellano. But not just that, a cry for help as well; the conjuration to see this through for him. "Unlike the other gods of Afterlife, I still yield the pain of losing my love. It never ended when I arrived here. I live within the hollowness inside."

My focus shifts to the rising cold within myself, shivering against it. To be stuck in that, the void of a rotten past, is unfathomable.

"Our lifespans were cut short after what happened to Kairos," Verina cuts in. "Due to the eternal death of a bonded deity, the mind of the reigning god of Afterlife corrupts much sooner than the others. To prevent madness from seeping into the Heavens, we all agreed to shorten our reign. In the event of another god losing their soul bond to a permanent ending, madness would not overtake them before their transition into the Shadowlands."

So Prosenth not only bears the pain of a love lost, but the guilt of indirectly killing the other deities and all those after them prematurely. When Lilliana said that the Nine was collected of not just ancient gods, but those who had a great impact on the Heavens, I assumed she meant those with positive influences on my world, but I suppose not.

Either way, Cato's mind remains intact. The Nine appears unaware of this, which leads me to believe that Lilliana created Cato and kept his existence a secret. But why?

Perhaps it was the one exception she was willing to make, knowing the importance of keeping life and death circular in the Heavens as it is on Earth—deeming wisdom essential enough to avoid the Law of Reincarnation. But if she went against the other gods to complete her goal out of fear that they would disagree ... maybe that means she will help me do the same.

I need to get her alone.

"It's time to vote," my Soul Mother announces. "All in favor of Anewla's title being returned, along with her previous role in the Heavens as goddess of Beginnings?"

"Agreed," Verina confirms.

"Agreed," Prosenth mimics.

A man with a thick beard and winged eyeliner comes after. "Denied," he says.

Who the fuck is this guy?

There is no chance for me to question his absurd decision before the rest of the Nine place their votes. None of which deny.

"Majority rules. It is done." Lilliana is quick to move on. At the other side of her, Kysi's quizzical gaze lowers on the man that was averse to our cause. "Next, all in favor of humans existing within the Heavens after their death?"

Same as before, all agree except the bearded man.

"Now," she continues, "shall the reigning god of Afterlife be granted six-hundred additional years, along with a soul bond to the goddess of Beginnings?"

Kysi shifts where he is seated. The caving in my chest is not due to the empty, chilling void, but the impending disconnect—a tether sewn by the hands of destiny, only to be torn apart by the mistake of man. He runs a hand through his hair, tousling it right before meeting my gaze. I wish I could reach him—hold his hand and repeat my promise in the woods.

"Our tie isn't broken," I speak to him, blinking back wetness under my lashes, "it just moved realms."

In the hilt of Kysi's features, a devotion lay. His chin tilts down in a nod of concurrence. I sense not just the dedication within himself to see my statement true, but also an ardency to test the validity of my vow. After centuries with a man that I was not fated for—opposite of, actually—to then be tied to him after finally getting away ... Kysi is worried it will ruin us completely.

But what choice do we have?

I do not humor the thought that this was meant to be—that this is the universe's way of separating us or the Heavens simply changing its mind about our connection on a whim. Still, the pang of not having that pull between us, having it with *Hellano* of all people, is enough to make my throat hard and ears ring.

A membranous twitch in my wings pulls focus in the room. I twist my neck, craning in the direction of everyone's hovering eyes.

Like sunlight upon spilled oil, my feathers glimmer rainbows.

A sad smile peaks on Kysi. His striking green irises brighten. "I love you too."

So, that is what it is. Similar to how they darken with anger, they shine with love. It must be from the bond. I wonder if they will shimmer for the god of Afterlife when this is all over; the thought makes me cringe.

"Denied," the bearded man states. I am not surprised. In fact, a small, selfish part of me—uncaring of the potential consequences if we did not follow through on our end of the deal with Hellano—is okay with his vote this time.

"Agreed," Prosenth utters. Another vote that I could have guessed.

The muscles in Kysi's neck strain. His chest neither rises nor falls as he imprisons the air within his lungs—waiting near the deathbed of our connection.

"Denied," says an unfamiliar voice.

That is—what? Why would they—

"Denied." Another casts their vote.

What is this, pity? Have they witnessed the cloak of affection between me and Kysi and decided not to disrupt what we so evidently wish to keep? Perhaps they know of a way around the god of Bargaining's deals, a way to help—

Lilliana's silent snicker snags my attention. "Denied."

Trepidation swims into my skin like poison from a needle. They yield no commiseration, have no methods to aid Kysi in escaping whatever will happen to him when we go back to Hellano empty handed.

With my base knowledge and limited education from the Ancient Library, I have never heard of the god of Bargaining not being able to keep his end of the deal. Considering the way his face has turned into alabaster stone, he has not either.

This is their way of punishing him for betrayal. Karma. Manipulate one bargain, and then find yourself in one impossible to execute. They will help me save the universe, sure, but not without Kysi paying the price for putting it in jeopardy.

When my title was taken and I could not complete my duties, the Heavens nearly ripped my soul from my body—pieces if it *were* taken. If Kysi cannot fulfill his responsibility of keeping his end of the deal—the deal *I* forced him to make ...

"Please," I mutter across the circular table.

Lilliana folds her fingers together. "Majority against. It is done."

Without a farewell, the Nine begin to rise and glide to the exit.

The flush of my blotchy skin heats the air, my breath turning from automatic to manual as I try to keep it steady against the whirling panic. What if I cannot find a way to call to the Heavens? What if I cannot override their decision?

A rough-hewn hand firmly holds my jaw, tilting my head to the side. I follow its warmth without a fight. Kysi's sleeves are rolled halfway up his arms, the white button down creased from our day together. His features are a buoy of light in the furious sea of my mind, a safe house against my whirling doubts.

He bends at the knees, leveling with me. "It's going to be fine, angel. *I* am going to be fine."

I search his face for the answer, finding nothing but a desperate attempt to convince me of his empty words. His sensual lips are taut with emotion—a silent wish to ease the turmoil churning inside me.

Maybe it was being with Hellano. Maybe it is the fact that I am missing pieces of my soul. It does not matter what traumatic blow tilted the scales of my moral compass; it only matters that they have shifted.

Lilliana knows how to fix this. I know she does. All I need to do is get her alone. Make her talk.

By any means necessary.

Chapter 15

Verina was the only one to stay behind, having volunteered to escort us to our bedchamber. Despite voting against us, she exudes sympathy. Pity.

As we exit into the hall, Kysi's hand finds mine. Each detail of the Shadowlands—although rather exquisite—does not leave me awestruck now, simply curious. Through the chilling mass in my chest and past the tangled web of my desperate objective, I take in the intricate exhibits around me.

The reverent scenery yields relics, artifacts, and descriptive tablets of past gods that line the walls—chronicles of their reign.

This vast museum doubles as a home. Beyond the galleries, I catch glimpses through serene alcoves nestled in quaint entryways. Deities lounge in some, relaxed against silken cushions. Others serve as communal areas, where laughter echoes through the corridor as gods share stories and connect in harmonic balance. To my surprise, we even pass a few sparring chambers where they battle for sport.

Not everyone is clad in robes. The ensemble of their dress varies with each personality we pass. Some wear gowns of chiffon that hang over cowl necklines or cold shoulders, while others fashion themselves for comfort—although elegantly so, sustaining a sense of uniformity all the same. Our attention snags many, but not enough so that it causes a distraction.

There is a peaceful repose to this realm. If not for my attachment to humans and the motivation to not just save them but redeem myself for the way they suffered by my hand, I might fancy living here. Later in life, that is.

"The Council of Shadows," I voice to Verina who saunters in front of me, "it's different from the Nine?"

She pivots slightly. "Indeed. The council comes together for the issues of this realm. The Nine gather for matters of the Heavens."

"That man—the pessimist," Kysi mentions beside me, "who is he?"

Verina's cloak sways in contrast to her form as we follow her up a set of marble stairs. "Drayxi, the first god of Afterlife," she answers. "He is against calling to the Spirits of the Sky. Given the consequence of our last vote, I no longer question why."

The upper floor gives way to a lengthy row of chandeliers. An assortment of doors lay beneath, all of which are ensconced with unique carvings. They vary in material—from deep cherrywood to heavy, charcoal-gray slabs. As we pass them by, I notice a pattern in their illustrious faces.

While each one is unique in their own regard, they all maintain the essence of what kind of soul resides within.

A mighty oak is carved into one, with branches for birds to rest and fawns to take shade. Wildflowers are etched near the roots, sharing the knoll that carries them; undoubtedly a chamber for one of my previous Soul Mothers.

Its neighbor lays ajar, bordered by piles of bones that surround a smiling skull. The hollow sockets eye me as if it covets my own skeleton to add to its collection.

Fitting for a god of Afterlife.

"Against it even now, as the realms are at risk?" Kysi probes, questioning the logic behind Drayxi's decision as I glance through the crack of the macabre bedchamber door.

The glance was so quick, so swift that I wondered if I even saw it at all.

There, Prosenth sat with a tome in hand, fingers gripping the leathery skin. But he was not reading, no, rather peering at me with those tortured eyes. Not sullen, I would say, but bitter with the refusal to accept the outcome of today's vote.

I am with you, I heard through the brief silence.

Perhaps it is wishful thinking, perhaps I saw what I merely *wished* to see. However, Prosenth was the only one to vote in favor ... the only one who may be just as desperate as I am.

Verina pauses near an oak door adorned with the outlines of a landscape. The beaming sun splits through mountains and over a riverbed, where black bears bathe and large, antlered moose quench their thirst.

"Perhaps not. Drayxi and Lilliana typically discuss the ritual in more detail after the votes have been cast. If changes are made, the Nine are collected once more."

"Will we be made aware of any changes?" I query.

The cloaked woman twists the knob engraved in laurel patterns, opening the bedchamber door. "That I do not know. The consumption of chaos that plagues Earth leaves us with little time to argue minute details. However, if the deal you made with Hellano is up for debate once more, I'll be sure to alert the two of you."

I am thankful for the gesture, as I know it is not required of her—nor was escorting us to our suites, which saved us the awkwardness of a stranger guiding our way in an already strange place.

"You mentioned a ritual. When is that scheduled to occur?" The pane-less windows cast a dimming light over the floor, helping me little with the claustrophobia of my persistent anxiety.

"With haste, in due time. Someone will call for you when the darkness has passed. Until then, rest." She offers a sentimental glance before sliding the door shut behind her, filling the still room with its echo.

A high beamed, wooden canopy surrounds plush bedding on the far wall. Vertical to the short footboard, a fan spins lazily at the apex of a tall, angled ceiling. Peeking from a room adjacent to the sleeping area, the crystalline pool in a bathing chamber awaits company.

As the blank sky darkens the world, speckles of light appear like cascading stars. They trail the outline of the windows and ceiling, growing brighter in contrast to the changing atmosphere. Some twinkle, almost in greeting.

"What are you thinking?" Kysi tucks a strand of hair behind my ear before covering my cheek in his palm. I lean into it.

What if what I saw in Prosenth was a mirage—an illusion constructed by a frenzied mind searching for answers in a place that advises you to abandon hope?

I shrug in response, deciding not to disclose what could have simply been a daydream.

"Try," he urges, nearly in a whisper.

Releasing a sigh, I pull a response from what I *do* know. "I'm sorry that I forced you to do it. It's my fault. Maybe we could have convinced Hellano to settle for something else, maybe he would have—"

"There was no convincing him," Kysi interjects, "and no convincing the Nine."

My forehead meets with his chest in defeat. The warmth of his sculpted body is firm, inviting.

The vibration of his throat waves over the top of my head. "Your wings are as dark as night, Anewla."

"A fitting fashion statement," I quip, voice muffled by the fabric of his shirt.

Kysi lifts my head to plant kisses along the contour of my face. "I can think of a better one," he croons between each peck, eyes brightening.

A grin tugs in the corners of my mouth. "Oh?"

Teasing fingers trail the hem of my dress, slipping beneath it to graze the skin of my thigh. "Nudity has always been my personal favorite." They glide upward, hooking the band of my underwear. "You wear it so well."

If I were to ask for the root of this arousal, he would lack honesty. I know what drives his fingers to pull them down, what motivates each greedy touch of his lips.

This may very well be our last night.

Kysi would deny it to spare my feelings, spout something off about how my presence alone is enough to get him going—how he does not *need* a reason to make love to me. As true as that may be, it would not change the fact that he is preparing for the end and yearning to spend it with me.

I reach for the buttons of his shirt. His tongue slides over mine as he helps me with them, tugging it off to expose the panes of his torso.

"Bed. Now," Kysi barks.

I oblige with anticipation, watching as he stalks over to where I lay. The clicking of his belt is followed by the hiss of its release. He tosses it over me, landing above my head.

That green illumination swallows me whole, as if I am their power source. I widen my legs to the silent command of his glare, my center glimmering against the freckled light above. The vines of my dress roll up to my hips, leaving my lower half wholly bare.

I tremble at the sight of him kneeling. A thud sounds as his knees hit the floor, the warmth of his palms running up my legs before tightening around my waist. He jerks me closer to the edge in one swift motion, hardly containing the craving that consumes him.

"You're so ..." Kysi hums over my labia, his index teasing the wetness, "responsive. It *intoxicates* me." Each syllable meets my core like a breeze with a secret, swirling the tempest in my stomach. His tongue begins near my entrance, gliding through my lips to the thrumming bundle of nerves at the summit of my desire.

A piece of my soul rests near his, and his with mine, but when our bodies collide, *that* is what allows them to truly swim together. Dance.

The tether between us tightens, along with the knot in my core. I let it pull me, giving in to the natural rise and fall of my hips.

Kysi stills between my legs, forcing me to work myself on his generous tongue. The command is not verbal, yet it is still heard through each flick he gives against my undulating waist.

You wanna' cum? Work for it, baby.

Reaching down, I fist his hair to steady him above me. Kysi groans as I find my rhythm, approving of my efforts to release.

The taut and tangled mess in my base unravels, spiraling outward into each limb as I writhe over the cloud of bedding. His grip strangles each thigh as he leans in, drawing out my orgasm.

At last, he rises, prowling over my breathless form with purpose. The ropes of his arms confine me in a prison of passion—one that judges me with a life sentence.

Kysi's hand snakes to the back of my leg, lifting it above his shoulder as he lines himself up. Thick lashes of lust observe the way my eyes fall back as he presses in, reveling in how I come apart from his touch. He emits an exhaustive drone that circles the air as he claims my body with an insatiable type of possession. Territorial. Domineering. Protective. Kysi takes me with a frenzied desire, drinking me in like the last drying oasis.

He tenses then, tumbling over a pinnacle as he releases into me, holding my leg with an unbreakable grip.

Kysi chased that high for hours, unable to detach himself from the spiral of love making, clinging to it. Not that I am complaining. If it were not for my suspicions with Prosenth, I would indulge with him until the light returned. But I must make sure that it is just a suspicion and nothing more. So, after a while, I coaxed him to follow sleep's beckoning hand.

The bedchamber door opens silently as I tiptoe into the hall. Above, the chandeliers sparkle with grace, enchanting the abandoned corridor. Faint murmurs echo from below as deities stay awake, enjoying the quiet void of night.

I do not appreciate the way my steps seem to reverberate, despite my attempts to move with stealth. The lurking threat of being noticed by a member of the Nine quickens my pace toward the destination awaiting me at the end of the corridor. The face of each door is like a sentinel, watching. Waiting.

Stones of bone come into view, piling up around that macabre skull. The twinkle overhead gleams off the vertex of the cranium. Its hollowed orbs seem to follow me as I close in; soulless eyes like a blackened crystal ball—harbingers of a ghastly omen.

Its teeth, however, smirk with the invitation to enter; twist the knob of its skeletal hand, encase it in my own like the handshake of a bargain—one that might save my soulmate.

I do not knock on Death's door.

As soon as my palm cradles the handle, the heavy slab turns weightless. It hangs ajar, summoning me to join the darkness beyond.

CHAPTER 16

My pulse becomes that of a hummingbird's when muffled voices rise under a closing distance. My body acts on instinct as I weave past the threshold.

Some childish, silly part of me imagines that it was the skull's doing—that somehow it prompted their arrival to push me through the yawning canal of the door.

A liquid midnight—just like that of the lonely limbo in which I traveled through to arrive here—swallows me like an asp, its unfused mandibles effortlessly engulfing me for digestion.

What is frightening me? Is the thick night a reminder of the nothingness in a permanent ending, the same one that has chased me around an infinite track? Or is it the horrific awareness that it is no longer following me, but rather Kysi, closing in on him with the promise of extinction?

The dark yields to an amber glow, pulling me from the apprehensive spiral. It burnishes a cluttered space, littered to the brim with bric-a-bracs and curios. A stale scent lingers, proof of neglect. A nest of sadness, each ornament an attempt to fill the vacant void that I have grown to recently know; except I have the luxury of lidding it with my lover's touch.

I suppose if that were not an option—if I was forced to live with the chill—I might resort to hoarding as well. Even if it did nothing, even if it were simply the closest thing to help that I could find.

"You came," a voice permeates the quiet. Prosenth releases the light dial at his bedside and leans against the steel frame. His shoulders are naked, with smooth skin that flickers against a candle's flame. For a moment, I swear something twinkled in the depths of his gaze.

Hope.

It is contagious, airborne. The feeling imbeds in the base of my spine, creeping to the atlas of my neck—so potent that I can almost taste it crackling on my tongue.

What I saw was real. He *is* with me.

"You called," I answer, standing in a patch of bare floor.

"Thank gods for your intuitiveness." Prosenth tilts his chin to the chair he once sat in hours before. Fabric is strewn over the back, but the seat remains empty. "That robe, could you hand it to me please? There's something I would like to show you."

I cross puddles of clothes and oddities on the way; empty goblets stained with maroon, drawings and sketches of one face, over and over, and books scattered about, lacking dust despite the obvious carelessness everything else here endures.

That is another thing I would do—consume knowledge or stories as well as things. Anything to escape.

It hisses off the lilac back rest, soft and heavy in my hand. He extends his arms and prompts me to throw, so I gently toss it across the room.

Prosenth heaves it over his head. He then stands, doing a lazy stretch before bending to shuffle through his nest of garments. The bedding lays bare in his wake, as if it already misses him. I barely detect the slits in the back of the fabric, made for both winged and bare-back deities. "Have another here somewhere," he mutters while chucking articles from his littered wardrobe. I dodge a pair of dress pants. "Ah, here," he says, having found a twin to his attire. "Put this on and follow me."

Prudently, I take the cloak from his outstretched hand. Part of me does not want to put it on, to be associated with the Nine in the slightest after what they decided today, but I understand the necessity. It would be unwise if the only two members opposed to the outcome of today's meeting were seen wandering the halls and speaking in hushed tones. Two members of the council, however, and no nocturnal onlookers would bat an eye.

The velvet material settles over the onyx locks of my hair. It weighs down my shoulders like a burden. The scent does not match that of the environment, but rather carries a hint of cardamom—out of place in a space that lacks freshness.

Given the way Prosenth held it out to me, and how he wears his now, I get the idea that him and this garb have spent many nights staring each other down. Loathing one another due to differing aims. And the cloak always got what it wanted once joined with its seven loyal allies ... To have a position of power and be useless in it to your own suffering, to stare at the embodiment of what could save you and get *nothing* out of it.

The hallway is even more hushed when we glide out from the bedchamber, as if the endless night beyond is waiting to hear what whispers we may share.

"Where are we going?" I ask quietly.

Prosenth does not so much as turn to address me when he responds, "Taking a stroll down memory lane."

The twists and turns of the Shadowlands work to dizzy me, the only reprieve being in the wide staircase that leads to what I cannot yet see.

Prosenth does not have wings. To avoid being rude, I accompany him on the trek upward. He climbs them with ease, the physical toll having no effect on his form. After a while, the burning in my thighs matches that in my lungs, possessing me to halt and lean against the cool, clear quartz wall.

I square my eyes to his. "If I still held my title and power, this would not be an issue." It is important to me that he is aware that climbing up so many stairs would have any near-mortal winded.

"Sure, yeah," he pronounces in such a way that I question if it was sarcasm I heard muttered, but not enough to pry. "Why don't I meet you at the top?"

With a raspy breath I straighten my back, staring at the steps that await. Pride turns me ignorant, because I refuse his offer just so I can prove to myself—and to him—that for a fallen goddess, I am not completely broken and weak.

When he swings his head to urge us on, I know the glance he offers is one of understanding. I have been through a lot and despite a much-needed rest, here I am, refusing to give up on something so irrelevant to the bigger picture.

When the marble flattens beneath our feet, I fight the urge to sprawl over it. "Thank gods," I croak, leaning to rest my hands on my knees.

Through the reflection below us, I spot amusement and a glint of respect across Prosenth's visage.

When I finally lift my head, I take in the gargantuan set of double doors. They lay open, inviting us to cross over its chasmal threshold and surpass the skywalk on the other side; a skywalk attached to nothing but us, and whatever structure is waiting at its opposite end.

Whatever illuminates the bridge is hidden, but it is lit perfectly to ward off the nihility that encompasses it.

Stepping onto the arch invokes a fear of heights, even though the vast nothingness gives little suggestion to what is up and what is down—the only reference being the bridge in which we stride ... me slower than he. The black world around us gobbles up the sound of our footsteps, hungry for what more we may be able to feed it. Its essence is a paradoxical sense of omnipresence and isolation.

"Has anyone tried," my voice shakes with how fast it disappears after parting from my lips, "going out there?"

Prosenth bites his cheek and nods. "The Shadowlands has everything one would need to thrive—community, entertainment, delectable foods, and breathtaking art. Still, the conscious mind holds onto the innate curiosity to find out what is beyond. The answer?" No hint of feeling lay in his orotund pitch. "Nothing."

Like a dropped stone disrupting the balance of water, my gut quivers. "They ... never returned?"

His brows magnetize. "If you were to spread those feathers and soar from this bridge, you would float into nothing for a while." He looks out into the abyss. "It invokes a sense of regret and dread—pure, unadulterated dread. Because what a foolish thing to do, leaving the one piece of civilization for *nothing*? When you are engulfed in the belly of its oblivion, you begin to second guess which way you are standing. It will feel as though you are falling slowly, spiraling in an empty lake. Then, just as you are about to give in to despair, you'll spot it. A freckle in the distance. Verina described it as a visage of desperation. Even after she landed on the opposite side of the platform from which she departed, she remained frightened and confused. It took weeks to convince her that we were not a figment of her imagination—a madness that she fell into."

The nihility around us, the one that swallows our conversation like fruit from the tree of knowledge, devoured a deity in its darkness only to regurgitate them on the other side.

I grind my teeth uneasily.

For a man who used to reign as the god of Afterlife, Prosenth speaks of my Soul Mother with admiration. "Verina has always been strong with a brilliant mind. She *wanted* to test the limits of this realm. Brought forth the case to the Council of Shadows herself. After she returned and everyone witnessed what it did to her, no one has gone out there since."

As if summoned by the retelling, a speck emerges in the distance. Sharp spires and turrets are the first to impale the piceous sky, slowly rising as we stride across the vast threshold. Domes of rich indigo rest among the quills of the structure. It gives way to a majestic edifice, with grand arcades and gold-flecked balconies that overlook the strip of opalescent stone we cross. Glinting from crannies and breaches, water cascades from the luminary body into steaming pools below. It is a true display of marvel craftsmanship, a splash of beauty in the gruesome, blank galaxy.

"Garden of Memories," Prosenth informs. "A repository for the things we wish to never forget to immortality. It is rather strenuous to house so many memories within yourself and easy for them to slip away from you with time, so the special ones—the ones we never want to risk losing—we store here." I match his quickening pace. "Kairos could never leave my mind, but I hold him here still, just to see him again. It is the most tangible evidence of our love that I have."

With a hard swallow, I promise myself to paint this place with my memories of Kysi when I die. My first offering would be the way the sun kissed his skin in the woods, and the box he held in his hand.

As we close in and stride over the haloing lazy river, I spot images in the reflection. Paints and canvases in disarray as a deity spins with inspiration, laughter with another atop the crystalline bridges in the Heavens, tokens given by lovers.

"They are free here," Prosenth says, "but always hear their beckoning call. Happy to be looked at once more. Happy to be remembered again."

The air is sweet and kind. I battle a euphoric tear that threatens to release like the waterfalls above. It is hard to explain ... this place makes me *feel*.

"The first time I came here and realized that I could share my memories of Kairos, I wasted no time surrounding myself with the images of our life. They formed spheres and swam around me in a calm storm, as if they missed me—as if *he* missed me. Then ... I fell to my knees and sobbed."

That is when the tear breaks free. I let it fall.

As we reach the door to the Garden of Memories, it opens unprompted, welcoming us to a planetarium of lights and orbs and stars that twinkle and float, filled with the whispers of reminiscences. A spiral walkway lines the great rotunda, reaching heavenward to the stained-glass dome above. Paintings come to life on every surface of the wall, capturing beloved experiences in a theater of wonder. For a place that is meant to be observed, its beauty is unapologetic.

"I have spent ages here," Prosenth goes on while leading us to the base of the spiraling pathway, beginning our ascension to the images above. "I would search through the memories of others while

Kairos—or his globes of the past—drifted beside me. One day, I found something ... interesting."

If I were to speak, my voice would undoubtedly crack with emotion. So, I raise a brow over my wet lashes.

"I cannot call upon another's memory, but I can learn their patterns. Like living beings, they each have schedules and homes. Whether it is in the canal outside or a small, neglected corner, they reside in their own personal common place. They leave occasionally, as if they have somewhere to be. I have noticed a pattern in many, including the one you are about to witness."

By now we are halfway up the rotunda, as if the farther we ascend the farther back in time we go. Prosenth slows beside me, pivoting to view the display of stories that dance on the wall like puppet shows, or moving pictures in a children's book.

Prosenth points. "There. See that? That is the god of Mortals, Beale." The crook of his finger leads my gaze to the image of a tan male, with eyes of thick chocolate and disheveled hair to match. "He was close friends with the god of Bargaining, Zapheen."

Beside him is another male, this one of fair skin and golden-brown hair. He is shoving the other, Beale, in a forest—the same one behind Kysi's estate, I realize—laughing as if they are about to fall over.

I had no idea that the god of Mortals and Bargaining used to be two separate souls. This is proof of a successful soul transference, meaning that Hellano's previous assumption that day in my kitchen was true; my death would wholly converge my spirit with his.

"Being allies with the god of Mortals, Zapheen was granted passage to Earth, where him and Beale would do everything under the sun. Hiking, sailing," Prosenth huffs, "seeing how much mortal liquor it would take to get drunk enough to woo and bed human women in one of Beale's many luxurious homes."

The painting depicts the two men peering out into a landscape atop snowy mountains, then floating in the middle of an endless sea, their sailboat drifting against the shadows of the horizon. Finally, it illustrates them dancing on wobbly feet among beautiful ladies.

"Zapheen lied with many females, but only one stuck with him." Prosenth narrates the story as it goes on to reveal a woman with sharp features and soft eyes. Native, with hair of liquid night tucked into plaits that line the length of her spine. Power and strength lay within her set jaw, beholding her beauty to any viewer. "Beale witnessed the woman's impact on Zapheen and kept the gates to Earth open for him. While the god of Bargaining courted her, he came to know the struggles she faced, the pain she suffered; deep and ancestral. So, he went to the god of Agony to bargain."

The picture shifts into a room lined with blood-red carpet and blackened walls, nearly as consuming as the emptiness outside. Lounging on a curve-backed sofa was a pale man with curious eyes, straightening his spine to the oncoming Zapheen.

"The deal was to never invoke suffering upon the girl again. In return, he would offer the god of Agony his title when it came time for her to pass away."

With a wry smile, the pale man takes Zapheen's palm in a tight grip, shaking in agreement.

"When Beale had received word of the bargain they made, he became burdened with the responsibility of reporting it to the goddess of Beginnings and the god of Afterlife, because the god of Agony making deals that go against the duty of his soul are cause for concern—signs of a corrupting deity. So, he went to them and did not tell Zapheen, in fear of his outrage.

"After confronting the goddess of Beginnings and the god of Afterlife with the bargain that was made, the two decided to send the god of Agony to the Shadowlands prematurely to wipe away the potential errors within him—any glint of erroneousness rooting in his spirit—and made one anew."

Clouds of smoke engulf the god of Agony, ones that I recognize could only belong to the god of Afterlife. When it clears and slinks away, a new figure stands in his place, blinked into existence.

"Without the knowledge of what Beale went to do, Zapheen had no opportunity to prevent it from happening so that he could one day withhold his end of the deal. Because of this, he was spared."

Zapheen is then in what is now Kysi's chateau, biting words at his friend.

"Beale convinced him that he did not need to make that bargain, that they could work together to make her life fruitful and whole with the abilities that they both shared. So, that is what they did.

"Through the passage to Earth that Beale left open for him, Zapheen remained by the woman as she aged. After a long, fulfilling life she slipped into death's waiting palm."

Zapheen appears sullen at the loss of his lover. His features remain downcast as he finds Beale to share the news, who clasps him on the shoulder with an empathetic hand. Their eyes meet and Zapheen begins mouthing words I cannot hear.

"Having no desire to exist without his beloved, Zapheen relinquished his title to Beale. It required no ritual, no fancy script. He willingly gave up the only thing that belonged to him, and hoped he would find her again on another plane of existence. From this, the god of Mortals and Bargaining came to be. When Beale passed into the Shadowlands, he planted these memories to preserve his dear friend for eternity."

I blink at the fading pictures and turn to where Prosenth now faces me. "Zapheen was spared because the bargain became *unattainable* to him. Out of his control. Kysi made the deal with Hellano knowing that it would come down to a vote ... but if we were to interrupt the ritual, read from our own script and change the outcome, Kysi would have no opportunity to fix it—so long as you do not tell him of our plans before they happen."

Balls of light hang overhead, dancing under the midnight sky. They cast shadows over his still features, alluding to a repressed desperation, a hope to convince, and the anticipation to achieve.

He is not suggesting that we disrupt the ritual to ensure Kysi withholds his end of the deal, otherwise he would not be asking that

I keep this idea between us. However, given the story that he has shared with me today, whatever it is he wants in return would still spare Kysi from what consequence may come from making a bad bargain. Additionally, if I do not agree with him, the chances of him helping me find the ritual sight and intercepting it to obtain *my* goals would be like grasping at a handful of straws the same length.

That lump in my throat has subsided by now, so I speak up, "What do you want?"

For the first time, Prosenth's mouth curves upwards into a methodical grin. An orb the color of sea foam emerges, as if brought to us by his smile alone. "I want," he extends a hand and points within the orb at the same face that spreads across his bedchamber like confetti, "him."

CHAPTER 17

My instructions were clear: when the faint bell rings, it is time to get up.

It echoes in the distance, coaxing me to slip from Kysi's limp grasp. My gaze lingers upon his slumbering side profile—ruffled onyx hair, the handsome curve of his soft lips.

I will save him—save us.

Prosenth left a cloak for me in his room. When the hood swings over my head, I blend in among the crowd in the hall. There are just enough council members about that no one gives me a second glance. My wings should not draw attention either, not unless something drastic happens that changes my mood. Even then, I would make a valiant effort to keep a lid on my emotions.

I walk in circles up and down the same two hallways. After ten minutes or so, the crowd begins to disperse as gods and goddesses begin their daily routines, whatever those might be.

A throat clears behind me. I do not look back, simply await Prosenth to fall in step to my right.

"They have already begun," he mutters with a quickening pace, urging us onward.

Through an archtop door on the second floor yields a curved hallway. A forest green sofa lines the crescent wall with circular, plum accent pillows. A mustiness fills the air, as if we are the first to enter this portion of the Shadowlands in a long, long time.

A vacant room opens to us. At its end, no spirits rest in the cubbies of the wine cellar. If this place existed on Earth, I imagine it would be lined with cobwebs and dust bunnies.

"The Nine have done their best to make this area less appealing to others, as it harbors a pathway to the ritual site. Partially destroyed, someone of my size could never fit through the band of tunnels." Prosenth begins striding past the walls, eyeing them up and down.

I raise my eyebrows in question, flicking a thumb to the wings.

He huffs, "You'll see. Here." A thrown gesture lands on a blank space of wall.

I scrunch my face and step forward, searching for what he sees that I do not.

Just there, lined in the near-pristine surface lay a petite fissure, so thin and straight that it could pass as a strand of sandy hair.

"Follow my lead," Prosenth instructs, pressing his hands to one side of the fracture. I mirror his form on the opposite end. Together, we press against the smooth granite. The weak link tremors under the pressure until finally giving way, doing the rest of the work for us.

A corridor opens with a low hum, revealing an unlit passage. It is not the height that disallows Prosenth's entry, but the width. Far too narrow for his broad shoulders, and crooked with broken stones.

"This is where we part ways. Remember?"

"Left, straight, right twice, straight," I recall.

He nods to confirm. "Off you go, then."

I step into the tight space, flexing to close the appendages at my backside. Prosenth wastes no time shoving the hidden access closed behind me.

Blinking to focus on the newfound dark, I press my palms to the jagged rock at either side of me. I am careful not to trip on the stones scattered beneath, sliding my feet slowly through the tunnel.

Left.

The digits of my fingers scuff against the protrusion of cleaved rock. I pass by another bend to my left, the gap seeming even smaller than before.

Right.

Claustrophobia greets me in the form of a crumbling ceiling, inducing a labored sigh. My cloak becomes an added, unnecessary weight against my struggle to fit.

Right again.

The corner is sharp and suffocating, forcing me on all fours to continue onward. Before I do, I shimmy to relieve myself of this incessant piece of garb, sliding my arms inside and gripping the hem, pulling it directly up and over. All I need to do is go straight now.

Doubt creeps into my mind as I am lowered into an army crawl, squeezing my feathers together.

This is any winged creature's nightmare. I cannot breathe, I cannot move, the rough-hewn walls are pressing and pressing and—

What ... is that?

Not the silver-blue that peeks through small breaks in the collapsed exit, but that *sensation*.

Warmth.

I move toward the speckled light that grows brighter and bigger as I become warmer with each pull of my forearm on the gravelly floor. Muffled voices emerge between the fallen chunks of stone.

"How kind of you to join us," a husky voice rumbles—the man who consistently voted against us, Drayxi.

I paw as quietly as I can at the debris blocking my field of view. Shifting one, I peer through and feel the kiss of heat that radiates from afar.

An ethereal fire licks the air in the center of the room, its sapphire and steely flames whip with purpose. The shadows are painted across the theater, undulating in a dance. I look down upon concentric seating encircling the Nine that double as stairs toward a solitary exit.

All but two members are dressed in their ceremonial robes. Lilliana and Drayxi, however, wear nothing but undergarments as they hover over copper-hued basins that rest empty upon pedestals, waiting to be serviced.

"You know I love fanning the flame, father," Prosenth responds at last. "Allow me."

Pushing from the altar, Drayxi strides to the side where his cloak lay. Prosenth replaces him in front of the bowl, undressing until he matches Lilliana's nudeness.

Two hooded elders close in on them. Simultaneously, they raise their arms to the sky, wielding daggers with wavy blades.

I give an audible gasp—although not loud enough to be heard—as they slash the weapons across the deity's chests.

The wound does not faze either of them, they merely lean forward to allow the container to collect every ounce of the crimson blood.

A third council member, standing by the deep blue flames, takes a piece of parchment from the pocket of their robe and begins to read, "And so, the Heavens shall be made anew—a place for all beings to reside in a kingdom within a new world, where Anewla, the goddess of Beginnings, will reign as the Ultimate Queen."

The blood-filled bowls are taken from each pedestal, their carriers traveling toward the flickering heat. By the time they are halfway there, both Lilliana's and Prosenth's wounds have healed.

"May Anewla have access to travel to and from the realms, with her title and power returned."

The first seed has successfully been planted.

Prosenth changed the script sometime between our departure from the Garden of Memories and the break of light. The original words were, *May Anewla have access to travel to and from* this *realm, with her title and power returned.* The crackling fire and shuffling feet made his edit go by entirely unnoticed.

The speaker continues, "Lilliana, first incarnate of life, spills her blood to the Spirits of the Sky for this cause. Prosenth, third incarnate of death, spills his blood to the Spirits of the Sky for this cause."

So, it is not the Heavens that heeds our calls, but Sky Spirits; entities of grander power than any of us.

As the speaker rolls up the parchment and places it into the inner pocket of her robe, the individuals beside her tilt the basins forward and into the dancing flames.

My icy veins thaw against the roar of fire that nearly reaches where I gawk from the ceiling. I lift my hand against the molten roar of brightness, sweat lines my brow. For it to warm the chill in bones, it must be made of the same material that binds souls.

The flames die down in the same moment my nerves awaken. They crack and spark like useless flint strikers, unable to come alive and reach their full potential.

Prosenth's eyes find mine. "*Now!*" he mouths with urgency. Pursing my lips, I nod and close my eyes.

I have never phased before, but it does not take much effort on my part to find that familiar drag and let it snag my core. It sucks me into a vacuum, one where realms feel as though they lay within one another, separated by a thin mesh.

Trails of smoke spin from where I land across splintering boards. My back erupts with pain as my wings flap to hide from the world. Shattered bricks scatter over the heap of debris beneath my clenched hands.

Perhaps I made a misstep, landed where I was not supposed to—somewhere that is currently being broadcasted in my living room.

BOOM!

My ears ring against a crack of thunder that bellows through a thick ether of smog. Lightning struck mere yards from where I now stand, rattling the ground with an angry smite.

The fog stains my skin and dress as it drifts passed me like a lonely ghost. Another *BOOM* lands just a few feet away, sweeping the uneven ground from under me.

I skitter away from the jolt in a panic, kicking my legs against the rubble. The lightning illuminates a binding of paper at my side, its remnants illustrating a familiar face.

Heather's patient file.

No ... *No, no, no.*

I regain my feet, frantic and shaking. With a pitch that threatens to steal my voice, I scream into the chaos, "HELLANO!"

The sooner I find him, the sooner I can bring him to the Heavens and transfer what broken pieces of my soul reside in him, back to me. Then, we can put an end to this madness.

"ANEWLA!" Cutting through the fog is a male voice, but not Hellano's.

Cato.

I follow it just as I did Kysi's when we arrived in the Shadowlands.

The ground shakes under another bolt of electricity. I teeter but find balance, cautiously climbing across the wreckage. Watching my step, I notice insects scattering to safety—wherever that might be. Scanning their movements briefly, I hesitate to observe their capricious patterns.

They are not in fact searching for refuge. Locusts do not hop, but sluggishly crawl, leaving gooey strings in their wake. As soon they excrete these sacs, their movements cease.

I swallow the urge to vomit at the sight of them hatching.

Not all of them survive the rapid growth, but those that do repeat the process of what I just witnessed; crawling away at pace that gradually slows, birthing offspring, dying.

The essence of life rushes to keep up with death's greed, forcing itself upon the insects before they have a chance to die. I shuffle away when one crawls over the tip of my pinky, fixating on the call of my name once more.

There in the distance, two figures emerge through the haze. One desperately pulls at another, who jerks back in protest and remains where they kneel upon the ground. They once again attempt to lead the figure elsewhere, and as they do, their head tilts back. "ANEWLA!"

The pollution stings my lungs, but my vision becomes clearer as I close in on them.

Meena's snow-white hair is stained charcoal, draping over the limp body within her arms.

My knees buckle.

The goddess of Pleasure's tears drip across Mona's face, gathering ash in their path down her cheek.

"Meena we have to go!" Cato tugs once more, but she resists, snatching her arm away to pet Mona's hair with a trembling hand. He throws a look in my direction—an urgent plea.

Where the hell is Hellano?

Reaching forward, I grip Meena's jaw and force her eyes to mine. Her lips quiver with tightness. "Not fair," she mumbles with puffy eyes.

My heart cracks like a boom in the distance. Meena did nothing, had no part in any of this, yet the pain it has caused sinks an achor of guilt in my gut. "Not fair," I validate, penetrating her shivering eyes with mine. "But the New World awaits you in the next realm ... as does Mona."

Meena's head shakes through my grip, perplexed.

"The call has already been made," I promise. "She's there."

Behind her glassy eyes, she settles into this resolution. Nodding with a sniffle, she ever so gently lowers Mona from her embrace. As she does so, Cato snatches her and phases into the New World. Her fading yelp echoes over where they leave me ... alone.

With my dead friend.

I failed her—failed them all. I came back from the Heavens to a falling world, then returned from the Shadowlands to see it wholly pulverized.

There is nothing behind her deep brown eyes. The same ones that used to narrow at me when I did something foolish or squint when she suspected that I was keeping a secret, simply stare without intent—lost in a destination she can never return from.

The bristle of a dense shadow slinks across where she mindlessly glares. The tip softens in the air, dissipating into the fog that suffocates the world. The phenomenon cascades down its length, growing and fading in the firmament. I follow it.

More black tendrils greet me as I trail the slithers of swimming darkness—swimming *away* from one communal source.

Each tumble I take towards the origin of their escape brings forth more threads of shadow, twisting and curling in an anxious attempt to straighten out and disperse. Ahead, they grow closer together into a single mass.

Hellano.

I press on, batting my lashes to focus. Nothing—I see nothing but a primal power that devours him. Like a failing heart under a defibrillator, his smothered body convulses as another boom erupts in the distance. Electric light filters through, flashing Hellano's faint outline through the dark clouds that bathe him.

I hesitate to reach for him, horrified that when I do—when I place myself in his hungry, polluted atmosphere—they will pull me in, leaving me to absorb into their nothingness.

Swallowing the fear with a thick gulp, I plunge my hand forward.

Searching for Hellano through the thickness of his power feels like wading through a bog. I do not stop pushing through until my fingers hit something solid.

I wrap them around the circumference of his arm and search through the mesh fabric of our layered realms.

Eight years I have lived muted, weakened. Eight years trapped in a mortal body, forced to reside in a foreign realm that has now suffered the cost of my unnatural descent.

As we blink into my home in the Heavens—no, the New World—the spark in my nerves finally catches fire.

Warmth, *my* warmth, flows through me like a liquid IV, wholly extinguishing the ice in its path. I am a blooming flower coming undone after a harsh winter. My power pours through me in fluttering ripples, settling in my bones. Home at last.

A full, deep breath spills into my chest. Rejuvenating. Restorative. Reviving.

The breath of life.

In front of where I kneel, the darkness around Hellano dwindles. He jolts upright, swooshing air out of his pressurized lungs—evidence of my fragmented soul decompressing. His lashes tilt upwards as he frantically scans the room to gather where he is and what has happened.

The room ...

It is mine, but ... not mine. The dais we arrived upon clacks with shapes that settle into the parquet floor. Fat beams of sunlight emerge through panes of towering windows.

As we speak, the New World is forming.

Vibrations of rustling leaves and the shaking hides of wildlife welcome us. My snow leopard arches her back into a satisfying stretch, releasing a whining yawn. A jackrabbit passes. The birds sing. My own personal kingdom greets me giddily with its purrs and yips.

"I understand ..." Hellano whispers beside me, awestruck at all the moving parts; the numerous species as well as transforming architecture. It is as if experiencing life has allowed him to comprehend the beauty of it now. Witnessing, *feeling* how much it was hindered against the nature of his power. Now it exists before him for all that it is. Vibrant. Loving.

In this moment, gazing into his hazel eyes as they track a fawn that frolics around my precious lightning bugs, I realize that this change does not merely come upon the Heavens, but also upon us—our souls.

History will *not* repeat itself. We can stand together in harmony, appreciating the essence of our purposes. Without me giving the first breath, he can never take the last. It is because he takes that I can give—present more beings with the opportunity to experience what it means to be alive.

We will not follow the tradition of loathing one another as our past lives have done. Part of me wonders if *that* is why I was able to love him at the start—because what if this was always meant to happen?

Hellano's glossy eyes find mine. A smile erupts from him then—a *real* smile. Genuine, broad, something I have never witnessed from him until now. He wears it well.

"I have to go." I squeeze his hand—the first touch we have shared in what feels like centuries. He responds with a nod as his attention returns once again to the display of wildlife.

Searching for that suction once more, I leave him to bask in the beauty with a newfound sense of pride.

Unity between the opposites of our nature has happened for the first time in history; without a soul bond.

And when I return, the New World will be waiting.

Chapter 18

I was a strong goddess. It was necessary to consistently create an abundance of life for Hellano to end.

Flora has always been the easiest to wield. Anything sedimentary is a challenge. When it comes to my abilities regarding Earth, it all came naturally.

Animals are not too difficult. Once they are created, they yield to me—an army at my disposal. But my connection to them is not one of a queen, but a mother. I refuse to use them to do my dirty work.

I land near the exit of the theater amidst an ongoing quarrel. Taking in the scene, Lilliana paces in front of a kneeling Prosenth—forced to the ground by two members of the Nine. His mouth has been gagged, seemingly by a chunk of fabric torn from his own cloak.

With clenched fists, my Soul Mother strides back and forth in front of him. Her caramel hair trails the length of her bare spine, kissed by the moonlight of the argent and cobalt flames. "You are willing to risk the dangers of interrupting the speaker—risk the Sky Spirits twisting your intent as they have done in your past, all so you can be bonded with your natural opposite? *Fool.*" Her striking tone is thickly riddled with annoyance and disappointment.

Stage two of our plan is cleared: distract the Nine until I return.

Prosenth's perceived anger is a marvelous act. Behind his performance, desperation appears to be a tangled thread with no end. Knowing what he is trying to accomplish, that part is genuine.

Beads of sweat line my forehead as shadows from the mythical fire climb the wall behind them. For a moment, I could have sworn I saw figures in their outlines—two, to be exact.

"The Council of Shadows will decide what to do with you later," she scowls, turning to find the speaker and move on with the ritual ... but spots me at the door instead.

Her stillness alerts the remaining elders. They turn to me in unison, and I become the main focal point in this hot, heavy room.

"What the hell is she doing here?" Drayxi's rough timbre cleaves the silence.

A dawning realization befalls Lilliana. She whips around to where Prosenth kneels, watching, mouth agape as he flings the gag from his mouth—its delicate impact inaudible over the crackle of the spindling fire.

"I'm sorry, Lilly. I really am." Prosenth flicks his gaze to me and gives a nod.

My foot hits the ground with a mighty stomp. The hanging vines at my thighs obey my command to attack, spiraling down the length of my leg. They spread like a disease, entrenching the ground in webs of green.

Rather than becoming languid from my time as a near-mortal, my power buzzes with vitality. It is as if my descent has left it spinning; faster and faster until the moment I return to release it from the gravity of its orbit. Every fiber of my being wants to let it wholly free, let it bring this entire structure down, but as I notice fissures forming in the stone floor, I reel it back in.

I am not here to destroy anything. Just accomplish a task.

A net of tendrils cascades down the sharp, angled steps, heading straight for the Nine. The two at Prosenth's side release him and stagger back, inching away from my snare. Swiftly, he jolts from his knees and strikes the one to his left, stealing their wavy blade as they fall to the ground.

By the time Prosenth reaches the basin on the podium, their ankles have been caught in the tissues of my trap. I tilt my chin, urging the ramblers to rise up their threshing figures. Barks of protest transform into shrieks of panic as the plants wrap over their robes like eviscerating chains, pinning velvet to their skin with an iron grip.

"Stop!" Lilliana wails over the commotion. She does not fight against the flora suffocating her body, as if she still remembers what it is like to wield the power—the strength. Her eyes sparkle against the flickering light. "Whatever you want, I'll give it to you ... Just don't—don't speak to them."

"Cover their mouths." Prosenth ignores her from where he hovers over the basin. As he slides the dagger across his chest, thick blood spills in its wake. "Hurry," he urges, "before they have a chance to speak over us."

As I turn back to Lilliana, her odious expression is bone-chilling. Tangled vines crawl up her torso like a spider preparing its meal. She does not fight back like the others, just glares at me as her neck and lips become veiny with verdancy. Around me, the other members receive the same—bound mouths as well as bodies. The latticework is thick enough that not even their throaty growls would be audible over the popping fire.

It sickens me to do it—to separate the weaves across her chest so Prosenth can cut into it and steal her blood. I want to look away as he does it, want to focus on the blue and silver flames, the branches of vines at my feet, the shadows that widen and dance around the room—but I am pinned against the way she simply *stares*. Stares like a goddess of Wrath, still against her rage.

If only I could spare her from this and do it myself, slit my own chest ... but Prosenth stated it had to be a member of the Nine. The Sky Spirits will not accept just anyone's blood.

Prosenth places the basin on the podium beside his ... and then I wrap my power around him as well.

"Anewla." His voice is a spinning wheel of caution and fright. Through the quivering call, he worries that I will not withhold my end of the deal we made—that I will take what *I* want and leave him with nothing.

Prosenth took a chance to trust me. Right now, regret shows in his tight lips. Thick leaves cover them as I silence him.

Death deserves a place here. The principals of it, the order it brings to realms—it is necessary in this life as it is in the previous.

Balance.

Not to mention, the Shadowlands is basically an army of unkill-able, ancient deities. That does not bode well with a new Queen just one world away.

"Not a soul in either the New World or the Shadowlands may be plagued with aging, but all realms will abide by the fundamental law of life and death."

Lilliana, unmoved and staring, sheds a single tear.

"May Kairos arrive to the Shadowlands without his power, mending the broken soul bond in the god of Afterlife for all those before him and all those to come."

Prosenth's shoulders slacken at that, eyes hanging heavy with relief.

The god of Afterlife ...

"I have never truly lived," Hellano had said. *"Never truly loved."*

"Grant Hellano an additional six-hundred years as god of After-life," I add to my list of demands. If his soul bond is mended, then his mind will not corrupt anytime soon. He can start over. Live. Love.

"Give me this, and may it be the last wish that you grant."

I do hear their muffled cries then, humming over the busy fire. As I stretch thick vines around the bowls next to where Prosenth is restrained, those two shadow figures that I almost did not see before return. I track their movements on the wall as I bring forth the deity's blood. Raspy screams fade as the elders hush, pulling their attention to the Sky Spirits' display.

No distinct features can be deciphered in the darkness of their silhouettes, but I can still witness the beauty in them. If Hellano and I are the foundation to life and death, these beings must be the ones that formed our spirits, along with soul bonds ... and the Heavens itself.

"Prosenth, third incarnate of Afterlife, spills his blood to the Spirits of the Sky for this cause." The figures accelerate their dance with each syllable I pronounce. "Lilliana, first incarnate of life, spills her blood to the Spirits of the Sky for this cause."

They urge me on, twirling in a euphoric display, almost as if they are eager to retire at last.

I tilt the bowls toward the flames, barely managing to pour a single droplet before it roars to life, swamping nearly the entire theater in its path. Heat licks my skin as I tumble back, hitting the stone floor now carpeted in green.

It wanes after consuming my offering, smaller and smaller as the light grows dim. Then, the ethereal fire snuffs out, engulfing the room in darkness.

Fire is life. It breathes. It eats. It is born, and it dies.

Just like the rest of us.

I ignite a flame in my palm and send it into the pit of embers. The silver and blue that illuminated the ritual site moments ago is now replaced by a natural, amber fire.

Breathing deep, I search within myself for the symbols to create. The formulas remain hidden ... Did the Sky Spirits deny my request for Kairos?

Something pulls then. It comes from across the room. For the first time, the answer lies not with me, but in Prosenth.

He peers into the waves of heat, gleaming with the dew of sweat. Inside of him, a great deal of love is left for Kairos. Tragic, to have carried it for so long without him.

When I take a small piece of that love Prosenth's eyebrows tilt with confusion, feeling the twinge of my power—the essence of life—in motion. Closing my eyelids, I make sure to cross my t's and dot my i's. Kairos shall be just as he was.

When they open, a figure stands in the middle of the flames. A man. He lifts his hands, sending them through the licking heat—perplexed.

Prosenth staggers when I free him, standing to inch closer to the fire. "Kai?"

A stone drops in me at how he pronounces it just like I do—Ky.

Kairos lifts his chin, searching past the flickering beams of burned orange. His tone is smooth, yet cautious. "Prosenth?"

Struggling to respond against the overwhelming emotions, Prosenth does nothing but balk. The sound of his name through the lips of his lover is an anchor that holds him in place against an urge to lunge forward.

All Prosenth can do is witness and weep.

A smoky foot extends onto the webbed stone followed by the rest of Kairos's body. The naked man peers at his mate, whose cries have turned into breathy sobs. Prosenth trembles as they come together. His cheek presses against the area over Kairos's heart—as if to hear that it is truly beating.

"I'm here." Kairos pulls him in. "I'm right here."

Seeing them embrace and reconnect, it makes me long for Kysi. I must return to him so we can meet the world that I have built for us—for everyone.

"Forgive me," I say to them all dryly. "After spending hundreds of years attached to the reigning god of Afterlife, I may have adopted some of his stubbornness. You see, when I want something—I *take* it." The verdant roots slither backwards, freeing the Nine and shrinking into the hem of my dress. "All is fair in bargains and soul bonds."

Lilliana gasps for air before me, shifting my victorious demeanor into a statue of concern. "What did you do Anewla!" she cries through rapid breaths.

I cannot answer.

My bones turn into the granite beneath my feet; not at the sound of those still struggling to breathe, but the lack thereof from the others.

The ones that remain limp on the ground.

"Are they …?" Kairos questions, taking in the scene.

No. No, they cannot be.

I step with great haste toward where Drayxi lay unmoving. Nudging his heavy arm, I watch it fall to the floor.

"You suffocated them!" Lilliana thrashes against the air, gesturing towards the flaccid figures. She meets Verina a few strides away, who is frozen in shock save for her attempts to gather oxygen. Lilliana lends her a comforting hand and then averts her attention to me, death wishing.

"I didn't—"

"What, you didn't mean to?" she snarls, whipping her head to Prosenth next. "And *you*! You *helped* her!" The burden of betrayal weighs on her shoulders—she thought of him as an ally.

Prosenth is slow to recover from the emotion of regaining his partner. "You would have done the same if it were you," is all he says in response. There is no regret, even after I went behind his back and asked the Sky Spirits for more than what we agreed upon. Kairos is worth it to him—worth everything.

"I would never do *this*!" Lilliana throws her arms up with a bitter fling, gesturing to her now dead comrades. Then, she points a shaking finger at me. "You ... YOU. WILL. FALL."

Chills run down the length of my spine.

I may beat Lilliana in brute power, but she triumphs in knowledge. The threat with her would reside in trickery and deceit.

Prosenth nods from afar, face still damp as he motions for me to take my leave. He will clean this up. I have done enough damage.

My teleportation only extends to jumping realms, unless I learned how to phase within them. So, I am forced to travel back to the bedchamber by foot. I suppose I could fly, but it does not appear that is something many deities do here. Apparently when dead, one does not find themselves in a hurry often. I stride with a brisk pace instead, unable to contain my avidity to bring this information to Kysi—tell him that he is going to be okay, that I made sure of it.

It must still be relatively early in the day, because Kysi is slumped the way he always is when resting: on his stomach with arms under the pillow.

Crawling atop the tangled bedding, I plant kisses along his back. "Ky," I muse, "time to go. I'll explain everything after the jump. But tell me first, how does King of the New World sound?"

No response. Not even a tired grumble.

"Ky?" He rolls to me when I pull on his arm—dead weight. "Kysi, stop it."

That handsome face is wholly blank. Still, like the black hole of night.

Panic whirls in my stomach, my shoulder blades, the back of my head. It swims faster with each second he does not respond. I shake his shoulders, watching the way his limp body absorbs the movement like waves in the middle of a hopeless, isolating sea.

Prosenth lied.

I press one hand against the side of Kysi's neck, my tears beginning to fall across his nose, his cheeks. The other pushes over his left pec. They search for a beat.

237

All I can think about is flying through these halls, finding Prosenth, and sending him into the next realm just like I did the others. I will let this entire building crumble in the void. Force every person to withstand the madness of nihility if it means that he would *suffer*.

But I will not leave Kysi here alone. They would take him to use against me as punishment—not let me bring him home. Prosenth will do anything to keep his mate, that has been made clear.

After I phase Kysi into the New World, I will return to torture Kairos before Prosenth's very eyes. Kill him slowly, keeping him on the edge of death until his partner begs. I would force him into the Garden of Memories and make him reclaim those orbs, leaving him with not even the image of the man he once again lost. Then, I will leave him to sit and remember Kairos until pieces start to fade—until he is driving himself mad with the images of a person he cannot recall—

A faint, slow tick chimes against my palm.

The breath I was holding finally comes lose in one relieved swoosh. Trailing pecks across his jawline, I send a thank you to the Spirits of the Sky.

He is alive. Perhaps balancing on a tightrope to avoid the permanent ending, but alive.

I lean into him, absorbing his woodsy overtones, and leave nothing but a hateful tear behind.

Fireflies swim around where we land on the hovering pallet of my bed. I slide from Kysi, gently situating him in the most comfortable position I can manage. After folding his hands in the divvy of his chest, I kiss him farewell and slide from the sheets.

Hundreds of thousands of unique imprints lay ready in my mind—all sorted neatly for me to choose from. I call upon Thorne, a mighty Red Wolf with paws the size of dinner plates, to guard Kysi.

No one is to get close enough to touch him—even breathe on him—until I return. Thorne's imprint thickens in response to my summoning. The wolf is coming.

My bedchamber is nearly unrecognizable. A wardrobe is tucked in a recess near the bathing chamber that was never there before, yet familiar threads and fabrics hang ready to be worn.

There are two sets of glass double doors, the first leading to a sitting room with muted floral cushions and a kindling fire. A sterling silver tea set rests atop a quant, chestnut coffee table. From towering plants near the walls to strings of them above, the space is adorned with potted greenery.

Onward, attached to the second set of glass doors, blush curtains dance in the breeze. They lay open to reveal a balcony that bathes in the warm sunlight. Chatter hums from outside.

Lots of it.

Slowly, I move across the threshold. Past the lit fireplace and through the veranda, the sun's kisses dry the wetness from face—which hopefully does not appear as astonished as I am at the sight of what is below.

Thousands upon thousands of individuals stand in and past the courtyard. The crowd stretches past where my line of sight is cut off by rolling hills.

It is not just humans that begin to spot me on the railing, but other winged creatures as well. Not gods or goddesses—no, these beings are something else. Humans, animals, plants, deities—everything has a discerning quality that classifies us as what we are. Our *nature*. Theirs is as clear as the cloudless sky.

Angels. Demons.

Peering down at them, I take notice of all the different colors and styles of wings. Some soar like bats, while others hover with appendages that flutter in a blur.

In the courtyard and closest to the estate—no, not an estate ... a whole godsdamn palace—Cato stands near Meena, who holds a protective arm around Mona.

My legs weaken at the sight of her here. The relief.

"The Queen!" an unknown voice shouts. It leads to an uproar that spreads through the masses in waves. Starlings chirp around me, holding the weight of a diadem at their feet made of solid gemstone. The hues change with each movement in the daylight as the birds place it over my hair with gentle care.

Through the reflection of the marble railing, I notice petite stems erupt over the crown. They bud into a lovely array of foxglove.

I am about to wave, because I cannot simply disappear before their eyes without at least greeting them, but then another shriek comes across the yard.

"Our King!"

The stiffness in me begins to slacken. Perhaps Prosenth really was telling the truth, and it only took bringing Kysi to the New World to set everything in place. I shift sideways, eager to meet my awakened soulmate. My King.

Hellano emerges onto the platform, a jeweled crown twinkling over his molten hair. It is made up of the same material as mine, however his does not bloom.

The god of Afterlife snakes an arm around my midsection and lifts a proud hand to the masses. "Careful," he warns, "first impressions are so important."

I bite back the will to strike, refusing to allow the kingdom's first vision of their Queen to be an act of violence. The people of the New World are elated to see both myself and Hellano. Families reconnecting with loved ones, new creatures exploring the fresh air.

"You wear my mate's crown," I growl through a clenched smile.

"This crown is where it belongs, as I am meant to be your equal *and* your mate, isn't that right?"

Bastard. He knows that I am still bonded to Kysi, can sense the tie missing between us.

I wave to the people. "I'll kill you."

"And divide the kingdom?" He tsks, "That's not very noble of you, my Queen." Hellano nudges the back of my arm, lifting it higher. "Now, don't make a fool of yourself on the first day."

I thought he changed.

My darkened wings are paid no mind. After all, it is my first appearance—how would they know it is a display of dread and loathing? But Cato notices, as does Meena and Mona. From the sea of faces, theirs are the only ones shadowed with concern.

I may be unable to call upon the Spirits of the Sky now, but I vow to find another way to wake Kysi from this seemingly endless slumber.

Hellano will pay. Prosenth will pay. I will save the true King and get my revenge ...

All while reigning as Queen of the New World.

Part Two

✦

THE FALSE KING

CHAPTER 19

The two twin suns of my Red Wolf's eyes track Hellano as we stride back into the bedchamber. Thorne's coat is a blaze in motion, rippling with crimson and gold. Hellano pays him no mind, sending his focus to Kysi, who lays motionless in bed.

"I'm sorry," he says, placing a palm to the dip in my back. "I understand why you fought to keep the connection ... I know firsthand how controlling soul ties can be—how they can drive you to do horrible things. It was the bond's way of protecting itself." He turns to me then, wiping hair from my shoulder. "Not your fault."

Although Hellano and I are not soul bound, and that is ultimately the reason why Kysi sleeps, I would not be able to tell by the way he peers down at me with consuming adoration.

It makes me want to vomit.

"That crown does not belong to you." It comes out as nearly a whisper as I stand before him. My anger is calm ... calculating.

"It does, my flower." Hellano's voice is low, meeting mine with a sullen urge to help me understand. "We are *equals*. Always have been, always will be. It is the nature of us." His thumb reaches up, grazing the side of my jaw. "I'm sorry about Kysi, and I mean that. The hardest part about that godsforsaken deal was seeing the devastation on your face when I shook his hand. I see it now; in the way your brows are slightly knitted. The way your lips threaten to part and release a cry. What can I do to make it go away?"

I loathe how after all these years, he still knows my tells. "Take. It. Off."

"You know I can't do that. Ruling the Heavens with you is my soul duty—"

"This is *not* the Heavens anymore."

"Just because you give it a different name and move things around doesn't mean a thing," he retorts.

Reaching my hand up, I swat his away from my face. "I have to go."

"Go? Anewla, you can't *go*, you're the Queen. The people are waiting for you to formally address them *right now*. You are the creator of the New World; it demands your presence."

I bite the inside of my cheek, aggravated. Unfortunately, Hellano is correct. Because I do not know how long my trip back to the Shadowlands will be, it is best that I do not disappear without a word.

"Given the warm welcome that you just received on that balcony, I take it you have already spoken to them."

He grinds his teeth. "Like any King would."

"Gods." I turn my back to him and stride to the exit. Taking a deep breath, I paint a vibrant, hopeful picture on my face. I cannot allow my people to know that anything is amiss. The kingdom is new, therefore fragile. They will have no knowledge of what is wrong until *after* they see it straightened out—when Kysi takes his rightful place on the throne.

"Well, go on," I mumble, gesturing to the door. "Take me to where I am expected."

My house is no longer filled with flora and fauna, but uniformed men and women—angels, demons, and humans alike—that walk with purpose before parting to bow before us. It is not the figures that take me back, but the architecture. Just how the Heavens would build homes for gods that perfectly match the essence of their purpose, my home has shifted into a palace designed for Kysi and I. It exudes the both of us—from trailing ivy lining the walls to his pine scent that swims between the people I walk by.

"They came from another pocket of the universe, one where they held no physical forms," Hellano says in step beside me, nodding to the new beings of our world. "Just as gods are born with the innate knowledge of their surroundings—where they are and what they are doing—these beings arrived here with the same benefit."

"You've already spoken to them?" I ask.

"A few, yes, but there is no limit to the knowledge yet to be discovered in our changed realm. Oh, and—" He extends a hand and pinches my elbow.

"Ow! You ass," I growl, rubbing my arm.

Hellano leans in. "*Ow.*"

… shit.

Pain—there is *pain* in the New World.

"Whatever you requested of the Heavens, it had its own ideas as well. Let's hope there aren't any other negative surprises awaiting us," Hellano mumbles while ushering me through a set of towering arch top doors.

The front entrance of the royal palace is nothing short of divine. Delicate vines wrap columns supporting balconies overhead, their emerald leaves shimmering with dew. A honeysuckle aroma sweeps through the arcade, cascading down the alabaster stairs at either side of me. Vibrant orchids and rich, purple peonies nestle in the corners of the steps as they curve into a grandiose courtyard below.

Lush trees border the area, with branches that are weighed down by succulent fruits. Their roots twist through the earth and mingle with the rocky pathway, leading to a tiered fountain at the center where lily pads sway against the trickle of water.

Amidst the beauty is a sea of staring people. Their attention impales me like spears of frostbite, ridding me of movement.

The Sky Spirits must have a sense of humor, because I do not remember having a fear of public speaking before interrupting that ritual.

From recesses in the castle walls, two large avians swoop down and perch atop the railing before me. As if born from the same mother, they move in sync as their translucent feathers embrace one another, spiraling into a cone to broadcast my voice.

If only I could speak.

Locked like a deadbolt, I remain latched to the solid ground. Unable to pry my heels from the slab beneath.

Unable to breathe.

Unable to blink.

My head begins to lose weight the longer that sweet honeysuckle is trapped within my lungs.

Like a calm current drawing me out of rapid water, familiar skin takes hold of my arm. It is a touch that I would recognize in the event that all of my other senses were stolen. The unique shape and texture … it prompts me to let go of the air trapped inside.

"If it's too much," Hellano utters through my hair, "you don't have to, flower."

I am unable to decipher whether the interaction is comforting or infuriating. Either way, it is enough to force my feet forward.

The assembly stiffens in response to my full emergence, somehow providing me with even more of their focus than before. It takes an effort to find what muscles in the back of my throat are required to steady my tone.

"Together we gather as not mere viewers of history, but makers of it." The words boom over countless still heads. "Bearing witness to the dawn of a new era, let us explore its boundless discoveries and opportunities. This realm will become the product of our intent, so let us build a prosperous future—a *real* Heaven—for all to share. Welcome … to the New World."

A heartbeat passes before roars of celebration cleave the silence. The noise drowns my anxiety, loud enough to make my presence not feel so overbearing.

Apparently, addressing the nation was not the only thing on the agenda for today.

Hellano insisted that we choose the members of 'our' council, which I was not wholly opposed to. I must ensure the kingdom will be in good hands when I depart for the Shadowlands.

Meena was chosen to provide insight on how we can strive to give our citizens the most joyous life. Not only that, but she is also to be our head of Medicine and Research—Hellano's suggestion. With pain being adopted in this realm, it is essential that we learn what new plants, animals, and foods may do harm.

I did not object when Hellano stated that we should have Luther, the god of Agony, on our council. In order to understand pleasure, we must also know torment. Additionally, Luther is to represent the angels and demons—their collective motivations and ideas—and give a report of their well-being during council meetings.

Which leads me to Mona, the head of Human Affairs. There is no better person to speak on behalf of humans than one as selfless and kind as her. Despite having no children of her own, she is a natural nurturer—I mean, she opened her home to me after I smashed the hood of her car. Humans will be lucky to have her watching out for them.

The council would not be complete without Cato, our official Knowledge Seeker. The nature of this responsibility will have him working closely with Meena, but he is to also continue studying a wide range of topics and bring forth information that may prove beneficial to ruling the New World.

"I'll send word to them and schedule our first meeting," Hellano says. This professionalism he displays—a *natural* ability to lead and manage—infuriates me. Is he doing this to prove to me that the crown belongs to him, or does the behavior originate from him genuinely believing it to be true?

"*Solely* due to the nature of our titles, I will grant you a seat on the council once Kysi wakes and claims his rightful place on the—"

A hand clasps over my mouth as Hellano pulls me through the nearest door. Brooms and mops rattle as we stumble inside a closet. If it were not for sunlight streaming through the small window behind me, darkness would wholly consume us.

Apparently, the Spirits of the Sky must have thought muck and grime would make a good edition to the New World, given the cleaning supplies that surround us on shelves.

We were never exempt from picking up after ourselves, but dust bunnies never settled, dirt never accumulated ... now, I can see speckles of dandruff floating against the light.

"Imagine a scale with unlimited, teetering sides," Hellano says with little patience in his tone, hand still clasped over my mouth, "a single thing—a single *word* overheard by the wrong person, and one of those sides gains enough weight to dismantle the entire structure. Is that what you want for our kingdom, Anewla? *Your* kingdom?"

The scent of warm berries forces their way around me like a constrictor; a smell I used to soak in every time we danced ... every time we embraced.

The itch to lurch forward and bite his palm is pressing, but he lowers it before I give in to the impulse. "How can the *truth* be bad for my kingdom?"

He scoffs, baring his teeth. "The truth? I'll show you the truth."

Hefty fingers lock into mine like a vise as Hellano pushes the closet door open. I am unaware of whether heads are turning due to our quickening pace, or simply because we are the ones wearing crowns. I flick a glance at Hellano, whose demeanor exudes nothing but aloofness despite the rush of our legs.

I was in love with a wonderful actor. Perhaps that is what caught me in his trap to begin with ... and why I never saw my descent coming.

Deep within the palace, we halt in front of a set of double doors. Although larger than its neighbors, its form remains quaint—not overbearing in appearance despite the intricate etchings in the wood.

Swirls of violets and golds allude to a detailed galaxy. Below it rests thick woods, their roots tangled across the forest floor. Within the bark of the trees, a woman is mounted atop a silver mare, her long dark hair drifting in the wind.

"The room you arrived in, it is your private corridors. We both have them. But ..." Hellano tugs on the long, golden handles, splitting the detailed image in half. "We also have a shared chamber."

Across the threshold rests an expansive mattress topped with deep green silks. Lush rugs lay before it, their fluff nearly as inviting as the bed. A pristine kitchen lay to the left—the half-open concept is split by a fireplace that protrudes from the wall and casts a warm glow over both spaces. The chimney, like before, is crafted with an array of gemstones. Although they flicker beautifully from the natural fire beneath, I know they await their time in the sun once it returns from under the horizon. Everything appears to be in order ... at first.

There is a faint twinkling overhead. Conservative, yet humble enough to pull your attention. The sight caves my chest in.

Like a geode broken open, the ceiling is adorned with icicles of pewter and purple—just like the stairs leading to Hellano's estate, and the ones that accent different parts of his home. The breathtaking rock formations drift throughout the space like a beautiful cave canal, stretching throughout the room and leading to others I have yet to explore. They trickle from each corner of the wall, invading the bedchamber like the plague.

This is not right. Kysi's essence is here, fitting into the space as if it belongs. Hellano's ... his resides like it has forced its way in. It is as though stealing Kysi's crown set this into motion—confused the New World during the creation of the palace.

"What have you done," is all I can manage to utter, appalled.

He releases a breath of disbelief, gesturing to the ceiling. "Anewla, this is *proof*. Proof by the Heavens, the New World—whatever you want to call it. Proof that I am to reign beside you as our souls have done for all of existence."

Just as death is inescapable, so is Hellano. Perhaps dealing with him is my natural punishment for killing members of the Nine, or allowing Earth to fall into chaos.

It is my fault ... how could I have not been more specific to the Sky Spirits?

Hellano softens beside me at the sight of my frigidness. I cannot look back at him, not with my gaze tethered to those hideously beautiful crystals above our heads.

"Anewla, I am not doing this to hurt you. I am still—"

I whip to face him then, eyes wet with beads that threaten to fall. "Don't you *dare*," I bite through a breaking voice, "say another word."

Sheer manipulation. Utter lies. The audacity for him to throw words around like that after *everything*. Nothing could rid me of the pain he caused, the pain that resurfaces with every look in his hazel eyes—the same ones that pretended to worship me for hundreds of years, that carried my image in them as if reflecting anything else would be a sin ... the ones that fixated on mine every time he went on and on about how much he loved his flower.

I have to leave, get away before my lungs threaten to collapse under the weight of trapped air.

Hellano lifts a gentle hand. "Please ... forgive me—"

I phase away before his touch has the chance to send me to my knees.

CHAPTER 20

The lack of clothes and clutter leads me to believe that I have landed in the wrong room. However, when the lingering scent of staleness severs the dissipating freshness of the New World, I know that I am right where I intended to jump ...

And Prosenth has fled.

The only evidence of him rests on the pillow of his perfectly made bed—abandoned now ... yet better cared for because of it. I stride over, plucking the piece of parchment from the cushion.

All is fair in bargains and soul bonds.

Mother. *Fucker.*

Against my bubbling vexation, I violently throw the paper; it merely drifts to the floor in a fluttering spiral, almost as if to mock me.

"Do not try to find him," a steady voice echoes in the now empty room, "because you'll never be able to in these endless halls."

Turning, I see Verina comfortably sitting on Prosenth's lilac chair.

"You know *nothing* about what he has done." Lips purse, I refrain from igniting a threatening flame in my palm. Heat emanates in my ears, my cheeks. It spins and boils like poison in a cauldron.

"Oh, but I do," she says, trailing a nail around the arm, "who do you think helped him?"

Thinking back, Prosenth spoke of Verina with a sense of respect and admiration. It is clear now that they care for one another, probably have for many millennia.

My gaze lowers, hardening. "You risked your life for the cause?" I ask distrustfully.

Verina merely huffs, "Gods no. How was I supposed to know you'd start murdering our ancestors?"

I swallow the guilt. "That was an accident."

"Consider your current predicament a natural consequence."

The tips of my fingers spark against my rising desperation. They pop in the atmosphere before I can smother them, drawing Verina's attention to my hand.

With the camber of her neck, she plainly stares. "Lilliana has stepped down from her position as Head of Council after your little charade." Deep brown eyes float up to mine. "It is now *my* responsibility to deal with you here. So, I'll offer you a deal; do not go after Prosenth, and I will tell you how to wake your mate."

Revenge is not worth losing the valuable information she has to offer. "Tell me what you know, and I won't go after him ... *unless* it deems untrue."

She straightens her spine. "Very well. The *real* reason Zapheen was spared is because the god of Agony was *also* unable to fulfill his side of the agreement. Hellano completed his duty by sending you both to the Shadowlands, therefore Kysi *had* to make good on his word."

So, when both parties cannot participate, the bargain becomes null and void.

"The solution is simple," Verina goes on, "convince Hellano to settle on the outcome of the deal, and Kysi will wake."

Easy enough ... in theory. "How am I supposed to accomplish that? Hellano has stolen his crown, he has no motive to settle."

Verina's cloak swooshes as she stands. "That would be your problem. Now, if you'll excuse me, I have a mountain of issues to solve thanks to the changes you have made, as well as your homicidal exit. So,"—she waves me away— "off you go."

I steady my glare. "If this doesn't work—"

"Then by all means, pay me a visit and I'll point you to Prosenth," she says with forced politeness.

I want to hesitate, unsure of whether I should trust this, but each second Kysi lays comatose on my bed feels like pelts of compressed adamant around my heart.

With a breath in, I grasp the pull and jump.

The sound of popping flames is first to greet me in the New World. Hellano stands facing the window, his bare back flickering against the light. Grey, drawstring sweatpants hang low around his hips as he stares through the glass and into the distant, twinkling city beyond; ready to go to bed alone, just as he has done for the last eight years.

"If you could wake him," I speak into the silence, "what would it cost?"

Hair of liquid fire shifts against the dark of night as he faces me. If his eyes were heat, I would be set aflame. "... Can I wake him?" The words are smooth, caring.

"If you wanted to ... but I know that you don't, so,"—nervousness shifts my weight to the other side— "what would it take?"

The panes of Hellano's powerful chest rise with a full breath as he steps away from the window. His gaze never wavers while he draws near, soaking deeper in the vision of me with each step he takes. "I did change, you know." Reaching forward, he takes my hand and places it between the mounds of his bare skin. I am about to pull away, but then I feel it—the warmth. "The ice is gone ... you made it go away."

A ray of hope emerges; maybe he will settle after all.

That voice ... it is sweeter than the honey hue of his eyes and smoother than the silks lining the bed behind us. It reminds me of whispers once shared under tangled blankets and good morning greetings after long nights of intimacy. Those memories may leave after millenniums in the Shadowlands, but right now they are carved deep in my mind as if by a talented whittler.

Perhaps that is how he can speak so lovingly despite our stark disagreement. Now that the void within him is gone—due to the return of Kairos in the next realm—all that is left is the love he had for me before. We may not be bonded, but hundreds of years with a person would tie you to them in one way or another.

Hellano lifts his other hand, wiping a single drop of wetness I was unaware had fallen. "I will spend my remaining lifespan on my knees before you if that is what it takes to gain your forgiveness. What I have done was a sin so horrendous that we must not forget the lesson; shifting the balance between us affects everything. Which is why I cannot wake Kysi. I will not put my position at risk—will not chance the downfall of a realm we both wish to keep."

I press my fingers to his skin, and he melts at the touch. "What if ... you keep the crown?" I suggest, illuding to the idea that we could settle; Kysi's crown for Kysi's life.

Hellano cranes his neck, slight amusement knitting his brow. "I can still tell when you are lying."

My jaw tightens. He knows that no matter what, even if I *was* willing to let him reign beside me, it would not matter. The moment Kysi wakes, he will be dedicated to fulfilling the position that was originally meant for him. Because I love him and wish the same, it would not take much convincing for me to withdraw my end of the agreement and help him steal the crown.

I jerk my hand away. "I hate you," I spit.

Although stung, Hellano swallows the insult. "That is not true either, my flower."

Not yet ready to return to my private suite, I instead roamed the halls before retiring for the evening. Since the staff had thinned due to the night growing late, the setting became more comfortable for not just me, but my furry companions. Lana paid me a visit, purring and rubbing against my leg—well, more like my hip given her sheer size. She nearly knocked me over.

It prompted the guards to come to my aid, but one hiss from my snow leopard had them trembling with their palms on the hilt of their weapons.

How silly, to think *I* would need saving. It was apparent that the guards were unaware of who exactly their monarch was. So, I ordered Lana to stand down and asked through her unique imprint if she would allow them to scratch her ear. The look she gave me was one a teenager might throw an ignorant parent, but she obliged.

Once the tension had settled, I gave them my name and asked for theirs. Hylan and Typa, a male angel and female demon, had useful information to share about the New World, especially regarding the cities within it.

Gourmara is a culinary district to the west, contrived of mostly human souls. Known for its diverse array of dishes, it houses restaurants of all ethnic backgrounds that beings from everywhere gather to enjoy. Behind the city is a relaxing forest where cabins and cottages lounge amidst the towering trees. The perfect ingredients are stationed at their disposal in gardens throughout the wood, ready to be picked and procured into delectable treats.

The Gallery Enclave is an art district to the east, known for its creative intellect and breathtaking views. One goes there to feel inspired and renewed. From painters to composers to dancers, the Enclave thrives on unique ideas and various forms of self-expression. Although it is primarily populated by angels, beings of all kinds travel to marvel in the city's wonder.

Revelry Row is to the north, a place with endless entertainment. Concerts, theaters, and clubs make up a city that never sleeps. Despite the residences mainly consisting of demons, angels from the Enclave often travel to perform as well as humans from Gourmara that gather to indulge in a night out. The city is mostly active when the sun is away, as many demons are nocturnal by choice.

Finally, we have the Capital, where the royal palace rests atop a knoll that faces its kingdom with pride. It serves as a melting pot for all the fresh souls of the New World. Residing in the southernmost part of the lands, nothing but training grounds and rocky cliffsides sit behind it.

If it were up to me, these cities would not consist mostly of their own species, but rather blend with the other beings in a diverse array of characters. I suppose like calls to like, and in a new realm these creatures find comfort settling near one another.

After the long conversation with Hylan and Typa, they escorted me back to my bedchamber and wished me goodnight.

But the sun has returned, and I have barely slept.

It was impossible to tear my gaze away from the way Kysi's eyes moved behind his lids. Every time I almost fell asleep, his chest would expand in a breath that would jerk me awake to observe him. At last, I rise to dress myself for the day, but not without departing from him with a kiss.

I wish those mortal fairytales were real; then he may have woken up.

My new wardrobe is deeper than I imagined it would be. Some outfits I recognize, but most are foreign. The walls are painted a deep blue-black that fades into ivory at the end of the extravagant tunnel. It works to bring focus to the rows of color coordinated fabrics, beginning with a velvet gown as white as a swan and fading into every shade of the rainbow. At the far end, apparel of deep midnight rests on either side of a full-length mirror. A boudoir is nestled in the wall to its right, and on the other side, a room divider peeks out from where the clothes end.

A woman appears in the reflection behind me. "You have a council meeting in less than an hour."

A yelp ignites from the base of my throat. I whirl to face her as she bows to greet me formally. What golden hair is not pinned to her skull, drapes loosely over her petite shoulders. Two wings extend from either side of her spine, like that of a dragonfly.

"Who are you?" I question.

"My name is Harlynn; I am here to assist you." Her voice is chirpy and optimistic. She slides past me and trails the garments as if she picked most of them out herself.

"No, no, no," she mumbles to the dresses. "After your meeting you are scheduled to announce the first annual Spring Festival at the Gallery Enclave." Plucking a sea green, sleeveless gown from the rack, she eyes me questioningly.

"That one's fine," I say with a nod. "Spring Festival?" It feels so foolish to ask a question that I should already know the answer to, but luckily Harlynn does not express the same insecurity that I feel. Instead, she gestures toward the divider in the corner.

"The Spring Festival is an annual celebration of the dawn of the New World. You and the King are to travel through each city and indulge in what they have to offer—their culture, food, and entertainment."

The satin slides over my figure comfortably, with thin pieces that hang across each arm, leaving my shoulders bare. The border is embroidered with marigolds and larkspur just a shade darker.

When I step out, Harlynn motions for me to sit at the boudoir. It reminds me of the one I used to cherish on Earth, not so much in style but rather shape.

"When is the festival?" I ask as she begins plucking at my hair.

Taking pins from the drawer, she splits one with her teeth before tucking a portion back. "Two weeks' time, Your Majesty."

I would prefer a more casual title whilst in the comfort of my own home—or at least my own private corridors. "Please, Anewla is fine between the two of us."

A grin tugs at the corners of her lips. "Very well."

Carefully, Harlynn retrieves the royal crown. I had placed it in an ornate box found in the sitting room. It was clearly meant for the diadem, with silk threaded around a perfect mold of its circumference.

The flowers over it vanished once I took it off last night, returning to the solid gemstone beneath. As Harlynn gently places it over my hair, they sprout once more into a different array of colors. Mainly blue petals now with bits of coral peeking through, a nice accent to the light green gown.

Fresh like the open sea, my attire is a contrast to the element I naturally wield—fire. Perhaps it is to give the impression of a light-hearted, gentle Queen; not one that commits manslaughter to the past lives of multiple hierarchal gods.

Let us hope it is convincing enough.

Silence lay steadily across the obsidian table in the council chamber. The dome ceiling casts a calm ray of sunshine over the space, alluding to a sense of peace that in fact feels irretrievable.

The goddess of Pleasure sheds a quiet tear for the fate of her dear friend, while I hold nothing but contempt for the false King sitting across from me. Fashioned in my same color scheme, Hellano never lowers his eyes from mine—never backing down. With my threatening gaze, I imagine the way he would look in a cell, shackled for the remaining six hundred years I so graciously *gave* him.

Luther's lack of noise differs from the others. Everything I have told the room is new information to him, and although I never mentioned that Kysi was meant to reign beside me—begrudgingly heeding Hellano's warning about a scale with many teetering sides—I question whether the god of Agony is putting the pieces together as he sits rubbing his chiseled chin.

Kysi's tie to Earth makes his essence similar to mine, but anyone that *knows* him or takes the time to truly observe the castle's details would be able to put it together; just as I believe Cato, Meena, and Mona have.

Hellano may have bits of himself here, like the rock ceiling of our 'shared' bedchamber, but that was merely an error due to his thievery of the crown.

Our members of council accepted their positions without trouble, although I think that may be because most were eager to gain an audience with us—to be updated.

"Most humans are content," Mona says after clearing her throat. "However, whispers of distrust are circulating over the god of Afterlife."

I notice how she does not refer to Hellano as her superior ... and so does he.

"It has to do with their imagine of Lucifer, a biblical entity—"

"I am aware of the devil, Mona." Annoyance lingers in Hellano's tone.

She takes a breath. "Those who believe you to be this character fear you as leader ... some have even gone so far to say they may be in hell."

Mumbling obscenities, Hellano pinches the bridge of his nose.

"Their assumption of his character wouldn't be that far off," Meena says behind a sniffle, peering daggers at the man across from me.

The false King clenches his fists over the slab of table. "Am I the only one seeing reason here?"

I chime in next. "Perhaps that means you're in the wrong—"

"He's not though," Cato interrupts. With eyes as wide as saucers, my focus shifts to him. "I want Kysi to wake as well, but we both know the moment he does it is only a matter of time before he attempts to take the crown." His abysmal eyes demand attention. "There are more lives in your hands now; more beings that depend on you. Humanity has been set back *seven hundred* years, Anewla. Kysi may be paralyzed from his failure as the god of Bargaining, but he still has a job to do as the god of Mortals. The sooner you accept that, the sooner you can begin helping him rebuild the human realm—pull your focus into creating more life for him to aid."

Divine Duplicity ... it is the phenomenon in which deities have two consciences within themselves. One is dedicated to their purpose, while the other is meant to experience existence. I can push into that Divine Duplicity at any time; see from the lens of a different eye that does nothing but create. I did it so often when I was with Hellano—forced that part of me to make more life. I do not need to tap into it here, not unless I want to create something from nothing, like a blooming flower that never needed a seed. The existing flora and fauna of this world require no more than a thought to manipulate.

I have been so focused on waking Kysi that I never thought to check on Earth. As I peer into the white pearls of Cato's eyes, I consciously enter through the glass wall of my mind and into the part of me that breeds beginnings.

Civilization cannot progress when life lags behind. So, I think through those mental equations, double checking my work as I give the mortal world a gentle push.

When a boom of life takes place, nothing but good fortune surrounds it. Relationships coil together like knitted twine the moment conception occurs between mates, and thousands of dormant seeds break open with tendrils of green.

Kysi can feel it, can sense what I have done. I know this because I feel him too ... in the way survivors embrace after the end of the world ... the way an orphaned fawn drinks milk from a mare in a dark, ashen field.

I have cried so much recently. This time I embrace the tears.

A wide bridge made of dark oak arches across a lazy river. The waterway snakes through scattered trees, leading to where the leaves part to an open area.

"Like Lila," Harlynn says, nodding in that direction. "And if you continue past it, you'll eventually reach the Ancient Library where it sits between the Enclave and the Row."

Figures on horseback crane their necks to peer at us from below, offering wide waves of greeting. I return the gesture with the brightest smile I can muster.

Due to Mona's lack of extra appendages, her and Meena departed early and are waiting for us in the city. They claimed that it was important for them to have time to scope out the area before I entered, but I think they were simply eager to spend half the day exploring together. The latter is what prompted me to send them off this morning rather than have Cato phase them in. Although my party will need to travel via teleportation after this speech—it would take more than a day's time to fly from the Enclave to Gourmara—I still wanted to take this initial journey to begin familiarizing myself with the kingdom's geography.

Cato and Luther are accompanying Hellano to Revelry Row, where he is to give a similar speech to the residents. Afterwards, we will meet at Gourmara and stand together before the humans to share the same news with them. The idea is that by appearing united with his opposite, those who associate him with the devil, no matter how closely he may resemble the entity, will no longer fear their lives here in the New World.

The thought of standing unified beside Hellano repulses me, but the well-being of my people is more important. Sacrifice—that is part of what it means to rule.

Hills part to reveal a city that blends seamlessly with knolls scattered throughout. The Gallery Enclave was curated with respect for the land, not infringing on its beauty for the sake of civilization. Countless windows twinkle like reflective confetti against the daylight, each structure unique in shape and style. Some buildings branch from the hills as if crafted by a giant sculptor, their walls curved to accent the earth and draw focus to other, more vibrant parts of the city.

Entering the Enclave is like walking through a kaleidoscope of color. Spires and glass arches line either side of the street, glittering off the mosaic tiles carefully placed between the stone pathways. They swirl with arrows and letters to guide citizens through the labyrinth. Without this advantage, one may easily get lost in the way buildings are colored to hypnotize and disorient.

As we stride forward, what appears to be a distant mountain shifts into a clothier the moment its painted brick opens to an exiting consumer.

Beautiful and dangerously illusory to the naked eye.

It is only when the customer notices me and bows that I spot the others. The city's immaculate details served to distract me thus far, but now my focus absorbs the people. From rooftops to balconies to lines on either side of me, they all lower to pay respects to their new monarch. If it were not for the guards and Harlynn nearby, I would probably attempt to hide amidst the art—find an area to blend into.

The directions underfoot lead us to an elegant square. A long body of water spans its center, where koi fish nip at the air and cause ripples to echo. At the end, a grand podium sits under pennants that sway in the breeze. The leaves of Magnolia and Crabapple trees rustle with waves of hello.

Mona and Meena stand to the side, nodding to me with a grin as if to say, "All clear."

The podium seems to grow farther and farther away, despite how I have met a standstill. Thumping sounds in my ears—heart beginning to race as Harlynn sends a quizzical glance over her shoulder, curious at the holdup.

A traitorous part of me wishes Hellano were here, maybe then anger would fuel me to stomp to the stage rather than stand here like an imbecile.

Their eyes, so penetrating and still, transform the back of my ribs into a raging tempest. The air is fresh on my skin but unreachable to my lungs. I need ... I need ...

I need Kysi.

Dipping into my other self, I push life once more in the mortal realm. I can almost feel it hum in response. The love and connection between sullen creatures ... it is like being wrapped in a cocoon so thick that there is no room for anything else—no possibility of the comfort being intruded upon or stolen.

When I open my eyes, the podium is not so far.

Similar avians sit perched just as before, their wings a megaphone for the masses. Some individuals rise to hover in the air, seeking to get a better view as I climb the dais and face them.

I nearly gasp at how this position perfectly aligns the lilac, cerulean, and forest green shades of the storefronts and townhouses. They come together in the form of a thriving planet, one that beams with purple rays of euphoria—delighted to *begin*.

To say that it is inspiring would be an understatement, an insult to a masterpiece that not only motivates its viewer to take hold of this world and make it their own but *demands* it. Who am I to refuse?

Once a Fallen Goddess, now the Queen of gods—the monarch of a whole godsdamn realm—all because I looked destiny in the eye and spat in it; I made it yield to *me*.

Just as I will make Hellano.

A toothy grin emerges. "My beautiful kingdom, I have arrived to announce the official celebration of our newfound home. In a fortnight, the first annual Spring Festival will take place in all corners of the New World."

It is so easy to speak to them now that the truth is about to be revealed ... now that Hellano is about to fall against the honesty of his uprising.

My finger reaches towards this house of cards. "So much sudden change has occurred, and you all have embraced it gracefully. Although there are many more to come as we continue to grow and thrive, there is one in particular that I am ..."

Thick clouds roll over the sun, darkening the skies. "... eager to share," my voice trails off as I follow their gaze overhead, bearing witness to the black mass that blankets the Enclave like a morbid omen.

That alluring image of a flourishing world is snuffed out by invasive shadows that spread like a hungry wildfire.

Whispers of concern bounce through the square as the thick smoke above parts to allow light through, illuminating the silhouette of a sculpted man with a mighty wingspan. Damning red hair pierces through the white light of day as the god of Afterlife descends upon the city, his stolen crown gleaming against its will.

Hellano slides across the stage with serpentine grace, feathers settling against the rush of wind. The citizens applaud his marvelous entrance, having not expected their King to visit today.

He smiles and lifts a hand to them before turning to envelope me in a tight embrace. "*Fine*," he sneers, "but it will come at a price."

"*Fine*," I respond into his ear as he parts from me.

Taking my place at the podium, Hellano elegantly addresses the citizens with a speech of his own. "Angels, demons, and humans alike, your Queen and I are elated to begin this journey as not mere rulers of the New World, but fellow citizens—allies and friends of the people, striving to maintain the integrity and goodwill that will carry us into the future. We shall work alongside you to curate a paradise for all."

His words invoke a merry cheer. Even a human grins with hopeful eyes.

"So, allow me to announce another joyous occasion on the horizon." Hellano turns to extend a hand to me.

With all the power I can forge, I take it and step forward.

Pulling me into his side, he shouts through the square, "A royal wedding!"

The grip around my midsection tightens against the sudden tremors that rattle my bones; a warning to stand tall and act accordingly.

His declaration is absorbed by an uproar of excitement and praise. Everyone celebrates ...

While the face of destiny wipes its eye and bites back.

CHAPTER 21

The city of Gourmara greets us with countless trays of savory foods and sweet treats, each person hoping for one of us to reach over and try their dish. Hellano loves the attention—no surprise there—and is delighted to taste what they have to offer.

Despite wishing that I could indulge myself, I do not think I am capable of keeping anything down.

It is a mixture of avidity and doom; the knowledge that Kysi will be waking soon and the emergence of my soon-to-be marriage. It may sicken me to do it, may be a constant battle of fighting the way my face wishes to express the disgust that I so passionately feel for this monster, but when Kysi wakes ... dealing with Hellano will get easier, because I will have my mate to get me through it.

So, I will reign next to the god of Afterlife. I will hold his hand in front of the masses. I will play the role of elated bride.

Whatever it takes to have Kysi back—have him and *keep* him.

With the edge of the forest behind me and the city ahead, I strain to paint the face of a powerful and confident ruler. Hellano does most of the talking with a voice that could melt the angriest blizzard—inviting and safe.

Merely a show, like the rest of him. *Fake.*

Although the cobblestone streets are full, curtains shift from apartments above eateries, taverns, and inns; undoubtedly filled with those too frightened to take part in the festivities. The knowledge of their fear weighs heavy on my shoulders.

Even I can see that this bias towards him is unfair. Hellano may be the false King, but he has not done anything to hurt the New World thus far. I would never allow such a thing, but part of me wonders if I will ever have to worry about it at all.

He truly does seem to care for this kingdom.

So, in time, I believe those fearful will eventually come out of the shadows and into a realm waiting to be embraced in all its wonder. For now, all I can do is offer a hopeful smile and act as if all is well.

Hellano may be the devil in my eyes, but he should not be in theirs.

When we return to the council room after the big announcement, my grip tightens around Cato's arm. "You brought him to the Enclave?" The question comes out more like an irritated statement.

The god of Wisdom offers an apologetic glance. "He said you had trouble speaking last time and wanted to check on you."

Facing Hellano, I find that his eyes are already on me. "How'd you know I was going to tell them about Kysi?"

The false King leans forward. "I *didn't.*"

Cato shifts against the newfound silence. "I'll ... phase the others into the Grand Hall," he utters before blinking away, leaving the both of us suspended in an air of tension.

So, Hellano really was concerned about my anxiety.

The room feels smaller against his tired, yearning gaze. "I heard what you were about to say when I arrived overhead." An indistinguishable type of sadness litters his tone. "Anewla, I still—" he reels in the words, not wishing to upset me, "*care* for you deeply. And I know this is foolish of me to wish for, but I hope that one day you will allow me to love you with a warm heart ... in all the ways that broken bond never allowed me to before."

I am unable to keep myself from slipping into the past, back to when that face—so gentle and coaxing—would have prompted me to slide into his lap and kiss his cheeks. Despite how much I hate to acknowledge it, Hellano did love me then.

It would be a lie to say that I never missed him. Not *him*, just ... who I thought he was.

"Don't hold your breath," I force out the words and watch how they sting.

A sigh of defeat falls out. "*I* may not be able to make you happy anymore, but ... he can."

My muscles sink under a sudden weight.

"Last night got me thinking," Hellano goes on, "trying to figure out a solution for the both of us ... If you sign my contract and legally bind yourself to an unending union with me, thus solidifying my position as King of the New World, I will agree to wake Kysi."

Motionless on my bed, my mate lays for the second day having not even *seen* this realm I have created for us. Unable to hold me in the safety of his arms. Unable to gaze at me with eyes that glow every time they land upon mine.

Two days ... my wings have not brightened in two days. "Where do I sign?"

Hellano peers not at me, but the ring fashioned on my left hand.

"I won't take it off." I hold it to my chest, pulling his focus. Of course, if refusing would be a deal breaker, then I would be forced to comply. "Don't make me."

With a sad smile he says, "Just thinking of a band to match."

Thorne lays at the foot of my bed, back after a quick walk. The wolf knows that he is free to go but stays to comfort me anyway.

Hellano needs more time to finish writing the contract, no doubt to ensure that there are no loopholes I might find.

With an arm draped across his broad chest, I hold Kysi while visiting the other side of my mind.

Earth looks greener already, healthier. When it comes to animals and humans, however, there is only so much that I can do. I am bound by the Law of Gestation—assumingly created *after* the god of Time received a permanent ending—which states that everything forming in the mortal realm takes time. And I have a feeling that when Cato mentioned humanity being seven hundred years behind, he meant *with* my help.

If only I refrained mentioning to the Sky Spirits that Kairos's soul shall never be reincarnated ... Earth might be much better off right now.

Yet, I still push with all my might.

Millions of buds' blossom. Ribbons of pollen trail across the windless skies. Everything faces the sun, like the flowers he got me on our first date. I can almost feel the rays of heat through Kysi's body. So warm ... so kind.

Running my palm down, I meet it with the limp hand that rests over a slow-beating heart. I slide my fingers between his and lay my cheek over the arch of his shoulder.

One more night like this ... one more night.

I dream of the woods, of a forest that hugs me with a man doing the same. There is fresh, vibrant life in all directions. A fawn grazes. A distant mare gallops, mane flying tendrils in the air.

It is a wholesome peace.

Back to my mate, I soak in the hills of his arms and torso. Familiar and soft, despite the firmness beneath. The air is sweet, rich with the aroma of ripe blueberries.

Berries ...

Rigid between tight arms, I gradually turn.

Hellano pulls his gaze from the land, finding mine frozen upon him. The environment shifts in the reflection of hazel pearls as a rough hand cups my jaw. "Don't be sad, my flower," he coos, guiding my face to the forest once more. "You can always make more."

The branches are stripped bare, displaying a darkening sky between their sullen boughs. The horse no longer runs. The fawn no longer eats. Motionless they lay atop dead grass, lifeless like the world around them.

The sheets were damp with sweat when I woke.

Now, Hellano sits across from me in the council chamber, his velvet black vest glittering against a deep plum tunic. He is the only one without papers in his hands. A master copy of the contract—the one we are all meant to sign—waits for us at the center of the table.

I am jittery, nervous, tangled like wool under a microscope. My efforts to suppress the overwhelming emotions prove pointless against the *tap, tap, tapping* of the ink pen between my fingers as I dissect Hellano's proposal.

Every member of council holds their own copy of this deal, observing it intently. Even Hellano's assistant is present, as well as Harlynn, holding identical documents. Their reason for being here was made known upon reading the first paragraph.

Anyone closely related to King Hellano and Queen Anewla shall swear to secrecy. Failure to do so will result in your immediate dismissal from the royal palace. Once signed, breaking this agreement shall be punishable by private execution.

How fitting, for a *King of Death*.

It then states that my relationship with Kysi is not to be made public. Only the people who place their names at the bottom of the original contract are allowed to know of our love, which will result in eight total signatures if all agree to the false King's terms and conditions.

The truth of my connection with Kysi is being pushed inside a prison cell lined with dead bolts. One of them locks when Cato is the first to reach forward and scribble his name. The god of Wisdom does not so much as glance in my direction as he sets his pen down.

Most of the contract consists of details regarding the ceremony. It is to include traditions adopted by humans, angels, and demons. Due to the latter two lacking bodily forms in their previous realms, there was no way for them to express the connection some of their souls shared with others. Now that they are here in the New World, the beings have already created their own unique rituals to wed.

Although our knowledge of these ceremonies is limited, Hellano would still like to implement all cultures in the royal wedding to display a sense of togetherness in the nation.

Imagining this marriage as a promise to the kingdom—one of dedication to unity and peace—makes it easier to stomach.

My focus is stolen momentarily when Luther reaches for the master copy. After sliding it back, Meena takes it next. They both appear confident in their decision.

The union will ultimately resemble a human wedding, with an aisle to walk down as well as rings and vows to exchange. There will only be two distinct differences in the ceremony; a playful game to start, adopted by the angelic community, where both soon-to-be spouses race to bow before one another. Whoever does so first, loves and respects the other more. We will then trade rings and empty promises, and afterwards comes a demonic tradition that I think will be quite enjoyable; Hellano and I are to cut a thin line across the other's hand before joining them together.

I will make mine hurt.

These are sweet, symbolic rituals ... it is a shame that I will be unable to partake in them with a genuine heart. Perhaps Kysi and I will have our own private ceremony, so I can experience it like my people do.

The next paragraph sends heat into my ears.

"When the god of Afterlife retires from his reign," I recite with a sharp tongue, "the crown will then pass on to his successor, and this shall be so for all incarnates of Death to come." My jaw clenches as I raise my head. "Are you kidding me? What if your successor does not wish to be King, or worse, what if they are an unjust ruler?"

A knuckle pops under the weight of Hellano's thumb as he drapes an ankle over his knee. "Keep reading."

At first glance, I did not think that Hellano's assistant had wings—figuring that perhaps like gods, not all demons have them—but when he reaches for the papers in the center of the table, I notice the way they hang under his arms. It is only then that I realize the pattern in these creature's appendages. Typa, the guard I spoke with my first night here, had membranous, dark wings at her back. Featherless, unlike Hellano's, and coming to a spike at the tip of the apex. Gathering this, I conclude that all demon wings probably have the same macabre essence.

With a sigh, I carry on.

"The goddess of Beginnings is to use her ability to travel realms and bring Hellano, god of Afterlife, back from the Shadowlands after his reincarnation in order to continue reigning as King of the New World until his successor is fit to rule." How am I not surprised that Hellano would find a way to exploit my novel abilities for his own gain? I scan the council, bewildered at how the majority could agree so easily.

"I would prefer his successor not come to power wholly inexperienced," Luther answers in response to my stricken expression.

That opinion is valid, but I do not for one second believe that Hellano is doing this for any reason other than to stay in power longer. I give him an additional six hundred years, and he finds a way to lengthen his sentence.

Bastard.

Mumbling obscenities, I finish the final paragraph and place the contract flat before me.

Every instinct urges me to reach for the master copy—hurry and pull Kysi from this endless slumber no matter what the cost. What would have to be in this document for me to refuse? Where is the line drawn?

Truth be told, there was never one to begin with.

The original feels heavier in my hand, despite being identical to the one I read through. I manage to write neatly against a shaking hand. Typically, my signature has swirls around the A's, but this time I lack the will to do anything but the bare minimum. It is a silent tell of my hesitation and entrapment; anyone who views it will know where my heart was when agreeing ... not that it would make a difference anyway.

Sliding the contract away from me prompts Mona and Harlynn to sign. Now, all that is left is Hellano.

He holds it like a treasure, a victory against the odds that have been stacked against him. Reviewing each name to ensure the spelling is correct and the letters are legible, he then picks up the pen with calm grace. It hisses against the paper as he writes.

A distant howl erupts as Thorne's imprint pulses in my mind.

Kysi has awoken.

CHAPTER 22

Never have I moved so quickly. Bursting through the bedchamber door, I find my mate upright in bed, breathing heavily as if awakened by a gasp. To witness Kysi move on his own accord feels like the sun rising after a horrifying, sleepless night. A piece of onyx hair falls across his brow at my disruption. The wings behind me lift their hue as he turns with eyes that brighten like a beckoning lighthouse.

"You were gone," I choke out, feeling lighter with each step toward him.

Reaching forward, Kysi pulls me closer by the hips, wrapping his firm arms around my back as I fall into his lap. "Don't cry." The whisper grazes through my hair. "I'm right here."

Even if I could obey this loving command, I would refuse. These tears are welcome, and to push them away would be a disservice. They deserve to fall. These droplets of joy have fought to run down my face the moment I found him near death in the Shadowlands.

Warm palms encase my face as my mate wipes the tears away with kisses.

A laugh escapes. "That is so gross, Ky."

"Oh, come on, angel. I've kissed you in far more inappropriate ways," he teases while tucking hair behind my ear.

The door slams, whipping our focus to the council intruding upon our reunion. Everyone but Hellano and Cato pile in, the former probably too disinterested to witness Kysi's exit from stasis.

"Ugh, someone put him back to sleep. Nobody wants to hear about that," Meena grumbles before allowing a grin to emerge. "Welcome back, Kysi."

I slide off as he stands to embrace his friend, Mona's observant eyes lingering at the way Meena sinks into the touch.

"Thanks, Meen-ie," he responds.

Mona then clasps his shoulder, prompting them to part. "Good to see you up and running again," she says before speaking to the others on my behalf. "I think we can all stop gawking and find someplace else to be."

Thank gods for best friends.

Luther, Harlynn, Hellano's assistant—they all take in the secret they have sworn to keep as the god of Mortals and Bargaining returns to my side and pulls me close.

Harlynn's eyes dart between the two of us as the others file out respectively. "Just ... call if I am needed," she says before scuttling away.

When privacy returns, Kysi shifts to me. "Who was that?"

I drape my arms over sculpted shoulders, relishing the grip he has on my waist. "An *assistant*."

Brows raise. "We get those now?"

"Apparently so." I follow his eyes to the flower diadem atop my head, cursing myself for not taking it off before he woke.

"It suits you, *Your Majesty*." A grin spreads. Before another word can be said, I pluck it from my hair. "How interesting," he comments, witnessing how the petite flowers slide away to the bare gem beneath. "What else is new?"

I am not ready to share the contract. Basking in the euphoria of his return sounds like a much better way to spend my night.

"Join me in the bath?" I suggest in an attempt to divert his attention.

When his gaze lowers to my blush linen gown, I know that the distraction worked. "You know you don't have to ask."

The water runs warm across my fingers as it rises in the cedar tub. A rock wall lay behind it with succulents tucked between protruding stones. The cove lighting provides a comforting ambience, cozy against the steam grazing the air.

Kysi's bare pecs rise and fall evenly now. When I am met with an outstretched hand from where I sit on the lip of the tub, reaching for it is the easiest decision I have made in days. It is one that requires no hesitation—hardly a conscious thought.

He undresses me slowly, absorbing the curves of my breasts as the fabric slides over them. When the dress falls from my chest and gathers at the waist, he does not push it down farther. Not yet.

Kysi's finger leaves chills in its wake as it glides over my skin. Hovering at the pinnacle of my breast, it circles like the heat collecting in the base of my stomach.

"I felt you on Earth. Your presence," he croons, slightly pinching my skin and watching how it pulls my back into an arch. "Felt you in sleep too, with your arms over me. Gods, how I hated not being able to move." Green eyes hang heavy with desire. "Tortured by my inability to touch you."

The hand falls, dipping behind the gown. His lips part when I release a moan, relishing in how responsive I am.

"You had a bad dream last night," he says, gliding a finger through my slick center. "I could feel you restless beside me. I wanted nothing more than to wake you. Distract you." Leaning in, Kysi's voice lowers as the trail of pleasure ceases between my thighs. "Do you want me to show you *how*?"

A simple nod is not enough to please him.

"Use your words, angel," he coaxes, calling to me with each blink that flashes across those wicked, feline eyes.

"I want you to show me how," I breathe out, "please."

My desperate request is met with a satisfied smirk. "Good girl," Kysi lilts, pushing the dress over my hips at last. "Get in the bath."

Making love to a soulmate is like hanging in a cloud of soft, warm touches. Waves hit the wall of the tub with each stroke, hypnotizing like a swaying stopwatch when mixed with the sound of my lover's groans of satisfaction. It buzzes over my tongue as we kiss, and through exhaustive exhales whispers of worship flow.

"Look at you." Kysi's heavy gaze drags up from where I astride him. "My Queen."

My hair still drips with water as I lunge for Kysi's arm in the sitting room. He was just on his way to the balcony to take in the landscape for the first time. The glittering lights of the distant city naturally attract attention, so the quizzical expression he gives me is called for.

"You can't go out there."

He turns slightly. "And why not?"

I can already feel my heart sputtering, hear it in my ears. "Because ... well, I had to wake you—somehow."

Facing me fully, deep onyx eyebrows magnetize in question. "What do you mean, Anewla?" his tone implies racing thoughts, undoubtedly running through worst case scenarios.

"There was a contract ... with demands in exchange for your wake."

Noticing my unease, Kysi closes the gap between us by pulling me toward him. "It's okay, angel. I'm sure we can handle whatever it is the Nine insisted upon."

My cheek meets the soft cotton of his shirt. "Except it was not the Nine who made demands ... or even held the power to bring you back."

He stiffens like a pillar of steel. "Don't tell me."

"I wish I didn't have to."

The hum of a heated voice rattles my cheek. "What did he want?"

When I lift my head, I am met with irises of phthalo green. Foreign, the shadow to a doorway in my mate that I have yet to see; different from the cages of arousal he often keeps at bay. That could not hurt anyone, as it stems from a passionate love.

What he struggles to contain now—forged by a molten rage—carries a violent, deadly impulse thrumming to be set free. His look is a silent order, one urging me to come out with it.

"Hellano is to rule beside me," I let out, watching him harden on the inside and out, "and we are to marry."

Time moves slow against the anticipation of his response. Thick lividity seeps from Kysi's every pore, oozing out in streams of crimson hatred. Words push through clenched teeth. "What is it with that man and stealing what's *mine*?" The fingers around my face nearly tremble as they slide away. "Where is he? I'd like to have a word."

Attempting to strike a deal with Hellano now is pointless, but the god of Bargaining seems determined to try.

"Probably his office downstairs. Maybe the council room a few hallways over." Kysi pivots from me, making a beeline for the exit.

"He's not going to agree to anything, Ky," I say, trailing behind.

No response. Like the day I assaulted him with a skillet, I am wholly ignored. Swinging open the bedchamber door, Kysi scans the guards lining the hall with a motive.

Then ... he shifts.

Straight onyx hair lengthens and spirals into curls of brown. His cheeks—once defined and structured—become plump, forming a round face. Light skin darkens from the kiss of a phantom sun.

In a blink, Mona stands before me.

The change was so rapid that by the time heads shift in our direction, all they see is the head of Human Affairs alongside the Queen.

Mona's visage spots a human soldier posted near the railing of wide stairs. Passing them by in only my robe, I pad to keep up with Kysi. "I shouldn't have to tell you that mimicking friends is *off* limits," I mumble in a low pitch, not wishing to alert those standing in uniform.

In order to phase, you must first know where you are going. So, if Kysi knew where Hellano's office or the council room was, he would have simply teleported there.

As far as to why he is masking himself as Mona, I lack the slightest idea. Kysi can only take on the appearance of mortals. Being their god, I know he must have an arsenal of faces to choose from. Why hers?

Closing in on the human, 'Mona' gives an order. "Take me to the *King*."

The way my friends voice sounds more like her than she does ... is horrifyingly impressive.

Like a python constricting a bobcat, the innocent man locks under the god of Mortals' will. Glamoured.

I will never forget when Kysi did it to me. It felt like a rope was cinched around my waist, the other end held by a gentle, coaxing hand.

In this man's case, that same hand does not pull slightly, but *yanks* with the force of a wrathful god. Past the illusion of a tired and aloof face, the soldier's hickory eyes store a palpable fear.

"Let him go," I order. "*Now.*"

Once again, nothing.

To push someone from the front seat of their mind is an invasion even the King of Death would deem immoral. How could Kysi do this to a harmless man—a species that he loves?

The floor below is busier. We pass courtiers—members hired by the council to work beneath them—with binders of information, undoubtedly channeling into whichever office Meena, Luther, and Mona have been assigned.

Cato did not want one for himself. "*The library is my worksta-tion,*" he had said.

I have never actually seen Hellano's office, only know of its lo-cation. A sharp right brings us through a tunnel of sparkling rock, its ceiling arched and hanging with crystalline spires. Dozens of my reflections pass by as I follow my disguised mate.

Once again, I am struck by the way Hellano's essence has intruded upon my home. This time it does not make me queasy. My nausea rather sprouts from the suspense that thickens the air.

"Back to your post," Mona commands the poor man that brought us here.

Curved walls form a room in the shape of a teardrop, its tip meeting behind a grandiose workstation. Painted bundles of gold burst through midnight and mulberry around us, exploding like stars in a distant galaxy.

The stolen diadem tilts up as Hellano lowers his pen onto the stone desk. "Mona," he greets, his gaze falling upon me—the robe tight around my figure. "My Queen."

"I need to speak with you," Mona requests, sending a panicked glance at the stationed guards. "Privately."

Worry shadows his features. Hellano must be regretting his decision to wake Kysi in this moment, given the way his expression seems to be racing through a million different possibilities.

My dripping hair and disheveled attire only enables this charade of urgency.

With a nod from their ruler, the guards file out.

"What's happened?" Hellano glances past Mona, hazel eyes sharp on the state of my undress. Having rushed away from what appears to be an intimate and vulnerable moment does not give off the right impression. "Did he hurt you?" he asks in a voice that seeks to comfort despite its threatening undertones.

Mona stretches then, growing in height as well as width; shoulders broadening into a towering man. "What did you just say?" Kysi questions with a hiss that is all his own.

The transformation dawns on Hellano but does not plague him with concern. Calmly he stands, pushing off the desk with stiff fingers. "If you wanted an audience with me, all you had to do was ask."

But Kysi is too heated to speak, too blinded by rage to reason. Then, the space he occupies empties without warning as he phases behind the desk.

Behind Hellano.

There is no time for me to scream. No time to warn or beg him to move ... before Kysi reaches either hand around the false King's skull and jerks it to the side.

Like crisp fallen leaves under a stepping boot, the *crack* of Hellano's neck is nearly as loud as the one in my heart.

The crown falls just as he does. It is then that I realize my mate has not returned wholly unchanged from his time in stasis. The Kysi I knew would never steal the appearance of an ally without their permission, bend the will of an innocent man, and become so uncontrollably violent.

It is as if what happened has left a wound upon his soul.

My throat bobs against the pressure of a heavy dread; Kysi came back different ... and a man I spent lifetimes lying beside—laughing beside—is now dead.

CHAPTER 23

Hellano was never skilled at braiding hair. Uncoordinated fingers would get tangled between strands, but patience never abandoned him.

I would complain about having too much of it, mumbling about taking a kitchen knife—likely one often used for when he would cut and serve me ripe fruit—to chop it off and get it out of my way. Have a lighter head.

"*You just need a break from it is all,*" he would say while rising to his knees on the bed. Behind me, sturdy hands would gather up locks of my midnight hair and begin tucking them into messy plaits. The ridges of his torso would occasionally graze my back in comforting sweeps, and the muscles in my scalp would ease from the attention. It worked to soothe my frustration, and later I was always thankful that he guided me away from the ledge of that impulse.

By the time his work was finished, there were always more bumps around the braids than in them.

Every time, I would chuckle at the sight of how silly I looked in the mirror. He would laugh too, in crashing waves so deep and rich. Flicking the bundled hair—more like frazzled rope—over my shoulders, soft lips would then find my cheeks.

"*Even my flimsy fingers cannot impose on your beauty,*" he once said into a kiss, just before eyes of liquid gold fell onto mine with such intent that I wondered if he were counting my eyelashes.

"*Never wilt, my flower,*" he stated next.

Now, those same eyes that were spun by the burning sun, the ones that hold trees in their speckles of brown, are just as Mona's was when I found her among the wreckage of Earth's descent.

Cold. Void.

In this moment, I wilt.

Such hypocrisy I have held to insist that he step down from his natural position; all to make him experience what it is like to have power stripped away.

Except my reason has been rooted in revenge, while his was from the influence of a growing, miserable blizzard ... and the will to keep living.

Tears drip, splatting across a still hand that once held mine. A strand of hair slips from my shoulder to touch him.

Now I know why Kysi disguised himself. Just as I refrained from striking Hellano on the balcony when I landed in the New World, he did not wish for his first appearance to be an act of violence. Instead of refraining like I did, he bypassed his moral code by stealing our friend's face and taking away a person's free will, so no one would witness him complete the act.

Breathy sobs fill the room, muffled against the surface of Hellano's vest as I fall apart against it. If my pain could reach the Spirits of the Sky, it would be loud enough to rattle the beds in which they lay.

Kysi simply stares, the revelation of my heartbroken response taking root within both of us.

Twice in just a few days, I have lost a man that I care for. And yes, I do still care for Hellano. I realize that now.

It was not easier the first time around.

What I have learned from this, is that time does not cease like I wish it would. It does, however, move at an insufferably slow pace ... as if to taunt me with the sheer distance of a future in which I *might* live happily without him.

My descent was the biggest opposition Hellano and I ever faced. Arguments in our past lingered from mere stubbornness, as I believe he thought this to be as well.

The bigger the push, the harder the fall.

Eventually, we would have reconciled. If not by romantic companionship, then friendship at the very least.

Because we were friends. Best friends. I never truly believed we would remain enemies, nor accepted the thought. Humored it, sure, but solely out of anger. Like impulsive words one wishes they could swallow after releasing ... I can think of three that I would give anything to take back.

I hate you.

"Angel," a soft voice pokes at the serpent of grief coiled within my lungs, "had your tears been expected I would never—"

"'Lano gained nothing from waking you," I bitterly intone. "He already wore the crown for a nation that accepted him as King."

Kysi does not move, lashes unblinking as his gaze flicks to the diadem that lay across scattered papers upon the workstation.

"*Don't* touch it," I warn. It matters little who he is to me now; no one so weak to impulses such as these shall rule in my territory. And right now, the only places I want that godsdamn crown is at my feet—shattered into a million pieces.

Balance becomes lost to Kysi as he teeters back, arms flying out to steady himself. Peering at what nearly tripped him, I see dense shadows—thick enough to give the illusion of solid matter—encasing his ankles in a vise. They crawl up the length of his calves, pinning his trousers against the sandy skin beneath.

"The fuck?" Kysi whispers to himself, battling against the restraints at his feet as well as the confusion in his mind.

The god of Afterlife's hand is barely lifted beside me, wrist twisted to face the god of Mortals and Bargaining. Piceous smoke seeps from it like leaking tar with a vengeful purpose. Darting to Hellano's once empty eyes, I find them overflowing with dissension.

The only time a phaser cannot teleport is if they are incapacitated—too ill or drunk to function—or trapped against the inescapable kiss of Death. Kysi is powerless now that the morbid smog has reached him, unable to avoid the inevitable defeat of my natural opposite.

297

Instinct lurches me forward to encase Hellano's body in my arms. "Don't 'Lano," I beg of him, "please."

The broad panes beneath me expand in a breath, and to my surprise, everything stills.

When the Sky Spirits accepted my request and granted him an additional six hundred years, they did so with the promise that he would receive it in full.

Standing in the walls of an impenetrable force, a caustic realization envelopes Kysi ...

Hellano cannot die.

A calmness blankets my private suite, although I can feel Kysi's presence in the way my skin pebbles upon entering. Darkness lay about, disrupted by the flicker of firelight through the double doors of the living room.

Tink goes ice against glass as my mate comes into view. Kysi sluggishly sips amber liquid—filled more than a finger digit deep—from a lowball. A lonely strand of hair sullenly drapes over a dark brow. It has been hours now that he has stayed up. Waiting.

I spent that time at Hellano's bedside in the shared chamber, watching and pacing as Meena worked with him. Progress has already been made, the range of motion returning in his hands and feet. The goddess of Pleasure believes that with regular healing sessions, Hellano will be walking in time for the festival.

The guards know nothing of the attack. I also refuse to tell them that their King has suddenly fallen ill. That excuse may make the kingdom look weak, having a sick ruler so soon after its birth. According to the palace, King Hellano simply has urgent and private matters that demand his attention.

Ice clinks together. "So, death comes for all but the embodiment of itself," Kysi speaks. "Irony is a poet."

Hovering in the threshold I ask, "What happened to you in sleep?"

Acknowledgement of the shift in his behavior is blatant on his expression, despite his attempts to conceal it. Inhaling deep, he begins. "I was trapped ... trapped in a singular, solitary piece of Divine Duplicity. Stuck within the portion of ourselves that only acts to fulfill a purpose. An endless labor, one that may have been tolerable had I not known sentience." The onyx band upon his index finger glistens against the flames while he tenses a hand, uncomfortable at the thought. "While I was there, amidst the inescapable duty of my other self, the knowledge of my lost life sought to drive me mad. Everything I wanted but never got," he says with an unwavering gaze upon me, "all the years I had left but would never receive—gone. Just memories remained ... mere reminiscences of a life wasted waiting for all that I longed for to fall into place. Regret, too. It was thick and hot, like molten sap. Suffocating. So much time spent staring from afar in the Ancient Library, time that I could have spent trying to connect with you, or visiting with Meena, *anything* but hovering and waiting like a ghost. I was a ghost for most of my life, until the inevitable sleep in which I had no choice in the matter. And when the mania of that entrapment threatened to consume me, it was your presence that pulled me from the fog of misery." Dull eyes brighten against the ginger waves of heat that warm the air. "I was a kite catching wind into the clouds of despair ... and you were the line that kept me grounded."

There is a pull in my diaphragm that coaxes me forward, urges me to comfort at the sight of his sunken shoulders ... but I remain still.

"In sleep I was stuck in the cage of a never-ending task, with memories of a man that lived a life meant to be *mine* ... and awake I am met with an even more horrendous continuation of that curse, one in which Hellano covetously fights to rid me of all that I live for. Stealing my mate for a second time, binding her to a deal she wants no part of. A deal that traps our kingdom—*my* people—under him. How can you blame me for my actions? How can you look at me like that, like I'm a stranger?"

I rip my gaze away then, blinking at the floor while contemplating a response. "Your feelings are valid Ky. The way you responded to them wasn't."

Kysi scoffs, running a hand through frazzled hair. "Please, Anewla. You cannot expect me to sit idly by and allow him to shove us into a fucking broom closet—allow him to reign over humans instead of *me*, their own god—"

Blood pulls into my cheeks. "That is exactly what I expect of you. Because Hellano has not harmed a single mortal soul, meanwhile you strip the mind of a man on your first day."

His remark is quick—a silent admission of guilt. "It was necessary for the cause. Hellano's death would have set us free, fixed everything!"

"Just as my descent was supposed to?"

Lips of muted terracotta purse at the question—struck. Tension swirls between us, thickening with each heartbeat that passes. "This disappointment of yours," voice deep and brittle, "this demeanor of hurt and betrayal, it all rests upon one simple fact that I was unaware of before. A single truth." A solid rod of suspense tethers our focus. "You still love him."

The look he gives is dizzying. It pushes into my soul as if to gather up my spirit and tuck it under a protective arm, away from the god of Afterlife. Away from the enemy. It yearns to be wrong, to be told that my heart could rest nowhere but the palm of his gentle hand.

I understand why he did it. If things were slightly different, if my feelings had remained in balance with my previous actions and thoughts, Kysi would not be seen as the villain. Instead, he would be a savior from the agreement that binds me, a noble King that conquered death for his people.

Kysi would have been a hero ... if the statement that lingers in the booming silence were not irrevocably true.

Behind taut features, a chasm of hurt stretches deeper with each fleeting moment his claim goes undenied.

When he steps forward, I track his movement. "Where are you going?"

Kysi shifts a shoulder to bypass me. "A walk."

A long-held breath escapes. This should not be the end of our conversation. "Ky—"

BUM goes the bedchamber door.

Pinching the bridge of my nose against a rising headache, I stand teetering on whether or not I should follow him. After all, a phaser on a stroll is like a bird crawling; something is obviously wrong for them to be doing so. When minutes tick by and I have yet to decide, I conclude that he is likely far within the palace walls by now.

My bed is barren and cold as I drift to sleep, the room quiet and still against the kindling fire that slowly dims into utter darkness. I try to wait for Kysi, but part of me is unsure if he will return at all.

A hopeful sensation of stirring sheets and a warm body meets me in a dream. The soft touch of my mate's skin as he nestles into my back, soughing words so soothing and sweet. "Forgive me, angel," sounds in the walls of my unconscious mind.

Nothing more than the faith of a future reconciliation.

The following days have been easier. Strained, against the stubbornness of my mate, but easier.

Aside from the contract binding Hellano to the throne, I have multiple reasons to accept him as King of the New World. Not only does this nation recognize him as such, but scheming to stage a coup would have lasting impacts on the health of our monarchy. As long as Hellano's reign remains benign, I have no real issue ruling beside him.

Kysi was less than amused when I placed him on the council as my official advisor, but he reluctantly obeyed. It is the closest solution to our predicament that I can muster; a role that involves working alongside the Queen in all aspects of her position. Not to mention that it serves to maintain the secrecy of our relationship. This way, no suspicion will arise at the sight of us often together.

Except we have not been together ... not much. When it is time to retire for the evening, Kysi states that he wishes to visit the districts and explore the kingdom. My efforts to accompany him have been useless, as he swiftly kisses my cheek and phases away before I have the chance to ask. Each morning, I find myself alone still, only to later spot him bustling about the castle—keeping busy.

Avoidance. That is all it boils down to.

"How are you?" I ask Mona through the boudoir mirror as Harlynn sticks pins around the budded diadem. It bloomed flowers of deep crimson this time, complimenting the matching gown that pours over my legs like a bleeding river.

"Fine, actually," she states while picking through the left rack. "My family is settled in Gourmara, although some have fallen victim to the conspiracy that they are living under the devil's rule." Eyes of deep brown flick to the powerful shade Harlynn donned me in today. "Other than that, all is well." She plucks a flaxen corset from the selection. "Can I wear this?"

"What's mine is yours," I respond.

Harlynn's focus darts from my friend to the line of clothes. With an anxious chuckle, she pats my shoulders as a silent 'all done' before shuffling over. "Perhaps not with that blouse, dear."

No offense is taken, just the raise of a brow as she watches the angel sift through silks and cottons to find the best alternative.

Twisting in the upholstered, velvet chair, I face Mona directly. "I'm sorry about your death."

She waves me off, accepting the ivory tunic Harlynn offers. "Considering how grim and broken Earth was in the end, I think I prefer to live where the air is always fresh, and the views are too pretty to capture in a painting."

"And your duty as head of Human Affairs, are you content with it? Kysi can absorb the position—"

"No, no. Keeps me busy. I need that, need to work. Been doing it since—"

"You were fourteen in your mother's café," I finish with a smirk. "Well, please, tell me if the New World is not suiting you and I will make whatever arrangements necessary."

"So fancy," she teases, stepping out from the divider with a content, smug expression.

Harlynn was right to suggest the billowy undershirt. There is something about wearing a friend's clothes that make outfits much more appealing. I would often feel just as confident after raiding Mona's closet back on Earth.

That feels like forever ago now.

"What about you?" she asks, patting herself down in front of the mirror.

My posture slackens. "Managing."

What more is there to say? Kysi is adjusting to his role slower than melting ice in a lingering winter, and Hellano—although much stronger than before—can hardly sit upright without support, according to Meena.

I have made efforts to visit him every day since the incident, but each time his eyes were heavy if not closed entirely. The healing sessions take a toll on Hellano's energy, but nonetheless, Meena claims that he works with stubborn ardency. Great improvements are made each day.

"Your beauty is devastating," a modulated voice drifts into the closet. "That ring really ties it all together, don't you think Harlynn?"

Fashioned in black from head to toe, Kysi wears a buttoned shirt with rolled up sleeves, tucked neatly into trousers an even darker shade of night.

My assistant clears her throat. "It certainly does not go against my choice of style."

Waving a hand at the extravagant materials, he says, "How kind of you to say." Shifting to me once more, he bows with the stature of a true professional. "My Queen."

I stand, walking to meet him at the threshold. "You know you don't have to act that way around them."

"I am aware, my love. Just ... practicing," he replies with forced optimism. "We—or rather, *you*—are needed in the throne room. I assume my duties as advisor include accompanying you to these events, yes?"

"That would be correct." I take his hand in mine, coaxing his green eyes to brighten. "When you think about it, you're basically ruling beside me—just *secretly*." I wiggle my eyebrows in hopes that a smile will come of it.

He humors me with a quirk of a grin. "A secret King ... what could go wrong?"

It is rather crowded in the palace today. Employers from each city have arrived to present the names of their businesses, along with a gift, in hopes that Hellano and I will visit their establishment on our journey through the districts on the day of the Spring Festival.

Kysi briefly explained the New World's economic system on our way to the throne room. I should not be surprised, given all the other transformations the Sky Spirits made, but I am regardless.

I open my palm to Kysi's outstretched hand as we walk. Vitric platinum, gold, and baby blue pieces clink together as they fall into my grasp. Like flat marbles, they are delicate and transparent, shimmering without the need for a light source.

"They call them soul shards, as their unique nature reminds angels and demons of how their spirits used to linger in bubbles such as these," Kysi states, leaning in with a low tone. "I found mountains of them under the palace."

Dropping the shards in the hidden pocket of my dress, I whisper, "You were just able to *walk* in?" Not that I have a problem with my mate accessing the royal fortune. But if he stumbled across them so easily, perhaps it means the castle could use an upgrade on security.

"Not to worry," he reassures, "I found Cato and ran some tests. *I* can enter through the thick slab of door or phase in. He can do neither. I assume the same law applies to you, and whoever else the Sky Spirits deem worthy enough."

Surely, the Spirits of the Sky made no mistake in their choice of who gets to enter the treasury. Still, a layer of unease prickles my arms at the lack of knowing.

Although fresh air circulates throughout the throne room, the atmosphere is heavy against the multitude of eyes that land between the tall oak doors on either side of me. A sudden silence cuts through the commotion, leaving nothing but the whisper of wind in its wake. If I were able to inhale, only one breath would pass before their heads dip low into deep bows—and there they stay.

Unmoved, like statues they remain. Waiting. It is not the crowd that locks me in a cage of angst this time, but what lies beyond the cloudy marble beneath us.

Towering sequoias stretch through an open ceiling, a clear sky peaking through the canopy of leaves. Sun beams slip through the branches, casting rays across magnificent seats carved—no, *grown*—into the bodies of the trees. A room beautifully crafted by the Sky Spirits, if not for the one stain upon their handy work that sends my stomach into a summersault.

To the left, under a dark shadow, is a third tree. It appears ... burned. As if the moment Hellano stole Kysi's crown, it disrupted the natural growth and forced the New World to try again—make one anew.

Three trees, the light neglecting the crisp, blackened one—like trying to cover up a mistake.

Kysi's presence is what grants me the courage to step forward, my heels *click clacking* upon the reflective pool of stone as I pass. Birds chirp within the trees. A serpent scurries across the protruding roots at the base of the throne.

As I ascend the dais with my secret lover just behind, I think about how in another life, another universe, we might be meeting these seats—two, instead of a third donning the room with a nasty scar—hand in hand with matching smiles and diadems.

The throne greets me like a pet to a master, its mighty trunk shivering with anticipation. Not the kind of hum noticeable by peers, no. Only the embodiment of life could sense a behavior so subtle. An excitement.

It is layered with a pad of moss that releases an earthy fragrance the moment I nestle into the alcove of wood—wet leaves and morning dew, mixed with the fresh wildflowers of spring.

My back is warm against it, the heat of sunlight swimming through the phloem like a creek at the pinnacle of summer. As I run my hand over the smooth arm, I notice a shy friend peeking their tiny head over the armrest.

Kysi cannot accompany me in this, cannot sit beside me in the matching throne to the right but instead is forced to stand on the sideline. Due to Hellano's physical state, he is unable to take the place next to me as well. So, I extend a finger of invitation to the serpent, coaxing it to slide across my hand and join me ... just so I do not have to sit before all of these people alone.

Similar to how the god of Mortals and Bargaining can force his will upon humans, I yield the same power to animals. But it is love that forbids me from doing so, as the snake's timid personality suggests it may not wish for a place in the spotlight. Just as my other children are given the same benefit, the serpent has the choice to decline.

There is a brief hesitation, but my little friend rallies the courage to obey. Scales glide between my fingers in a loving embrace, just before their petite head tucks bashfully under my palm.

If this tiny reptile can be brave, then so shall I.

My focus shifts once more to the bending figures before speaking, "You may rise."

There is no shortage of work in the districts, as businessmen and women continued to name their establishments and gifts long throughout the day. Harlynn labored with efficiency below the dais, organizing their offerings into categories and subcategories. Renwick, Hellano's assistant, ushered each citizen forward in turn.

Although the throne was rather snug, my back is stiff as well as bottom sore. Surely, Kysi's feet ache all the same. Having explored the cities more thoroughly than I within the last few days, he offered suggestions here and there on the more unique and practical places to visit on the day of the festival, stating which ones would be ideal given their location and services.

Museums at the Gallery Enclave, followed by dinner in Gourmara. Then, the celebration will continue in the city that specializes in parties, Revelry Row.

Hellano is awake now, back resting against the cherrywood bed frame. His smile is a slash of white as I place a basket over his paralyzed legs; berries and fresh bread for us to share ... just like before.

"Think I still got it?" he asks, twisting a blueberry between his index and thumb.

The question ignites a scoff. "I doubt it."

Hellano tilts his wrist back, aiming. "Open wide, then."

Rolling my eyes, I oblige. Mouth agape from the grin it just held, pearls of sweet honey peer upon me with the memories of our old playful game. Hellano used to land shots from across the room like they were nothing, but he is out of practice and recovering now.

When the berry bounces off my cheek, I cannot help but laugh.

"It's these arms," he says with a chuckle, "still don't have full control of them."

"Alright," I respond, moving a few inches closer. "Try again."

A sweet expression becomes him, with the hint of something more. After plucking a raspberry from the basket, he motions with a slow, tantalizing finger. "Come a little closer, flower."

The request would bring me to arm's reach, but I comply, nonetheless.

After lifting the fruit to prepare another toss, Hellano's gaze snags to my open mouth. Throat bobbing with a nervous swallow, the drupelet never takes flight. Instead, an arm stretches out to me.

The brush of his thumb is soft against my bottom lip as a cold cluster of beads falls over my tongue, begging to be savored. Just as his expression does at this moment, thumb idly tracing a line while holding my chin up. There is a hidden sadness behind the gold in his gaze, but on the surface lies a firm longing.

"Oh, how I have missed you, my flower," he utters, hand moving with such slowness as it cups my face. "The touch of your skin, the waves of your hair ... my remaining lifespan shall be used to cherish these features like a holy tome to a man of new faith."

With a sad smile, I withdraw. "When did you become a poet?"

"The day you fell," Hellano claims without hesitation, "because that day ... I fell too."

CHAPTER 24

To signify the connection between our opposing titles, Hellano and I are to be fashioned in black and white today. Personally, I would prefer to wear a dress made of vines and flowers to the Spring Festival, but I suppose painting the picture of a healthy, unified kingdom is not something worthy of complaint.

Kysi leans against the full-length mirror before me, watching as Harlynn pins another section of my bleached tunic to the dark corset fit snugly over it.

She is adamantly determined to prevent the fabric from rustling and becoming sloppy during our escapades through the districts, despite my efforts to explain that it would matter little.

"Remember," the angel says, "you are engaged. Your public interactions with the King should reflect that. So, try to act like you love him."

Kysi makes no effort to stifle his huff.

If thoughts could be seen, my eyes would have rolled back far enough to witness the image of my annoyance. "Harlynn, would you give us a moment please?"

With the click of her tongue, she responds, "We have a strict schedule today, Your Majesty. I just have a few more pins—"

"Five minutes"—I throw her a sympathetic glance— "please."

Sighing causes a thin strand of yellow to fall from behind her ear. "Oh, alright ... five minutes." With a quick bow, she makes for the door.

So much willfulness in such a little body, that woman.

I blow out a breath, wiping invisible dust from the corset. "That black band"—nodding to his hand— "where did you get it?"

Peering down in question, Kysi twists the piece of jewelry. "It was a parting gift from your predecessor. I never take it off."

That day in the throne room, a bald man from the Row offered me an elaborate carcanet of topaz and peridot. It was breathtaking, just like the jewels attached to his ears, lips, eyebrows, and nose.

It was not easy finding Cato. After pointlessly searching the library, I decided to sit and wait for him in the hidden annex. He phased me to the man's home during midday when Revelry Row is at its quietest. I felt bad for waking the demon but luckily, he was not put off by my interruption in the slightest.

I talked with Hugo for a while before requesting his services. Excitement and pride made his jeweled face sparkle at the thought of crafting for the Queen's 'special friend'. It took him only a day to finish, and although he did not wish for payment, I ensured that he was generously reimbursed.

Stepping from the circular pedestal, I meet the drawer of my boudoir and pull. A quaint box stares back, patiently waiting just where I left it. Retrieving the gift, I close in on my mate. "It's a good thing I got you one to match—sort of." Raising the little cube of carved wood draws his attention. "Open it."

A handsome grin emerges alongside a questioning look. After taking it, the box opens with a pop.

Laying on a bed of moss is a carefully crafted band of obsidian. There is a demarcation of gold interrupted by speckles of emerald, blurring the division between saffron and black.

Kysi's tangled mood flakes away at the sight. "If you missed me, you could have just said so," he teases, pulling me closer. "You're not worried someone will notice the similarities between ours?"

My shoulders shrug. "Coincidences happen."

Although our rings have similar colors, I designed his in a way that does not call for a second look. Only one peering closely at them would notice how they complement each other.

"Our bond is unbroken because I made it so," I remind, "and I would do it over and over again to keep it—keep you."

A warm knuckle grazes mine as I slide it over his finger. It fits just as well as our hands do when we hold them; our arms when we embrace; our lips when we kiss.

Just to prove it, I push off my heels and connect with his mouth.

A palm presses against the side of my head, arm spanning between my wings and up my back to pull me firmly against his sculpted frame. To be close again after weeks of separation—aside from quick kisses and loose hugs—heats my face. The forest-green fabric of his shirt wrinkles against my grip as I reciprocate the pull.

Coalescing like clouds in a coming storm, our soul tie responds to the fortnight without affection. It weaves our spirits as if in fear that it may lose the other side of itself, may be without it for hundreds of years once more. To part would be painful, but somehow Kysi finds the strength.

"I am this close to ruining Harlynn's handiwork," he sensually intones.

A chuckle erupts. "She is the only one that would mind."

As if summoned by the end of a timer, footsteps approach; light ones that could only belong to a blonde-haired ball of planners and tight schedules.

The door swings open and her eyes go wide. "Your *hair*! Oh, Anewla, how could you let this happen? Hurry, hurry, sit. I can fix you. *You*"—she glares daggers at my advisor— "out!"

Massive chatter vibrates through the windows as I stride down the ornate hall on the second floor. Frazzled nerves forbid me from looking, but my curiosity demands to know how many eyes will be facing me once we step out into the open air.

A horrifying number, it appears.

A sea of heads, all murmuring with excitement as they peer towards the imperial staircase overlooking the courtyard. The sight tenses my clammy hands as I whip my focus forward, attempting to blink away the agoraphobia.

It only serves to flash the image in my mind repeatedly—the way their crowded bodies cascade down the hill into the Capital. If any souls linger inside their homes, I can only assume it is due to the same issue I am forced to face. Except in my case, I am the main attraction—the ant under a magnifying glass, this kingdom the eye observing my every movement, every follicle of hair clinging to my shoulders as if it too is panicked.

The King of the New World comes into view from below, craning his neck to absorb those frightened strands. Hellano winces at the turn, still sore from the assault but otherwise in perfect health. Under a vest as dark as soot, he wears a tunic whiter than a dove.

"Gods, Anewla. You're as pale as a sheet," he says with concern.

"I'm fine." But my voice implies otherwise. As I descend onto the first floor, the council comes into view behind the King.

They will accompany us as members of the royal court, their crucial roles demanding an official presence. Having my friends nearby today is a relief. Their mere proximity slightly lulls my heart rate.

All nod except one, who cannot pull focus from the back of Hellano's head. Spinning my gift over his finger, Kysi seems to be reminding himself of our sacred bond—or, attempting to. Given the tight lips and set jaw, I can only imagine the hateful thoughts underneath those wisps of onyx hair.

Vile roach, likely one of them.

I meet my opposite at the door with a nervous swallow. Heavy palaver ensues beyond it, inducing a tremor in my knees. Breathing becomes a challenge, and for some reason—out of everyone in this room—I look to Harlynn for help. Someone so put together must know what to do.

She sucks in air, giving me a silent order to mimic. My inhalation is ragged, but I manage to complete it. With the wave of her petite hand, she motions for me to step closer to the King.

Act in love—right. Be a couple.

When Hellano takes my hand and places it into the warm crease of his arm, it calms the tempest in my muscles. I latch on and squeeze his bicep to remain steady.

Harlynn and Renwick both reach for the bulky handle of the fortress doors, light splitting through the widening crack. It is a test to smile against the crescendo of celebration.

"Don't let me fall, 'Lano," I beg. Nothing would trigger a deep isolation more than embarrassing myself in front of the entire city. While my attention rests frozen upon the wisteria-lined railing of the staircase, there is a shift in my peripheral.

Pearls of hazel gaze at my profile. "Never again," he promises, guiding me into a step.

I have Hellano to thank for doing the majority of socializing. Outgoing and a sucker for attention, he drinks in the smiles and distracts the people from me as much as possible. Each question he asks them while we trek through the courtyard is genuine, curious.

What is your name? What do you do? Is there anything you need here?

Most do not have an answer to the last one, but the few that do are listened to with intent. Renwick pencils their words to the side, absorbing each sentence like a sponge for Hellano to study later.

Glancing around, I find Mona and Meena together. They introduce themselves with grace, but some sideways glances do not go unnoticed.

Not for the fact that they are both women, but because a goddess with divine beauty holds the hand of a mere human.

Come to think of it, no marriage between different species has occurred in the New World to my knowledge thus far.

Perhaps my friends can one day make history.

Kysi shakes hands with a mortal woman, who fawns over his every mannerism. Those around her are captivated as well, as if glamour is not needed for humans to naturally gravitate towards their god.

Every time I look forward, I can feel his gaze upon me.

Upon us.

Cato and Luther chat as well, although the former appears rather uncomfortable to be so far away from books.

The first order of business the god of Wisdom has enacted is the collection of scribes for the purpose of distributing knowledge throughout the kingdom, thus making it easier to access. Original copies are never to leave the labyrinth of shelves—they *can't*.

But there is no rule against copying them.

"*Learning is a right*," he had said when presenting me with the idea. As if I would ever dream of refusing.

There are plenty of prying questions regarding the King and Queen's upcoming nuptials. Hellano casually responds to the latest one by tucking me into his side and claiming that a honeymoon is a luxury we sacrifice so our precious denizens can indulge in such vacations without worry, for as long and as often as they would like. It is the same answer I would have given, although delivered with an unmatched elegance.

Every corner of the Gallery Enclave is teeming with unique merchandise. People display detailed paintings right off the main walk, as well as intricately molded pottery and stylish apparel. All is eye-catching, each article demanding attention.

Hellano keeps a tight grip on my hand, pointing with his other at the items he wishes to purchase. Not for the sake of materialism, but to support the individual artists.

Gourmara is not so welcoming this time around.

The divide between supporters and skeptics has evened out over the last two weeks—for what reason, I cannot say. Many do not celebrate, but leer from afar as if the breeze is putrid.

Only I can see the way it pangs Hellano. He offers a sweet smile after I squeeze his hand in comfort.

Dinner is served under a veranda of trumpet vines. Tiny bulbs of baby blue twinkle between the ginger flowers, brightening with the setting sun. Venison falls apart over my tastebuds, melted butter swimming in a smokey sauce. Nothing short of exquisite ... Kysi advised well.

Food in the New World holds flavor like clouds before a dangerous rain, the meats richer and pastries sweeter than anything Earth could offer. Hellano serves me bites from his plate: risotto mixed with wild forged mushrooms. As we laugh through mouthfuls of intoxicating cuisines, I find myself studying the way his skin reflects the sienna ambience.

Out of all the glances thrown our way, all the staring I battle to ignore, Kysi's is the hardest to move past. I am unable to directly see his lingering eyes as the council eats around us, but I can feel them. The way they glide down my back, over my arms, landing on a teardrop over a gold band.

The prick even takes credit for that, I imagine he thinks.

When we arrive at the Row, it is as if night has come alive. Lanterns sway over the cobblestone path and neon lights illuminate through the glass of music shops and tattoo parlors, all open to the crowded streets.

Many take notice of the King and I as we stride through, though they do not balk. Perhaps it is their drunkenness, or the guards that follow from a distance that keep them away. But I would not be surprised if the city was too enchanting to miss for long.

When the god of Afterlife pulls me into his side, I tell myself—have been telling myself since this morning—that it is just for show. To uphold the ruse of an engagement forged without ultimatums, but one crafted from love and devotion, along with the first mutual purpose between our souls: ruling a kingdom.

Every road sings a different tune. From rhythmic jazz to bumping percussions, all energies and tastes are accommodated for. Hellano veers left, leading our group into an alley of twirling bodies. Music echoes in the petite square, bouncing off the windows of void apartment homes.

When the King pivots and lifts my hand—his own settling at the base of my spine—I am hesitant to participate. Although the cacophony of Revelry Row eases the edges of my frayed nerves, I still have no desire for exposure.

"Picture us like before—if it helps," he says while taking the first step into a waltz.

The suggestion sends me back to a time when all the comfort in the Heavens laid within the confines of his arms.

I take his advice to maintain the mirage of our romantic duality.

Dancing did not come to us naturally. It took decades to successfully avoid stepping on each other's toes and stumbling into walls and furniture. Every blunder was followed by laughter, and all the missteps were blamed on our opposite nature. We never gave up on the challenge; perpetually determined to conquer asynchronization together.

Now, we flow like moonlight over rippling water. The ebb of our spinning feet picks up where they left off, as if the last eight years were nothing but a bad dream. It is impossible to keep my imagination from drifting, from pretending that our nightly traipse was never interrupted by a grievous bargain ... that our love was not catastrophic enough to invoke such a deal.

It seems his thoughts have drifted alongside mine, because as I lay my head upon his relaxing shoulder, he says, "It's different this time—my love for you. Not crowded behind coldness but smothered in warmth. My soul may be whole now ... but I could never be complete without you."

There is a flutter that rages against a tight band around my heart; a lingering love for Hellano at odds with the bond tying me to another. I yearn to respond, even if I am unsure how.

Out of respect for my mate, I remain passive.

Prompted by the transition of a beating anthem, a mortal child lunges toward us. A wide grin—spacious between missing teeth—displays giddy excitement. Just like her eyes as they meet mine.

Another fists the collar of her shirt, hauling her back to the sidelines. Surely concerned the child would be a bother, the guardian whispers reprimanding words that sink the girl's expression into a pitiful visage.

The notion that any person should think twice about approaching us is a seed that must not sprout. Not here—not in the heaven I made for them.

Remembering this morning, I think of Meena and Mona. Multiple withheld a censorious condemnation at the sight of their affection—a glorious goddess with a common human. My friend is beautiful in her own right, but I suspect the contrast between mortal and divine beauty matters little against the belief that our species should not intertwine.

One of the few things I disliked on Earth; society would always waver in the face of new concepts. Push against it.

But I shall never circumvent my past or blur the truth. Their Queen once scrubbed the cupboards of that human's home; one she so graciously allowed me into.

Hellano is left behind when I advance across the square. Tiny, almond-shaped eyes lift at the sight of my oncoming frame. The pointillism of freckles patterns her face, little legs zealously fidgeting.

I bend and level with the girl, who appears no older than seven. "King Hellano has found himself tired, which means I am in need of a new partner. Would you mind?"

A giggle erupts. "No, your High Knees."

A smile spreads as her guardian nudges her from behind. "Oh!" she exclaims before offering a curtsy, conforming to royal etiquette. I copy the stance, then walk with her into a pocket of space.

Standing to the side, Hellano's expression is one of pride. It leaves a sinuous grin in its wake.

The girl shuffles below me, unfazed by her own incoordination and unforgiving in her sense of self. I envy the way my lack of a childhood kept me from experiencing the world through rose-colored glasses.

Perhaps I could try; catch a glimpse of it through her.

A boisterous cackle bubbles from the child's throat when I mimic the silly movements. Together we twirl, her auburn curls swaying against the breeze of our spins.

Amidst the freedom of our dance, I wonder if one day that authentic part of herself will pass on. Do children grow up in the New World, or are they encapsulated in bodies left in the previous realm?

A blessing and a curse it would be, if so. Only time will tell what the Sky Spirits have decided.

The song comes to an end, and we resume the statures of proper ladies—a stark contrast from the wacky two-step. The girl's euphoria is contagious, forbidding my smile to escape long after my chuckles are contained.

The surrounding space is scarce. Revelers have halted to bear witness to this unlikely pair.

Unaffected by the attention, the girl smiles and bows like we are the end of a groundbreaking performance. Through blush lenses, I bend alongside her.

To my surprise, the applause is deafening.

With a face brighter than gloss under the sun, the child scurries away. Max capacity returns to the center square as the celebration continues, this time with frequently switching partners. Someone snags my inner elbow, sweeping me into the commotion.

Their presence is not overbearing now but reserved in judgement. Having no knowledge of when my fright will reawaken in panic, I take advantage of fear's vacancy and embrace freedom.

Humans and angels and demons become a dizzying array of acceptance. It feels as though we have done something—the girl and I. Brought these beings together. It may not extend to the rest of the New World, or even the Row, but in this little courtyard ... a good seed was planted.

A familiar muscle loops in my arm. "How 'bout a private dance?" Kysi's voice is a whisper against the booming music, only reaching my ears.

Tilting my chin, I ask, "How do you plan to manage that?"

His jaw is cut with an insatiable need. "Two blocks over. Meet me in the theater."

Like a church bell muffled by thundering skies, caution pangs in the depths of my psyche. However, the adventurous part of myself trudges on—pushes me to indulge in forbidden kisses.

Every individual I danced with had twinkling irises, reflections from the strung lights above. Kysi lacks this trait, eyes enhanced with a vibrancy that would mirror nothing. When I nod in agreement, their radiance breaches low-hanging lashes.

When we unlink to switch partners, Kysi's amorous demeanor shifts to friendly as he greets the next person with a handsome smile. A single streak of black hair kisses his forehead, button down shirt rustled from the busy day.

If the theater could sing, it would be a siren song.

Through the twists and turns of the capering group, I find Hellano roaring with laughter. Cato chuckles beside him, white hair lacking volume as if it is the only part of him fatigued. They will surely be here a while, enjoying the performance.

Passing Mona at the corner of the alley, I mumble, "Off to ... get advised." Just in case someone needs to find me.

She snorts. "Yeah, okay."

The sky opens to a cloud of glittery fuchsia and indigo, painting the scintillating galaxy like an art piece from the Enclave. Despite consistently emerging with sparkling billows of color, the overhead night never offers the New World the same picture as before.

Beneath it lies a grand amphitheater, swarthy with inactivity against the bustling city. Perhaps the only setting unoccupied, untouched.

Because who would sit and watch a play on a night like this, or any night in Revelry Row for that matter? No, no—the stage is meant for daylight, when citizens want entertainment without the hustle.

Deep scarlet curtains drape from pillars above; two on opposing sides, with private rooms at their ends to hide props and actors. It is a stage that can be perceived from many different angles. A centerpiece to the Row.

Given the festival, I would assume reaching the stage unnoticed would be a challenge, but the surrounding area lacks activity. Almost as if forgotten.

After ascending the perron adjoining a private room, the door clicks shut at my back. Gloomy is the air that teases silhouettes of dead streetlamps and benches.

Not a sound pierces the space, only the distant hum of revelers.

Beyond the ingress to the stage lay a forest of oak trees. Their bodies are capricious, allowing a wide berth between each spine. No doubt perfectly placed for the opening scene of tomorrow's show, so the audience will not miss a single action.

Above, however, their branches mingle. Burned yellow peeps through the verdant canopy. If the power of life were foreign to me, these detailed sculptures may have convinced me they were real.

A rumble disrupts the quiet woods, cascading through the synthetic bark like a howling wind. "What an impeccable ... *performance* you have given today."

Pristine dress shoes clack over the polished floorboards as Kysi steps forward, untouched by gaiety.

I cross my arms, defensive. "You heard Harlynn this morning."

His teeth are bright against the ebony atmosphere, mouth curling into a caustic grin. "Ah, yes. '*Try to act like you love him.*'" The distance between us shrinks like the subject of a bully. "But you don't need to try, do you? Nor act."

My feet remain firmly planted. "Is that why you called me here, to argue?"

A tiresome sigh escapes. "No, my angel. That is not why I asked you to come." With only a hand's width between us, my mate slackens at the sight of my coiling attitude. "But does admitting jealousy make me the bad guy?"

Just like that, the sight of his internal struggle and heartache melts any ounce of annoyance. Hooking a finger through a belt loop, I pull him against me. "I think it makes you honest."

A deep and penetrating gaze strips me bare. "Honesty," he says, focus flicking to my parted lips. "An important trait for bonded souls, yes?"

I look down with thickening dejection. Kysi wishes for me to be truthful—hash out the issue of my resurfaced fondness for Hellano and figure out what it means moving forward.

The pressure of that conversation is not what bothers me, but rather his doubt in the depth of my devotion.

My connection to Kysi is like the relentless pull of a river's current. Different from Hellano's that is stubborn and deep, like a boulder rooted in solid ground.

One of them moves me, the other I cannot move.

But it is the flow of Kysi that I follow, let sweep me in the glaucous pool of his idolatry. It is hard to imagine anything else, has been since submerging myself in its silky caress. The water rages when we part. Angry and spiteful, as if we have stolen its birthright. But near—near it settles like a soothing babe, calm and content. A place you could float in for eternity.

Saying goodbye to Hellano will feel like choking on barbed wire, but I fear it must be done. The public appearances shall go on, but not in a way that blurs the lines of what is real. Hellano will understand, I am sure ... if I ask it of him.

Kysi's attention swings behind my arm, where a wing grazes my elbow. It takes a moment to make out the cascading rainbows against the dull room. Their appearance softens the rigid line of his back, shoulders sinking like branches relieved of heavy snow.

Soft lips catch mine when he dips low. Together they embrace with a loosening grip on patience, the need for proper intimacy shoving its way to the forefront of our desire.

Like spirits to a drunkard, I drown in myself in the tender waters of Kysi's touch. Deeper I dive into the depths, my only connection to the surface in the grip that I hold at the nape of his neck.

Our bodies conform to one another with an aggressive arousal. Colorful feathers hug artificial wood as Kysi pins me to an oak, his solid form looming at my front. A hardening mass teases my center through the barrier of cotton and polyester. His feverish mouth heats my every pore, and through them an addictive tongue is lively with deprivation—identical to the broad chest pounding against my forearm.

His steel length buries between my covered thighs. "I could take you right now," Kysi growls.

"What's stopping you?" I breathe, eager to continue.

Now, in the confines of his arms—that soothing river—a dry breeze catches my hair. It pulls me to the surface against my will, towards the break of daylight.

But dawn is many hours away ...

I lift my lashes to see him clear as the morning sky, expression softened with guilt; conflict stirring behind bee-stung lips and taut brows.

"Honesty," he admits.

Past the onyx strands of his hair hang bulbs of light. Subtle, but bright enough to reveal everything under the blanket of green overhead.

A bashful wind picks up once more, guiding a shining curl off my shoulder. It pulls my focus along with it ... straight past the raised curtains and into the overwhelming, silent crowd.

What humans do not gawk at the unfaithful Queen blink away a haze, only to follow suit shortly after.

Was it truly our separation that aggravated the bond between my mate and I, or was it instead battling the future—this moment—knowing the damage that would ensue, the scar it would leave upon us?

The night of our first fight, I dreamt that he came to bed and asked for forgiveness. Now I know that was, in fact, real. Except the apology was not meant for the disagreement hours prior, but what he planned to do. This ... expose the lie.

"Our King!" a human proclaims. "The true King!"

Uproars of retribution, of righting the giant *wrong* that has stained this realm, echo through the theater on all sides.

Trapped in this scene of infidelity, it occurs to me that Kysi's question of honesty between bonded pairs was not directed at me, but himself.

The truth of his actions settles in me like drying cement. Those nights 'exploring' the New World were in fact spent pushing the conspiracy of a devil king and rallying his people to appear at this very moment.

Kysi could only manipulate mortals to arrive here, but what better way to gather other beings than to collect a faithful crowd, one that would undoubtedly incite curious revelers to follow for the sheer possibility of being entertained.

And they have been given the ultimate show.

This display solidifies the fallacy of Hellano's satanic nature, which could still be dealt with had Kysi not painted himself as the savior he so blatantly wishes to be. But why? Is it so important for him to rule that he would take it by force? Would this greed remain if only I held power, or does he do this solely because it is his enemy that I reign beside?

The division this will cause—the consequences ... it tramples the good seed I planted mere moments ago.

Only when I attempt to flee do I notice the resurrection of my buzzing nerves. They rebel against my mental command to run and hide, refusing to rid me of this literal spotlight.

If not for the frost in my bones, I may have collapsed upon finding the council wide-eyed and still near the alley I snuck away from.

At their center, Hellano absorbs the image of my flushed skin; the way Kysi remains firmly against me, shirt disheveled and hair just the same.

Then, the arms imprisoning me tighten as Kysi pulls me into the void of teleportation.

CHAPTER 25

Eggplant cushions surround a solid mass of quartz, its surface veiny with shimmering gold. The space is cluttered with wealth, goblets and shards peeking from under sofas and side tables. One holds a crystal decanter filled with liquid bronze; identical to what Kysi sipped the day he snapped Hellano's neck.

Whether he found it here during the hours I paced at his enemy's bedside or brought it sometime after our argument, I cannot say. Either way, its presence sends a message of isolating intoxication.

My mate winces when we part, palming a shoulder. After taking a breath to collect himself, a ringed hand lowers to reveal scorch marks burned through the smooth fabric of his shirt.

"Feisty," he says, shaking off the pain. "I expected as much."

I squint at Kysi's audacity. Hurting him was unintentional, though my anger pushes against the thought. "You betrayed me."

The response is quick and snippy. "Apologies for not rolling over and submitting like a dog, *Your Majesty*. That was what you expected, after all." I trail him sauntering about, the treasury coming into full view.

Kysi was not exaggerating when he said mountains of soul shards lay under the palace. Behind him they pile high like walls in a maze, gemstones and jewelry poking through the faint glow of currency. There is no need for lanterns or chandeliers; their lazy light collectively wards off shadows. In the distance, weapons line the marble wall. Daggers and spears, bows and short swords that crisscross. The air is cool and sterile. Dustless and new.

One would think such opulence would be exempt from messiness, but this place feels like a hoarding dragon's lair.

Pop goes the tips of my fingers at Kysi's words, vexation tugging at the leash of my dwindling patience. "Greed steals the riches of men," I spit. "You've taken your people at the expense of a unified world, but is it worth the cost—worth *me*?"

His set jaw twitches. "Nothing is worth more—"

"Then WHY?"

A heartbeat of silence passes before Kysi bends, snatching an item from the crowded quartz table. "Because of this!"

At the end of his outstretched arm is a diadem darker than tar, with curling waves ascending from the base. With a defeated shrug, I ask, "And what is that?"

"Hellano's crown."

This confession makes me hesitate. Hearing Kysi insinuate that Hellano is meant to be a king comes as a shock, knowing how much he wishes to see that man suffer. My astonishment is short lived, however, overshadowed by frustration that exits in a grunt.

Rearing back, I kick a black circlet across the untidy floor. "Look around! This room is filled with fancy headbands and expensive junk!"

"Not like this one, *none* are like this one," he claims. "It is my crown that he currently wears—that he *stole*. Your *king* has been lying this entire time, just to continue standing in the life *I* was meant to lead."

Kysi is not falling into mania, but stubbornly descending—consciously taking every downward step. Glancing at the glistening treasures, I find too much. Sparkling dresses upon headless figures and rings only fit for the strongest of hands, this saferoom has it all. Someone desperate to find a solution is bound to subconsciously conjure up the answer in a place that has everything.

But that would still not justify the secrecy. Our conversation that night in my private suite determined his course of action. After ordering him to stand down and silently admitting my love for his nemesis, Kysi knew I would take no part in his plan to separate this realm. Fully aware that my wishes exclude division in the New World, he continued with the objective anyway.

"Get out."

The soul bond quakes against the silence following my command, like a taut rope threatening to snap.

Denial grips Kysi. "Don't say that—"

"Leave the castle. Do not return until you have brought peace back to my world."

Faded green hovers upon me in a heartbreaking stare. "Was it *ever* meant to be ours?"

There are many responses swimming in my mind, the biggest being that I had no knowledge he would wake from stasis changed. *My* mate lacked the selfishness it would take to harm an entire kingdom out of jealousy. He was willing to do anything just to have me but can no longer settle on what he spent centuries hoping for.

That quivering tether between us vibrates with pressure. This moment feels like a busy highway to a foreign visitor—dangerous and impossible to navigate.

Just like before, the right words never come to me.

The visage of heavy anguish upon his face awakens the deepest part of myself. It is a piece lacking boundaries and self-respect, concerned with nothing but finding a way back under the passion of his kisses again and the loving space between his arms.

A human psychologist once explained that ego is like a man on horseback. Although the animal is superior in strength, the rider is responsible for controlling it. That is all this yearning part of me is—just a horse getting spooked.

Kysi's throat bobs with a swallow. "Goodbye, Anewla."

The crack in my heart is a roaring whip of thunder when he blinks out of sight.

The seat to my right is void in the council chamber. Kysi's absence is unsettling, despite how much I was expecting it.

Cato has buried himself in the Ancient Library, so lost to us that the message of this meeting never made it to him at all.

Meena complains about his lack of attendance. "That man will be with me one second and gone the next," she says. "He does it at the most random times, but almost *always* when I need his assistance the most. Would've been nice to have his guidance after Hellano's attack, but I was left high and dry."

The god of Wisdom is a natural recluse. I understand the way social situations can become a bit overstimulating. When your purpose pulls you in one direction, it is a call nearly impossible to deny. But this behavior cannot continue, his position here is far too valuable.

"I'll speak with him," I promise, "establish a proper line of communication somehow." Perhaps if I built a grand library full of copied texts in the palace, he would stick around more.

The events of my infidelity have traveled across the continent, leaving a wave of division in its wake. Businesses in Revelry Row have already begun shunning those in support of the god of Mortals and Bargaining, calling them 'anti-equalists' for their resistance against a balanced monarchy. Knowing the devastation Earth inhabits, these individuals believe our realm's equilibrium resides in the unity between myself and Hellano. They hold a moral obligation to protect their new way of life.

Those in support of Kysi are majorly human, though opposing species can be found in either group. Most believe the only true safety lies under their god's reign, especially after the pain Hellano and I caused in their earlier lives. For them, it is a matter of protection against our reckless sense of power.

"Gourmara is withdrawing, declaring themselves and everything to the west a new nation," Mona announces to my left. "The Kingdom of Groveheart."

"They have no power to do such things," Hellano states. "We should station troops in the city, remind them that *claiming* independence does not automatically grant it to them."

Meena chimes in next. "It would only make matters worse. Tensions would rise, riots would follow—"

"The goal is to remain unified," the king retorts, "by any means necessary."

That statement hooks my attention across the pristine obsidian table. "Just what are you suggesting, we batter them into submission?"

Golden pearls stick to my frame. "I am only proposing that we resist *their* resistance."

Even if they claim otherwise, Kysi's followers are still my people. A ruler whose nation is forced into obedience is no ruler at all, but a tyrant. My failure to the New World is a gaping wound, but I cannot allow it to fester.

My distant mate's words echo from the previous night. "*Was it ever meant to be ours?*"

Not just mine and his, but everyone's.

My tone opposes debate. "If independence is what they seek, then we let them go."

Mind racing ahead, I can read the way Hellano feels this action will paint us as weak. Not just to the fresh neighboring kingdom but also the citizens that choose to remain. This is fine, I care not of mere *thoughts*. If Groveheart takes advantage of this mercy—withdrawing just to attack—then I will pass the god of Afterlife a big red button.

Hellano speaks of his desire to keep the New World together. Words teeming with patriotism, he expresses how everything would have stabilized had the god of Mortals and Bargaining not conspired against us. If only humans had the time to bear witness to Hellano's fairness, all would have been made well.

But Kysi wove the whispers of conspiracy through a wheel of deceit, all for his own personal gain.

"Continue your reign of kindness," I tell him. "Do not for one second display who they think you are. Time will bring truth; we must have patience."

With a nod he complies. "Yes, my Queen."

Fatigue pursues me in the following days like a ravished hellhound, giving chase at all hours but the night. Insomnia relieves the beast so it can rest, leaving me deprived of that very sleep.

Although my intentions are to serve *all* people of the New World, I no longer reign over it entirely. Bordering Groveheart now lays the Kingdom of Celestia, where Hellano and I rule.

Rumors circle the events of the Spring Festival. Some believe that I only stay in Celestia on behalf of Kysi; a pawn for him to rule both kingdoms. Others think I was manipulated on stage and physically violated, so he could further brainwash 'anti-equalists' and pave his path to power. Another idea, or rather a concern, is that I have yet to decide where my loyalties lie and may abandon this kingdom for the other.

Despite what each one believes, the majority of Celestians are tense with doubt at the thought of Hellano and I parting, worried that it would bring chaos to this realm as it has on Earth. In response to this, Harlynn has moved the royal wedding forward.

I am to marry in one week.

Thorne currently snoozes at my feet, a massive paw twitching in response to a dream. The wolf appeared unsummoned, his loyal nature hoping to aid me in these tiresome nights. But all I have received from this wholesome act is jealousy.

His snoring is envious.

Kysi must have come to bed in the weeks leading to his banishment, otherwise sleep would be possible to maintain. This trouble began his first night away, when I awoke to a foreign atmosphere. The skin of my back felt … confused. Like it lost something.

The sickness of solitude has worsened since.

Meena left for Groveheart hours ago, to work alongside her friend in his newfound position.

With her went Mona.

That was the real pang of heartache. Opening the bedchamber door to my friend in a qualm, her lover silently waiting in the distance, told me everything I needed to know.

I waited still, watching as Mona wrung her hands and stumbled over words, dodging the confession. After finally coming out with it to confirm my assumption, I had to pretend that it did not twist the dagger in my chest.

"*I would follow her in every lifetime*," she said with glossy eyes. "*Please understand.*"

The lump in my throat made it difficult to respond. All I could manage was a whisper as I pulled her close, soaking in our goodbye through her spirals of brown hair. "*Your heart could never anger me*," I promised. "*I owe it far too much.*"

That makes three gone. Four, if I count Cato's disappearance.

The god of Wisdom has not been seen since the festival days ago. I am beginning to think he left for Groveheart as well, taking with him copied texts so he can fulfill his purpose away from the Ancient Library.

My thoughts are interrupted by a furry companion jerking awake, legs kicking to get underneath his hefty body. I assume it is the result of a dream that took a daunting turn, but then his yellow eyes face the exit with predatory focus.

Knock knock, goes the door in the dead of night. A warning growl responds.

"Just me," Hellano says through wood. "Not that Thorne really cares."

It is humorous how overconfident this animal is. Scenting Hellano from afar, he knowingly growled at the King of Death—as if he would stand a chance against the deity in combat. "Settle down," I soothe the swellheaded wolf. "Why don't you go nap on the sofa?"

Hellano enters to the sound of my grumbling companion. After giving the king a sideways glance, Thorne ambles into the living room.

"You're Mother Nature," he says while striding over, "can't you get me on his good side?"

A chuckle falls out to my surprise. How one could escape at a time like this is beyond me. "What are you doing here, 'Lano?"

"Other than hearing the news of our dwindling council"—the bed dips as he sits— "you lack vitality, my flower."

"How very observant."

A sculpted arm drapes over my legs as he props himself up, gray t-shirt clinging to his frame like a jealous lover. Dull moonlight paints his skin blue, gifting his appearance with a deathly handsome filter.

This proximity threatens to unlock imprisoned emotions. Feelings that are unwelcome and confusing, like the impending acceptance that those I care for are really gone ... and being unable to distinguish whether this longing for Hellano is genuine, or simply compensation to my lonely heart.

"Talk to me," he urges. "I'm right here."

The expression that follows is one that I have seen many times in our past. It is the same as an open hand, a beckoning call for connection. Safety and comfort are promises in his gaze ... so I open the cell of my broken self.

He reaches for me when my lips part with a cry.

Blotches of darkness stain his pewter shirt as tears fall. Warm arms circle my back, holding tight with care. Through sobs of grief and guilt, Hellano's mellifluous voice works to soothe.

History does indeed repeat itself. Like before, the cocoon of his body provides all the comfort in the world. Firm pillows of love are the panes of his chest, collecting my sadness to drive away—forbidding despair to settle.

But the past only returns in part, for the newfound warmth pulsing against my wet face swears that it is gentle and kind.

Our eyes meet through a thin space, and I cannot deny that it is me who hangs the tension we both hesitate to give into.

Compensation for my lonely heart or not, it is impossible to care at the sight of lips that once worshipped my every pore ... and seek to do so once more.

Hellano does not deny me the kiss.

It is sweeter than ever before, and not just in the lingering hints of strawberries that coat his tongue from a late-night snack.

I was never able to reach all of him during the naked moments of our past; the door I believed he consciously kept closed was really a gaping hole he sought to fill. But now the entrance is open to a yawning canal of deep love. Not void ... overflowing.

Endless in a different way—endless for me.

A lazy moan tumbles from my lips as I guide him closer; a silent plea to be pleasured again. These kisses ignite much more than I expected, leaving me trembling to experience all the ways he could cherish my body with his soul intact.

For eight years, sex with Hellano dangled from the Heavens. Memories of it—the rhythm and sounds—mocked the abstinence following my descent. The anger I held did nothing to combat this problem, only introduced me to masochism. Although that desire left alongside my resentment, it makes me wonder what gifts my absence may have brought him.

Flush with his powerful form, each swirl of our tongues sends me deeper into that infinitely open chasm. Atop me, Hellano is blatantly hardened and ready. Instinct drives my hips forward, brushing against the member between my thighs with a begging force.

Our mouths separate against my will, and I raise my eyelids to find him peering down at me as if I hung the moon. But behind those features of admiration, Hellano fights a moral battle.

"When the dust settles," he says with steady cadence, "I will still be here." Leaning down, soft kisses line my nose and eyebrows. "Until then, allow me to admire you in sleep."

The ache in my stomach misses his heartlessness; at least then, it would get a reprieve. My higher self—the one currently reeling in the disobedient horse that is my id—falls into each peck planted upon my face with gracious thanks.

After nodding with acceptance, Hellano slides over and pulls me into his side. Slow strokes line my arm that coax me to drift. Insomnia cowers in his presence, growing smaller the farther it flees.

"'Lano?" I call in a quiet hum.

"Yes, my flower?"

"Where did you find the crown?"

A finger halts near my elbow. "Why do you ask?"

"Curiosity," I say with one foot in consciousness.

The tracking on my triceps resumes. "Cato handed it to me—said it was mine."

Odd. Kysi said that Cato was unable to enter the treasury, which means the crown could not have spawned alongside the other—unless of course, one of them was lying.

Through the delusion of upcoming dreams, the lines of current events connect into an unsettling image.

The god of Wisdom defended Hellano in the first council meeting, yet never showed to aid in his recovery after Kysi's attack. All throughout the Spring Festival he appeared anxious and uncomfortable. Nonverbal until the very end, when he began cracking jokes to Hellano at the exact moment Kysi summoned me to the theater.

The revelation yanks me from the caress of sleep.

"He's playing both sides," I exhale.

Hellano rises beside me. "What?"

"Cato—he's been helping you *and* Kysi since the very beginning, driving the wedge of your discord deeper. He's not missing ... he's hiding."

If the New World's divide was a gluttonous beast, it was Cato that spoon-fed its insatiable hunger. Knowing his secret was soon to be unearthed, he retreated. But, why?

Confusion is too thick for betrayal to take root. Or perhaps this is denial; an inability to acknowledge or accept that everything is crumbling around me like sand between fingers—falling apart as it feels I may.

CHAPTER 26

The tiny serpent that lives in the tree of my throne willingly weaves its scaled body between my painted nails. They match a royal blue dress, its chiffon neckline glittering like a starry sky.

Elegant Celestian attire.

I have a feeling that my future outfits will remain as patriotic as this one, perhaps with the other shades my kingdom has adopted: saffron and indigo.

Chatter buzzes in the throne room, where mine and Hellano's engagement celebration is currently underway. Only those chosen for hire are in attendance, which is more than I expected. Apparently, every aspect of our wedding requires teams of people.

The group holding binders of sketches, dressed as if they murder those brave enough to disobey color theory, are clearly the designers Harlynn chose to style my gown for the ceremony.

Florists congregate on the right of them, expressing a sweet and enlightening aroma that wades where they hover.

Culinary afficionados gather near the food banquet along the far wall, analyzing the meats and their tenderness. A few human faces join them, to my relief. It is painful to imagine how quickly meals will grow bland here without both fresh ingredients and a mortal touch. If trade with Groveheart is not established soon, it is likely that fine cuisines will become a rarity in Celestia.

Among carafes of ice water and fizzing punch, I take note of a beverage rather popular among our demon guests.

"Is that tomato juice?" I ask Hellano.

His spine straightens. "Not exactly." Throwing an empathetic glance my way, he goes on to say, "Pigs blood—it's a delicacy among their kind. Now you know why Renwick always reeks of iron."

Stifling a gag, I look to where his assistant chats harmlessly with Harlynn. That explains too why the demon's lips are consistently blushed. Swallowing nausea, I remind myself to lack judgement. With new species comes new cultural norms—there are bound to be a few requiring mental adjustments on my part.

Harlynn's attention finds me, eyes going straight to the dark circles under my own. She spent all morning lecturing about the importance of beauty sleep while attempting to disguise my fatigue, but no amount of powder could cover how worn down I appear.

Panic overcame me shortly after the unveiling of Cato's actions. I wanted to leave for the Ancient Library at that very moment and search for the traitor myself. Hellano settled my racing thoughts with a more logical approach.

Not only would it have taken most of the remaining night to get there, but it would have also been a waste of precious time. Cato would not hide in the one place he is expected to be. Even if we knew his whereabouts, catching him would be an entirely different challenge.

So, Hellano suggested that we level the playing field; learn the art of teleportation ourselves. Once mastered, finding him will be a reachable goal.

Although it takes many years of deep meditation to master this talent, it is our hope that my ability to jump through realms will accelerate the process. Surely, one aspect of phasing will not be so different from the next. The sooner I learn to teleport *within* worlds, the sooner I can teach Hellano as well.

Because neither Cato nor Kysi's purpose rests in pioneering, Hellano did not send them to explore the New World after its birth. Instead, a team of volunteer travelers took on the responsibility. A group of skilled woodsmen and cartographers currently venture these lands with plans to return in half a year with their findings.

But now Kysi has a kingdom of his own, along with this dangerous advantage over us. With the ability to discover in one day what voyagers could in months, the King of Groveheart yields the power to grow his nation much larger than our own.

So, Hellano and I laid idle until the break of dawn, swimming deeper in the voids of our minds. Now, as we sit upon these thrones—consciously ignoring the scorched one's stain—we mentally hang over the surface of meditation. It will be a constant effort to strengthen that muscle while simultaneously managing our daytime responsibilities.

I did, however, insist that we visit the Ancient Library tonight. Not in search of the god of Wisdom, but a motive.

Cato was my ally, there had to be a catalyst for his betrayal.

My attention snags at an approaching human. One of the chefs. She bends low into a bow, light brown hair pulled tightly against her skull. Not a strand or split end free.

"It is an honor to serve you both on the day of your union," she says with focus upon the floor.

"You may rise," Hellano responds. "To what do we owe this pleasure?"

Eyes much darker than her imprisoned hair meet mine, then his. "My name is Anna Agnello. My father, Matteo Agnello, is a painter at the Enclave."

Rubbing his tired chin, Hellano thinks aloud. "Matteo Agnello. Yes ... his art hangs above my mantle. Black and white koi fish circling one another." The king nods to me. "Yin and yang. It is a fine piece."

Anna gleams with pride. "His work never succeeded in our previous lives. After decades of failure, I watched him put down the brush and abandon his passion. After turning away from it, my father dulled ... no longer walked with purpose."

"Shame," Hellano says. "May that continue no more in the Kingdom of Celestia."

A grin emerges then. "It has already ceased, Your Majesty. On the day of the Spring Festival, everyone witnessed you admire his art—find meaning in those fish. Since then, every canvas has sold. The orders continue. He is in no shortage of work, and never have I seen him so whole." There is a twist of empathy in her features. "My King ... Satan never existed to me on Earth, nor does he in this life."

A piece of my aching heart heals upon witnessing their shared smiles.

"Your faith is priceless, Anna," he replies. "May your father's passion forever prosper."

"As well as your marriage." She bows adieu. "The marks will suit you both beautifully."

I tilt my head. "I beg your pardon?"

"Your tattoos, my Queen."

What in gods name is she talking about? "Right," I bluff. "Yes, thank you."

Hellano and I are left equally perplexed. Renwick takes note of the confusion, and hurries over to whisper answers. When the explanation befalls the king, he throws a gesture at me.

A metallic scent hits my nose as the assistant comes close, bending to share the information. "The mark of the wed is a symbol that seals your union in flesh. It develops on the neck of newlyweds amidst their consummation."

My gaze falls upon Hellano. After coming down from my desperate arousal the night before, I was thankful that he halted what could have been a damaging act. Eight years may be a long time apart, but we have only just reconciled. It is too soon to give him those pieces of myself again, and I can see in his expression that he too wishes for any future intimacy to be genuine.

Like litter in a collapsing metropolis, our obstacles continue to grow. A look of sympathy is shared between us, and with it the promise of togetherness. No matter how high the waves may rise or how angry the clouds roll overhead, we will weather each downpour in tandem.

Cato's annex is an organized type of messy. The piles of books in each corner are symmetrical and straight, multiple rows stacking waist-high. Fat pillows and soft blankets accompany the assemblage, which helps little with our fatigue. Drowsiness burdens my wings with added weight, the long flight here leaving them all the more drained.

"Harlynn is good at makeup," Hellano yawns while skimming through a novel. "She could draw the tattoos on."

"The exact same every day?" I question his logic, trailing the spines of ancient stories. "One droplet of rain or itch to your jugular would wipe away the handiwork, and I would prefer to avoid another lecture from her."

In all honesty, I like that about Harlynn. Not the rants she gives me, but the structure. Her presence brings comfort to the mayhem that engulfs every other aspect of my life.

Stability in a storm—that is what she is to me.

"Does it even rain here?" Hellano mumbles.

I shrug and continue the search. There is no time to sort through all these texts, so I will have to settle for those that stand out.

Hours tick by with no progress. Nothing of meaning peeks through the veil of this mystery, even as I replay the events in my brain over and over, straining to connect even the smallest detail that might get us somewhere.

From this pondering I have concluded how the events most likely occurred:

Cato found a crown in the treasury that could pass for Kysi's. He then gave it to Hellano, knowing it would paint him as a villain and thief. Hellano, whose soul duty remains in ruling this realm with me, thought nothing of the god of Wisdom handing it over. In fact, it further proved his stance.

Then, Cato just so *happened* to be nearby when Kysi stumbled upon the treasury. Faking his inability to enter, Cato knew that when Kysi came across the other crown, it would solidify his belief that Hellano was working against him.

By now, the towers of tales lay in disarray. I admit that it is poor investigating not to place everything back in its original spot, but exhaustion has left us rather careless.

Splayed on the floor, black wings stretched far above his head, Hellano groans. "What are the chances I learn to teleport now, and just phase us to bed?"

Rubbing my eyes puts swimming stars in my vision. "No harm in trying," I say, extending my ankle. He takes it with a lazy grip.

Silence.

"It didn't work."

With a huff for a laugh, I help him rise. "Maybe next time."

Hellano does well at keeping the pressure of discouragement at bay, but I can still feel it following me as we depart from the annex empty-handed.

It is from sheer will alone that my feathers continue to flap over the shelves. As they pass under me, I am reminded of the day I found the god of Wisdom.

Kysi and I were the first people Cato had seen in ages, yet he was disinterested in our arrival. Sitting on the floor surrounded by open books, the immeasurable number of years Cato spent in isolation prior to our meeting seemed happily spent.

As I spot the aisle we met drawing closer—this area of the library familiar to me now—I question whether my influence in his social emergence it is what drove him away.

There, amidst the line of perfectly flush rows, a singular spine pokes out farther than the rest.

Perplexment influences Hellano to accompany me downward. "We just grasping at straws now?"

Being unaware of the sentimentality this aisle beholds, Hellano lacks intrigue in my arbitrary discovery.

But this is no coincidence, I know it in the protruding title that stares back at me like a prophetic curse.

A Victor's Demise.

The leather-bound pages are heavy. In them, I graze through the story of a champion's fall, at last reaching the gruesome fate they were always meant to have. It feels like a hate letter, a message that I deserve all the misfortunes of this world ... that I am destined to bear them.

Under the final paragraph of the epilogue ... is a note.

.

Friend turned foe
Through blue waves of woe
Fear the falling snow, as it does the thaw
For useless is a bite from a frozen maw

.

The first part is clear; Cato now considers himself an enemy. Blue waves of woe and falling snow are surely his eyes—the tears they have privately shed. It leads me to believe that Earth's chaos was too much for him to witness, *seeing* rather than *reading* of the destruction must have changed a piece of him, broken it.

I may have more empathy if this poem lacked threats.

Fear the falling snow—his pain. The 'useless bite' is assumed to be my upcoming retaliation to whatever it is he has planned.

Was it his moral compass that planted the seed of this riddle, disallowing him to strike without so much as offering a warning? Maybe madness has finally caught up with him—that being another negative outcome from the ritual.

The god of Wisdom gone mad ... with all that power of knowledge. It sends a chill through the still air.

Chapter 27

Harlynn has poked me thrice since I donned this flamboyant gown. Dozens of petite diamonds spread across the bend of my right shoulder, placed perfectly by the uptight assistant.

Unbeknownst to her, she is what holds me together today. Although I am aware forgiveness would be freely given if I happened to ruin the kohl lining my eyes, I still bury the urge to weep. There is silence between us, and hovering in the air are a thousand sympathies. Her lips never part to express them—save for the occasional grunt of frustration when the pin hits my skin, followed by a quick apology.

I am averse to the mirror this morning. Stunning is the woman staring back, but tableaus of sorrow are often still beautiful. My feathers are as black as the turmoil inside, but only because I allow it. Here in the privacy of my wardrobe, I do not use the gift brought to me by consistent meditation to stifle their colors.

Silver-white crystals cover the bust of my wedding dress. They fade into violet and aqua; darkening passed an ombre of plum and navy-blue. Gold scatters around my calves—amidst the amethyst and tanzanite—eluding to patient stars that sit unmoved for eternity.

Because nothing screams 'I love you' like nationalism.

"How would you have done it?" Harlynn asks, sticking another gem to the nook of my neck. "If circumstances were different."

Blinking at the thought, I realize that I had yet to consider it. "I suppose the presence of nature would be more of a priority, although I remain thankful that the ceremony's location is outside. A thick forest would be ideal. Private, save for the wildlife wishing to observe." The vision comes with a sigh. "The air would breathe for you."

"Sounds lovely," she says with a sad smile.

If the display of patriotism was not paramount, I know that Harlynn would have done everything to make this day my dream come true. But Celestia needs hope, and it is I who must deliver.

As I peer through the mirror at this foreign version of myself, draped in jewels rather than juniper, I finally understand Hellano's Soul Father.

Drayxi, first incarnate of Death, voted against all proposals from the council. He consistently opposed the ritual, but actively participated when it was time to ensure its perfect execution. He must have known what I am only just realizing.

The largest bargain is one made with the Spirits of the Sky, and they do not give without taking.

Who knew the price of a New World would be my unified kingdom. My friends. My mate.

Perhaps even myself.

Songbirds carry a tune at the far side of the palace; an invitation to step into the vast gardens ahead. The open exit before me is quiet against the music. I cannot yet see the crowds in wait.

But I know they are there. Beyond the bend in the rocky pathway, passed the arrangements of dahlias and poppies, azaleas and carnations, bell flowers and forget-me-nots, are fields of freshly cut grass that hold an infinite collection of occupied seats.

I press on against the thunderous ballad in my chest. Butterflies and bees chaperon me forward, serving as a distraction from the peering audience.

A gazebo emerges at the center of the gardens; ivory stone lined with the trellis of green, rising pillars stalked by blood-red roses. Between them stands the image of forever.

Tailored perfectly to his form, a suit of shadowed twilight compliments Hellano's broad torso. Cuff links and lapel pins hold the emblem of our nation; a crescent moon hugging the beaming sun. This symbol represents the moonlight and daybreak of each passing day, tributing our dedication to always move forward with dignity.

The crown atop his head remains unbothered by blossoms, unlike mine that sprouts with petals the colors of our kingdom. I am unable to resist comparing it with the diadem Kysi claimed was his—noting the way it would much better suit his purpose and power.

Hazel eyes trail the dark hem of my gown. They wander up slowly, roaming each obsidian curl left untucked from my braid, at last hesitating over my burgundy lips. The king extends a hand to guide me under the alabaster roof, where pairs of curled wings sit perched on every corner. Ready to share each word with the attendees.

The broadcasting birds keep Hellano from speaking his mind, but the way I am absorbed by his lingering gaze—like strong wine to an empty stomach, warm and fierce—tells me the swallowed comment was rather scandalous. When the natural blush hits my face, he knows the message was still received.

Silent communication is a skill that came to us with time. By now, our body language has become its own secret dialect.

As stated in the contract I signed, the ceremony is to begin with an angelic tradition; the first one to bow loves and respects their partner more. It is I who will give the curtsy, as practiced in the rehearsals prior. Although I truly feel this way for Hellano, the act is meant to be a statement to the masses after the events of the Spring Festival ... that my reign is here.

Just before I dip low before him, Hellano clears his throat and bends—beating me to it.

Murmurs pour over the grounds, though none yield disappointment. Except maybe Harlynn's, wherever she is, probably rubbing her temples at the fact we have already strayed from the script.

The naked crown points skyward once more as he rises with a cheeky grin.

I retrieve Hellano's wedding band from the hidden pocket of my dress. Chosen with care, a tree's life cycle lay etched upon the gold, illustrating the significance of our paralleled connection. As it slides over the knuckles of his finger, the inscription inside remains a mystery to him.

Dauntless is my love, for it is the one thing you cannot end.

Our vows were prepared in private. Only Harlynn and Renwick know what was written. They made us memorize and recite the letters until their execution required no conscious thought.

Because the last thing we need is for me to choke.

"My beloved Hellano," I begin, voice echoing over the lands, "I stand before you, the bringer of death, with an infinite promise. To always cherish the stillness between heartbeats, treasure every ending as the path to a new beginning, and never fear your darkness ... as it is the soil from which life is reborn.

"The ancestral separation between our souls has faced our love and cowered, freeing us from the demarcation of hatred. I promise to wield our allegiance with noble intent, and reign beside you with devotion from now until my final breath. Which will be yours, and only yours, to take."

Each syllable consumes him like the very shadows inside, stretching his jacket with a deep inhale. Hellano's throat bobs as he reels himself in, reaching into his own pocket next.

Out comes another band of gold, this one with patterns I struggle to perceive. Most of the face is engraved with black streaks, leaving untouched saffron in seemingly random places. When my mind finally puts the image together, a gasp breaks free.

Lying on its side, a skull stares into a growth of life. Sprouting from its eyes and coiling from its mouth is healthy vegetation—budding flora and bundles of herbs. Work so precise could only be done by one demon in the Row, and this time, Hugo has truly outdone himself.

It fits perfectly alongside Kysi's, which I have not yet brought myself to part with.

"Darling Anewla," Hellano speaks, "my previous lives envy how darkness forever yields to purifying light, whereas I give it thanks. For yours guides me when I am lost and warms me when I am cold.

"I promise to cradle your creations before granting them rest, remembering that it was you who gave them form. I swear to walk alongside you not as an enemy of beginnings, but its most faithful witness. Through you, I have learned not just the beauty of life ... but how to live."

Curse him for pulling a tear from my ducts in front of so many people.

With wavering control in my tone, I continue. "Hellano, god of Afterlife and King of Celestia, if I vow to be your discipline and reason, your grace and understanding, your just mind and heart, do you promise to be mine from now until the end of eternity?"

"I do," he answers without hesitation. "Anewla, goddess of Beginnings and Queen of Celestia, if I vow to be your discipline and reason, your grace and understanding, your just mind and heart, do you promise to be mine from now until the end of eternity?"

As I part my lips to agree, a knot forms inside my vocal cords—silencing them.

Hellano waits expectantly, bemusement rising with each speechless tick of time.

Only raspy air escapes, as if plagued by an impetuous illness. Two rings glint over my hand as it searches for the mass in my throat, grasping at the skin to find nothing amiss. The invisible, dense ball coils so tightly that I wonder how air proceeds to my lungs unshaken.

Frightened to be suddenly mute, I look to Hellano for aid. Red brows knit at the sight of my petrification, patently concerned. I reach for my future husband, who opens his arms and takes a step toward me.

Commotion from startled guests halts our union.

It is not them that guide me to the source of their shock, but the steadying tides of a once vicious river. Easy goes the hurricane in my diaphragm ... the crashing waves in my heart.

Leaning in, Hellano whispers with urgency. "The birds—make them go."

The array of distinct animal imprints would take others a lifetime to sort through, but I manage it in less than a second.

Flee, I tell them, and away they fly.

Coal waves swirl from a blackened diadem that rests over equally dark hair. Kysi stands with a sinister charm, flicking a dust bunny off the shoulder of his sharp, verdant jacket. "I promise to love you through vicious waters," his sunken voice rolls out.

The wad in my voice unravels, releasing me of its grasp.

"Come on, Anewla," he lazily lilts. "You know the rest."

I gulp, reliving the joyous day that just governed my utterance. "Keeping you mine and never letting go."

Glaring are the green eyes upon me, splenetic and cross. "We made a *deal*."

CHAPTER 28

The forest behind Kysi's chateau remains the sole witness of our agreement. Warm rays beamed through veiny branches above, kissing our skin with its blessing. Grass clung to our bodies like shells in sand, whispering reverence into our pores.

"Then we have a deal," I had stated, carving our oaths into Kysi's sedimentary power. Never did I think this profound act of love would work against me.

A possessive tug draws me closer to my groom. "I spared your life," Hellano snarls. "Free her immediately or I'll renounce that mercy."

Instinct claws under my skin, demanding that I guard my mate, protect him. With stagnant feet, I hopelessly pray to the slumbering spirits above that Hellano does not wield his shadows. In that instance, I am unsure whether I could refrain from succumbing to the will of my soul bond.

Kysi's hands go up in satirical defense. Mottles of emerald on his fourth finger reflect in the midday sun. "I am afraid the deal binds me as well," he smugly states, "as ridding her of our vows would go against my side of the agreement."

Through countless craning necks I spot Harlynn, front and center, gripping Renwick's shoulder in a panic. Violent tension eats at the air like decay does a corpse. Both men are feet apart, but their adversity is nose to nose. I must take control—forbid them from subjecting these people to the trauma their outbursts would induce.

The god of Bargaining is made aware when a client attempts to escape their contract. Had I known this ceremonial script was going to alert Kysi, I would have made Harlynn phrase it differently. Nothing Hellano and I have displayed thus far contrasted with my promise in the forest; it was claiming myself *his* that rang the bell in Kysi. I am unaware if the notification required him to arrive and investigate, or if he simply showed up to cause a scene.

"We know the way out of your bargains," I remind. "Hellano and I *are* capable of marrying ... all you have to do is settle. *Share*."

A barking laugh expels. "Sorry angel. I am no polygamist."

Hellano seethes. "You wouldn't be an active participant."

Kysi's amusement flakes away, attention flicking to me. "I have a better idea," tone softer than mist across a quiet lake, my mate presses to persuade. "Our distance is not feasible. The soul tie will forever hale, insisting upon our entwinement. So, let's skip this nonsense and get to the inevitable scene where you come home with me."

The bond calls out like a neglected child searching for care, begging that I accept Kysi's proposal.

Cato once said that soul bound lovers cannot stay parted. I had no knowledge of the tether between Kysi and I before my descent, which stifled the pull on my end. However, its revelation was an idle ember catching wind deep within, unfurling into a mighty flame.

But one thing stronger than the connection our spirits share is the *duty* our souls are bound to. I know that mine is to serve the New World, and abandoning Celestia would not be in its best interest. Humans left my reign, so I shall not force it upon them again, but instead serve from afar with goodwill. Here I can mediate between the nations and their kings, using my power to maintain civility.

"This is my home," I tell him. "But make no mistake, I will always care for your people as I do my own."

A scoff of disbelief. "You can't honestly wish to stay. Anewla, this isn't you," he contests, gesturing to my sparkly attire, "dressing up like one of Hellano's rocks—his property."

The grip on my hip tightens with impatience. "Watch your tongue," Hellano snips. "The contract has been broken; she acts on her own accord."

It may be in his mind, but certainly not mine. Not only did I give him my word, but the contents of that document are sensical. I plan to see it through.

Kysi reluctantly hovers, forcing the question through gritted teeth. "Fine. Anewla ... is this truly what you want?"

The knot in my throat does not derive from his influence, but my pain.

"Yes." The utter is barely audible.

Kysi hardens, expression falling from a cliff of hope. With flat cadence, he repeats words that were spoken to us by the man at my side on the day of *our* union. "Enjoy your honeymoon."

Then he vanishes, and the raging waters ensue once more.

Monochrome fish circle one another above the mantle in the shared bedchamber. The painting holds immaculate detail, each gill analogous in its form. Hellano was right; it is fine art.

After summoning the birds to return, my husband soothed the masses. According to them, the King of Groveheart only came to give congratulations and wish our marriage well.

I scratch the thin cut on my hand. "We shared blood. How is *that* not sealing our union in flesh?"

Hellano's laughter spills out, rolling his shoulders. "That'd certainly make things easier," he comments, returning to the couch with a drink in each hand.

With a sigh, I find the spot beside him. We have yet to come up with a solution to this 'mark of the wed' issue, and now the pressure to fuck and forget is weighing heavy.

When he offers me the drink, I accept it with a hefty swig.

"You think second base would give us, like, temporary tattoos?" he japes.

A cackle erupts, intensifying the burn in my throat. "Only one way to find out."

Hellano's smile is slow to depart as he settles, suspended in my gaze.

Once upon a time, all inches of myself were familiar with the touch of his full lips. Last week when he stopped my advances, I had just enough of their attention to resurface the details of their tantalizing torture. I remember how they would temp and tease, guide me to the edge of a spiraling climax and hold me there until I begged for freefall. Different parts of me ache at the sight of them: arms, stomach, thighs. Even my calves miss the kisses he gave when my ankles were wrapped around his neck.

As I peer at that alluring mouth, alcohol warming my gut, I want nothing more than to feel it over my skin again. My physical needs battle the rampant pressure in my mind. Vacillation is a mental intruder; one my libido works to shove outside and lock behind a tremendous door.

It pounds upon the barrier when I reach for him, connecting us in a provocative kiss. The residual bitterness on my tongue is shared with intensity, sweeping over hints of leftover apple from the afterparty.

Louder and louder the banging persists, beating like a steel drum, yet my tenacity remains too stubborn to halt. I move with haste and mount Hellano's waist, as if to outrun the hesitancy. Pawing at the buttons of his shirt, each one undone is accounted for.

Two, three, four.

Tink, tink goes the buckle of his belt. Hands trail from my hips. I want them low, but upwards they rise. Past my sides and over my arms, they disregard my breasts to encompass my face; get my attention in the gentlest of ways.

With a shaking head, I silently beg not to be interrupted. The violent percussions in the depths of my thoughts might catch up with me ... make me face them.

But Hellano can sense how this is not right. Not me.

I should have known he would refuse. This characteristic of his, although inconvenient at times, is one of his most respectable qualities.

My consent is never good enough. What Hellano truly requires is the purest form of participation—no motives aside from connecting. Making love is more pleasurable, anything else is beneath him—beneath us.

"You don't actually care about the mark," he states, forehead against mine.

A sad type of annoyance surfaces. I hide the dismay in my palms, face shrouded from its display. Through this cover of darkness and into the cranny of my psyche, the hinges of that thundering door shatter to reveal what really stands in the downpour beyond.

Kysi.

Holding the same struck expression from our last shared gaze. Paralyzed with bane melancholy, he bores through the broken threshold of my mind with a screaming need. Unable to enter still.

A tepid warmth wraps my knuckles, lowering my hands. "Talk to me, flower."

I sniff. "It's the bond ... all tied up. I'm sorry, I just want it to stop—need it to stop." Stumbling over the words, I propose, "Maybe if—if I just talked to him. Tried to find common ground somehow."

Hellano pecks at the tips of my fingers, thinking. "If that will help you, we can leave right now."

Any attempt to negotiate whatever truce I offer would only loop them into an argument. His presence would be a hinderance to the goal. Even if that were not the case, this conversation belongs to Kysi and I.

"Celestia should not be left," I say, collecting myself as I slide from his lap. "You stay."

His hand lifts, pressing to the dip in my side. Uncertainty lingers under patient lids. "When will you be back?"

Through that steady tone I find an internal struggle. Hellano somewhat understands my discomfort and the motivation to pacify it. However, he struggles to accept the fact that I, his new bride, am leaving to visit the enemy king—my soulmate—on the night of our wedding.

"This time tomorrow"—I squeeze his arm to reassure— "we'll pick up where we left off." Doubt peeps through every movement as the king follows me to the armoire. "We may have to seal our union a few times," I tease to lighten the mood, "you know, just to make sure the tattoos are permanent."

Broad shoulders slacken then, along with the ridges in his bare stomach. A soft grin follows as he watches me sifting through clothes. "Thoroughness is imperative in our line of work."

Clouds scarcely veil the moons and stars tonight, so a plum cloak should work to effectively conceal my identity. Dark enough to appear as a speck in one's eye and gone with a blink. I drape it over breathable clothes, wings hissing through the slits.

On the outskirts of the Heartain Forest—the vast woodlands beginning at the backside of Gourmara—lays a great manor crafted from the finest nightspruce wood; a material that rivals the strength of steel, impenetrable to foes as the wind is to mountains.

According to our sources, Kysi is stationed there.

Surely surrounded with guards, waltzing across the front steps is out of the question. I will circle above, seek out a point of entry. With plenty of trees to bend and animals to rustle, creating a distraction will be effortless.

The palace grounds are consistently beautiful no matter which direction they are viewed. Through spotless glass—the same window panes I found Hellano peering out of when I returned from the Shadowlands—groves scatter. They house empty fields where horses graze when awake, and through them, the distant Capital City gradually darkens while falling asleep.

The window splits open, inviting the quiet world in. A reluctant grip encompasses my waist as I clutch the sill, supporting my weight while I heave myself over. Our chamber is on the second floor, but the ground below appears miles away. With feet planted on the ornamental ledge, I turn to give a final farewell.

Hellano's grip tightens. "Careful."

"I got it," I assure.

Ivy borders the window like a frame to a charming portrait. Hellano is the muse, ruffled hair more hypnotizing than any flames I could conjure. Golden eyes tint with rich caramel in this light, near his pupils. I love bearing witness to the way they change. Brown glints against the morning sun and fades with the day. Green only emerges in the moonlight on occasion, when mixed with the warmth of an indoor glow.

Tonight, they are devastating.

Heartbeats pass through an impalpable string, tethering us to an unwanted goodbye. I must do this—must unravel this tangled mess for inner peace, so I can live without a tempest in my chest.

I lean forward, clasping the back of Hellano's neck to draw him into a kiss. The act of affection is a promise to return. It is not me that Hellano distrusts; the extent of my loyalty was proven once before. The bond, however, possesses none of his faith.

"One day," I remind. "I swear it, 'Lano."

Kysi will comply, I know it. Because we finally came together, our separation now is surely worse than the centuries apart. Like a wall raised between magnets, no barrier is left to absorb our pull. He needs relief too. It was painted in his stature; a rigidness calmed by my presence.

My wings are a quick purr as I release Hellano. The castle becomes a fading cluster of spires with each clap of my feathers, my husband a mere pinpoint within it.

The wind is a sharp chill. Echoes of it breach my clothes and graze pebbled skin beneath. It is the first time I have noticed a change in climate, which leads me to Hellano's question last week in the Ancient Library about rainfall in the New World. Since then, I have paid more attention to the skies each day. Some hold heavy clouds, others just the galaxy.

I would say it does rain by assumption, although not from necessity. Beings require no sustenance here, only indulge for enjoyment. It is a nice thought—the New World offering water as nothing more than a treat to plants.

For safe measure, I cling to the spread-out billows of sparkling fuchsia and lilac. Just until I am away from the Capital and surrounding towns.

Steady gusts work in my favor in spite of their bitter bite. This demands less physical strain and speeds travel time, so I suppose shivering is payment for the advantages. The views help as well. They are a distraction from the cold as the late hours tick by. When nature becomes pungent and layered, I know Groveheart is drawing near.

Silver-blue tints the land with humble elegance. Networks of rivers cascade along moss-covered rocks, the fresh water unhurried to brooks and bluffs. Antlered deer hurdle across, their bodies reflecting underneath as they gallop freely towards the mosaic of shadows that make up the forest floor.

It is just as homely as the open air and scattered wildflowers of Celestia.

The landscape is enough to hook any sightseer, but instead I hover and squint with a different purpose. Surveying pointed shades of jade and sage, only a few precipices jut from the towering trees. It is unlikely that Kysi's residence would be visible from here; there is much more forest to cross. I observe the terrain as a precautionary measure, to familiarize myself with foreign land before progressing deeper into it.

Since the stags have leaped away, all is quiet and calm. A stream trickles faintly in my ears. Tranquil and serene.

Something shifts in my periphery. A glint, barely noticeable. Quick, so quick ... Head cambering, I whip toward the oncoming blur.

A tiny comet—no more than the size of a marble—pierces my wing.

Pain explodes. Every muscle seizes in white-hot agony. The sky falters as I tumble, horizon rolling at a quickening pace. The forest grows larger with each downward spiral, closer to its threatening pinnacle. I grasp the crisp air in a panic, fighting uselessly to regain composure.

Catch me! I call to the trees.

The order is muffled, like someone shoved a gag in the mouth of my mental command. Evergreens stretch their limbs too late, scraping my body to get a grip.

Catch me, catch me, catch me!

No signal. They cannot hear. Their imprints are fading, blending, syncing together in my head until I am unable to decipher flora from fauna ... unable to find them at all.

Each cut from a bough is a saving grace. It slows my descent, lessening the impact—although not enough to escape the blunt-force collision.

My skull slams against a firm bed of detritus, wing twitching like a short-circuit.

A cry sharp enough to shatter glass rattles my throat. Flocks burst from their nests above to escape the clamor. Leaves and branches sway not from a breeze but my shaken mind, swimming together in a haze. Instinct tells me to feel for damage, but my arms will not move. Eyelids gain weight as my body sinks into a stupor.

Rustling sounds overhead, more than just disturbed wildlife ... Murmurs. Rushed whispers. Footsteps crack the fallen debris around me, but I cannot turn to see. The biggest struggle I face is keeping my lashes raised, catching only a glimpse of oncoming figures before losing all awareness.

CHAPTER 29

The lack of moisture on my tongue becomes extra dry at the sound of a repetitive drip. I pry it from the roof of my mouth, batting my eyes against a buried ache in my temple. A sharp, grating screech follows my movement as I roll to the side. It scrapes against the cold floor, rough and obtrusive. A hammer of hurt pangs in my skull as the tenor bounces off the walls; stuck in a death knell of reverberating pitch and pain.

Through smeared vision I spot a white glow surrounded by greedy darkness. Focus finds me with each blink, sight clearing to a dreary venue.

A square of light seeps through a solitary exit ... absent of handles. I am boxed in a tomb of granite save for the jagged ceiling of untouched rock. It beads with condensation, crying in the corner with a continual splat. A table and chair sit unoccupied to the side, made of metal and stone like the rest of this dungeon.

Bits of freshly broken gravel scrape my arms as I strain to sit up. The screeching drags once more.

I wince from the sting in my wings and the throb in my brain, finding the noise not to be some far-off wail, but the bellow of chains.

Wrapping my wrists and covering my hands, latches sprout links united by locks at my ankles. They come together as one on the floor, trapped by a protruding semicircle of steel.

What ... *the fuck*.

Is this Cato's doing? No—his strike would be sneaky. He would act alone. I imagine the god of Wisdom would lead me down a pretty path, perhaps one I have walked a million times, to provide a false sense of security before disguising a snare in plain sight.

Unless I am wrong ... What if he orchestrated my capture by whispers of stretched truths and fear mongering, leaving others to execute the rest?

Split the kingdom and steal their Queen.

But why? It cannot be power he craves; Cato wishes to read, not rule. Maybe madness pushes deities away from their soul purpose, detaches them from its leash.

Nothing lays at my disposal here. No roots to spread or thorns to grow. However, I do not *need* nature's presence. It is mine to form.

I could develop vines from my palms to fill these bindings until the pressure makes them pop, but all the bones in my hands would likely shatter before their surface would see a crack.

Any maneuverable body part would do; life erupts from all parts of me. A flick of the chin or a tilt in my elbow could work if I focus hard enough.

Every strength has its weakness, and my access to Divine Duplicity in this realm comes with limitations. Hands are the easiest to create with. Feet are a close second. The rest do not come to me so easily.

Either way, these whole-hand cuffs are far too solid for splinters to puncture, or anything else I can think of mustering.

Deep breaths. I must clear my mind, cultivate ideas rather than fear. Although I have yet to solve the puzzle of phasing, meditation has offered additional gifts. My wings are pitch-black, and masking their expression would be a pointless waste of energy. However, I will cling to a seed of calm within for mental clarity, leaving them to lighten on their own.

Inhale.

First, I must warm myself. Comfortable bodies fuel focused minds, and this room may as well hang swine.

I never enjoyed the end of summer. A parky breeze matters little to me, but the lower the temperature, the more difficult it is to manipulate life forms. When things grow cold, they become sluggish and harder to move.

When things freeze, they die.

It made no difference to me on Earth without my abilities. However, each year reminded me that when the leaves fell, it was Hellano's time. Life's annual return was always a relief that my power was still in use, and at the very least, he was sharing it with his own.

Divine Duplicity dislikes the cold more than I do. The side of myself that infinitely burns, breeds, and begins stands at the ready when unbothered. It is farther now. Agitated. This is why I did not call upon it during my flight to Groveheart; it was pointless to waste energy on stifling a small discomfort.

With added concentration, I can make it to the border of my split conscience and reach through the veil, take hold of heat to soothe my quivering bones.

Exhale.

It is there, stationed and working as always. Never allowed rest. Forever mechanical.

Lifting an imaginary hand, I grasp the curtain to enter ...

It does not move.

I pull harder with a grimace.

Let me in.

My seed of calm flees to a brewing terror as I yank again with all my might.

LET ME IN.

No flimsier than the stone of my cell, this fortress gate remains closed.

The fall ... I remember the fall. How the trees could not hear my cries for help.

What have they done to me?

There was something in that bullet—something that revoked my communication with nature ... along with my means to create it.

Light pours from the yawning exit, haloing a sturdy frame. Black boots hug the bottom of tactical pants that belt in a matching short sleeve. Pallid grey webs curve upwards between ebony digits of a demon's wings, creating a pointed U behind their head. Stepping in the cell, stiff features make up a foreign face.

The woman walks forward, hands clasped at her back. "It is world domination that you seek"—*Bump … bump … bump* go her approaching feet— "and shall never obtain."

Most angels and demons remained in Celestia during the New World's divide, but not all.

My parched throat responds, "I came for no other reason than to make peace with your king."

A cynical smirk arches as she leans in. "I bow to no one, goddess of Beginnings."

Not a willing citizen for either kingdom … "What do you want?"

"The Imperial Army demands a world free from divine government. A realm where laws are obeyed by the masses that make them."

I crane my neck. "Did mortals not leave my reign in peace?"

The chair screams as she pulls it out, sitting with fists on her thighs. "To serve another deity."

"Not to serve." I shake my head. "To be looked after, cared for."

Jaw clenched, the woman hisses, "We are not children in need of a keeper."

I withdraw, considering the best response. "Our positions over each nation serve to comfort the common person. Is that not the goal of all societies?"

"Who defines comfort?"

Interesting point, but still refutable. "The demeanor of the people."

A scoff. "You cannot see us all."

The fact she is here proves her point. An army of imperials certainly never flagged my radar. "You want separation from gods? Fine. Go find a barren plot and build."

"The terms of our land is currently"—head teetering for the right words— "under negotiation. Your capture will be a great service to us."

It sounds like her plan is to use me against Kysi and Hellano. "Leaving does not suffice, I see."

"Only some arrived in your kingdom when the New World was forged. Others were here. Watching. Learning." By 'here' she must mean we are not currently in either kingdom. The woman's elbows meet her knees as she shifts forward. "I have heard the stories of your reckless destruction and thirst for sovereignty ... I know what you did to the Spirits of the Sky."

My chest sinks, lips tight to conceal what I do not yet know to say.

"Wisdom is a liberator," she quips, "and the one thing more powerful than you."

I surge toward her, caught by manacles. "Where is Cato? Let me see him."

The woman does not flinch, just apathetically blinks. "So typical of you deities to bark orders. It is not a luxury you possess now."

My knuckles are white inside these shackles. It would be immoral to blame Cato for his insanity, especially when I am its catalyst. I must remind myself that the hatred I feel is not for him, but this wretched predicament.

"The kings will not trade their kingdoms—not even for me," I tell her.

"I do not expect them to. You are the pebble damning an avalanche, all we had to do was pluck you."

Crossed with confusion, I pry, "What the hell does that mean?"

Her gaze upon me does not waver. "Who is there to blame for your disappearance if not Kysi? A jealous soulmate that refuses to free the Queen of Celestia. Or Hellano, who used her status to further solidify his position, only to cage her when the job was done." The imperialist stands, beelining for the door. "It's only a matter of time before they wage war to save you. After waiting for their numbers to dwindle, our army will deliver the final blow." Back to me, her feathery hair sways in its ponytail with the twist of her chin. "The kingdoms *will* fall, Anewla ... and so will your kings."

Alone I am left with the perpetual drip of water, seemingly louder than it was before.

CHAPTER 30

The light from the window never goes off. Sometimes I wish it would, so the immersion of darkness would grant me the freedom to make-believe. To pretend I am home ... not to a place but with a presence. Two of them.

The persistent glow seeps through my closed lids as I twist my rings with a thumb and forefinger inside the bindings. I am thankful to still have them, yet terrified of what that means. My captors are unbothered by the hope they carry. I am allowed to cling to it because they believe it will get me nowhere, that it is useless here.

I beg to differ.

While fidgeting with the bands I remind myself of one thing: the mark of the wed.

The moment Kysi sees that Hellano does not have it, he will know that my disappearance came from a third party. I have nothing to worry about. They will not go to war ... they will find me.

Death is not what I fear. If the Imperials were trying to kill me, they would have aimed for the head. It would lack sense to do so anyway, because my soul would simply form a new body. Perhaps someone a little confused with the current political climate, but a renewed replacement, nonetheless.

When the door opens today, two men pile in. They each have wings the shade of coal, the tall one with talons that curve like a scythe at the pinnacles. The shorter one's hang from below his arms, like Renwick's, and poke through slits between a white coat. In their purposeful strides, it is apparent that work takes priority over hygiene, because both of their heads could use a good wash. Pens and notepads are carried in their lab jackets, patting the breast pockets with every step.

They must be the creators of that bullet.

"Color me impressed with your little invention," I humor them. "What's your secret, a native plant at the edge of the world? A potion of your tears?" How else will I keep my spirits up, if not by the use of sarcasm?

One clicks a light in my eye. "Pupils receptive."

"Magnificent," goes his partner with greasy black hair. "I'll pluck. You hold."

The taller blonde nods, bulky hands firm as they force me to lay flat on my stomach. "Down you go."

"Hey!" I fight with little success, still throbbing and weak after being shot. A knee meets the middle of my shoulder blades, and my arms are glued to the floor. "Don't touch me!"

I may as well be a fish in the hands of a goliath.

The dark-haired man kneels above my outstretched pennon. "Apologies, but we are on a tight schedule."

Fingers slide behind a handful of inky feathers. He grips them at the base and my eyes slam shut.

A wet crack sounds, barely audible over my outcry. Rivulets of warmth slither from the empty sockets of my skin.

Feathers fall on their own sometimes. Few have ripped loose by accident over the centuries, caught on clothes or shut in a door. Nothing more than stubbing a toe or breaking a nail—annoying above all else.

But this ... this is agony. My fading divinity had to of muted the pain of smashing on the hood of Mona's car, because even *that* was more forgiving.

Glass clinks and something presses against the flooding wound. A blood sample, no doubt. I cannot look. Even if I tried, my vision would be too blurry to see.

"I would've cooperated, you know," I lie through gritted teeth, knowing damn well the second they reached for me I was swatting like a tomcat at the vet.

Blondie huffs, "Our time with you is limited. It will not be taken for granted."

So, this vacation with the Imperials is temporary. I can only assume my reunion with Cato will come soon enough, after they overthrow the nations and claim their independence.

A trade. The powerless Queen for a government free from divine rule. When it comes to the scientists, their motivations are clear; I am an experiment. Which raises the question, what puzzle are they trying to solve? Is Cato also searching for the answer?

Another fist takes hold of a cluster and pulls.

I wince, a low growl vibrating the pit of my throat as I wade through vicious waves of pain. A wet drop falls from behind my lids.

"It's easier this way for you as well," goes the feather plucker, "like ripping a band aid off."

I crane my neck to stare daggers, rage boiling my tears. The black hole in my wing is clearly visible now; veins of deep purple trail from the site and extend passed feathers still intact.

A disappointed sigh falls from the man kneeling beside me. "Bead absorbed. Retrieval unsuccessful."

"It was a long shot anyway," his partner responds. "Remove the remaining feathers and we'll monitor the area."

Spit flies from my baseless threat. "Pull one more and I'll sprout burs in your fucking prostates, pigs."

"Yikes," the other comments before shifting focus to his colleague. "We'll do it gradually. Don't want to aggravate the appendage any more than it is."

I scurry to sit when they stand together. Cold air licks my fresh wounds. The tall one opens his coat and pulls out a dainty potted plant. "Here" —he places the cactus on the table— "to spruce the place up."

Fucking asshole. Nothing screams "helpless" like putting ammunition in front of an unarmed prisoner.

A shadow swims from the window of the door before it swings open to reveal the woman from yesterday. She stands as tight as a bowstring, stalky and muscular. "Dev. Wren," she greets the men, "how is the project coming along?"

"On track, Miss Priscilla," the bastard with a bundle of feathers replies.

"As expected from the minds of you both." She enters, her curved jaw ticking as her penetrating gaze lands upon me. When the men leave, silence hovers for only a moment. "Aren't they brilliant? My favorite minds in all the New World. Aside from Cato's, of course."

It would be a lie to claim I tremor from the cold. In reality it is my miserably ripped flesh. "I will laugh when your plan crumbles."

A brow quirks. "You sound so sure."

"You'll find out soon. Perhaps even by tomorrow," I reference Hellano's bare neck.

Priscilla thrums patient fingers over the table. "Ah, yes ... the mark of the wed." Anxiety hitches at her untroubled attitude. "It would have been easier if your soul bond held out until *after* you fucked the Celestian King, but we knew it could force you to seek out Kysi at any time." A satisfied grin covers her mouth. "Take some words and throw them around—say them *just* right ... and you have vows in disguise. With a belly full of ambrosia to make his libido sing, the god of Afterlife should be married again by the end of tonight."

The Heavens will return before Hellano beds a random person—not while committed to another. "You could bathe him in brandy, and he still wouldn't touch the likes of you."

"Perhaps," Priscilla softly intones, "but Hellano's heart will be aching at the thought of you choosing to stay in Groveheart with your soulmate. Vulnerable and alone, a trusted someone will arrive to comfort him. They'll serve him spirits and feed his mind hidden promises. After guiding the conversation to get what they need, all that's left will be to conjugate the marriage."

Now it may be anger that I shake with. She wants to twist Hellano's words and then seduce him to create a fake mark using someone we know ... someone we trust.

"It will work," Priscilla says, face smug and proud. "Harlynn can be *very* convincing."

Chapter 31

I can't say when the droplets stopped falling. A stagnant puddle leers, gently reflecting the glow from the window. Why does the sound go on in my head?

Drip, drip, drip.

No water plummets. No ripples appear. Yet, it continues ...

Time blends together now. If I had to guess how long it has been, I would say three weeks. Give or take three weeks.

Persistent discomfort is a torture of its own. My right wing is wholly bare and substantially lighter than its counterpart, which leaves me in a constant state of imbalance. Simply switching positions to keep my limbs from going numb causes the room to spin.

I wish I could suffocate my innate will to live. It forces me to continue a battle with despair, despite how weary I have become. Like a cancerous body feeding itself to go on, I sit in a limbo of hopeless resilience.

All I could think about was smashing that spiked succulent over Priscilla's downy brown hair. The image of her cheek sliced by the shattered clay pot; needles buried across her temple. I replay it in my head. Faster. Harder. Over and over.

She comes when the scientists finish picking and prodding, to taunt me for personal satisfaction—poke at her caged pet. It is easy to disregard the verbal attacks on my naked wing and overall pathetic appearance. Mentions of Hellano and Kysi, however, are not so skillfully ignored.

Especially when she speaks of how handsome the former looks with tattoos.

Visions of Harlynn tilting the glass to Hellano's bee-stung lips haunt my dreams. My imagination is robbed of all but the picture of gold hair draped over him in a state of helpless inebriation.

My current torment pales in comparison to what awaits her. When I am free, I will grip her painted neck and dangle her over the ledge of existence, until reincarnation forces me to let go and gift her the mercy of death.

Priscilla prides herself on how flawless everything is unfolding. Rumors of Hellano's treachery have spread through Groveheart like a disease. Kysi's jealous greed is known in all of Celestia. Peace is slipping through the cracks of my kingdoms. Drumbeats of war echo over the lands from the marching boots of soldiers preparing to attack.

All in line to fight for the Queen.

Mortals lack the ability to fly, so Celestia has the advantage of air. However, not a single angel or demon has experienced war.

Groveheart has numbers of battle experts at their disposal; people who have served the military in their previous lives on Earth.

If there is one thing I know about the human population, it is that war is a second nature.

Being chained in a cell gives a person plenty of time to think. That is all I have done. All I can do.

I understand Kysi now. His actions.

As if the physical and psychological torment were not enough, guilt is also leeched upon my heart. I never heard him out, never *truly* listened.

He was right all along. There was never meant to be one kingdom. Priscilla's homeland is proof of that. If there are more civilizations out there like I suspect, naturally many are destined to reign.

Hellano's purpose to rule is engrained in his spirit, which is why he fought diligently for the crown. There was no other choice for him; nothing is more powerful than what drives the soul. I was so foolish to think Kysi's time in stasis had turned him malignant. It was not that at all ...

Kysi adopted the fate to be King of Groveheart when the eternal flames vanished at the last ritual.

For centuries my mate lived in the shadows. He suffered loneliness and heartache to respect the life I was leading, only to act when the cries of praying humans were too loud to bear. He would not have left me and split a nation if there was no imminent threat. It had to be an inescapable urge. A *soul duty.*

"You're a woman of science," a grating, deep voice sounds, "wouldn't you lunge at the opportunity to uncover groundbreaking discoveries?"

I lower my gaze to Dev. "Not at the expense of ethics."

Two fingers are firm on my wrist while he counts my pulse. "There's nothing you would abandon ethics for?"

I wiggle my hands inside the steel cuffs to keep blood flowing. "Just because you have the ability to innovate doesn't always mean you should. Not everything works in favor of the world. Some treasures are better left buried."

Dev's wing follows his arm as he lifts a finger. "I suppose." Back and forth he moves it in front of my face, but I keep my glare on him steady. A brown deeper than soaked soil flicks upwards to meet my eyes. He drops the arm in defeat. "My work does not belong *underground*, Dr. Delphine."

I will never get used to them calling me that.

"*Our* work," Wren cuts in at the table where he scribbles notes on a pad. "Your eidetic memory may lead this project, but my theorems pave the path."

"How could I forget?" Dev chimes and they both chuckle. "I don't expect you to fully understand," he says to me with soft pity. "You studied brains. We study bodies. Apples and oranges."

"What *is* your work exactly?" The chains drag as I cross my arms.

Wren flicks the notepad closed and pockets it. "If Priscilla hasn't told you, you're not supposed to know."

I roll my eyes and instantly regret it. The constant ache behind my brows tends to flare with sudden orbital movement. "Can I at least get something for this migraine? I *know* one of you probably"—I suggestively sniff—"indulges in a thing or two to make the nights go by. My bets on you, big bird."

Wren chuffs. "Would if I could, but you know just as I to avoid unnecessary variables in any experiment. You wouldn't micro-dose a control group, would you? Didn't think so."

A groan releases, and I lay my head on the stone wall. "What you gain in curiosity, you lack in compassion."

They hover for a moment. "We are genuinely sorry, Dr. Delphine."

I can't explain why part of me believes them.

Like clockwork, Priscilla enters after they depart. Sweat blotches her uniform, and the roots of her hair are damp. Combat training must have gotten the best of her today, because impatience tightens her features. As usual, I close my eyes and try to tune her out.

"I didn't want to execute these plans." She gets straight to the point. "But I couldn't *ignore* the god of *Wisdom*. So, I strategized. It was all precautionary ... until those travelers arrived to outline my city like a fucking blueprint for the Ultimate Queen."

My lashes slowly lift to her stiff, livid stare. "What did you do to them?"

The imperial sits in the chair, knees wide and arms crossed. There is a shadow of satisfaction from inciting a reaction out of me that she fails to mask. "We couldn't risk one nation winning the first battle with too many soldiers left. Nightfall needed more men."

Nightfall. The City of Imperials. Her home—my prison.

"A treaty was made."

My breath hitches. That means ... there *are* more cities. More occupied land. Enough to find one to *ally* with.

Good gods. The New World is far bigger than any of us know.

Priscilla avidly bounces her knee. "There are hordes in the Ferathore Mountains that make carnage look civilized. Clans of feral angels and demons ready to sink their teeth into anything with a beating heart." The silence between each word absorbs my trep-idation. "It doesn't matter what species you are. They are always hunting. If not for blood, then bones to whittle. Skin to craft. Hair to weave. I was nearly torn apart before they heard my proposal."

How unfortunate.

"There are too many clans to count, but those that could, rallied their leaders and met me on a patch of unclaimed territory. I offered them annual human prey in exchange for their allegiance in the war."

That breath becomes trapped in my chest. Is that what she is fighting for? The one thing she knows gods will never allow—*I* will never allow: dominance over another species?

She shrugs. "They refused at first, but that's because they only knew the savory taste of animals. Not the sweet blood of humans."

"You didn't—" I pull the links taut as denial seeps in.

"I did," Priscilla barks, "and when they were done feasting upon your colonizers, picking their teeth with the bones of their fingers, I had to convince them not to invade Groveheart for more."

My voice wavers, "Those men were *not* there to prompt an invasion."

Priscilla cambers her chin, eyes in satiric resolution. "Oh? That's a shame, then." She waves a nonchalant hand. "Well, treaty's made—no stopping it now."

Rage spreads from my ribs, seizing every muscle. The imprints in my mind look like a watercolor painting left in the rain, but through their blurred lines I find that godsdamn cactus.

Blind the bitch.

A solid spine shoots out. Priscilla's head falls back, and her arms rise to cover her face. I wait for a cry of pain, a mumble of profanity, but no noise emits.

Slowly, the imperial lowers her hands and grips the needle embedded into her *cheek bone*.

Damn it.

She shifted at the last second. The tiny spear is only an inch from the bullseye. I watch as she pulls it out without a wince and levels it with her pale blue eyes.

"Two months," she utters under a breath, so quiet that I barely hear.

It all makes sense now—why they left the plant, why she comes every day to provoke me. It has not been weeks since my capture ... it's been *months*.

Their poison is temporary ... and I just told them how long the effects last.

Daylight falls upon the joyous faces of my lovers. They chase me in the empty throne room, their crowns tight in my hands. Laughter is shared in a melody of emotion as we spin between the regal seats. It is blissful to them and my unconscious self, but through layers of sleep the reminder of their voices weighs down my chest.

I flee their playful advances. The soft breeze drifting through the open ceiling flags Kysi's shirt as he flanks left, trapping me between him and Hellano. My husband's smile is genuine and bright, contagious and handsome. His head falls back with a chuckle that melts my very being.

A yelp sounds with a tug from my midsection as my mate swings me from the dais. Kysi's arm is firm around my waist, familiar and comforting. The touch heals me in ways no medicine could.

I am hauled near the center sequoia. Hellano leans against it as Kysi places me on solid ground and pulls my back to his chest. It is just as warm as when I held no heat within myself, and his shaved jaw grazes my ear as he leans down to kiss my cheek.

When I turn my head to grant him my lips, he takes them deeply and tugs the diadems from my grasp. A giggle bubbles from my mouth to his, the edges perked up as he raises the black crown to Hellano.

They are not enemies here. It is a sight I never thought would be seen, even in the pit of my slumbering imagination. My lovers lift the pieces to their heads, and the moving parts of their troubled past halt. The crowns are at home ... and so are they in them.

Hellano turns to me and lifts a hand. His thumb runs back and forth near my ear as he dips to share a kiss that is soft and sweet, like the raspberries we ate in the shared bedchamber.

Our lips part, and the room is suddenly full. Angels, demons, and humans, they all lower their heads. Those not fashioned in the colors of Celestia wear shades of brown and green for Groveheart. Kysi and Hellano split from where I stand, walking in opposite directions.

Anxiety spikes. Are they leaving? What has happened to make them repel once more?

Kysi stops at the throne to my left, adjusting the lapel of his jacket as he takes the seat.

And to my right ...

The scorched sequoia, the *dead* tree, practically hugs Hellano in the shadows of its black bark as he lowers into it with humble confidence.

It was never a stain. Never a mistake.

I lower myself in the center throne ...

"You may rise," our voices thunder.

They left the cactus.

If all I could do was shoot one little needle and *miss* after hearing what Priscilla did to those innocent voyagers, I am no *real* threat. Yet.

They expect me to use it to test my limits, see if I can escape so they can document how horribly I fail. Chart how much I was able to achieve before getting caught. I refuse to do anything until I am confident in my success, and that is why I have done absolutely nothing but meditate for the last four days.

Unbeknownst to my captors, I am storing every ounce of my energy. In their presence I play the role of an exhausted damsel, weakened by that small act of defiance. I will not underestimate them, however. No inessential time is to be wasted. If I wait too long to act, I run the risk of exposing myself. Lying does not come easily, and they may catch on to my scheming if I am not careful.

I just need a little more time. A day, maybe. Then, I will cross the bridge to Divine Duplicity and attempt to lift the veil again.

"You've known me for a few months now," Wren says while working through equations on his pad. Both the men wear safety goggles now. "Do I display qualities of obsessive-compulsive disorder?"

Not particularly. "The worst I have seen," I reply and watch his eyes go wide.

"She's messing with you," Dev grumbles as he monitors how steadily my chest rises and falls.

I suck in air and hold it out of pettiness.

He humphs, annoyed. "You never make it easy, do you?"

I release the sigh in a swoosh that winds his hair. "No."

Wren shifts uncomfortably in the chair. The curved claws at the tips of his wings cast a shadow over the table. "Alright then. Dev, come take a look at this, will you?" He turns the notepad to his colleague, who strides over and glances at it for a split second before blinking to take a mental picture.

Dev's mouth parts in astonishment and tilts upwards. The men gape at each other ... and Dev nods.

They leave in a rush.

Fuck. Fuck, fuck, *fuck!*

The puzzle that's had them stumped has just been solved. I am out of time. They won. My kingdoms—

No. NO. It could be one breakthrough on the course of many. It could be a single step in the long road ahead.

It is still not worth the risk. I need to get out of here *tonight* with what little time I might have left. I have not attempted to use my abilities the slightest over the last ninety-six hours. Hopefully I have gathered enough energy to pack a punch.

Priscilla's words dissipate before they reach me. She circles where I sit, her calm tone no more than a fading hum in the background. I am aware of nothing but the repeating thump of her boots. They are the swinging pendulum that carries me deeper into a meditative sinkhole.

Bump. Bump. Bump.

Inhale. Exhale. Talking buzzes around me but does not resonate. It is incomprehensible.

Bump ... Bump ...

My thumb grazes the wedding bands in the confines of the shackles. I pull from the hope they give—it *is* useful here.

...

Silence. Without opening my eyes, I can sense her before me. The atmosphere shifts as Priscilla bends down. Hair on my arms arch. The back of my neck tingles. Her warm breath hits my nose and this time, I hear her loud and clear.

"War has begun."

CHAPTER 32

Divine Duplicity is farther than before.

Fog lingers with each breath as I travel through the faded path of my mind. It is empty and dark, a road only I can wander. The air is resistant but submits to the gentle hand I have lifted to guide me.

I know why the Capital lays between Groveheart and Celestia, why it naturally carries a blend of species.

It is my territory. Home to the Guardian of the New World—the Ultimate Queen, and anyone else in search of one themselves. It borders the kingdoms of my lovers as it is meant to, so they may reign beside me on common ground.

Such a hopeful picture threatened by bloodshed and tragedy.

The veil nears. I see it ahead. Feel it.

It stands unmoved like a fortress gate, locking the recipe for life inside as one would their most prized possession. My legs grow heavier with each step forward.

It has been two hours since Priscilla relayed the news. I continue to doubt whether I should have waited just a second longer and collected what extra energy I could squeeze out of myself, but patience is a parchment in the wind. Hesitation may gnaw at my psyche, but I have not looked back once since beginning this mental journey.

My reaching hand palms the wall of Divine Duplicity. Everything I need to escape lies on the other side. Everything I need to stop this war. Stop the men I love from destroying themselves.

When I test the curtain, there is a little give.

It is not sedimentary like before, but rather flexible. It follows my force as I tug, stretching as elastic would. I brace my foot on the supple barrier and fill my lungs, straining backwards until tremors rattle my joints.

Sweat breaks over my forehead from where I sit with crossed legs on the dungeon floor. This is taking too much energy. It may consume all that I have before splitting open … *if* it opens.

All that I made, all that I started, is falling apart at the seams mere months after the last ritual. It could all go away if those silver-blue flames were still burning. If I had not driven away the Spirits of the—

I hit the ground with a jarring thud. It echoes in my mind and bounces off the wall in all places but one.

A small rip looms above. In it are the whispers of a thousand beating hearts. A rooster's call at the break of dawn. Eggs hatching and infants crying.

In it is the beginning of all.

I rise at its vanguard. The cut is thin, hardly big enough for my hand. I steady my feet beneath me and push my fingers in, pressing weight into my shoulder to drive them deeper.

The tips tingle as contact is made with a crumb of raw power.

I sort the rush of symbols in my head, work through the equation. Atoms merge. Molecules form. My eyes flutter open to the tangible charge in the air. Newfound matter pressurizes to form nascent beings. Their pigment changes to blend with the granite floor, camouflaging the two bodies. Loose gravel trembles and comes together, hardening into the final digits of their pointed legs.

The abrupt exhaustion leaves me gasping. I blink rapidly to keep the encroaching faintness at bay. Stars swim in my vision like a meteor shower. It was too much, too draining. Rock is the most difficult to move. I have never birthed anything new with it before. But Divine Duplicity only gave me so much. I had to take advantage of the environment.

The room falters as their imprints lay flat against the blurred canvas of others. Twin arachnids survey the cell with curiosity.

"The locks," I lethargically sough, "pick the locks."

Their limbs are long and low to the ground. The speared ends clink with each step. My newborn spiders climb over my shin and locate the clasps quickly, sticking their appendages in the petite keyhole. *Tink. Tink tink.* They work together as if sharing a mind. I rest my head on the wall while I wait and release my muscles from all tension.

A hollow snap jerks me awake. The bindings on my hands and feet fall free, and they taste the air for the first time in months. They are visibly cleaner than the skin left uncovered, and my rings stare back at me like the white flag of my enemies.

How long was I asleep?

An imprint swells. Only a bit ... good. No time to waste.

There is no handle on the door, but my two tiny liberators can slink through the bottom and tell me what the other side looks like. That is exactly what they do.

Ideally, a handle that pushes down would be the easiest to deal with, but luck never swings too far my way. I am relieved to learn that it is not another lock that requires picking, but a knob in need of a twist. We can work with that.

My knees shake violently as I stand. I hover to let them settle—remember what it is like to bear weight and walk. One baby step. Two.

Drag the chains in the corner, I instruct. Priscilla is too precautionary to leave my cell unguarded. This way, when the imperials come to investigate and the door swings open to the right, all they will see are links leading into the dark shadow behind it. It will require a step inside to check if I am still bound.

How many were there?

Two, that they could see, but the hallway turns a corner where there are likely more.

The spiders move with haste, shooting thick webs from the tips of their abdomens to haul the manacles over. I wearily make it to the wall near the door, so I too can be draped in shadows when they peer in the threshold.

Open the door and restrain the guards.

I can almost hear them mischievously snicker as they creep beneath the door once more. A moment later, a strand of light beams over the floor and gradually grows wider. Mumbles sound in the hall from both directions. Footsteps follow.

My heart gallops faster the closer they come. A nervous sweat spans my shoulders.

"They said she would try," chimes a voice I do not recognize. Another huffs in response. There isn't enough oxygen in the room to fill my lungs when the seeping light outlines their silhouettes.

Chains rattle as my spiders bait them like a game of cat and mouse.

"Nice party trick," one says, taking the first step inside. "What did you do, use the cactus roots?"

I see their mountainous bodies in front of me as one nudges the other and points to the untouched plant on the table. They did not think that I was strong enough to create yet, only manipulate what is already there. "Hm. How did—"

The arachnids carry malice in their hiss, leaping from the ground as if gravity is a *suggestion*. They latch onto the guard's faces, their joints burrowing a circle in their skin. Pale strings spray in their mouth and nose as they stumble and claw at the attackers.

I slip from the darkness and close the prison door to muffle their cries. The snicket is empty and quiet, the ceiling unkept just like the one in my cell. Jagged and cold, as if they knew rock and ice were weaknesses of mine.

Of course they did ... thanks to Cato.

Through the window, the soldiers silently battle. One hits the table with their thigh and falls to the floor, tripping their comrade.

Webs of white encompass their heads to blind and suffocate. The guard with bulbous arms goes limp, and the spider plucks their legs from the fluffy bed of silk.

Don't kill them. I do not know these people, not really. They could be acting to protect themselves from a threat they were brainwashed into believing. Sparing them will plant a seed of truth.

The sinister insect pauses over the man's neck, grumbling as she reaches a single limb back and pops an air hole in her victim's mouth.

Thank you.

The remaining soldier lifts a weak hand and grips the body of my newborn child, but instead of pulling ... he squeezes.

I cover my mouth to hush a sob. Blood and guts shoot through tight fingers just before they go flaccid. Grief restricts my ribcage. The insect was my first ally in months, and its short life was sacrificed to save me.

Sticky threads line the doorknob as I twist and push. The twin stomps past me, carrying pain in her strides.

I'm sorry ... the guard—

Her unique fingerprint angrily bounces. The spider defies my gentle command with a thundering NO.

Not all lives are mine to spare. *Alright ... For your sister.*

Those night watchmen had nothing of use on them. Not a key or a map, only identical batons too heavy for me to carry. My spider, who I have nicknamed Violent, is hardly visible as she camouflages herself with the floor. The stone tips of her legs do not match her body, but the slate-gray mixes with the fallen debris from the ceiling. From here, it looks like pebbles are drifting on their own.

Violent goes around the curved corner and relays what she sees. Two doors on the right and a set straight ahead. The coast is clear for now.

I crouch under the first window, inching up to peek for a millisecond. Rows of bunks hold slumbering bodies, and I cannot tell whether they belong to more members of the Imperial Army or laboratory staff. I do not hover to ponder it.

Violent slips into the next corridor at the end of the hall to scope out what is ahead. As I pass the second door, I do not need to glance through glass to know what is inside. I can hear it—hear *them.*

"Even without the dangers, I don't know how long it will take," Wren speaks with a layer of concern.

"You excel both in physical stature and mental sharpness," Dev assures. "This will be a walk in the park compared to our work thus far."

"Our work thus far involved equations, not manhunts. If someone could accompany me—"

"NO—no, you must go alone!" Severity blankets Dev's voice. "Remember what Dr. Delphine said? Some things are better left undiscovered. This revelation *cannot* be released to the public. Secrecy is of the upmost importance! If we had aid, this would have been solved weeks ago. We must not compromise all that we have done when we are so close! You can do this. I will have the bead reconstructed by the time you return. Then, we will alter the ingredients for compatibility to reproduce it. I cannot do it without you."

Dev and Wren ... they did not create the poison that stole my power. It was either found or given to them. They have been studying it, chemically breaking it down to analyze its makeup. At last, they achieved this, and now Wren is leaving to collect the materials for more.

Violent sends information through her individual mark ... She found the way out.

To get there, I must avoid the imperials on patrol. On the other side of the same wall that holds the exit before me, another pair of double doors rest in the center of the walkway. In front of it are two rooms divided by another hallway that hits a T, circling around each chamber. Where the top of the T begins, straight across from that center set of double doors, is a thick slab of iron with a vault wheel on its belly. That is the door to freedom.

"We have time," Dev goes on. "There is another bead if we need—two when I rebuild the sample." A heartbeat of silence. "Go, Wren. Find the elements. I'll be waiting alongside our work for your return."

It is not just guards I must steer clear of, but Wren. I have to move before he comes out and finds me.

Tell me when the watchmen rotate again.

Seconds pass. My cheeks flush when steps pad on the other side of the door. Just as I am about to call for Violent again, her imprint twitches.

I slip through the exit into the main halls. They are bright white and barren just as before, which helps none with how easily my pitch-black hair and dirty skin could be seen. I stick out like a gods-damn flare in the dark.

Assuming the escape hatch is locked, Violent will need to keep it from wholly shutting after Wren leaves. She will crawl ahead and send me queues to progress, hold the door, and out we will go. All while fighting indolent muscles, crippling vertigo, and anxiety-induced nausea.

Easy. Piece of cake. Not a problem.

Gods, it is so hard to breathe.

I force an inhale and move at Violent's command, banking right towards the set of doors in the middle of the hall. I spot the end of a boot string ahead, and trail forward to stay behind the imperial on duty. Heated chatter sounds in the room to my left. Boots stomp farther down the strip around the corner behind me. I pick up the pace.

The exit … it is in the distance to my left, down the narrow path that splits the two chambers. It is tall and hefty, a beacon for safe havens with green pastures and clear skies. The grand wheel hanging out stares back at me like the all-seeing eye of a great curator.

Violent warns me to move, and I shuffle past it quietly and turn left into another runway of white.

My movements cease at the sight of a woman ahead. Her rigid posture faces the same direction I do as she marches forward, taking the bend at the end of the hallway that circles back.

This hospital, or bunker, or whatever the hell this place is, reminds me of a maze where one continues to pass the same landmark despite going different routes. The halls all round-robin back to one another in confusing tunnels.

By the time I take the same corner, I see the promise of freedom once more. This is where I must leave Violent so she can bar the door after Wren walks through. I will continue to follow the woman ahead until I can circle back and slip free.

I peek my head from the edge, finding the set of doors I passed earlier straight in front of the exit. Stern voices go back and forth in the room diagonally to me. I take a step in the main hall—

My stomach lurches at the swinging doors. I rear back, pinning my mutilated wings against the wall. My hand palms my mouth to silence quivering breaths.

That was Wren that I saw—dressed in a fur-lined coat rather than medical gear. Which means the door I eavesdropped through was merely a side entrance to the lab connected to this main area.

Heavy boots thud louder. I press against the wall like it will absorb me—hide my visage from the blinding bars of light above. If I turn back now, I am likely to meet a guard making another round, except I would run into their front instead of their back.

In this moment I pray. If the Sky Spirits can hear, if they care about this realm in the slightest, they will keep Wren's focus forward.

He comes into view, so close I can almost reach out and grab him. His strides eat the space between each step as he climbs the short stairs to the massive exit. He reaches forward, hand gripping the wheel. The thump of distant feet echo down the hall in which I came.

I can hardly hold a laugh of disbelief. I am about to be the luckiest godsdamn soul in all the New World. I am about to escape.

Wren hesitates.

His fingers drift from the circular handle and pat the pocket of his thick coat. Head tilted down as if searching for a forgotten item, Wren turns on his heels before finding the missing piece of parchment in his jean pocket. The scientist pivots back around to leave.

Our eyes meet.

Whatever hope I held in my wedding rings, what faith I had in my own success, shrivels and dies.

He stares. I stare. The day has come for me to try and break free just as they expected me to, and I failed ... just as they expected me to.

Wren's mouth falls open to call out. I lift a hand, and to my surprise, it stops him.

The guard around the corner draws closer with each blink. My vision becomes glossy at the edges as desperation floods my senses.

Please, I mouth. I search his face to find an ounce, a single fucking speck, of anything benign lurking beneath.

Conflict. I see it there. In the lines of his brows, the way his lips slowly close.

Maybe it is the paper of hope he holds within his hand—the list of materials on it that makes him merciful. Maybe it is the way he always blinked when Dev would pluck a feather. Or how he was the first to leave my cell. Every. Single. Time.

Wren sees how close I have gotten, eyes darting from the vault to the lab, then back to me. With a hard swallow, he turns and twists the mighty exit door.

A freezing wind barrels in. The scientist grips the frame to steady himself against the current. Sleet swims through the cave canal like a winter vortex.

It dawns on me then that Dev and Wren were never *dirty*. Priscilla was never dotted in *sweat* ... it was melted ice from the spiraling flakes beyond.

Fear the falling snow.

Wren does not glance my way when he pulls the vault behind him ... and leaves it just slightly cracked.

He really is letting me go.

I wait. Focus on the steady stomps that close in. I need to make one more round to put enough space between us before opening that door a second time and alerting the entire bunker. There is a chance the guards will think it is Wren returning for something, but not one that I am willing to risk freedom on. When I open that hatch, I must fight with everything I have to get out before they reach me. Violent is strong for her size, she can pull me with her webs or hold them off until I can make it through the tunnel. Once I leave the cave the wind won't be so strong; it is the burrow this structure was built into that causes the funnel of ice and air.

I go around one more time. Violent crawls near my feet. Thank gods the wheel looks the same whether it is turned one way or the other, because then the guards may have noticed it was unlocked.

In these months, I have done more than beat death. I beat powerless torture.

Ready? I will need Violent to slip through the crack and help me pull. It will no doubt be heavy.

Her imprint flutters. She is ready.

One ... two ... three.

We book it to the iron slab and I yank the wheel so hard it feels my shoulders may pop from their sockets. It moves dreadfully slow, but I only need it open far enough to fit my wings. Flurries fly in from a thin split of fresh air.

"You'll die out there."

Every nerve ending curls. My forlorn will to succeed begs that I continue pulling, but my brain forces me to look back.

Dev stands at the other end of bleached walls. He inches closer from the laboratory's main entrance. A metal rod is raised from the end of his outstretched arm and forks in two. Between the parallel prongs a holster is drawn to the mad savant's cheek, where he holds another bead between tight fingers.

"You're not even wearing shoes." He stalks forward, white coat motionless around preying legs. "You'll freeze before morning."

The uniformed woman I was trailing halts at the scene. Another guard comes into view next, stopping to cautiously observe.

"That's your last one, isn't it?" I tilt my chin to the weapon. "You dissected the other—"

"I can bring it back," he claims with uncertainty at the hilt of his burr.

I squeeze the handle when he takes another step, which stops him for a moment. My gaze narrows. "Reconstructing the chemical makeup of any material is an extremely delicate task, and this is ... what the fuck even is that thing Dev?"

A vein near his temple bulges. "It is the savior of my people! It is the only thing that protects us from your kind!"

"Gods. Are. No. Threat!" I repeat for the countless time. "And when you fail to reproduce that abomination, you will see! When you cannot weaken the deities of this realm into submission and are forced to live among them as they are, you *will* see."

Dev shakes his head. "You don't want the same things we do."

Humans. They want humans. The Imperials know I would never sit idly by while they use them as blood bags. They seek the freedom to rid others of theirs.

I cannot keep my bottom lip from shaking. "You don't want that ... you want to *learn*. I can create an endless number of species for you to study. I'll birth oddities of nature that will hold your attention for centuries. Drop the bead, Dev. Let me leave."

Rich brown eyes bore into me. I search them as I did Wren's, digging deeper and deeper for that spark of morality.

413

They darken, and I know it is not there.

Save yourself, I tell Violent. They must not find her, or she will die under a light on a table. When my spider's defiance swells in my mind, I do what I always told myself would be unforgivable ... I *force* her to flee.

A wetness drags across my cheek at her writhing imprint.

My innate will to live, the same one I wished to smother, perishes at last.

Dev is right. I will die out there, but sometimes the worst thing someone could ever do is the best thing they could have done.

I will not survive this ... but by gods my daughter will be born from wrath and resistance. She will wear the snarl I leave behind and avenge my death with each blow she lands upon the foundation of Nightfall.

I may be weak, but the goddess of Beginnings cannot say goodbye without a parting gift.

With a sharp inhale and a mite of power, I rear back and *spit* in the face of my captor. Saliva flies while I wrench the door open. It hardens into a toothpick of nightspruce, and I can tell by Dev's cry of pain that I hit the target this time.

The gap in the door, where snowflakes dance and wind whips, is now big enough to fit my frame. I lunge toward certain death and hope that Hellano does not sense my downfall, and if he does, at least know that I went on my own accord. For him. For Kysi. For the New World.

The canal to gloomy redemption freezes. No ... not the canal.

Me.

Something feels clogged in my neck. It seeps in and inflates my throat, as if the altitude ahead is dangerous to breathe. Gravity pushes me back, and I reach for my ears and nose. Have I started bleeding again? Gods, it feels like that was lifetimes ago.

My face is dry ... but my fingers wave across branches under my skin. I follow their bumps, swaying like a drunkard as the adrenaline wanes, to a marble-sized hole at the apex of my back.

The room quakes and my balance falters. Stairs slam their teeth in my side before gravity pins me to the floor. My world turns sideways as an overwhelming, all-consuming agony punctures each digit of my spine. Electricity ebbs through the marrow of my skeleton, a static burn that floods ligaments and seeps into every sinew.

Divine Duplicity mends a tiny rip, without so much as leaving a scar.

Dev's hand violently shakes as he drops the empty rod and clutches an eye. Imperials pile out from the room to his left, lead by Priscilla. I can hear her voice boom, but am robbed of the ability to comprehend. Soldiers race to me as if rabid dogs bite at their heels. The first ones step over my body to reach the door. I do not realize what a comforting distraction the freezing breeze on my back is until it's gone. A million clicks lock the vault. Each one sounds like a life lost to war; the end of calamity annihilated.

I choke like a fish without water. A fire ignites in my lungs. Calloused grips seize my arms and legs. I am lifted and carried away in a rush, passing where Priscilla fists the collar of Dev's coat.

"If she dies, we lose!" she howls. The yelling fades as I am lugged through the laboratory doors. Endless exploding stars border my vision and burst brighter with every failed attempt to breathe.

My perception becomes a slide projector of images as I fade in and out. One minute I am surrounded by imperials, the next Dev is leaning over me. Blood runs down his face, eyelid pinned shut by a fat splinter. He pushes through pain, prioritizing my viability over his injury. Whatever gentleness he offered before is gone, as he shoves a clear tube down my throat with so much force it tears the lining of my esophagus.

Sterile air sprinkles the inferno in my chest. The slight reprieve is all my body needs to let go of consciousness.

I am neither haunted nor contented by dreams. As if my brain is too beaten down to conjure them up, nothing but oblivion reaches me. It is still an indication of my unwanted survival; the Shadowlands do not greet me yet.

I wiggle my fingers against soft cotton. There is an acidic odor that chaps the edges of my dry nostrils. A wave of soreness passes my tongue when I instinctively try to swallow. It prompts my lashes to flutter, and the first thing I see is a plastic hose snaking from my pried open mouth. It spans my torso, running off the bed to a machine that huffs every couple of seconds.

Vials fill shelves with colorful liquid, some bubbling with vitality. Books that do not stand between them are lain sprawled upon crowded countertops, accompanied by what looks to be centrifuges and microscopes. Other machines I do not recognize, but their naked wires and gears carry the same dreadful purpose.

I languidly push myself upright, finding that I am not bound or cuffed or chained. The only thing attached to me is the pipe sending fresh air into my chest.

A page flips. Piled with more books and scattered papers, a round table sits by the side door. Splattered red stains a long pale jacket. Strands of hair poke from the plaster wrapping Dev's head. He blinks an umber eye to store the image of text for later, his other hidden behind layers of absorbent swath. Another page turns.

Priscilla's words echo, *"If she dies, we lose!"*

With torpid smoothness, I lift a hand to the lifeline between my lips. In one fluid movement, I wrest it from deep within my chest. I hack and rasp, feeling it lift from near my diaphragm and drag up my breastbone. Dev is near me in a trice, but the tube is already out. I throw it across the floor.

To my surprise, the chemist is still at my bedside—watching. That solitary eye is transfixed upon my thorax, waiting for the rise and fall.

Unbidden, it comes.

Dev's shoulders alleviate tension. A hand runs through locks of unbound hair before falling to his side. "I should bind you to that bed," he quips.

I blink. "Why haven't you?" my voice is a withered leaf, raspy and coarse.

"Priscilla and her power moves." He wipes a stain on his forearm as if it is a piece of lint. "You'll see the next time you try to leave."

My brows magnetize. "So ... I could try right now?"

His hand lifts to the double doors before me. "Be my guest." The thought does not concern him in the least.

I sluggishly swing my legs to the side. "What happened?"

A question the man seems almost excited to answer. He even extends a hand to help me stand. I ignore it. "I have colleagues in Nightfall that specialize in mortal research. Did you know humans have the power to project their consciousness to other planes of existence? They mostly do it without knowing, in dreams or periods of deep thought."

Mortal research, aka nonconsenting human subjects. I swat Dev away and put weight on my bare feet. They strain to keep me level, and the scientist keeps both arms out in case I tumble. It is not an act of care; I am merely his porcelain lab rat.

It is blatant curiosity that drags my legs forward, because I know with a palpable suspicion that escaping is no longer possible for me; they would not let me walk freely if it were.

He continues, holding the door open. "I think you did that."

"What are you—"

The halls hold scattered imperials. None make rounds—no need to with all the eyes about. Some sit on the floor with their heads against the wall. All appear bored until their faces turn to me, a battered spectacle of divine failure.

At the end of the main hall, brambles are bestrewn in a semicircle around the steely vault. Broken crumbs freckle their severed ends. I study the scene, frozen in place as Dev nods to a soldier. "Like mindless bacteria evading painful stimuli, I theorize that your divine nature responded to our threat using a critical defense mechanism."

The cumbersome wheel spins. It creeps open to reveal a yawning cavity gagged by dead brush. This was the rumble underfoot that tripped me ... a burst of rapid growth.

By his assumption, that would mean Divine Duplicity attempted to ensure either my death or survival; whatever avoids my recent and powerless dormancy. It dislikes the hardened borders, my inability to reach it. The bead Dev shot into my neck not only imprisons me, but it as well. Divine Duplicity followed the path back to me before the tear was sealed as a last-ditch effort to free itself.

The only exit ... is barricaded.

We are all trapped inside.

CHAPTER 33

Brew swirls in a beaker on the round table before me. My face is pallid in the pomegranate reflection, and someone brushed my hair while I slept. Dark veins bloom from behind my neck and climb the hills of my jawline to fade across sunken cheeks. They were swollen and bulging before, now they are level with my skin.

A decaying corpse would be more visually appealing.

A smudge blurs the top portion of my right wing and blends into the wall behind me. The other remains disgustingly bare, like a hairless cat intruding in personal space. I wince and look away before the nausea rolls in.

Wait—the blemish on the glass ... It moved *with* me.

If I were not frozen in this chair, I might have screamed. But all I can do is stare. Gape at my botched wing ... the one originally left untouched. It looks like a bite was taken out of the upper segment.

Vomit. I need to vomit, but that would require having food in my stomach.

"Take this"—Dev gestures to the cup—"for the pain."

Now he offers me medicine? Anger rattles my teeth. "What the fuck did you do to me?"

He falls into the opposing chair. "Saved you from a lifetime of backache." I am given an expression that implies he's owed thanks, and it brings me a hairpin away from smacking it off his face. "It cracked like ice on a lake when you hit the floor. Bent to a right angle. Would you prefer I let it heal crooked?"

Staring at my foreign appearance—one wing ripped naked and the other broken and bandaged from my failed escape attempt—I am unable to fathom permanently losing flight. Before, all it would take was patience for the feathers to grow back. Now ...

It is too draining to pretend I have strength anymore. My fortuitous act shatters like heated glass. Unashamed of who sees me break, I curl into myself and weep.

Erratic lamentations fill the lab. I fall apart hysterically; no corner of my mind is safe from this trauma. What is happening here will affect me forever. Nights surrounded by stars are over. Days spent kissing skies and chasing clouds are gone. I will never feel the sun's close embrace, the moon's cool face, the tickle of wind under the span of spread feathers again.

Never have I resonated so deeply with Hellano's purpose. Because right now ... death is all that I long for.

A tender touch caresses the shell of my sorrow. It softly leads my forearms down, exposing my ruddy cheeks and tear-filled pores. Dev kneels before me. Solace drifts from an eye so richly brown it reminds me of earth after heavy rain. His hand reaches up to my wet face, and I cannot decipher whether penitence eats at his conscience or if he does not regret his actions at all, just loathes their consequences. All decisions aside, at this moment he offers consolation.

A dense mass of emotional turmoil perches between my ribs. This man is a monster. My only option for a loving haven, a place to expel heartache, is in the same arms that constrict me purple.

It prompts a consuming anger that plunges me to the floor. Dev falls at the impact, catching himself leaning back. His torso becomes a target for my frail fists. I strike him repeatedly, screaming and crying to transfer a fraction of this debilitating misery. He does not stop me. I beat his chest without protest, like he knows it is less than what he deserves.

I do not just fight a heartless madman, but also the shameful urge to accept whatever comfort I can get. My fragile blows grow weaker as I gradually surrender to my desire and confide in another.

Sobs fill the fabric between his open coat, and he wraps me in a hug I am too weak to resist. It is a warm outlet, and my traitorous body and mind cling to it like a child nearly torn from their mother.

"Shh," he soothes, "I can fix them. I promise."

The first round of poison laid groundwork for the Imperials. They know how weak it made me. How weak it will make other deities. Dev claimed that Priscilla wanted to put me back in my cell after I saw the vault and he used this knowledge to convince her that I am of better use in the lab—more accessible to his research. Not an ounce of me believes it came from kindness. I assume it has something to do with the fact Wren is no longer here to keep him company. Dev made me swear not to touch anything, though. I made the promise with no intention of keeping it, but my new roommate has not left my side once.

Priscilla stares back at me from the round table. It is the first time I have seen her since the barricade. She must have been scrambling, pacing alongside her major officials. It would be contrary to her current comportment, however; the Imperial Army leader lacks the slightest concern. There is nothing in the frozen sea of her gaze. Calm water, stagnant and dangerous.

"There is information to deliver. Updates. Status reports. A missed deadline will not go unnoticed. Someone will come." Relaxed fingers intertwine upon the table. Her chest expands and deflates at a steady rate. "If you try anything until then, so much as fucking cough without excusing yourself, I will throw you right back in that prison where my comrade lays bloating on the floor." Her smooth cadence is low, almost a whisper. Hopefully, she does not notice the way bumps spread over my forearms.

A man lays dead in my old cell. The Imperials have not brought him out—have nowhere *to* bring him. Priscilla's stillness is the only indication that she may be mourning.

Her steely frame rises. "One more thing before I go," she says, staring down at me like the lowly subject of a queen. "You better hope that little bug is good at hide and seek. Otherwise, I am about to gain a new pet."

Lividity clamps my lips. I forced Violent to obey my command. However, I am unaware of where exactly she fled. Her imprint is gone now, blended together with the rest of them. My heart aches at the thought of her trying to call me and getting a busy signal.

When the bitch is gone, I shuffle to the bed beside Dev's and bury myself under Wren's blankets. The chemist peers into the lens of a bulky machine. His hands fill the holes on each side, tinkering with internal parts.

I will not mention Wren's mercy. When he finds out that I kept his secret, the first thin layer of trust will settle. There is no telling what the future holds, but I will stack bricks for a storm anyway.

A dull ache blooms over my backside. It grows stronger with each heartbeat. During my first two months here, I was given nothing for pain. Now that I am on my second dose of poison, Dev is more comfortable offering me relief. It does not come from a place of empathy; he likely wanted to test how the toxin responded to it.

"May I have more Redspire, please?" I coax with delicate syllables.

I am met with a contemplating glare. Despite his many facades of compassion, I know a genuine soft spot is forming for me when he bends his own rules at my request. "Oh, alright. But we must save as much as we can. You'll need it more than ever after the reconstructive surgery."

In a moment's notice, I am offered a small shot of the viscous balm. I take it without hesitation or complaint, and the ache dulls almost immediately. It lingers in the nooks and crannies of my spinal column, but it is easier to bear.

If boredom were a maze, I would have every exit and dead end memorized. I try to meditate, but my brain insists upon conjuring daydreams to cope. I see Kysi and Hellano in them. Hold their hands and kiss their faces. Someone more headstrong would fight these pointless fantasies for the sake of productivity—meditation holds power even for the powerless—but I cannot bring myself to part with them.

I imagine us laying under a tree with teardrop leaves. Plumes of sparkling indigo and bubblegum pink slowly drift behind the full branches above, where Kingfishers lounge in the crevice of a bough. My shoulders are boxed between my loves and their fingers are tangled in mine. I watch in silence as they point out passing birds and oddly shaped clouds, soaking in the calm hum of their voices like a wanderer would a rare spring. Kysi lifts an arm to point at another bird. When I follow his finger, I find not an animal but an arrow cleaving the sky.

No matter how hard I try to build impenetrable dreamscapes, reality always finds a crack to barrel into.

More soar above, coming from all directions. Each one released darkens the sun—cuts it to bleed and turns the air a crimson red. Ashen smoke billows in the distance. The Kingfishers flee when screams erupt.

I whip focus to my mate for direction or comfort, only to find his eyes glazed and still. Hellano's the same.

I am alone in the midst of war, the middle of the New World's collapse. It is karma for what I brought to Earth ... I must live inside the wreckage of my own making.

Just a daydream, just a daydream.

The world is how I left it, with covers over my knees and Dev peering through a lens.

The songbird of hope lies muted in my soul, its perch fatefully paralyzed. I cannot decipher if the torpid space within me comes from the animal's departure ... or its death. I coast in the empty space of my mind that always pushed me to carry on, waiting for that familiar wave to come, that native song to sing.

Stillness. Silence.

My wedding rings falter between fidgeting fingers and fall from my hand. They land side by side on the blanket across my legs, an infinity before me. I cannot help but think the coincidental place-ment *should* make me feel better. Instead, it feels like a cruel taunt.

I will be stuck here forever.

I sluggishly reach forward and break their connection. Just before I slide them over my knuckles once more, a discrepancy glints on the inside of Hellano's. Letters—an inscription I never noticed before.

Never wilt, my flower.

Clear pearls crowd the corners of my eyes. One falls with a blink, plummeting onto the covers with a quiet thump. I read it again and again. Countless times. Each one is protein for my malnourished heart.

I finally slide the rings back on and curl my left hand into my chest. In the pit of my being ... a chirping lullaby picks up.

Apparently, rebinding elements takes time. Sometimes the scientist will sit straight-backed at the round table with an eye closed and lips moving. It is utterly creepy, but I can only assume it is his process of skimming the pages he previously blinked into his mind. Other times, I am weighed and measured and poked and swabbed. I am afraid to sniff in fear he will say something like, "*If you must, please blow your nose into this collection cup so I can place it under my swanky microscope.*" In his defense, aerodynamics and structural engineering are not his specialty, and the operation he performed after I broke my wing is the extent of his hands-on experience. Dev wants to make sure that he performs the surgery properly.

It is a little nerve-wracking, the thought of having my wings reshaped by a novice surgeon. But when I think about their current state, I am not sure how it could possibly get any worse. I trust that he will do his best. Dev seems to enjoy the challenge, and it helps him pass the time while he waits for the machines to do their job.

I have concluded that because Wren is currently off collecting the materials needed to recreate the weapon, it must not grow naturally in this realm. Which means, it was given to them. But how did the first owner know how to craft it in the first place? How did they figure it out so quickly?

Cato is the only explanation. I theorize that Priscilla's "status reports" are meant to be delivered to him, and because Dev and Wren stated previously that their time with me is limited, I assume that means I am to be handed to the god of Wisdom once the kingdoms fall. Maybe when I see him, I'll find the answers. This thought makes me hope it will forever remain a mystery, because that would mean I got out of here and stopped the war.

"Why would Cato hand over three beads without telling you what they are made of?" I break the silence. "Where did they come from?"

Without so much as glancing my way, Dev responds, "They are of unknown origin. The secret of its makeup belongs solely to the Imperials—well, technically just me for now." He pulls a hand from inside the machine and taps his temple twice. "All stored up here. It is the one piece of knowledge the god of Wisdom must never know. Or any deity, for that matter."

Now I have more questions than before. Cato just ... acquired this poison, something that could destroy his own kind, and gave it to them? I suppose that is why they call it madness; there is no rhyme or reason.

"What's the deal between Cato and the Imperials?" As soon as the words are out, I realize I have pushed too far.

I can almost see the soft spot for me solidifying as Dev hardens. "I know what you're doing, Dr. Delphine. Stop trying to gather confidential information."

Of course he knows, because I was too fucking obvious about it. "Fine, don't answer." I brush it off. After a few heartbeats, I ask, "What's your favorite color? Or is that confidential too?"

Lips purse in annoyance. "Silver."

I twiddle my fingers. "Favorite food?"

"Blood."

... I refrain from asking what kind. "How did you meet Wren?"

At this, he pauses. The hint of a smirk arises as Dev thinks back. "Priscilla paired us for this task, and skillfully so, because his brain is magnificent. I fill the gaps in his formulas, but he lays the pieces in front of me. We work together like the strands of a double helix. Wren is quite the inventor as well. He built most of this lab equipment."

Spending months working alongside someone, sleeping five feet from them, would either bring people together or tear them apart. From the way Dev speaks of him, I would guess they have become close friends.

I wonder how much that would change if he knew that Wren had let me go ...

Medical instruments clink in Dev's elbow-length gloves as he takes them from an autoclave. My bed, or Wren's I should say, has fresh sheets for the operation. It is otherwise bare, save for straps that hang on either side. I nervously circle the round table, fidgeting with my hair and nails.

Numerous illustrations accompany an array of science books. The outline of my frame with different wings behind it. Various angles and close-ups of Dev's vision, with lines, numbers, and symbols clustered on every blank space of the pages.

One set of sketches stands out from the others. A journal of gadgets I have never seen, concepts of hardware with unknown purposes. The handwriting is softer, unlike Dev's rigid penmanship. It must be Wren's book of inventions.

"Ah, ah, ah," Dev barks from across the room. "That is an invasion of Wren's privacy."

I quirk a brow. "Then why is it open?"

He dodges the question like it was never asked. "Come and take your Redspire. It is time."

Apprehension returns. I will not be asleep for the surgery, just given a hefty dose of pain medication. That's why the restraints are on the bed ... to hold me down in case the balm is not potent enough.

Is it worth the potential pain? The New World is falling apart outside, and we are sitting ducks in a bunker with no escape. Why is this a concern? I want my wings to be fixed, but it feels selfish to care. Then again, boredom has a way of bringing forth purpose. What else would fill our spare time here? At least this feels productive.

I swallow my fear and gulp the medicine. It is thick and bitter. My senses dull before I get it halfway down, and by the end of it, Dev is holding the beaker for me. I collapse onto my stomach, and the chemist hauls my legs up the rest of the way before pinning my wings to trays on either side of me. There is no mental fatigue, just physical. I am numb everywhere.

We have gone over the procedure a million times. He made me memorize it so nothing would surprise me, but the sight of that bone saw still triggers my fight or flight. Adrenaline surges, but it is useless to my unresponsive limbs. I am thankful for this, because if by chance the Redspire is not strong enough to mask the pain, this extra rush will surely top it off.

A violent whizz fills the room. After slamming my eyes shut, I know it has made contact when the sound lowers an octave. No pain thus far, just an occasional pull or jerk.

Feeling woozy, I distract myself by once again building a dreamscape. I take my time with every detail. A filigree carved bedpost. An intruding wind that slow dances with the mesh canopy of curtains. They drift around us like waterfalls of silk, a soft privacy fence for our scandalous rendezvous.

Kysi's lips are warm on mine. Hellano's breath grazes my ear from behind, his chest teasing my back. Their hands explore in waves that grow with each glide over my breasts, my stomach, and around my hips. At last, they crash between my thighs and move in tandem. Each swipe pushes and pushes and pushes me up a steep hill.

Our skin is flushed with arousal. I dare not blink in this rumination. I hold the walls of it steady with every bit of mental strength, fixating on the curves of Kysi's broad shoulders. His perfectly carved nose, like the side of a captivating mountain. His jaw that rivals the beauty of a horizon. Onyx hair that tangles between each of my fingers as I move between them.

And Hellano, whose eyes remind me of a newborn galaxy bursting with color. The sun favors his skin and gifts it with radiancy. Even at night the glow stays, like he is entrusted with its light until morning breaks.

"Ask me for it," Kysi groans into my mouth. The command is meant for not just me ...

Hellano's sunken tone vibrates my neck. "Can I take her?"

Moments pass, and Kysi's lips leave my mouth and find my earlobe. "Your turn, angel," he croons.

The build-up has me teetering on a knife's point. "Can I take him, please?"

My mate's hand carries mine to his length. When I ask again without words, his eyes grow brighter. "Yes," he breathes, "make her writhe."

I sense Hellano lining up, moaning as the tip slides—

"What the hell are you doing?" An irate voice springs my eyes open. How could I have such promiscuous thoughts while being carved like whittler's wood?

Priscilla stands at Dev's backside. Blood splatters his coat and goggles. The bone saw is disregarded for a file, and he responds without turning to greet her. "I cannot focus with these grotesque extremities in my line of sight. They need reshaped."

It seems her ponytail is on a bit tight today. "You didn't think to tell me? Have you lost your mind?"

Has she been living under a rock?

I suppose so, since we are technically trapped in a cave.

She overlooks the scene. "You're wasting precious resources!"

"I will decide if a resource is wasted," the scientist barks.

Priscilla withholds a response. After all, she relies on Dev. Something swims beneath her soulless eyes as she grazes over my bleeding appendage. She takes a step forward. Then another.

Dev notices the movement and does a double-take before briskly pivoting between us. "It is you who have lost your wits! Her blood is toxic, and we do not yet know the consequences of ingesting it. Out! Get out this instant!"

You have got to be fucking kidding me. These creatures will drink blood from anything. What makes them so different from the Ferathore Clans they speak of?

Priscilla gulps, eyes darting from Dev to me.

"We finish this, and you can go back to getting your fix from a *clean* donor." The file is tightly held. "Go, Priscilla. Now!"

Her fists habitually clench. Nostrils flare with each inhale. Is she bathing in the smell? Is it coaxing her to feed? Quickly, Priscilla twists and takes long strides out.

The grating file on my bones resume.

Pressure fills my vertebrae when I put weight on my legs. It would be a crippling pain if not for Redspire, which is the only reason I am attempting to walk just two days after the operation, rather than weeks from now. When I awoke moments ago, it was a surprise to hear I had slept the entire time.

Thank gods for Dev at my front keeping my balance, because the moment I leave the bed I nearly fall forward. Most of my weight is carried in the front now. It will be an odd transition, but at least the hardest part is over.

"Do you drink from my kind, too?" I ask, gripping his forearms for balance. Dev does not wear his coat today. Too many blood stains. Instead, a deep blue shirt with a single breast pocket hugs his chest.

He hesitates before answering. "Divine blood is the most sought after of all species. Even if you weren't the first deity I have met, I am not sure I would indulge. It makes Priscilla ... different. She won't admit this herself, but I think she has developed a dependency for it."

So, Cato offers his blood to them as well. Another note to add to my preposterous list of things I do not understand. "I thought you knew the god of Wisdom?"

He shakes his head, leading me into a step. "Priscilla and Harlynn are the only ones who speak to him. I hear he is quite reclusive."

Her name sparks rage in a place I cannot pinpoint, so it must be everywhere. It's not until thumbs swing back and forth over my elbows that I realize I was squeezing Dev's arms.

"She was your friend," he dolefully states.

"I miscalculated." My tone is sharp as I try to focus on the task at hand and move my leg.

His trailing thumbs do not stop when I loosen my grip. "You did no such thing. One cannot foresee an outcome like that." I have no response. He leads me into another step after my throat clears. "Your flight will be limited. Don't expect to soar as you once did. With practice, say if you fall from a great height, they will save you."

My feet resist his gentle tug. I was just rearranged, chiseled and fucking *carved* under the impression they would be *fixed*. "What did you just say?"

He casually peers at our feet, waiting for me to continue this pitiful attempt at walking. "With your type of feathers—"

"Did you ever believe I would fly again, or did you just tell me it was possible so you could do another experiment?"

The gauze across his face slightly shifts when his brows furrow. "I never said—"

"You *promised*. You lied!" My nails leave red crescents on his skin. "You are here because of *me*. *I* brought you into this world, all of you!" I camber my chin to the door, where soldiers have been kicking pebbles in the halls for weeks. "Your heart is disgusting and cruel. At least Wren had enough compassion to leave the vault cracked for me, you can't even tell a truth!"

The words fall out before I can catch them. Dev stills, and the grazing on each of my elbows halts. "Wren did what?"

I steel myself and wait for regret to surface. It never does. "That's right. He saw me trying to escape. He let me go ... and he isn't coming back."

I throw that last part in just to piss him off.

The scientist tenses before me, shoulders a taut line. A brown eye scours the floor, the walls, my feeble frame before him. "No. He wouldn't throw it all away. You're trying to get in my head." He releases my arms and lets me wobble while my feet level out. "It won't work, *Dr. Delphine.* I cannot be manipulated so easily!"

My voice rises. "How else do you think I got that door open, huh? You can hear the wheel, and it was turned *once.* Ask the guards on duty that night!"

Dev thinks back, *knowing* I am right. Panic forms lines across his forehead. A hand reaches his hair as the truth settles. "My work," he whispers to himself. "My legacy."

Wren once reminded him that it was *their* work. Dev remembers—can't forget a thing—but has no plans of sharing the glory. Never did. This fact makes it easier for him to believe me ... he knows that if Wren knew, he would abandon the project Dev relies on him for.

They may be friends, and Dev may love him in his own way, but at the end of the day he always prioritizes himself.

My work. *My* legacy. Something lays in those words ...

An idea snares me. So simple—the solution is so simple. It may not work at all, but how have I not thought of trying before?

Each step I take toward my captor tilts the room. I trudge on shaking knees before a fall closes the distance. Dev catches me, bringing a foot back to stabilize us. The collar of his shirt bunches in my fists as I peer at him with desperate hope.

A mass swells in my throat, but it is weak just as I am. "I'm yours!" I blare in his face. "I'm yours, I'm yours, I'm yours! Yours and nobody else's!"

Percussions pound against my wrists. Either his heartbeat is fast, or time has slowed. Mouth agape, Dev peers at me with resolution. "I am no psychologist ... but trust me when I say you are *unwell*, Dr. Delphine." Everything I said before becomes nonsense to him now. A layer of pity slackens his posture, and he steadies us both once more. "That's enough walking for today. You should lay—"

BANG!

Through the wall where our empty beds rest, in the direction of the somber prison I used to live in, urgent cries and barking orders scatter around us like water through a broken dam.

Stomping feet clamor in the halls. Dev is immovably tense. "What is happening?" A wide eye zones in on me. "What did you do?"

Double doors swing open. A vein bulges in Priscilla's neck, her split ends curling from a stressed updo. She is flanked by a handful of imperials. They carry the same batons the guards wielded when I tried to escape, the ones too heavy for me to lift.

They disperse throughout the room. One with a shaved head swings her weapon around like a ball in a sock, beelining for a counter of lab equipment. She reels the weapon back and brings it down on a vital machine. Pieces go flying.

It is the first time I hear Dev cry. He rushes to the woman, grabbing her bicep to halt another blow. The scientist's shrieks are inaudible against the ruckus of pounding sticks. Chaos erupts like a choreographed play. The laboratory falls apart around us, gears and metal chunks soaring with each wailing crescendo that trumpets the halls.

Priscilla stalks me with nothing to lose. "If we die, you die with us."

I take a wavering step back as a pointless effort to keep distance. No way could I best her in my current state, not on foot or in combat.

A scream simmers between my collar bones, rising like the red in a thermometer as I watch the leader of the Imperial Army prey with a deadly purpose. Her half-lidded glare reminds me of a submerged iceberg, lethal and cold. My instincts search through imprints and snag none. I sprint with burning legs to the wall of Divine Duplicity and beat on the door. A single stride separates us, and that scream finally reaches a boil when my back hits the wall.

It never escapes. Priscilla winces and falters, palming the back of her neck. No one stands behind her; I find no visible source for her sudden pain.

Then I see her. Violent.

Slate-gray stones emerge from the dip in her shoulder. My spider doesn't blend in with her surroundings now—cannot with how quickly she moves. Ivory threads spill from her belly as she races around Priscilla's head. Her dangling ponytail is pinned to the back of her skull, mouth and nose covered to muffle her cries. In a frenzied panic, she chases the insect with her hands, but is too slow. Violent's movements are sporadic and unpredictable, yet each one appears carefully carried out.

Priscilla hits the floor, clawing at the webs that suffocate her. A slender man with tattoos stops damaging the lab, having noticed his superior's struggle. He drops the weapon in shock and rushes to her aid. I don't have a chance to see if I can lift it before Dev grabs the hilt.

The scientist wears outrage like a second skin, dragging the weapon across the room to the woman with the buzz-cut. She is too focused on her task to notice the way he circles it behind her. Her kidney's take a devastating blow. She hits the floor, but Dev doesn't stop. Over and over, he beats the soldier until her face is a blur of battered bones and blood. When she stops moving at last, his shoulder ticks in search of another victim. The slender man.

This room is a riot, a cacophony of noise and disorder. But outside, in the halls, it is quiet. I am the only one to notice, as everyone here continues to fight and destroy evidence. The square window on the side door is a portal to idyllic stillness. Too tranquil to make sense.

Outdoor serenity is short-lived when a man in uniform halts on the other side. His profile whips forward, desperately glaring to witness the hectic life rummaging the lab. His eyes meet mine, fear stricken with crow's feet in the corners. The man bares his teeth, his throat muscles jutting out. The expression is one of forced acceptance, like he knows he is about to die.

A set of hands wrap over the man's ears. The digits of ringed fingers hold tight to his face. I cannot hear the neck snap, but the sight of it twisting to an unnatural angle rings a familiar bell in my mind. The soldier drops like a marionette with cut strings, and his downfall gives way to the unforgiving killer.

Piceous cotton clings to coiled shoulders. Above them, midnight hair drapes in damp waves. They halo dour cheeks, darkly shadowed with the beginnings of a beard. A line stands between tilted brows, and beneath them—the only spots of color save for sandy skin—eyes of the purest green beam with a relentless vendetta. Had I known better, I would think a god of Revenge had come to collect long overdue debts.

Kysi stands as a pillar of adamant, fueled by smite and wrath. In a blink, he is gone—vanished from the hallway.

Through my peripheral, just a few paces away, another imperial hits the ground with a heavy *thud*.

CHAPTER 34

Sweat glistens over the ropes of Kysi's arms. He does not phase to each imperial soldier for slaughter. Instead, he stalks them like a panther, smooth and swift. There is a change to his form as well as portrait; he is leaner now ... trained. It shows with every movement, each swipe from a dagger I never witnessed him unsheathe.

Priscilla is already dead, thanks to Violent. As for the tattooed man that rushed to her aid, Dev took care of him. Fleeting moments pass before the scientist is the last enemy standing.

Kysi hesitates to strike, shifting focus from Dev's latest victim back to him. Slowly, green eyes drift around the room, taking in the battered machines and broken beakers that drip with multicolored elixirs. They scan over the blood-soaked lab coat in the corner before flicking to me. Not my eyes—no, Kysi avoids looking there—but the dark veins around my neck. Their ascent up the lower half of my face. Foreign wings that surely need new wrappings. Rings that I still wear.

Resolve casts a malignant shadow over the god of Mortals and Bargaining. He knows why Dev lacks a military uniform. Knows what this room is ... what it has done to me. When he faces my captor once more, all hesitation has vanished.

One step brings them a hand's width apart. Fisting the hilt of his blade with a grip none could pry open, Kysi plunges the dagger into Dev's stomach. He cries for a second time. It rattles the room, which I had not realized became so eerily silent.

Dev's knees hit the floor when Kysi pulls the weapon out. Not a fatal blow, just enough to grant my mate a taste of his pain to satiate a burning need for revenge. Dev makes no attempt to speak, no effort to beg. He knows how useless it would be. Nothing could be said to save himself, not after a higher power has seen what has been done to his mate.

The knife was dotted in blood before—quick kills. Now, it comes out a slick, deep crimson, like it had time to settle and collect. Kysi kneels, still towering over Dev's hunched over body, and grips the base of his hair to look him in the eye. With an unwavering glare, my mate lifts the saturated blade to his mouth.

Consuming blood will always make me woozy, but I am unable to look away as Kysi's lips pull the thick liquid from the knife ... and spits it in Dev's face.

"The only blood you will get from me and mine, is *your own*," the wrathful god growls. Malice streaks beneath Kysi's lashes as he grazes the dagger over Dev's freshly mottled swath. "Now tell me," he demands in a tone both dangerous and intoxicating, "what happened here?"

THE DESCENT

Whines erupt from every breath Dev takes, though he does not disobey to answer. "It was"—he winces through the words— "her."

At last, Kysi meets my gaze, as if my violence granted him the courage to face me with his own. Below his trembling concern and fury, satisfaction vibrates the air between us. Marvel and respect, especially when pinpricks cascade over my back and Violent emerges from behind my shoulder. Then, Kysi states as if it was never in question, "That's my girl."

When he peers at Dev, the impulse to finish the job swims through each flexed muscle. Reluctantly, he fists the collar of the man's cotton shirt and drags him like a ragdoll over the limp bodies between us.

Kysi wants nothing more than to kill him ... but his fate belongs to *me*.

The one who experimented on me for months, seeking to create power over all other species, kneels at my feet with tremors so aggressive that they shake the strands of his hair.

My mate turns to me. Anger and carnage flake away with the rigid lines of his posture, and he replaces it with a realm's worth of gentleness. Headlights of green illuminate his features, having brightened the second my face centered each pupil. If I still had feathers, they would undoubtedly display all colors.

Kysi lifts his arm carefully, like one would a tortured canine unfamiliar with a loving hand. The knife twists in his palm, leather handle held out for me to take.

It would be so easy to stab Dev in that empty space where his heart should be. His single umber eye lifts with a pleading apology. In it is the memory of a comforting embrace, all the empathies felt but never acted upon, all the events leading to this moment that may have altered the outcome.

"I'm ready ..." Dev whispers. A tear collects blood on its way down his face.

I tsk. "You assume my judgement is death ... but that is not in my nature." My pointed finger levels with his widening glare. For Dev, the worst punishment is his own wasted potential. "I sentence you to an eternity of solitary darkness."

Violent scurries down the length of my arm, straight for the scientist. Dev falls on his haunches, but not before my spider closes the distance in a leap.

Beings do not wither in this realm. They do not starve or dehydrate. All the photos in his brain, those with step-by-step instructions to his personal success, will be left to sit in limbo forever. The blind cannot craft weapons of war. They cannot rebuild chemical structures, even if all the pieces are lain before them. They cannot create what they cannot see. A brilliant mind ... destined to infinitely wander in a void. The only proof he was once not alone will rest in every fallen comrade he trips over. Every foul smell their rotting corpses emit. Until their stench dissipates and their bones turn to dust indistinguishable from the debris and pebbles littering the halls.

Rather than driving a long leg through his last remaining eye, Violent hovers above it. I hardly have time for confusion before she rears back, baring fangs to drive into the sclera. Her body wiggles as she feeds, and a horrible noise drones from the scientist. Dev instinctively swats her away, but each attempt is met with the needle points of her legs.

Sheer will does not pull me from the gruesome sight, but overbearing nausea. Even if my physical strength was not already compromised, the wave of sickness alone would be enough to falter my balance. Something finally comes of it as I stumble forward and hurl near Kysi's feet, painting his steel-toes in pomegranate-hued liquid.

Kysi slightly pivots to gather my hair. A rough-hewn hand spans my spine, working in slow motions up and down. The vomit continues, so forcefully that I gasp for air between each flood of resurfacing Redspire. The bed frame steadies me just long enough to finish puking, but my futile attempt to stand without it yields useless.

I have envisioned my mate's arms in countless different daydreams, relying on memory to imagine how they feel around me. My mind could never compare to his authentic touch as it spans my back and beneath my thighs. Kysi lifts me effortlessly, like I weigh no more than a piece of lint on his clothes. It is probably not far from the truth, considering how much muscle mass he seems to have gained, as well as how much I certainly have lost.

His grip tightens and words flow in a caress of vibrations. "How do you expect me to ever let you go again?"

I rest my forehead in the crook of his shoulder. "I don't."

Violent leaves Dev with his head in his hands, blood draining between fingers. My mate motions for her to come, and she climbs his shin with obedience. Saving me was more than enough to gain her trust; Kysi gained her fealty.

The King of Groveheart tenses. I cling to him like the very fabric of his shirt, anticipating the pull of teleportation to take me away from here.

His body heat vanishes, and gravity hauls me downward. Violent becomes airborne, legs splayed to grasp the surgical gown around my knees. I slam my eyes shut, waiting for the hard floor to jar my tailbone. Instead, I am jerked upright, back into Kysi's hold.

"I'm sorry," he pants, readjusting his grip, "I'm sorry. You're too weak to phase."

Before I can protest, he is moving out of the lab without a second thought, kicking the laboratory doors open to aim for the exit.

I have never seen so many bodies.

Not even when Earth collapsed. No, there was too much smoke and destruction to see clearly then. Even so, life and death battled one another. Now, there are just empty vehicles that once housed consciousnesses, feelings, and thoughts. All abandoned.

"Don't look at them." Kysi steps over limbs like they are fallen branches on a hiking trail. Climbing the steps to the vault, he reaches past my back and spins the wheel. His bicep works diligently beneath my new wings to pull the iron door. Chilled air kisses my skin through petite openings in the tangled vines, and Kysi gapes at the obtrusion.

"That mental space you were trapped inside during stasis, apparently mine bites when backed in a corner." Concern creeps through. "I'm never going to get out of here," I whisper to myself as a lump forms in my throat.

Kysi lowers us to the ground. With legs across his lap, I keep my grip tight around him. Hands cup my cheeks. "Look at me," he says, leveling his gaze. "I will not let you stay here a second longer than I can help. In order to do that, I have to go—"

I shake my head. "No. You can't leave me here alone." I can practically feel every glossy eye shift in my direction. "Use your knife. Cut us through." We both know it is far too thick ... but there must be another way. One that does not involve making me sit amidst dozens of corpses.

"Baby, I have to," he soothes, petting my hair. "Only for a moment. I will be right back, I swear it."

Kysi wants to get help. He is right to suggest this, and I know he would never abandon me. But he is here now, and I cannot stand to be left. What if this is all a horrible dream, another one of Dev's experiments? What if the moment he phases away, I will look around at the dead bodies and watch them rise to resume their duties as if nothing ever happened? The blood painting the walls will dry white. The scientist will open those doors with a clean wrap around the side of his head, seeing me clearly for what I truly am ... frightened and weak.

"Make a deal with me," Kysi urges. His thumb softly strokes near my ear. "If I am not back in thirty seconds, I will never kill in your name again. Your absence will not starve me, and your presence will cease to consume me. Your smile will lack the power to bring me to my knees. If I am not back in thirty seconds, then my heart is mine."

If this truly is real and not some woeful conjuration of my imagination, then Kysi would be forced to return. His soul will not sit idly by and let him betray a bargain if it can help it. He would have to come back, even if he did not want to, because everything he listed cannot be made true simply by stating it.

"Make the deal with me," he repeats. "Come on, angel."

Lowering my head, I blink slowly. "We have a deal."

Lips graze my cheek. The space around me becomes cold with his sudden disappearance, and alone I am left.

One, two, three, four. As I count the seconds, I count the motionless figures lying about. There is comfort under my fear; Nightfall has lost. Their biggest weapon is gone, and the Imperials have lost their leader, along with many other important military figures. Soon the war outside will be over, and I will march into the heart of that city to detain any remaining rebels and save what humans are still suffering at the hands of Dev's colleagues. Hellano and I will find Cato ... and we will reincarnate him.

I flinch at Kysi's abrupt return. "I only needed fifteen." He offers a side smile and drapes a blanket over me. A fleece coat wraps his frame now. I am lifted from the floor and returned to the feel of his forearms and chest. Together, we face the exit and wait.

Not a sound emits through the small gaps in the brush. "Who did you bring?"

Pockets of light snuff out one by one. Like withering bones, the vines snap and fall. Black smoke fills the canal and eats away at the barricade. It moves with purpose, retreating quickly when its meal is fully devoured.

Light returns. Tendrils swarm backwards in a race. Some snowflakes fall victims to their shrinking darkness and fade into them with the slightest touch. Inky ribbons retreat into palms that once held mine. Above them, through layers of warm clothes, broad shoulders slacken at the sight of me.

Hellano has paled since I last saw him. He wears gloom like an iron veil, but piercing through its metal lace comes the reprieve to suffering. He rushes forward, patting me down in Kysi's arms to make sure I am truly present.

"Flower," he utters in a light breath that suggests a boulder has rolled from his lungs, but anger still emanates. "May the Sky Spirits have mercy on your enemies, because I sure as hell won't." With urgency, he reaches to take me from Kysi's arms.

My mate tightens his hold. "Unfortunately, I didn't save any for you." He nods to the graveyard behind us. "Couldn't help myself."

Hellano disregards the statement and meets his enemy with a warning glare. "What's your plan here, Kysi? Carry her down the mountain on foot? In a blizzard? Give her to me." It is not a suggestion.

Releasing a disgruntled huff, Kysi responds, "Straight to Groveheart. Straight. There." The grip around me slowly loosens.

My husband rolls his eyes. "*We* will meet you at the manor."

Kysi's throat bobs with reluctance, but he gently transfers me to Hellano. A soft kiss is planted on my forehead. "I will be waiting, angel." A narrowed stare is thrown at the King of Celestia. "Very impatiently." Then, he blinks out of sight.

I can feel how different Hellano is through multiple articles of clothing. Just like Kysi, he too has grown. The product of war, no doubt. Has everyone else changed, too?

"Did they suffer?" my husband questions, peering into the bunker. It stares back like an unhinged jaw, having chewed me up just to spit me out.

"One will," I answer. "Can you close it?"

If Dev were to wander out, it is unlikely he would make it to civilization. Even if a winter storm did not blare outside of this shallow tunnel, it appears the Imperials hid me in a remote location far from the city. If he were to leave, he would surely die.

I want him to *rot*.

Hellano treks out of the cave's mouth. Hazel eyes turn back to scan the rock, and he nods his head. "I can close it."

Angling a hand from my ribs, condensed shadows dance through the angry snowfall. They part on all sides of the cave and burrow into the sediment, leaving gray dust in their wake. The yawning canal shakes with pressure, then crumbles in a heap of heavy stones. Give it an hour, maybe, and it will blend in with every other nook and cranny of this mountain.

No one goes in. No one comes out.

A broad palm nestles into my side once more. Hellano spreads his feathers and steps from the swirling cliffside. I slide my arms through the opening of his jacket for warmth.

Neither of us speak. Not that we would be able to hear much against the whipping wind, anyway. Words are unneeded. I understand his longing in the way he angles his chin on my head. I feel his love through each occasional squeeze around me.

I lose track of how long we fly. The storm grows kinder when the sun dips low, and calm hills of white can be seen in the distant landscape. Sleep somehow threatens to capture me in the cold.

"Rest." A warm breath hits my ear. "I've got you, flower."

For the first time in months, I sleep soundly.

CHAPTER 35

A satin cloud pins me down. The grand bed is cozy and warm. A woodsy scent filters the air; sandalwood and pine. Muffled voices go back and forth, faint enough to disguise words. The chatter is cleaved by a set of redwood doors with golden handles, surrounded by sage green walls with a cherry-brown trim. Paintings of laughing families accompany sculptures of dancing couples. None of their faces are discernable ... except those in one piece.

A vertical frame hangs beside the bathroom entrance. Long black hair haloes my smiling face. I am peering up at a handsome grin—the cause of my elation. My mate beams down at me in the portrait of us.

Kysi's manor is humbly beautiful from what I can tell. Past the picture, a rock shower stands mighty in the facilities. I can hardly see through the glass door from where I lay but make out Kysi's body wash in the corner. All is quiet save for the blurry conversation in the hall ... for a moment.

A quiet hum snags my attention to the other side of the room, where a small table rests by a window that spans most of the wall.

One meant for a private dinner inside, or a confidential meeting with a foreign adversary.

Alone in one of the two chairs, locks of daffodil strands sway against an arm that moves atop the polished surface. A pencil scratches paper. The humming continues.

With no Redspire in my stomach, I assume Meena is the reason why moving isn't painful. She must have worked on me while I slept, helped me just as she did Hellano after Kysi snapped his neck.

Harlynn will receive no such mercy.

She is barely turned around before I am on her. The chair bangs against the hardwood floor when I throw us to the ground. My heartbeat thuds in my skull, so loud that her scream is inaudible. Never have I itched to cause harm more than I do now. Not to Priscilla. Not even to Dev. Her pain is my morning sun and rising moon. It is ripe fruit and sweet wine. It is all the things that satisfy and soothe. A pacifier to many fortnights of loathing.

Harlynn's jugular strains underneath my crossed thumbs. The tighter I squeeze, the wider her mouth opens. Her dragonfly wings twitch and buzz. I dig my knees into the creases of her elbows to keep her down.

Was this how she straddled Hellano when she assaulted him? Or did she wait until he passed out from overconsumption?

A quick swipe across my belly yanks me into the air. I am swept from the angel, kicking and screaming to get back to her.

Harlynn rolls to the side and pushes herself on all fours. She palms her neck, and her torso expands rapidly in attempts to catch full breaths.

"She's on our side!" Kysi exclaims in my ear. "She's on our—"

I writhe in his grasp. "She raped Hellano!"

My arms become locked under an additional vise. I am forcefully turned in the other direction. Holding me in place with my mate, Hellano scans my face to gather my attention. His grip is firm but not too invasive.

"She didn't touch me." A single hand falls from my arm and cautiously rises. He hooks a finger in the collar of his burgundy sweater and pulls it down. "See? I'm fine, flower."

Thankful ecstasy steadies me against confusion's staggering blows. I let my finger trace the naked skin of his neck. Soft and bare. A blank canvas. "But ..." I look to Harlynn, who accepts Kysi's offer to stand and swipes hair from her face.

The only markings on her throat are the ones I inflicted.

"But she's one of them," I state with perplexity. "She's an Imperial."

"*Was* an Imperial," the angel hoarsely corrects. "I couldn't do it."

The room is still for a moment. How is it that my mate and husband can stand around like this woman can be trusted after everything she did, everything she kept from us? "How much blood is on your hands? How many lives have we lost because you helped Cato start a war?"

A tender grasp finds my chin and tilts it to the side. Hellano shakes his head while delivering the news, "There is no war."

My head swims. Priscilla lied ... to incite reactions from me to further advance Dev's research. Does that mean the voyagers were never eaten? Are there even clans in the Ferathore Mountains?

A light flurry falls like confetti through the window behind Harlynn. She looks at me with carefulness and uncertainty. "How do you expect me to believe a word you say?" Contempt trickles across each syllable I speak.

Her shoulders rise and fall. "You'll have to if you want to find Cato."

My jaw ticks at the sound of his name spoken aloud. "Tell me what you know."

According to the people of Celestia, Hellano is refusing to show his wedding mark until the lost Queen returns home to display hers alongside him. Every day since the night of our wedding, he has covered the area.

"Watching you let the humans go free was the first time I doubted my purpose in the Capital," Harlynn states from the table. Hellano and Kysi sit on either side of the bed. Both have yet to leave my side. "Bad people do good things for a number of reasons. Personal gain, public praise, boredom. I chalked it up to any one of those. But the reservation grew one night outside your bedchamber," she admits, thinking back. "I was in the hall—always tried to keep close by—when I overheard Mona's departure. Your own best friend was leaving for the enemy kingdom ... and you didn't even get mad. You *hugged* her."

Is empathy a foreign concept to *all* Imperials?

"I wasn't sure what to do after that, didn't know what the truth was," she says. "After your capture, when it was time to open the ambrosia and fulfill my duties ... I couldn't. I broke down and told Hellano everything."

She relays the information to me just as she did with him that following evening. I do not interrupt, just let the pieces come together. My lovers are quiet to my left and right, but my focus stays tethered on the angel.

Instead of Groveheart and Celestia going to war, they allied to search for the Ultimate Queen. Not even Harlynn knew where I was being held. She was left in the dark as a precautionary measure, in case she was tortured for the information. The council—all except Cato, of course—came together again. Invading Nightfall was too chancy; the kings wanted to avoid putting my life at risk. They also figured my presence in the city was too obvious.

Harlynn's knowledge about the beads is no more than Dev's. As far as she knows, Cato just had them. He offered them to Priscilla, along with his blood, to kickstart their rebellion.

"What about you?" My tone is laced with distrust. "Did you drink from him?"

My old assistant shifts uncomfortably in the chair. "Once."

I lift my brows and throw glances at the kings. They are unfazed by the information—already aware. It seems she really has told them everything.

"Cato said it would help … achieve our goal," she continues. "It makes us feel brave and powerful. Equal."

"You are equal," I chime in. "Perhaps not in fancy magic, but your heart beats just as mine."

Her sad smile is short lived. Bewilderment wades in its place. "The god of Wisdom claims you are a dangerous leader, a threat to those lacking divinity. Why would he lie?"

Madness is only a theory. It is possible that he simply changed his mind about me after witnessing Earth's chaos. Perhaps he disagreed with me dispelling the Spirits of the Sky, finding it too bold or heinous.

A sigh swooshes out. "I can't say for certain … I wish there weren't so many reasons to consider." Rather than harping on them a second longer, I get back to the matter at hand. "Why only once?"

She takes my hint to move on with the conversation. "I was worried that it would blow my cover, cause me to become too reckless. My given task was top priority."

If Priscilla was ever high in my presence, she masked it well. Perhaps not everyone has the same tolerance.

There are more holes for her to patch. "The Imperials want to enslave humans. Why were you happy that I let them go?"

A thin brow shoots up. "I don't need to enslave mortals to drink their blood. Not to sound vain, but there are plenty of men willing to let me indulge amid ... *other* activities. My motivations as an Imperial were solely to protect my kind."

There are men who would sell their souls if it meant receiving a crumb of attention from an attractive female, and considering Harlynn's undeniable beauty, I have no doubt there is truth to her statement. "I thought only demons *indulged*. After all, they have pointed canines. Plus, I haven't seen your kind sharing pig's blood with them."

Harlynn scrunches her nose. "Let's just say I have a type."

Kysi huffs. "Let me guess, AB Negative?"

She sarcastically squints. "I prefer brains over biceps. Don't worry, you're safe."

The King of Groveheart rubs the corner of his eye with an obvious middle finger. Harlynn ignores it. "My incisors are less noticeable, like small razor blades." She glances around awkwardly. "I am happy to answer additional questions about my anatomy, but if that is all ... when would you like to see the god of Wisdom?"

Against my personal preference, not particularly soon. "Once I am healed. 'Lano, can you help me train these wings?" His are not as pointed as my new ones, but they tilt upwards at the top. That has to count for something.

"I'd lay siege on a city for you," he states, "which is exactly what we should be doing in Nightfall."

"He's right," Kysi interjects, steeling his posture. "What they did is grounds for war. Now that you're safe, we can invade."

Did my mate and husband just … agree? Have the mountains learned to dance? Are the rivers flowing backwards? The falling snow outside feels like the indication of hell freezing over. For once, I disagree with *them*. "That would only prove their fear of deities wanting to expand power. The Imperials are not a threat anymore; their military is broken, and their trump card is shredded. Even still, we can bring our armies to stand guard outside their borders should things go south. Hellano and I will find and reincarnate Cato. Nightfall will remain an independent nation, and as long as they aren't enslaving anyone, we will *not* impose on how they choose to live."

My kings swallow any objections. Harlynn soaks up the plan like a sponge, then stands to address Hellano. "Renwick's hair is thinning from stress. You should get back to Celestia, tell the people the Queen is in recovery." She shifts to me. "Meena will arrive within the hour for a healing session. If you need anything … I'll be around."

Not sure how I feel about that last part, considering how little I trust her right now. It implies she has every intention of remaining my assistant. Then again, there is a saying about keeping enemies close.

When the door snicks shut, Hellano kneels at my bedside. My fingers go straight for his collar and snag it down, just to check one more time. A grin teases his mouth. "Have I mentioned how attractive you are when defending my honor?"

A laugh rolls out. "It's only hot when the victim is *guilty* … but I'll let you have this one."

The grin forms into a handsome smile slitted by white. He leans in. The kiss is soft, as if my lips are a house of cards. "Come with me." The whisper tickles my skin. "I can take care of you at home."

"I'm *right here*," Kysi cuts in, unamused.

Hellano's annoyance is palpable. I reach my palm to his scruffy jaw. "I can't return like this, 'Lano."

He inhales deep. "I figured you'd say that." Another kiss caresses my lips, and he squeezes my hand before rising.

Kysi does not delay in meeting him at the end of the bed, clearly eager to send the god of Afterlife away. Hellano does not instantly grasp his outstretched hand. "You'll find me back here in the morning," he promises Kysi, who does not deign to respond, just wiggles his fingers with impatience. My husband throws one last look my way. "Thank you ... for not wilting," he says before clasping Kysi's forearm and vanishing from the manor.

Little does he know that he is part of the reason why I didn't.

A sudden bounce erupts inches to my left, causing me to flinch. "Gods, he is so clingy," Kysi utters while lifting the coverlet to settle in beside me.

My mate's warmth happily invades my personal space. I raise a brow. "And you're not?"

A huff sends a strand of hair flying from his cheek. "Pfft, please. I'm in the mood for a nap. You just *happen* to be here."

"Is that so?" I cross my arms. "Alright then. Have a nice nap."

It takes a total of three seconds before a hand slides over my hip. I bark out a laugh, and his smooth chuckle sings in my ear. "This proves nothing."

Denying his affection would be senile. Our soul tie has soothed like a baby in the night, and I almost forgot how comforting the calm was. We nestle close, given peace at last. The percussions of his heart are hypnotizing. Our breaths become slow and lazy. Every inch of my face is touched by lips seeking to cherish me. Careful fingers draw spirals over my skin.

"I didn't know if it would work," I mutter. Kysi is propped on his side, cradling my head in the nook of his arm. "Breaking my vows."

My temple receives the next kiss. "When humans disobey bargains with me, their whereabouts ping like a marker in my mind. I didn't know if it worked the same with other gods—not until the wedding. It doesn't exactly. Your location was vague. Blurry."

I think back to the last time I saw him before my capture. "Did you have to jump around to find the ceremony?"

"No," he lilts. "I knew where it was."

I camber my chin to get his attention, pull him away from pecking my nose. "And how's that?"

A smirk tilts. "Nosiness."

After centuries of observing me from afar in the Ancient Library, I should have anticipated that he would keep tabs on me. "And the bunker?"

Kysi's expression falls as he remembers the recent past. "The moment I sensed the violation of our deal, I never phased more rapidly

461

in my life. Your presence felt like a shaking compass needle that steadied the closer I got." His eyes peer into mine, and it sounds like he is struggling to level his voice. "I need you to know that I never stopped looking. Every day I phased somewhere new to search for you. Although I am eternally grateful for the promises we made in the forest that day—because it is what brought you back to me sooner—I swear on my soul that without it, I would have eventually saved you. There is not a place in any realm you can escape me forever. I will always find you."

To anyone else, the statement might run chills down their spine. But when Kysi says it, all I hear is the promise of infinite devotion.

The kisses return along my jaw, soft and sweet. Each glide of his hand is greedy yet careful, like I am a porcelain doll with many cracks. Despite his failing efforts to hide arousal, Kysi does not physically progress. I am unaware of how well I could ... *perform* right now, given that I can hardly walk, but it doesn't take away from my own personal desire to explore him, feel his breath on the most intimate parts of me.

Apparently, I am also unskilled at concealing the urge, because Kysi coos in a sunken voice, "You're not ready for me, baby." Fingers trail my inner thigh. "But I can help you in other ways."

The sheer proximity nearly induces a moan, but as tempting as that may be, it is a line we cannot cross until a conversation is had. "Ky?"

Lips touch my neck, and the vibration tightens my core. "Yes, angel?"

"The mark."

Just like that, his heat dissipates. Seconds pass.

Kysi rolls on his back, staring at the ceiling. At first, I think he may not respond at all. A wall rises between us, and I curse myself for not basking in our peace a little longer. "You want it," he definitively states.

"Celestians need to know our marriage isn't a lie," I admit.

That sculpted jaw twitches. "Right."

"Ky." I release an exasperated sigh. "That doesn't mean that I don't love you. 'Lano and I may not be bonded, but I am tied to him in other ways." Truth be told, I am tangled to them both like the product of a seamstress with two left hands. It is quiet for a while. I am unable to tell whether he is angry, confused, or sullen. "Tell me you love me, too."

Shaggy dark hair shifts when he turns his head. "Nothing could stop me from loving you." Contentedness is difficult to find in the words. Is he upset that our bond is so strong? If this was an outcome he could have predicted, would he prefer I never saved it at the ritual?

"Stop doing that." Kysi jerks me from the mental spiral. I look at him in question. "I don't need telepathy to read your mind, not when your thoughts never make it passed facial expressions." He shifts on his side to face me. "I think you often forget that having a soul bond with someone doesn't equate to romance with them. I love you on my own. Always have ... always will."

I scan his features and come across nothing ingenuine. No response could truly honor the depth of my feelings, so instead of giving one, I reach forward to kiss him.

My advance is accepted, and our mouths meet with dense longing. His tongue savors mine in a jealous embrace, but the connection is cut short by the bedroom doors parting wide. Does no one knock?

Meena averts her gaze in an instant, whipping around to face the wall. "Tell me you are not ruining my progress because you can't *control* yourselves."

I miss Kysi's touch already.

"Relax, Meen-ie. We've been perfectly celibate." He props himself up on the sheets. "You know, for the goddess of Pleasure, you are frequently stressed."

She turns with a scoff. Winter hair follows her every movement. "Gee, I wonder why?" Her striking gaze never blinks on my mate.

He shrugs with a sheepish smirk before swinging off the bed to give her room.

I roll to my stomach on Meena's command. Her hands are quick to start, palming my shoulder blades beneath the bandaged wings.

She was not lying when she said healing Hellano took a toll on his energy, because it feels like every muscle is straining under her power. My blood is like a potion being stirred inside stiff veins. It is a sensation I never noticed when she tried to heal me before. Perhaps bleeding from my eyes and having chunks of my soul taken away were bigger focal points to my body, or maybe her abilities operate differently based on the injury.

My lashes turn to lead after a few short moments. Kysi sits nearby, visage becoming a blur with each blink.

"Sleep, angel. I'll be right here," the timbre is smooth, promising. Just like Hellano's when he carried me across the sky.

I willingly give in to another safe sleep.

CHAPTER 36

Swirling gauze leaves behind newborn feathers. Silver-gray and thirsty for air, my wings strive to spread and flap, but Meena's hair is a frozen waterfall too pretty to tousle.

I find her in the reflection of Kysi's bathroom mirror, contently observing the product of her power as she rids me of bandages for the last time. Peering at the woman, I find us not so different. I breed life. She mends it. Heals the sick. Comforts the weary. Encourages my children to laugh and love ... what greater gift is there? Meena does not help me because I am Kysi's mate or Mona's friend, but instead from a spirit driven by restoration.

She runs a damp cloth over my fragile quills. Such delicateness in a woman with bite. Pore-less skin the shade of a sunflower's eye, and an unapologetic temperament few have the confidence to carry. Her cadence sings of profound strength, given not by striking features, but rooted self-assurance. Meena is rightfully proud of who she is, because behind her divine appearance is an even more beautiful soul.

A repetitive thud hits the lower cabinets beside me. Mona sits on the counter, swinging a leg back and forth. She is clearly unaware of the noise—too busy sneering at Harlynn, who leans against the rock shower. My friend holds a tight grudge, has ever since the assistant's betrayal unearthed. Over the last week, more than a few words have been targeted at the angel. All were sharper than the teeth she bares.

We reunited days ago. Mona was following a lead to my disappearance in a small town northeast of Gourmara named Whermwood—a dead end, as they all had been—when Kysi phased her back to the manor. He and Hellano expressed that I was sleeping and suggested she wait, but not even two hierarchal gods could stop her from barreling through the bedchamber door.

Mona's swift entrance jerked me awake, and the planet spun slower when we found each other across the room. Spirals of mousy hair bounced around plump cheeks, and her features were tight from months of weaving worry. The sight careened me forward. Meena's medical instructions were left behind; I did not move slowly, and there was nothing gentle in the way we embraced.

"We should schedule a council meeting," Harlynn proposes, ignoring the daggers stared at her. "How does a week from today sound? Gives you more time to settle and recover. Then, we can discuss the plan for Nightfall."

A knuckle pops under Mona's thumb. "Council meetings are for trusted allies only."

Harlynn steels herself, but I interject before a remark parts her lips. "She is our link to Cato," I remind. "Her attendance is necessary."

That prompts an eye roll. "Fine. As long as she knows it isn't *wanted*."

Bluntness is Mona's blessing and curse. It is nice to have that trait in an ally—someone so defensive on my behalf, motivated by a platonic love potent enough to choke any in its atmosphere.

Relatives are a privilege my soul can never experience. And yet, family found me atop a blaring Honda Civic. Mona would often joke about how awful that day was. She spilled coffee on her blouse, cracked the screen of her phone, *and* missed her turn to the grocery store, which led her to one on the opposite end of town. To top it all off, she came out with a handful of bags to witness a lady fall from the sky and smash the hood of her newly detailed car.

And what did she do? She *comforted* me.

Mona loved me when I had no title, before divinity returned with a crown. She held me when I was powerless and promised I was far from it. She swore that strength is never stolen, because it always rests within. I may not have a mother or father to guide me, nor siblings to grow alongside, but Mona offered more than food to eat and a bed to sleep in. She offered sisterhood.

Harlyn scoffs. "Does she ever hold her tongue?"

Meena tosses gauze into a bin. "No," she amusingly intones, "that's what I like most about her."

A barking laugh escapes. I am surprised to hear it comes from me. Just days ago, laughter was more of a concept; an idea of intrinsic expression. But it is *real*. The evidence lies in its contagious echo.

Meena giggles a lovely note. Mona's shoulders roll in muted joy. Even Harlynn struggles to stifle her grin.

In this slice of shared happiness, I cling to the image of more to come.

Deep within the Heartian Forest, I strain to levitate an inch from the ground. Eleven days have passed since escaping the bunker, and weakness fades each passing night.

The shape of my changed limbs brings a challenge—no surprise there. It should get easier when my feathers are done growing. Their shortness has a silver lining; flight muscles beneath are working overtime. Long, thick quills would be a crutch, though their warmth sounds nice against the bitter chill.

Batting sable wings, Hellano hovers nearby—always does when not in the Capital. Snowflakes drift over rigid hair, fluttering past ruddy cheeks towards a draping lion's fur coat. Maroon shades full lips in a blood rush from the cold.

Royal duties occupy the kings each morning, and during that time, Meena tests the limits of her abilities. Although my body is healed, internal wounds remain. The goddess beads with sweat during every session; it is no easy feat ridding my veins of poison. I doubted she would be able to at all, because what sense does it make for her power to drive out what takes ours away? But when she dropped a small pot in my lap and demanded I focus, I'll be damned if the dirt inside did not tremble. Meena's power is miraculous, its only limitation remaining in death itself.

It took ten minutes for a tendril of green to sprout through, and by then my energy was drained. After a full night's sleep, when our sessions have concluded, I go back to the plant pup.

Today, I budded a soft pink lily.

"Don't hold your breath," Hellano instructs from between two Nightspruce trees. Their naked branches begin just above his head, stretching skyward like bony fingers in search of the sun's warmth.

My feet hit the sparkling powder beneath. A cold fog plumes from my breath like smoke over a train. "You broke my focus."

Wings tuck inwards, and snow muffles the sound of his boots hitting the ground. Hellano strides forward with a deathly handsome smirk. "You were turning into a cranberry, my Queen."

My racing heart would agree, but I cling to stubbornness. "That's my natural blush," I jape. "You'd kill to have this complexion."

His smooth chuckle heats the air, and I envy the mist grazing his lips on the way out.

A crisp *woosh* snags our attention. Kysi spots me a few yards away, where he phases next to a boulder. Arms cross inside a thick wool jacket as he leans against the rock. "Angel," he croons before addressing Hellano with little interest. "Terminator."

A fiery brow lifts. "He never stays gone long, does he?"

It is true that we do not have much time alone. After exercises with Meena, Kysi collects Hellano from the Capital so we can begin training. If the Heartian King's tasks are not yet finished, it is not long before they are. At most, Hellano and I make it through half a lesson before our privacy expires.

I shake my head to confirm. "It isn't easy being away, especially after what happened." The reason for his intrusiveness lays in the subtle panic of each return. Green eyes frantically dart until meeting mine, and shoulders slacken at the sight. Anxiety at work; the fear I may not be where expected. Fear I may become lost again.

Once the initial fright is pacified by proximity, a secondary motivation emerges. Without fail, after finding me safe and sound each day, Kysi's busy gaze flicks to the skin of my throat.

So far, my spouse and I have not abandoned all comfort to fuck in the freezing woods.

"I understand," Hellano soothes. The genuine response hints to a recent past. One that sprouts frostbite in the chest and drives you to no destination. However, empathy does not come only from the remembrance of a wounded soul. Hellano battles a similar need for my continual company.

I nervously glance away from his honey-hue eyes. Form-fitting leathers adorn my frame, much different than the heels and dresses I was once accustomed to. I was uncertain of Harlynn's choice of apparel, but as it turns out, they are remarkably effective at retaining body heat. "I don't think anything can keep me from him, 'Lano."

Drifting flurries slow to a dying breeze, as if the world brakes in wait of his reply ... "I know, flower." The tone lacks competition, unlike Kysi's thick possessiveness. Not that my mate has no right to be defensive; Hellano shrouded him for centuries in shadows he never had to wield from his palms.

What was it he said, before the world fell and the war of our souls ended? *"If I can't have all of you and be whole, I will settle for just a piece."*

Daylight slinks beneath the lowest hanging boughs—a subtle chime that its rays will depart soon. Until then, there is more work to do.

Collecting another breath, I rise from the ground a little higher. This time, I do not hold it in.

Moonbeams are veiled by a dismal storm as the three of us lay over Kysi's duvet. My satin nightgown is thin, but despite the pebbles lining my arms and legs, I am far from chilled. Boxed between two balmy auras, their shoulders are snug against mine.

My mate claims that ample relaxation is essential when learning teleportation, which is why his guided meditations are scheduled before bed. So far, this technique has been the opposite of helpful.

Not that these meetings are uncomfortable—far from it. Just ... so distracting.

Kysi held no objections when Hellano first joined us. After all, Groveheart and Celestia share a common enemy. Teaching him would prove beneficial. Also, I think he grows tired of phasing him to and from the royal palace each day.

"Don't search for the pull in the void of your mind. Call for it. Let it come to you," Kysi smoothly drawls. A hand leisurely lays on his sternum, the other tucked behind shaggy black hair. "This power is a timid creature you must coax into the light."

One would assume my strengthening divinity would make this process easier, regardless of the persistent distraction of two wildly attractive men, but I remain unsuccessful. Hellano inhales to my right, concentrating.

Logic taps an impatient foot as I struggle to focus between them. It is not just their closeness that gallops my heart, but the peacefulness of it. A shiny new fear emerges; the threat this slice of heaven—scented like a picnic in the forest, with a basket of berries and wildflowers that sweeten the air—will end. End and never return.

Kysi senses my struggle and lifts a lid. "It helps if you close your eyes, you know."

With a sigh, I refocus on the ceiling and try again. *Call* into the void of my mind? And say what, exactly? *Hey ... here teleportation. Pssp pssp.*

Oh, for gods sakes, Anewla. It's not a cat.

Their bodies are so warm. What charges the air like static, my crying libido? Shared heat mingles around me and leaves chills behind. A teasing draft in a windless room.

I pictured us together in the bunker, when my wings were pinned and sawed and filed. The vision drives itself forward, leaving me to chase after it with waving arms. Arousal is a hinderance to the goal.

It builds me up and leaves me frustrated—a knot in my core that grows tighter by the hour.

Unlimited access, that is what I want. What I *need*. Exploring hands and roaming kisses, a cataclysm to my senses. To release tension. Reset. It would certainly help me achieve *ample relaxation*. Yes, I cannot think of a more unwinding activity. To be full of one and choking on the other—

"That's enough for tonight." Kysi swings his legs over the bed. I force myself not to reach for him. "Same time tomorrow."

Gods, help me.

Hellano's lashes lift. Golden pearls target me. "I think I'm making progress. How are you feeling?"

Like I want to jump your bones. "Good. Making progress."

My husband offers a slight smile and kisses the center of my forehead ... The knell for ringing home chimes an odious bell.

A stone drops in my chest. Tragic is the fading warmth of their departure, a blanket ripped from a cozy nest. Kysi firmly holds me at the end of each day, and it never fails to satiate the longing for them both. But this pocket of time—the fleeting moment when two leave and one return—is more bitter than a mouthful of dandelion greens. It is the aftertaste of cold isolation. The lingering reminder of a cave with no compassion. For three seconds a day, I am alone, and for a reason I cannot place ... it is just as harrowing as before.

Hellano sharply halts after standing. A semblance of curiosity ebbs in the way he looks at me, and it is then I realize my instincts have acted on their own accord.

Upright and leaning forward, I find myself with a grip on his wrist. Kysi remarks the scene from the footboard, where they usually meet to phase east to the palace. Unease draws a line between the dark arches of his brows, disquieted at the concern I may choose to finally go home with my spouse. What worry wades in Kysi, hope does Hellano.

My voice shrinks and wavers. "Can you stay?"

Heartbeats pass before Hellano inhales hesitation, throwing an awkward glance in Kysi's direction.

"Please," I add. "I'll sleep better near both of you." A lie—being hot and bothered tends to flee the will to slumber—but I will say anything to get them back in this bed.

Hellano would agree if it were solely up to him. I see it in his stance. His eyes. Mate be damned, he wants us together. So, I turn to Kysi with a silent plea.

Moments linger like stretching shadows at twilight. I could digest his refusal, understand it. Being denied would make the ephemeral loneliness more bearable, because at least then I would be weathering it out of respect for a lover's comfort. But I must know how deep his hatred lies, must know if Kysi can let go of harbored grudges.

The windows to his soul resemble an empty meadow, wide open and vast. No walls. No caves. Just the loving light of day upon two fields of green ...

Muscles roll loose as he softens—no, melts—under the weight of my request. A sigh falls out, and abruptly, he turns. "If he snores, I take him back."

Blinking in stupefaction, I am the last to move. Hellano turns his hand in mine, wedding band glinting against the dull light. "I go where you guide me, darling wife."

Trudging to bed, Kysi quips, "Don't be offended when your *wife* clings to me all night. I can hardly pry her off in the mornings."

An irritated huff follows. "Oh, give it a rest, already."

Sheets lift on either side of me. *Don't get excited*, I tell myself. *It doesn't mean anything.*

Kysi swings a possessive arm behind my head, his bicep just beneath my neck. It cranes to span my chest, while Hellano's drapes over my stomach from where he settles on his side. The tangled limbs remind me of roots under a dense forest—grounding. The contiguity is paralyzing.

There is shame in accepting their comfort knowing what I previously settled for in place of it. I once attempted to force my misery on Dev—make him take it back. When the punches failed and anguish remained, I quickly succumbed to the scientist's embrace; if I could not transfer despair, perhaps I could steal some of his complacency. It was a futile hope.

It is ironic how affliction could not be shared then. Dev deserved to bear the burden of my pain, but it was frozen inside. Now, it thaws freely. Unable to be contained, a river of hurt washed away by affection. Love. If my suffering were a casket of jewels, these men are talented thieves.

Separate breaths cascade upon my skin—over my hair and across my shoulder—like lapping waves on a shore. "I love you," I say into the darkness.

The admission came without conscious thought, personalized for them both. They reciprocate simultaneously.

"I love you, angel."

"I love you, flower."

With those words, they rob that gem-filled grave dry.

CHAPTER 37

A carved grandfather clock ticks near the base of a curved staircase. The steps rise above an unlit fireplace to a mezzanine lined with archtop windows. It was easy getting into the manor's grand living space unnoticed. Most of the staff are home weathering the storm. It whistles the wind in threatening whispers.

Fear the falling snow.

Dread coils. The downfall accumulated faster than I could heal. Quicker than I could train. When the clock dings thrice, it feels more like the end of a countdown than the beginning of a scheduled council meeting.

The blizzard is a tight noose, and Cato could kick the stool from under me at any moment.

Sparks of frustration tickle my nails. A flame unfurls atop my fingertips. I flick it off, illuminating the council on its way into the fireplace. Warm light grows as it eats dry logs.

"You recover quickly, my Queen," the god of Agony comments near the mantle. He wears a burgundy tunic with bishop sleeves and a drawstring V-neck, the laces slackened to uncover chest hair. The shirt is held in by tight trousers that leave little to the imagination. Ironic, how the giver of my pain is the same person in my corner. It is not Luther's fault; his soul duty is just as persistent as the rest of ours.

I would hardly call myself recovered. Healed? Sure. But when it comes to flying, I am a pathetically heavy hen. This meeting cuts into flight lessons—which shall resume indoors when our business is adjourned—but I am not complaining. They are pointless. All-day meditation would be a better use of time. Without mastering teleportation, my immobility is slightly above a human's. Not to mention, if I were to step outside in the cold, Divine Duplicity would shrink and flee. Amidst weather this angry, it would be nearly impossible to reach.

Once, while reading the Law of All Gods in the Ancient Library, I discovered a god's access to raw power can be driven away by many different sources. The catalyst varies from deity to deity. So, to my fellow gods' advantage, freezing temperatures do not affect them like they do me. Truth be told, I am unsure what does for all except Hellano.

We never verbally disclosed the information—it is a topic gods leave unspoken, no matter how closely they are related—but we did not have to. Unlike our previous lives, who avoided one another like the plague, Hellano and I know enough about each other to place the pieces together. I gravitate towards fire, so the cold is my enemy. Considering my flames have never bothered him before—they may breathe and grow, but they also devour and destroy—and he always had a fascination for detailed stones and pretty gems, I assume his weakness is water. It makes sense; life on Earth first began in the seas and evolved from there.

However, not every deity is tied to the elements. Access to the veil of Divine Duplicity could be stifled by a specific emotion or event. Whatever sends it away is a closely guarded secret to our kind—our Achille's heel. Being the god of Wisdom, I question if Cato knows all of ours. The thought sends goosebumps down my spine.

Meena takes Luther's compliment for herself as she hikes red bottoms atop the sandalwood coffee table. The couch squeals as she leans back and tosses an arm around Mona. "Oh, it was nothing."

Luther smirks as he fiddles with a star pendant hanging over his breastbone. Copper painted fingernails drift from the jewelry and curtly gestures in her area. "Still conceited as always, goddess of Pleasure."

"Only as much as you are arrogant," she pokes fun.

I never paid much attention to their dynamic. Previous unions between us held little space for banter. Given their grins, and the memory of Meena forbidding Kysi from pointing blame at him when I bled on the floor of his estate, I get the impression they enjoy teasing each other. They are opposites just as Hellano and I are, and that fact does nothing but amuse them.

Harlynn sits straight-backed on the loveseat parallel to Meena and Mona. Butterfly clips fasten hair from her face, the rest falling against the back of her baby blue sweater. Dragonfly wings slowly open and close as she thinks aloud, "Luther should accompany us to Nightfall."

"Why?" Mona's glare is full of judgement. "Just as Meena has to touch a person to heal them, so does Luther when inducing pain. Cato isn't just going to let him walk up and shake his hand."

She is right. The day I returned to the Heavens, when my soul attempted to leave my body and caused my insides to leak, Kysi blamed Luther out of panic because we were dealing with powers not yet understood. *Natural* pain is not something he consciously invokes; it is the work of Divine Duplicity, and there is always a reason for it. All environmental and genetic factors have an input for the equation of agony. To induce pain from no source requires physical touch and a journey to the other side of his conscience.

"No," Harlynn's tone holds patience like an arrow in a quivering bowstring, "but it could throw him off. Buy us time." Eyes of roasted hazelnut reach me. "I can get you to Cato, but I can't stop him from disappearing. The god of Wisdom is driven by curiosity, right? Let's pique his interest."

Kysi leans against the arm of the couch beside her. The first button of his white dress shirt is undone, fair skin teasing to firm panes beneath. "Luther is not a threat to Cato, and he knows it. More importantly, he knows that *we know it too*. In the moments after we arrive, his head will fill with questions. 'Why is *he* here?', 'What are they planning?'"

The god of Agony puts a hand over his heart in defense. "I may not have extra bones on my back like you avians, nor the art of teleportation mastered, but I outmatch everyone here in physical combat."

I do pity young, wingless deities. They are considered the weakest among us in terms of capabilities. That is, until they become phasers. Luther was reincarnated less than a century ago; he is practically a child.

"Uppercuts aren't going to help us here, because again, you won't get within arm's reach of Cato." Hellano grips the back of the loveseat near Mona and leans weight into his arms. A fox fur sweater hugs his shoulders, and denim jeans frame muscular thighs.

One week ... That is how long I have been sleeping beside them. *Just* sleeping. My current point of sexual frustration has made me severely regret proposing the idea seven days ago. The buildup is driving me fucking crazy, and I may be forced to steal Meena's place of rest soon so Mona can hold me back from making any irrational decisions.

My spouse continues, "Just stand there and look pretty while I do what I do best."

Kill.

"I'm flattered you find my handsomeness more distracting than your ... *ropes of death*," Luther sarcastically voices.

"They aren't always so obvious," the god of Afterlife shares. I begin to search, assuming he let one loose to prove a point. "You'd be surprised at how much shade my little shadows can find to conceal themselves." Not a vein of black snakes over his hand, so it must be traveling between the cushions behind Mona's head.

Bingo.

A slither of night creeps from the sofa's corner. It snakes down the leg, delving into a crack between the floorboards and passing under the coffee table undetected. It slips between Harlynn's feet before I lose sight of where it is headed.

I am accustomed to their charades. Hellano often used them to play games, like juggling apples or inciting my snow leopard to pounce on them like a kitten would a laser. They used to chase me through rooms too, a dozen separate strings of black gunning to tickle my ribs.

Sometimes when we argued, it would end with me angrily storming off, but it was never long before ribbons of onyx came to find me. They would swipe hair from my face. Rub my back. Wrap between my fingers like a hand to hold.

Reconciliation was not their only reason to search me out. I could never forget the way they called me—curled in a coaxing motion to beckon me forward, through the halls and up the stairs—to where Hellano laid waiting in bed.

Other times were not so loving.

Since my birth, the reincarnation process has only happened once. To describe it in a single word: disturbing.

A visit from the souls of Life and Death truly meant one thing ... your time was up.

Hellano and I knew when his death was due. It felt like a rope fraying against a blade—an awareness. Luther's Soul Father was tense, as was I. After all, I had never seen anyone die before.

The previous god of Agony was sitting in the dining room of his estate when we arrived. There was a bottle of ambrosia on the table, next to splayed fingers he skillfully tapped a knife between. The god of Afterlife tried to hide the shadow, make it quick. But the deity caught it zip across the ceiling. He tried to flee, scared to die. It was the barbarity of it that motivated me to fulfill my purpose and replace him—not the purpose itself. I should have looked away. Should have covered my ears.

Hellano held me while I cried for days.

It was the first and only time I looked at us, and together we felt wrong.

Kysi jerks, snagging me back to the present. My mate swats his shoulder, and Hellano's tendril of black catches itself in the air. "Touch me with it again and you'll sleep in the storm."

Hellano japes, "And miss your cheerful hospitality? Wouldn't dream of it."

The council quiets at our admission to co-sleeping, although they appear to be holding back commentary like it is a rabid dog on a leash, too stunned to let it go. The wind is the down of a thistle in the heartbeats of silence.

"It's settled then," the King of Celestia gracefully carries on. "The god of Agony will join us."

"Not in bed." Luther winks. "Just so we're clear."

Kysi rubs his eyes. "I need ambrosia."

Mona seizes an opportunity. "Don't accept any from Harlynn or you'll be married by sunrise."

That arrow of impatience finally flies. "The only mark I'm about to give will be square on your nose if you don't shut your trap—"

Harsh words spray like rapid gunfire as the women stand. Hellano's hovering shadow acts as a barrier between them. Dress shoes click on the hard floor as Kysi plots a course to the bar area. Luther leans against the mantle and crosses his ankles. Meena checks her cuticles.

Where has our sense of uniformity fled? Maybe the looming conflict is at fault, or the recent months of strain and stress. Perhaps the manor is suffocating, and we are just victims of cabin fever.

"Enough!" Mouths shut and heads turn. I breathe deep, and it burns on the way out. Gods, my nerves are fried. "Wasting time is a luxury we cannot afford. Now, without the use of snide remarks or sarcasm, someone offer a suggestion on how the hell we are going to march an army through a blizzard."

A third of Celestia and Groveheart's defenses will join us. We will only speak to Cato with a protective beast at our backside—or in this case, surrounding the entire godsdamn city.

"Nightfall is encircled by mountains," Kysi returns with a drink in hand. "We'd have to travel through a split on the eastern side, given that most of my army cannot fly through the peaks."

Hellano nods. "If you've noticed, the blizzard has pockets of inactivity. I say we depart when it is calmer and stick to the outskirts of small towns so we can take shelter when the storm picks up. Soldiers can take different routes and travel in groups to avoid drawing unnecessary attention."

Right ... because Imperial's look like regular citizens. We wouldn't want to sound any alarms while heading north.

I drag focus to Harlynn, who blended in seamlessly right under our noses.

"We regroup on the other side of the mountains and close the distance together," Kysi simply states. A silence wades in wait of objections, but there are none.

He and Hellano must have discussed the plan many times prior. Otherwise, the conversation would not have gone so smoothly. I imagine the two kings sitting at the table in my mate's suite, going back and forth with tight faces.

"Why should my army be delayed so yours can play catch up? When we strike, it needs to be swift," the god of Afterlife would say.

"The only thing swift will be their deaths if my people aren't there. You know damn well how much war they have experienced, given you're the one who started them all," Kysi would retort. If I had to guess what drives his power away, it would be anger; it is hard to bargain when emotions are high.

Of course, Hellano would deny it, claiming it is not him who starts wars but ends them. The argument would spiral from there. But now, they speak like practiced associates.

Harlynn laces her fingers over her knees. "The stronghold in Nightfall is our destination. I will show you the window where Cato likely is, so Kysi can phase us inside."

"And if he's not there?" Mona questions.

The angel shrugs. "We wait. He'll come, because he has to."

"Um, elaborate?" she presses.

Harlynn's lips purse. "As emissary, I was scheduled to relay information at every opportunity. Cato was my transport. Our meeting place was a large, empty room. While I spoke with Priscilla, Cato busied himself by bringing copied texts from the Ancient Library. He did not do this only when I met with Priscilla, but during any idle minute in the day. Each time I saw his personal library, it was bigger. The god of Wisdom gravitates toward knowledge. If he is not there, it won't be long until he is."

So, even in mania, Cato is still driven by his purpose. The manor creaks against the tempest outside.

"How soon can we leave?" I ask the kings.

Their bodies tense at the question. It is clear they are not comfortable with me participating yet, given my lack of maneuverability, but they do not voice their concerns. A wise choice, because making me appear weak in front of our council would certainly ruffle my feathers.

"A day to address our commanding officers and plan the journey," Hellano states. "Another for them to relay the information. One more to prepare for departure. Then, it would be up to the storm."

Kysi nods in concurrence.

Anticipation thrums from my cranium to heels. Let's face it, waiting for me to move without the use of my feet is like watching water boil on a lukewarm stove. The snow is falling hard, and the timer for whatever Cato has planned could zero out any second.

"Be ready in three days," I tell the council. "Then, we leave at the first opportunity."

CHAPTER 38

Preparations for Nightfall will begin in the morning, therefore the kings will be unavailable in the coming days. Training will continue with Meena, and I have decided to shorten my wing exercises to focus on learning teleportation.

Hellano's departure to the Capital used to conclude our nightly meditations. Now that he returns at dawn instead, the lessons have no official end. On Kysi's orders, we are to continue until sleep invades. It undoubtedly increases productivity, but I believe he really did it to avoid awkward goodnights.

Per usual, particles of arousal muddle my brain like gnats on fruit. Tonight, as well as every other, my libido tethers me to consciousness. With enough self-discipline and the strength to stay settled rather than rub on them like a cat in heat, my urges should die from neglect after ... a while.

Just reach for them, my inner thoughts tempt. *You need the mark anyway.*

In truth, impending tattoos are not much of a concern anymore. If I wanted to wait, Hellano would conjure an excuse. Probably say something diplomatic like, *"As we have come to realize, no two wedding brands are identical. They do not solely display our love but distinguish us as individuals. Given recent events and the threat we face ahead, precautions are in order to protect the safety of the Ultimate Queen. In doing so, our marks shall remain confidential for the time being."* And of course, his outmatched charisma would leave the people throwing roses at his feet.

Knowing this, the mark of the wed still motivates me to give in, because it is the only reason I have aside from purely vulgar motivations.

A low pitch cracks the quiet. "You're killing me, Anewla." Green faintly glows through Kysi's closed lids. He lays on his stomach, arms under the pillow. Our legs are knotted beneath humid sheets.

"How? I'm not doing anything," I whisper with attitude, as if I have not spent the last twenty minutes squirming between them.

The glow illuminates a beautiful grin. "You are doing *many* things."

So ... Kysi also struggles to balance desire with the possible consequences of satiating it.

"You think we haven't noticed?" Hellano's sultry timbre grazes my ear from behind. "Your need is a ringing bell, and I am a godsdamn salivating dog."

My pulse thunders. "Oh ..." I stumble over words, engrossed in the warm breeze of their exhales.

The darkness is a blindfold—save for Kysi's orbital glimmer—but it could never hinder me from distinguishing the men. Their atmosphere holds a unique charge that my body responds to differently. Kysi softens my edges, Hellano sharpens them. Intimacy would be a sensory clash on my pores. Over my breasts. Between my thighs.

"Gods," Kysi utters and turns. A grip lands on my jaw, squaring my attention to a bright, lustful gaze. After over a fortnight of wrestling with carnal cravings, my mate yields.

My jaw tugs forward, and feverish lips melt into mine. His tongue flicks over my tastebuds, ravenous with greed. If I do not pull away now—calm the indecent chaos soon to pursue—I may not be able to at all.

Detaching myself feels like holding magnets a centimeter apart. "You don't need—"

"I am well aware," a primitive impatience rumbles his throat. "Now, unless it is to deny participation, *don't* interrupt me again."

Time slows to wait for a protest. I soak in the words, avidity growing alongside bewilderment.

Slowly, he brings my mouth back to his.

Hellano bunches the fabric of my nightgown. A kiss lands upon my shoulder, then another. Two hands meet the hem of my underwear.

Someone should name me the goddess of Manifestation, because what *the fuck* is happening right now?

Fueled by a festering passion, I lift my hips. Over my thighs and past my knees, their hands travel the distance back up my legs. Featherlight fingers sweep through me, inducing a moan that vibrates Kysi's tongue.

"Fuck," Hellano groans at my backside. His other hand reaches to steal my lips from Kysi, who instead takes my earlobe between his teeth.

Hungry words quake near my jugular. "You poor thing," my mate says, exploring my pitiful wetness with Hellano like it is the only territory they can smugly coexist.

Contradictory to the harmony between my legs, their mouths enter a battle for attention. Back and forth, rich and sweet, they fight for sloppy kisses. Hellano runs his index against my bundle of nerves, and Kysi teases my entrance. The combination lures my back to arch.

"She likes that," says the gravelly voice in front of me before my lips are stolen once more.

A sunken tone responds, "I know what she likes." It drifts into a breath that skims over my breast and travels down my ribs to the apex of my thighs.

It has been eight years since Hellano kissed me in my most sensitive area, and he does so as if waiting another second might be the only thing that could kill him.

"'Lano," I breathe into Kysi's mouth, and he tenses with heightening desire.

I both despise and worship Hellano's tongue, fighting the way it hurls me towards release so soon. I reach for his hair to steel myself—a guardrail in violent winds—only to find Kysi's fingers speared through the strands ... moving Hellano over my clit.

"No—no, not yet. Ky—" I want to savor it. Soak in it.

"Stubborn thing," he whispers through my teeth, noting the way I push against the orgasm. The sinewy arm spanning my body gets faster, speeding Hellano's pace. "Give us what we want."

Muscles seize to pleasure's vise. Whimpers and moans echo in the night, drawn out by their hovering motions.

Kysi stops claiming my mouth to witness me unfurl. "That's it," he praises, "let it out."

I return from the spiral with an overwhelming need to consume. Hellano's dark silhouette grows above me. I rise to meet him, running my hands down the length of his covered abs before grasping his shirt to lift. He submits to my advances, pivoting to let me straddle his waist. I feel every ridge of muscle made fresh in my absence, every new line he did not have months ago.

Kysi catches my nightgown from draping down, snagging it off me in one swift motion. Wholly bare, I roll against the bulge in Hellano's sweatpants and reach for another under my mate's waistband. He kneels adjacent to Hellano, reaching back to pull his shirt off.

Chiseled body on display, black hair falls back as he looks to the ceiling and bathes in the pleasure of my pumping hand. The image is enough to shatter me: a detailed statue of seductive divinity.

"Good girl," Kysi drawls.

Hellano's grip surrounds my hips, running me harder over his solid shaft. It builds me up, aching and pulsing for more of him. More of Kysi. More, more, *more.*

I tug Kysi's bottoms down and lift myself off Hellano's erection. He obeys my silent order and drops the final barrier between us. Skin on skin with molten blood, I imagine the air must be full of steam.

Hellano's length effortlessly slides into place, and drones of satisfaction fill the space as I inch onto his throbbing cock, lower and lower.

Sex in a well-lit room has the advantage of a clear show, but one perk the darkness brings is the elevation of other senses. So many touches—hands roaming and teasing and gliding—and none pass me by unaccounted for.

"It's a fucking wonder I survived without this," Hellano says, burying himself deeper. I lean forward as he drives into me, leveling with Kysi's pulsing member.

Taking my mate's hand in mine, I place it on the back of my hair, then steady my palms on Hellano's chest. Kysi knows what I want from him, and I will not move until he does it.

"Probably best if you choose the pace, angel," he suggests through breaths.

The hills under my hands rattle as Hellano groans out, "She's fine, trust me."

I grin in the dark and trail a thumb along my husband's jaw, remembering the countless times our coition became rather brutal. What is aggression if not passion in a mask? Angry sex was exhilarating—sometimes we would argue just to make up. It was never truly serious, only the roles we liked to play.

Pressure guides my head forward, and I open wide to take Kysi in.

Their prolonged hums are addictive. It trumps all simple plea-
sures combined. A land of milk and honey to bathe in, drown in.
Kysi quickens, gathering my hair in a tight fist. When Hellano meets
his speed with a firm grip on my waist, my eyes roll from the crushing
euphoria.

It is bliss to expel pent-up affection. A passionate, *"I've missed
you,"* dances in every thrust. Hellano takes control below, knowing
just the spot to hit. My abdomen coils, and there is no fighting the
climax this time.

My cries encompass Kysi's cock, which leaves him pumping in my
mouth with added vigor. The hint of salt reaches my tongue before
bursting into my throat. Moans are muffled by my need to swallow.
Just when I have taken it all in, Hellano stiffens under me.

Light is not required to know his brows are barely knitted. Lips
slightly parted. Abs flex against my palms, contracting with the rest
of him.

I take them both in, waiting for my foggy mind to clear into a
field of regret. But it does not manifest, not as we collapse beside one
another. Not as our sluggish limbs tangle.

Only one thing is missing, and that is weight on our shoulders.

Muted sunlight casts a silver-blue glow upon freshly cut hair. The
diadem found in the treasury circles Kysi's skull, its inky waves

travelling skyward. He turns from the window, catching my eye. Full lips tilt upward.

"I love to watch you wake," he coolly states, "but I love waking up to you more."

Blinking sleep away, I stretch in bed like a feline bathing in sunlight. "Such a heartthrob," I lilt.

His short laugh sings a soft tune. "What can I say? I had centuries to practice."

"Shh." A smile lifts my cheeks. "You'll wake him up."

Kysi arches a brow and steps patiently toward a snoozing Hellano. Meeting my spouse's bedside, he nudges his spine and snaps twice in his ear. "Wake up, terminator. Your stay has expired."

I squint at the stubborn Heartian King.

He shrugs. "Sorry angel, but his eviction is overdue. We are already behind schedule because I couldn't bear to wake you."

Hellano rolls over and rubs fatigue from his face. "I am no issue, it seems."

"Correct," my mate acknowledges. "Harlynn requested I drop her at the Capital, and Renwick gave me clothes to bring back since he has better things to do than wait for you all morning. Celestian attire waits on the dresser, just under the crown you maliciously stole, or rather, *accepted* from the enemy."

Tired arms flop over the covers. "You say that like you're not wearing what is *claimed* to be mine."

I wave my hand to stop their bickering. "Hang on, why did Harlynn need to go to the Capital?" Surely, she has not been left unsupervised.

"Apparently, the clothes I stocked for you are not meeting her standards." Seconds pass, and he notes my skepticism. "I can assure you, my love, Harlynn has been nothing but compliant since her admittance to espionage."

"We trust her," Hellano says hoarsely while pushing himself to sit, "despite having every right not to." Dark green bedding compliments his complexion. Golden eyes halt upon me. "Here I thought you couldn't get any prettier."

Transient curiosity cambers my neck, fleeting when I behold his own.

A linear mandala streaks his adam's apple. Rigid points change direction in no conceivable pattern. The longer I inspect it, the more I see. Countless polygons with no same shape or size.

Striking, just like the rest of him.

Snapping out of my daze, I lift the coverlet off my legs. I snag my discarded nightgown off the floor and swing it over my head before reaching the vanity.

Hellano's tattoo is sharp and cornered, whereas mine rounds with many spirals. A thousand tiny curls span the circumference of my throat. A marriage stamp unique to only me, crafted with its counterpart in mind. It possesses a sense of forever, bestowed upon an unlikely pair at the mercy of love.

Kysi nears my backside and brushes hair off my shoulder. A soft kiss is planted upon the ink. "You can pull off anything, can't you?" he asks, then leans forward to nab the other king's clothes. They soar to my sluggish husband, the gemstone crown airborne for a short time. "You've got three minutes."

The mascot of our demise leans on cream thermals, staring at me. Without its existence, our misfortune may have never come to pass. Two men seeking to rule ... and only one crown—or so Cato led us to believe.

But I had not yet come to that realization on the night of the Spring Festival, nor had Kysi, and disregarded him as being jealous when he attempted to explain his thoughts in the treasury.

"How generous of you," Hellano grumbles and pushes brawny arms through a tightly knitted sweater.

"Ky"—I nod to the diadem— "try it on."

My mate embraces me from behind. An intrigued look looms in the reflection. "Whatever for, my Queen?"

"Aren't you curious?" The question extends to Hellano as well, who loosely props his forearms on his knees. My crown is a similar block of stone to the one he came to wear ...

That is, until I put it on.

Sliding away, Kysi snags it and holds it up for inspection. "On occasion." I am met with a suspicious expression. "What do you think would grow?"

If Kysi's theory is wrong, then nothing.

Shadows envelop a black wave and pluck Kysi's headpiece away, clearing the path. "Probably weeds," Hellano taunts while reeling the piece of jewelry to him. "Let's see, shall we?"

Kysi mimics with annoyance while raising the solid crown. I watch it fall into place.

As if bearing witness to a fulfilling prophecy, my lips part in awe. Hundreds of tiny clovers bloom quickly, like the release of a long-held breath. The Heartian King holds me hostage in his ravishing tableau.

Kysi's behavior—the plotting and scheming and lying for a position he did not have—truly was from a soul responsibility he could not escape. Destiny cannot be stolen, and my mate is to be a *king*. The epiphany gallops my heart ... then palpitates with another dawning realization.

I believe Hellano's story; the god of Wisdom swore it was his to wear. But aside from a macabre poem in an endless library, and a bread trail of odd behaviors, there was no tangible evidence of Cato's betrayal. I was clinging to that, holding tight to the idea of simple misunderstandings. This, however—Kysi being the key to the crowded clover's freedom—is undeniable proof.

My mate was right when he claimed Hellano wore his crown, which means the god of Afterlife was never meant to have it.

The revelation impacts my husband like a steel drum. He blankly stares, taken back by the blatant transparency of his enemy's true form.

The black diadem spins slowly in the hovering shadows beside him. Since Kysi's first assumption was correct, maybe his second one is too ...

Are both gods meant to rule in the New World?

Hellano examines the piceous headpiece. By his will, dark smoke slowly brings it over red hair disheveled by sleep. The air thrums with anticipation, and I am bolted to the floor with immovable posture. Kysi and I adamantly observe it settle upon Hellano's scalp.

A pin drops in the deathly silent room.

Kysi gapes. "It's ... illusionary."

The waves appear to sway but never leave their stations. Their insides whirl with trapped shadows. If Hellano's palms were made of glass, I imagine this is what would lie beneath.

I once had a dream that my lovers reigned beside me. Chased inside the throne room, we went around and around the trio of trees. Later, I concluded that the castle holds Hellano's aura—just as it does mine and Kysi's—because it is *supposed* to. A place where they can reign over their kingdoms on common ground. A place where we can be together. The idea was nirvana—a realm tilted so far south makes it difficult to believe in such fantasies. But now, seeing the men as they should be, wipes the blur of that improbability away.

"Guess that confirms your notion," the Celestian King says, glued to his reflection in the vanity mirror. "Enjoy this while it lasts because it may be the only time you hear it, but ... you were right. It really is mine."

My throat is full of all but words.

Despite missing the kings to the marrow of my bones, I am thankful for their busyness. Blowing off steam the other day has helped me focus, along with the absence of their tantalizing distractions.

The kingdoms will be entrusted to Meena and Mona when we depart. Because the former spends her days mending me, my friend's availability is limited as she prepares to temporarily rule the nations. I have not seen her since the council meeting, and I hope to catch her for a goodbye.

Due to the lengthy downpour outside, we suspect the blizzard will rest at any moment. Its weather pattern is fairly unpredictable—we may have anywhere from two to twelve hours of inactivity before needing to seek shelter. During heavy snowfall, Kysi will teleport soldiers forward. However, he must be wary not to use too much energy. His invaluable skill must not be exhausted before we reach Nightfall.

"People were awfully confused when the kings showed up wearing different crowns," Harlynn mentions behind me in the bathroom where she braids a lilac vine into my hair. "Now, it seems they understand ... There is no denying the fate of their reigns."

I say nothing while she pins the thick plait into a halo. Not a strand is left out of place. She moves to the side, clicking a familiar box open. Silk surrounds a naked gemstone.

It is an odd feeling to switch roles so drastically ... Once a helpless experiment, now a monarch again.

I peer at the crown with pride, and determination spiderwebs near my sternum. Its sparkling spires is a cathedral of hope for my people. A promise of peace.

It fits snugly in the circle of my braid.

"And when they see you again," Harlynn goes on as the headpiece flourishes with virid moss, "there will be no denying the fate of yours."

I peer at her then—*really* look—in search of withheld truths in the lines of her face. My doubt in her is evident, but so is the want to forgive. She was my anchor in chaos, and now a different storm brews—one of uncertainty and fear—and there is nothing to keep me from drifting off in a sea of panic.

"I had something made for you," she says, breaking eye contact to exit the bathroom.

In the brief quiet, I find the manor does not creak from the tempest beyond ...

The path to Nightfall is clearing.

Harlynn's tolerated company is better than seconds of isolation, so I enter the bedchamber with haste. Sprawled upon the bed is a peat jumpsuit. Creamy lichen cascades across patches of moss to the cinched waist, where colorful fungi nestle. Indigo, soft pink, and blue caps shade the mushroom's short bodies. The legs are plump and billowy, making the ensemble appear similar to a gown while granting the advantage of maneuverability. A thick hood is attached to the neckline, near shoulders of tangled branches that stretch down the length of each arm.

It is breathtaking, but more importantly, it is *me*. I am confident in the confines of nature. Safer. It may be difficult to wield the material in the height of a snowstorm, but right now the blizzard is calming. I could use it if I need, without having to journey to Divine Duplicity. The moment I step outside, I know the road to raw power will narrow—even more so when the snowfall angrily picks up again. Alas, the gift of Life will always be as near as it can be.

The living material curls into my touch like a child against their mother. Much of myself was given, perhaps lost, in the drive to create heaven for all. After failure at every corner, I realize now the key to success lies not just in allegiance between kings, but loyalty to myself. Faith.

Skimming the natural fabric, I feel thin brambles latticed within.

"I know you can defend yourself just fine now," Harlynn mentions to my right, "but there is no harm in having your blades sharpened."

The angel's gift is not merely for show. It is also a weapon. Just in case.

"Thank you," are the first words I say to Harlynn in days.

Figures materialize near the window. I have grown accustomed to Kysi and Hellano phasing in and out. Harlynn, however, jerks with awareness.

"Ugh, it's no less creepy when you guys do it," the angel huffs in reference to the god of Wisdom.

The men pause at my appearance, eyes skimming over my hair. I am equally entranced by them in regal uniformity. They are similarly dressed save for differing colors. Each wears a jerkin over a warm doublet, with breeches that glide into leather riding boots below the knees.

Laurel patterns are embroidered into Kysi's forest-green vest. An ivory undershirt rolls from its borders. Pinned to his breast is a bronze brooch—Groveheart's crest: the tree of life. Our diadems match, and I cannot help but wonder if this historical day is why.

To its left, caged shadows greet me in waves upon Hellano's head. He too wears Celestia's badge near his heart; a crescent moon hugging the marigold sun. It clings to a royal blue vest that restricts the torso of his plum shirt.

"A goddess indeed," Hellano states with unwavering pupils. My cheeks flush.

Kysi comes to my side and kisses the blushed skin before noticing the attire chosen by Harlynn. He glances at her in approval. "You've outdone yourself."

"It was owed," she replies. "That and more."

I shake my head. "Your debt will be paid when you lead us to Cato and help restore peace to the New World. Only that will redeem you."

The angel sucks in a breath. "Fair enough." She tightens the band at the end of her braid and motions to the window, where snow no longer falls. "Let's get on with it, shall we?"

Heartbeats pass. The air thins from a dissipating stillness.

Hard raps reel our attention to the door, where Meena swiftly enters with a hefty clay pot held to her side. "One last exercise before you go," she says, already aware of our impending exit. Pale locks sway around her every step to the center of the room, where she places the pot on the floor. The goddess of Pleasure holds her hips, and elbows split through strands like rocks in a stream. "Don't hold back."

The room looks at me. A pink lily patiently watches on the table near the window. I peer into the soil and wonder what seed sleeps within.

Opening my palm to the ceiling, I curl my fingers in a dance. A stem sprouts and climbs the air with excitement, producing nodes that spread on its journey upward. The plant surpasses us in height and meets the roof, which does nothing to stop its growth. It continues unfazed in a perpendicular fashion. Ivory jasmine blooms throughout the body. Yellow pistils awaken to feed upon our exhales. I only hold back because I must, otherwise the growth would consume the entire suite. Closing my hand feels like stopping time. Everyone stills when the jasmine flowers stop spreading.

Slowly, those around me follow past the covered ceiling down the stalk and land on me. Although I am miles ahead in terms of recovery, my reluctance cannot be hidden.

"Our duties call once more, my flower," the god of Afterlife gently speaks. The remembrance of Luther's Soul Father flashes over him. "I promise to make his end swift."

My chest aches. I breathe deep, but it does nothing to soothe the tremors in my joints. The rattle in my bones. No amount of time, training, or meditation can prepare me for a god's reincarnation.

My biggest purpose happens to be my greatest aversion. Oh, how the Sky Spirits love irony.

I must remind myself that I am not losing Cato permanently; he will arrive in the Shadowlands. Though my reputation there proceeds me, perhaps I can see him when the dust settles ... Get some answers. Closure.

"Remember who you are, my love. It is not the end of a life, but the beginning of a new one," my mate says.

With a nod, I snag the outfit from the bed and rotate towards the bathroom to dress. "Go find Luther," I say over my shoulder to the kings. "Tell him it is time."

CHAPTER 39

The kings adopted horses.

A chocolate thoroughbred named Penumbra bravely stands a few paces behind my left shoulder. The King of Celestia is mounted upon her golden encrusted saddle.

I had not known my husband also went looking for me in the months of my disappearance. When he grew weary of flying, he would ride in search of his missing bride.

Horizontal to Penumbra is her sibling, Aurora. The mare's ears do not twitch. She hardly blinks. Like her sister, she is stationary. Aurora's auburn coat gleams under Kysi.

I learned today that when my mate's energy waned from phasing, he too would ride to find his lost soulmate.

Harlynn and Luther are mounted behind my lovers. The former is on the same side as the god of Afterlife, should his power be needed in the event of another betrayal.

The animal carrying me was offered by a stable hand who passed too quickly for questions. The moment I saw her, identical to the one illustrated on the shared bedchamber door in the castle, I knew she was mine.

Amity's mile-long mane drifts in the cold breeze. I run my hand across pewter fur as soft as silk, and she humbly huffs with approval.

Steeds of every Earth tone face me on the front grounds of the palace. Each rider is adorned in their native colors. Brown, green, purple, and blue splash against the blanket of white underfoot. Behind them, birds orbit turrets and swing into the crevices of balconies and window ledges—out to feel the sun's sweet grace. Winter left the once vibrant network of plants charred upon the castle's face. Even still, the background is a tapestry of home.

Hooves kick snow. The horses are eager to run; I best not keep them waiting.

"As previously stated by your kings," I address the legion with unbreakable cadence, "the city of Nightfall is home to the Imperial rebellion, consisting of angels and demons that seek to enslave human beings and drain deities of power. Without interference, we face the threat of a realm ruled by races only fit for their own. Our diverse blood holds the power to divide the world, but only if we discount the way it beats through same hearts ... Hearts that weep. Hearts that love. Hearts that beat with purpose and passion.

"I am not purely a queen or goddess. I am the Guardian of the New World. As its creator, my soul's purpose is to uphold the safety of all species. None shall live under my reign against their will, but *all* will yield where justice demands."

Silence. Seconds. Stillness.

Thump goes a fist over a heart. Another follows. Hylan and Typa begin a wave of responses, each soldier stamping their chests with a vow of loyalty. When all soldiers, both Heartian and Celestian, bear the same stance ... I pull on Amity's reins and head north.

It took four days to reach the outskirts of Nightfall. Everything went perfectly. We had long spurts of weather inactivity and no interruptions along the way, almost as if the Spirits of the Sky awoke from their mighty slumber to pave the path. There is just one problem ...

Nightfall is completely empty.

I am dumbfounded by how ... *normal* it looks aside from the vacancy. The stronghold juts from the upper right quadrant like a castle to a kingdom. Resting not far from the border wall, a quaint eatery's sign swings in the icy wind. I am too far to make out the name, but two crossed loaves are painted on the wood.

Farthest from where we stand, on the other side of the land, houses tuck into one another like neighborhoods for families rather than lairs for oppressive, bloodsucking spawns.

The army splits behind me, Harlynn, and the three other gods in our group to encircle the city. The mountains form a crescent shape at our backside. We traveled through a jagged canyon between them. It was quiet—no signs of *uncivilized* activity.

Harlynn squints past the stretch of granite surrounding the unoccupied land. "I don't understand ... Do you think they left after what happened in the bunker?"

"Possibly, in fear of being 'colonized by divine government', or so Priscilla said," I respond.

My gut trips into freefall. If we cannot find their new location, it is only a matter of time before they rebuild and strike again.

"Stick to the plan," Kysi chimes in. "If Cato is not in his personal study, maybe something there can lead us to him."

Godsdamn, this is starting to feel like a wild goose chase.

Harlynn guides us into a trot. After a ten-minute ride around the terrain's bend, we face the back end of the stronghold between frozen pines on the northernmost hillside. The angel dismounts. Dragonfly wings flicker to soften her landing.

"There." She points to thin rows of stained glass rising halfway from the base of the fortress. "Cato once mentioned how light withers books over a long period of time on Earth," Harlynn convinces. "He called it a tragedy. But here, in this realm, they are not damaged for simply being admired. The solitary issue he held with the Ancient Library was its lack of natural light. No windows, because it harbors endless secrets. He liked this place for the light. It made him feel like part of the moving world."

Amity snickers as I climb off the saddle. "Ironic, the way he seeks to destroy it now."

Kysi comes forth, fair skin blushed from the chill breeze. "You guys know the drill, no one get too grabby." The corners of his luscious mouth quirk up. "Except you, of course."

Unbelievable.

I huff a laugh and slap my palm over his jerkin. The others reach for his arms. Taking a deep inhale, my mate carries us across the hill, past the border wall and through the fortress windows in less than a second.

It smells of binding glue and leather. Clear walkways line the cluttered space, leading to workstations and alcoves.

Not enough shelves to hold his progress, it seems. Furniture is almost entirely hidden by untidiness. A living space can be made out under piles of books. The coffee table has no free space. Neither does the brown couch beside it.

I progress through the clutter at the forefront of the group. The stacks forming makeshift walls have none of similar height, and many tower over our heads. The tunnel of bound parchment forks into two walkways.

The left side leads to a spiraling staircase that trails to a mezzanine with more books. Those ones are shelved neatly between colorful beams of daylight.

At first glance, the other side appears to be a dead end. I find it a trick to the eye, nothing more than two cases open to another inside: an entrance to hallways leading deeper into the first floor.

Books tumble like a flock of startled birds in that direction. My heart skips and I veer to the right.

"Cato," I softly call, "is that you?"

My ears beat like the drums of war. No response comes, but the sound of rummaging ensues. I press forward. One leg drags the other as I close in. A quick denunciation mumbles around the corner. I turn the bend ...

There he is. The god of Wisdom. My old friend.

Thinner now. Weary. He kneels on a flowery rug between shelves, gathering tomes to restack. Vibrant white pearls drift past the floor, catching sight of my winter boots. Slowly they rise like a torturous confession on the tongue; an ugly truth to hopeful ears.

The first time I saw Cato, his eyes looked like they wanted to swallow me whole. It is the one part of him left unchanged.

Sunken cheeks drift into a prominent jawline that shades his neck. Dark circles hold up a depressing gaze. Light blonde hair is unkept, frizzy and tangled around his collarbones. His cream tunic is rustled. Sea-green wings curl into his back as he cautiously rises from the floor with a book in hand.

Hellano needs enough time to sneak a shadow across. I need enough time for closure.

"I'm sorry," I admit, and the ancient god stills. "I never asked if you wanted to help—if you wanted to be a part of the council. I never questioned if you craved anything apart from your purpose. Pulling you away from the Ancient Library was a mistake. I am your friend ... I would never intentionally sacrifice your happiness."

Not so much as a blink comes from him.

"Why the long face?" Kysi remarks beside me. He leans against a high-reaching case and crosses his arms. "Upset the evil plan didn't work?"

I straighten my spine at Cato's reaction. A wide breath inflates his chest. His tone is calm and low when he releases it. "No ... I'm sad that it *did*."

Another illusion reveals itself when a figure emerges from the shelves—or rather, the crack I never saw between them. A violet cloak swims around forthcoming feet. Hair the color of dead grass drapes over the bust. A crooked smile fractures my ribs.

"So ..." Lilliana saunters in with feline grace. "Rather than clashing kingdoms in the name of love, two loathsome kings banded together."

My first incarnate closes in on Cato and effortlessly slides the book from his grasp. It did not appear easy for him to let go of, however.

What is she doing here? Memories scatter into an investigation board that I scan for clues.

A lightbulb goes off.

"They've already started," Prosenth had said on our way to the ritual site. *"We have to hurry."*

Lilliana gave herself the same advantage I have: the ability to travel realms. The Heavens were about to be reshaped. She needed transit to the New World to ensure the Nine made the right decision ... ensure *I* was properly handling the role.

Then I broke into the ritual site and killed over half the Nine. Not just any retired gods, but ancient, hierarchal deities that have walked with her since the dawn of time.

Lilliana opens the book. Manicured nails flip through. "Hm. Where was I? Ah! Yes, here we are. *Oh!* This chapter is quite scandalous. Let's spare the red faces and skip ahead, shall we?"

Cato shrinks into himself.

I could not be more confused. It is not just me, either. A line of bewilderment forms between Hellano's brows, and Kysi tilts his head.

After humming past words, my Soul Mother clearly recites, "None shall live under my reign against their will, but *all* will obey where justice demands." She closes the pages. "I. Couldn't. Agree. More."

Panic freezes my lungs.

"What happened to you was a plot twist I never expected," said the god of Wisdom on the day we met.

Heat floods through my face. So hot with anger, the air likely wades above me. The story of my life—my *fucking* book the godsdamn Ancient Library had stocked with every secret, every finger reaching for the upper hand. They had it this whole time.

Cato was transcribing it for her. She has been tracking me. She knows *everything*.

Which means she knew we were coming.

CHAPTER 40

YOU. WILL. FALL.

Those were the last words Lilliana said to me. She gave herself the power to dismantle my reign as insurance for the Nine. The moment I proved myself unworthy to her and the last surviving members of council, mere moments after the eternal flames died, she knew it was a mistake.

"Anewla ..." Harlynn trembles behind me. "I swear on my life I have never seen this woman."

I am the final grain of sand falling through an hourglass, a fleeting blink away from turning around to rip the angel to shreds. What cause do I have to believe her? She remains an Imperial.

But then, before the sand speck can crash upon the shore of its neighbors, the hourglass turns upside down.

Cato speaks not with words, but a glance. At me. *Into* me with those infinite eyes. His chin tilts down a centimeter, unnoticeable to all but me. His lips barely mouth syllables I cannot piece together. Such a small, light action. It quickly passes.

Awareness lifts my hair like a porcupine's quill. I know not what Cato was trying to say, but this much is clear: he is not in control.

Lilliana has him trapped.

"I figured a monumental shift in the Heavens would involve *some* issues," my predecessor drones. "I did not foresee the need to interfere coming *right after* the ritual."

All it took was a few drops of blood and a request into cobalt flames, and the Spirits of the Sky gave her the ingredients to dismantle me: the ability to escape the Shadowlands, three beads that rid deities of power, and Cato. Her eyes and ears.

Her *puppet*.

Did he beg for help in glances I never looked twice upon? Was I too preoccupied to notice his silent cries? My friend, who I owe my very life, has been controlled this entire time and I was too selfish to notice. Did my descent to Earth really humble me, or am I still the heartless goddess I always was?

Hatred fuels my step forward. "You strip the will of your first born to *get back* at me? I am more different from you than my own opposite, the god of Afterlife."

Lilliana takes a step herself, passing Cato's shoulder. "You interrupted a dangerous ritual and brought mortality to our kind!" Her voice raises a pitch. "You are *corrupt!*"

Knuckles tighten. "Then why not kill me at first chance? Why seek to break apart the realm?"

The white in her eyes carries a gray tint as she looks at the kings. "It isn't *just* you."

Hellano scoffs. "Oh, so we're all corrupt? It sounds like the Sky Spirits failed to save you from insanity when you arrived in the New World. You're the eldest goddess of Beginnings; you're not supposed to be here."

Lilliana bites back, "Never have I seen corruption in more than one deity at a time. Something is wrong. The balance has shifted." Her angular jaw shakes with disapproval. "You must all perish for the sake of our collective existence."

Killing one deity point blank would be hard enough, but three? She did not like those odds. She needed to wear us down first. And it was working ...

Until Harlynn threw her plan off course.

This meeting had two outcomes: being brought by the Imperials as payment for independence or coming with a united army.

But the angel's loyalty is not yet determined. Harlynn may have refused to take advantage of Hellano, but that does not mean she would not reconcile the mistake by shoving us all into the enemy's blade later.

I glance at the King of Celestia, whose nose points to Cato. In his eyes there is no emptiness. In his heart there is no space. The ritual *mended* the god of Afterlife's soul. That is how I know Lilliana is wrong.

Greif festers in many ways. It can morph into fear. Delusion. Bitterness. Perhaps she carries all variations of it inside, like a virus spreading through a sea of people.

"You failed." Kysi pushes off the bookcase, drawing Lilliana's attention.

A ribbon of black emerges from the top of a case behind her. It swims in the air.

Hellano is going to kill her.

But following my eye, Cato finds the trail of shadow. His face pales.

Fuck.

With no consent in his actions, the god of Wisdom lurches to Lilliana. They stagger and lose footing, but their bodies never reach the floor.

Together, they phase out of sight.

Kysi kicks a wooden case and strains to collect himself. "Son of a bitch."

In a trice, our mission has gone from killing Cato to saving him.

I whirl around to face the others. Hellano reels in the shadow with frustration. Luther silently ponders. I cannot bring myself to look at Harlynn. There is no time to sort through the mysteries of her allegiance.

"One of us needs to find and guard my book in the Ancient Library," I suggest, "stop them from gaining the upper hand."

The angel's voice grates in my ears. "No, they want to separate you three. If anyone goes, we all need to—"

"Guys." The god of Agony fixates on nothing in particular. "I think I know why this city is empty."

All our postures become ramrod straight as Luther pulls focus from the air. "While we were moving out of the kingdoms ... Nightfall was moving *in*."

The shelves tilt. I am heavier now than I was moments ago. Dread churns in my gut, and I battle to remain upright.

We brought a third of our armies with us, which would leave enough men on the home front to safely guard it considering Nightfall's size. However, if the treaty between feral clans and the Imperials is true ...

My people are being slaughtered.

I cannot hear my chest crack, but it deeply does so. Slamming my eyes closed, I place brick after brick in the space of my mind. Those around me become lost on the other side. I let no sound in. No touch. Deeper I sink into meditation's cocoon. Inside the sedimentary blocks and away from the perception of others, I fucking *panic*. Threading fingers through my hair, I pace to the beat of my pounding chest.

Is that why our journey through the mountains was quiet? My brain demands that I go to the Ancient Library, but how can I when my people might need help—might be dying on land I swore to protect them on?

A dense gale rushes through the cracks of my enclosure. It spirals within and winds a lilac petal from my braid. Power whips at my skin like a million outstretched fingers begging me to reach for them.

I did not find teleportation. *It* found *me*.

With great strength, I spear my hand through the twister and grasp the potent force.

The atmosphere shifts into a burning cold. The wind circles differently now. It is not intentional like before but unpredictable. Glittering clouds gather in the distance. They roll under my vision as the horizon spins into a sprawling city below.

Colors twirl as I tumble from the sky. Indigo and fuchsia. White and maroon. Wing beats prove useless, so I urge the ivy in my clothes to spread and cushion my landing. But I am falling faster and faster. They will not be able to withstand the collision.

A flat-top building grows larger by the second ... It threatens to crush me on impact.

On this fated day, I descend yet again.

Death becomes imminent in the forms of flashing pictures. Butterflies dancing in the woods behind Kysi's estate. The colors in Hellano's eyes soon to meet extinction for mine. Meena's shiny hair and sharp tongue. And Mona ... I never said goodbye to Mona.

A hopeful current shoves me sideways. I juggle the gust and nearly drop it, but my once broken and battered wings catch it in their sails at the utmost defining moment.

The rotating plane levels in time for me to jerk left and dodge the corner of a multistory building. My skull bypasses the roof by six inches at *most*. Eyes wide, my muscles cry out as I attempt to slow myself down before crashing into the side of a music store. Angling my wings, I swerve hard to evade and tumble upon the top deck of an apartment home.

If not for the layer of snow and outdoor furniture covered in tarp hindering my speed, the decoratively carved parapet around the porch would have catapulted me into the streets below. It does, however, knock the breath from my lungs.

I grip the barrier. It is colder than a carcass in the rain, sucking the warmth from my palms. Blinking away flurries, I peer into the active city.

At last, my chest fills with a gasp.

Imperials adorned in fighting leathers attack my soldiers at every corner.

A woman with brown hair cut around her jaw plunges a longsword between the wings of a Celestian cadet. A window breaks above her and shards fall into the sparkling snow. A body soon follows and lands three feet away; this one does not wear a uniform.

The shattered windowsill frames a figure covered in animal pelts. Matted hair sticks to the female's cheeks. Tribal tattoos line her face. She peers at her crawling victim and bares two rows of fangs, filed for effortless devouring. Shells open over her shoulder blades when she jumps from the ledge. Beetle-like wings flitter to brace her landing. The organ caged in my ribs skips when she grasps the mortal man's ankle, yanking him back before bending to sink pointed teeth into his side.

The feral clans *are* real ... and Revelry Row is under attack.

CHAPTER 41

Families flee homes wearing not enough to ward off the riling winter. Shops are torn apart. Merchandise is strewn throughout in attempts to self-defend. Calamity strikes its adamant staff as the coming storm buries motionless bodies in white.

My soul bond soothes, which tells me Kysi is nearby. He must have come to my same conclusion to go straight for the nearest city to Nightfall. I search for him in the havoc, but how can I find anyone in this web of disarray?

A group of tar-colored threads poke out from an alley and slither like vipers towards the Imperials and their allies.

Hellano.

This is his element, of course he would make a dramatic entrance.

Before his shadows can reach the feral with beetle wings, her victim rears back and elbows her in the nose. The angel staggers, and the innocent man fights his pain with agonizing wails. The gaping wound in his ribs is clear from where I stand. Every movement is an incredible test of strength.

A few wide strides from Hellano, I spot a specter in the crowd. Someone nearly forgotten.

Ivan.

Mousy hair is freckled with fallen flakes. Brown eyes are too far to clearly see, but I know they are there. Kysi ditched his crown and used a default disguise to avoid drawing attention to himself. Smart.

A stark contrast from my shadow-wielding husband.

My breath hitches as Kysi—or rather, Ivan—ducks under the swinging fist of an Imperial. Once my mate recovers, he does not retaliate. Why?

Another jab leaves the Heartian King rolling to evade. His attention jerks not at his attacker but the wounded civilian, who grips a shard of glass in both hands and drives it into the beetle-winged woman.

Then, Kysi releases him and searches for another. Ivan's gaze surveys the area. I follow his line of sight to a woman on the corner. Her limbs have a mind of their own, warding off a fur-covered demon with a kitchen knife. Again, the Heartian King avoids another blow and quickly recovers. He constantly scans his surroundings, taking hold of any human in need.

The god of Mortals and Bargaining does not fight one battle ... he fights over half a dozen.

I alarm my children, and the animals hear my call to aid. Their imprints swell and shrink in waves. Birds swoop from their private nestles. Canines come out of hideaways—pets most likely. Ferals have no reason to go after them now that humans are a target. I can take advantage of that while I figure out a way down—

The imperial determined to kill Kysi tenses as if electricity is burrowed into their veins. They fall to reveal Luther behind them, who continues to prowl through the carnage unafraid. Fingers drift upon the napes of necks until recipients of his raw agony seize and drop, then onward he goes to the next.

Our group alone is powerful enough to take out a small army, but the city is *infested*. Our energy will eventually wane.

A high-pitched cry whips me around. I rush to the other end of the deck and lean over the railing. Auburn curls soar behind a fleeing child. A girl—the one I danced with at the Spring Festival—runs from a feral demon. His hood covers a hairless head. Features are sharp. There is not a shred of morality in his eyes.

An empty trellis hugs the stone beneath me. The wood is dry from the cold but if it holds me, I can make it to the girl.

I swing a foot over the deck and wedge it in a diamond-shaped hole. It bears okay. Bringing my other leg down, I dare a glance to see the girl scampering into an alley. The tameless man closes in.

Crawlers in my jumpsuit reach for the trellis to distribute my weight more evenly and speed the downward climb. The ground crunches under my boots, and I rush for the child.

Adrenaline is a breaking dam. Getting across the busy road is like running through racing traffic. I sidestep lunging shoulders and swinging blades to progress. The atmosphere seems to push against me as it does in nightmares when trying to escape something. It has been at least ten seconds since I lost sight of the girl. Worry knots between my collar bones.

I break into the alley and spot the demon hunched over near a bench. His hood has fallen back. Dozens of red droplets are inked into his bald skin, showering him in illustrious blood.

Gods, this man is fucking ruthless.

Senses spread to the bramble Harlynn weaved into my clothes. I diagonally slice my hand from top to bottom. Thorns break away and gather in the air as they split the space and puncture his right ear. Some imbed into his neck, but hey, we can't all be perfect.

The feral falls back and palms the injury. A trail of blood cascades down the end of his jaw. It beads identical to the designs on his bare head.

With a narrow gaze, my strides eat the distance. I raise a calm fist next, knuckles facing my target. Fingers flick open and tendrils bolt from my sleeve.

I won't bother the dogs with this one. I have him all on my own.

His expression transitions from shock to horror. His right hand is covered in silky red that leaves prints in the snow as he scurries backwards. It must be a scary sight—green tentacles coming for you.

Hardly different from Hellano's power ... just a lighter shade, really.

Killing comes easy when it gives others the right to live. My frightened prey swats at the growth, but his thumb gets caught in its hungry mouth. Reddish lips tremble over serrated teeth. He pulls his arm back to no avail. Hooked.

Vines press up and circle his head. I squeeze them over his skull, weaving tighter and tighter to trap out oxygen. Once the man stops flailing, ramblers shrink from his lifeless face.

The girl. She must be terrified—

The sparkle in her vacant eyes dies as the clouds veil the sun. He went for her jugular ... and got it. Poured blood melts ice. She wears purple pajamas with a chain-link pattern around the hems. Awoken by war in a heaven I created.

The dead demon left an indent in the ground where I kneel. Guilt is what brings me down. It is what wipes crimson from her cheek and gently closes her eyes. I am unaware if she would have grown up in this realm ... Now she will never have the chance to.

"Drayxi was stubborn," a voice calls into the alley.

Lilliana stands with the god of Wisdom at her side. Daylight loses a battle with the clouds above them. Her cloak catches in a breeze.

"I always hated that about him ... but he was *necessary*." Her sharp-edged tone wavers, "They were *all* necessary."

Words hitch in my throat. There are a million apologies to give and a million more arguments to counter with. Death was no concept to her. Its abrupt presence was traumatizing. She loved the Nine.

This is not about corruption. It is about revenge.

My predecessor steps forward.

Cato's loose tunic flags in the freezing current. His feet are planted, but the subtle urgency in his clenched jaw tells me that he is clawing at the cage of his body to escape.

My attention fuses with Lilliana's as I rise. "Look at how many lives you've taken. Look at this *child!*" My rigid index points to the tiny corpse.

She looks at me still and ambles onward. "Their lives are specks on a timeline my council held together. Our loyalty was to the eternal flame. You didn't just kill them. You killed *it.*"

"I *freed* it!" I raise a hand against her oncoming proximity. The ivy around my wrist hits a barrier an inch from my fingers. Something is holding it back, perhaps the worsening storm? I look up from the confusion, but not fast enough to stop her tight fist from barreling into my stomach. A sharp ache blooms from the point of injury.

"The Sky Spirits were a watchful eye on our universe," she seethes.

Boots pack the fresh bed of snow as she circles around me. Every time I blink, I find myself back in the bunker. In my prison. Surrounded by Priscilla's spiraling interrogations. Throbbing. Always sore.

"You closed it." Pressure shoves the back of my head into her lifted knee. A crack sounds. My eyes water and knees buckle.

Drip, drip, drip, goes my blood on the ice. Just like the leak in my old cell.

Lilliana speaks further. "One does not stay balanced on a tipping scale by remaining stagnant. They lean *against* it. When the universe tilts—and it *always* does—they are what kept it from spinning entirely. But the Spirits of the Sky cannot be wholly controlled. Every ritual had to be carefully executed," she explains before my kidney explodes with a blow from her boot.

A lean foxhound senses my danger and races into the passage. His tri-colored tail does not sway. The dog halts three yards away. He remains silent and does not charge my assailant, just cambers his head.

Please, I beg the canine. Nothing.

An amused laugh rolls Lilliana's shoulders. "They can't attack me! I am *you*."

The dog recognizes her soul. Sees it as my own.

I will myself to rise against the wind's pressure. Cato wrings his neck and shifts weight on either foot. Past him and into the murderous main street, a fallen sword lays in the road. I am not skilled with a blade, but it is better than nothing.

"You are *nothing* like me." Pivoting away, I break into a run for the weapon. I am a single lunge out of the alley when Cato releases an anguished cry that gets cut off. Instinct spins me around to check on him, but he is not there.

The ground is a rug pulled from under my feet. My back hits first, and the impact rattles my skeleton. Cato hovers above, lips drained of color. Metal clatters stone as he kicks the sword away.

Wrestling bodies fight to the death around us. Some take to the skies, where only one will come down alive. Lilliana walks out of the alley with the upmost patience. Disappointment dulls her tone. "Running from phasers is useless, daughter. You should know that."

Her round-toed shoe reels back and meets my temple. Hot pain cuts behind my eyes. A ringing sound vibrates my ears. Stars dance in the borders of my vision as Lilliana drops over me. Elbows locked, she wraps two frigid hands around my throat and squeezes.

I slam my fists into the creases of her arms, but they are as solid as iron. Air is sucked from my chest. Cato grips the back of his head and paces to the side. Failure lines the worried creases in his face. His mouth moves in whispers lost to the carnage—the same syllables he silently spoke in the private library earlier ...

A Victor's Demise. A Victor's Demise. A Victor's Demise.

The riddle ... It wasn't an expression of hatred—Cato was trying to warn me.

Like bargains are tricky, so is his forced loyalty to Lilliana. The god of Wisdom is unable to do anything in blatant contrast to her, but it seems his freedom lies in subtle messages. Small things with improbable success.

Cato must have believed I would not find the clue. By chance I did, it was expected to be misunderstood. Because I did not catch on to the riddle, Lilliana lacked concern. She kept a permanent eye on Cato after the Spring Festival to ensure no other hints would be left.

My captured friend marked a pebble and threw it into a forlorn lake, hoping I would somehow find it.

Bow-shaped lips form a tight line above me. I claw at Lilliana's velvet cloak with purple-tipped fingers. Tangle them in her hair.

Reach for her jaw and press against it with what strength my weakening muscles will allow.

·

Friend turned foe
Through blue waves of woe

·

"Like a mother-daughter bond, your past lives care about you," Kysi had said so long ago.

Not unconditionally, I have proven.

Divine Duplicity is far. My lungs are already burning. What choice do I have but to go after it? It matters none how low my chances of success are. If it is my only one, I will take it every time.

An inferno rages beneath my breastbone. I sink away from myself as she snarls in my face. The veil is a seed in the void of my mind. Distant.

I lunge for it.

All my decisions and experiences have led me to this ultimate test.

·

Fear the falling snow, as it does the thaw

·

A sense of calm acceptance caresses my being. Death does not scare me. If I fall victim to Hellano's essence, I know it will cradle me in its lake of nothing. A comfortable rest. Knowing this, my legs hurtle forward anyway.

The blaze above my diaphragm travels to my rushing legs. The entrance to Beginnings grows ahead. I can hear it from here, beautiful birdsong and the crackling of frost against a new sunny day.

But I am slipping. Melting away. Black strands lift from my messy updo on the journey to Divine Duplicity, as if the atmosphere is charged with static. They fall away in onyx waves. My skin drains color with every swing of my arms as I sprint towards the finish line. The veil is near ... but something is different about it.

I resist the impulse to stop and question when I see a figure between the open gates. Floating. Culminating. A fetus in a womb. My successor.

Brair, the goddess of Beginnings after me ... she is forming.

And I am falling apart.

Holes are punctured in the fabric of my being, plummeting through the floor under me and dropping from the sky above her. In a few heartbeats, I shall collapse on the welcome mat of my savior's domain.

My legs give out at the door ... I tumble inside.

Sweltering air awakens my nerves. Abstract symbols crowd me, more than I have ever seen. New life must be forged with a gentle hand, but I have no time for second guessing.

My skin pebbles against a grand awareness. Formulas combine in areas I do not touch, almost as if someone else is helping me solve them—using my soul as a conduit to create. That cannot be right. It is impossible ...

Unless the Sky Spirits no longer sleep.

When the idea reaches my thoughts, I know it to be true. What else would wake them, if not the internal struggle of their most important creation? The *Soul of Life* is at war with itself.

They effortlessly sort through the blueprint I laid. I step back in awe as a gargantuan imprint forms. Something is different about this one ... the Sky Spirits leave it with a piece of themselves—a gift.

Then, the Spirits of the Sky extend an outstretched finger and graze the imprint's surface. The brief touch shatters it into thousands of pieces that spread among the others.

Not just a new life ... a new *species*.

Minutes without oxygen have weakened my limbs, but it is the holes in my soul that make them unresponsive. I cannot move. I am too weak to settle the imprints and bring the beings into existence. Reincarnation is a creaky bridge between two cliffs, and I am teetering on the last cracked board.

So, grasping the last piece of myself before it falls away ... I take the leap and blink into the sky.

·

For useless is a bite from a frozen maw

·

Light streaks in comets of orange that erupt behind Lilliana's head. They are chased by a trail of black that turns falling snowflakes into ash. A dark wingspan opens on either side of my Soul Mother's skull. Larger it grows around her head, vast and wide. The color of soot.

The temperature rises.

Soldiers from all sides stumble away and grant us a wide birth. Lilliana slightly lets up on my throat to investigate. A straw of oxygen cuts through.

She turns to witness the commotion. Steam blooms from her backside as the wings close in, shading us with its silhouette. Terror has no time to reach her face before a monstrous mouth opens above us. A wave of heat burns a million tiny embers into my jumpsuit. Threads of lilac-twisted hair fall away from my braid, taking with it flowers of fire.

Lilliana is plucked from above me, and the cloudy sky greets me between disheveled buildings.

Behind the curtain of Divine Duplicity, fragments of myself fall away from Brair. Her body fades like the wind over sand and I am rained down upon and filled once again.

A strong grip encompasses my limbs and pulls me from the patch of melted snow. Cato helps me stand on wobbling knees. He breathes like he has been running for miles, released from the shackles of Lilliana's will.

There are no words. No warm embraces of victory or shouts of cheer. We are caught in the magnificent and horrifying wonder of a new animal race.

Air—sweet, precious air—extinguishes the flames in my chest. I do not wish to hear Lilliana cracking against two rows of fangs, so massive and sharp they would make a feral's mouth pale. It tremors the marrow in my bones to listen to gargles of blood suffocating her screams. But I cannot look away.

An enormous cranium armed with thick, leathery skin swivels in my direction. A row of horns snakes from both nostrils and ascends the cheekbones, passing sinister eyes and protruding from the skull.

Scales flare over a bulbous chest as the beast inhales. Crimson drips from a deadly jaw to talons jutting out of webbed feet. If the creature were to lift its slithery neck, it would easily be able to peek through third story windows into bedrooms and living spaces.

A rush of unease floods through me when the monstrous reptile levels its gaze. It does not respond to my fear like other animals would.

There is only one way this creature could devour my earliest predecessor—or any of them for that matter—and that is if it does not possess a biological obligation to serve and protect my soul.

What a gift the Sky Spirits left behind ... Fire is wild. Untamed. It has no master.

Dragons act on their *own* accord.

Which means their trust is not freely given; I must earn it.

I move a shaking leg, and Cato's grasp on my arm tightens. Concern etches into the lines of his features. Am I terrified? To death, but I keep my expression calm and nod for him to let me go.

It is difficult to walk. Still recuperating from the lack of oxygen, my muscles struggle to obey. A pounding headache pushes against my eyebrows from Lilliana's boot. Blood from my nose streaks my face, but the dragon's scalding breaths instantly dry it. Something between a purr and a growl rumbles behind its forked tongue.

I halt in front of electric-purple eyes that sparkle from the parting clouds above. They blink horizontally, observing. Waiting.

Inches from the apex of its nose, I lift my hand and dance a flame across my fingers. Empty pupils follow the drop of fire.

I reach for our connection. *You come from me and belong to yourself, just like your siblings in nature. If I ever go back on this word* ... Remnants of my past life stain its viscous maw. *Take me no differently than her.*

A stern huff spirals loose hair around the plait on my head. I crane my neck as the serpent rises to a staggering height and looms above, incredulously staring.

War rages in other parts of the city, but this pocket of the Row is dead silent. Soldiers from the kingdoms, the city, and the mountains do not dare move and risk drawing the beast's attention.

A cognizant wave undulates through soundwaves in the pit of its—no, *her* throat ...

"*Walk,*" the dragon speaks aloud.

Against hollering logic, I take the first leap of trust by turning my back to the creature and limp through the carnage.

Stone trembles underfoot as the serpent marches behind me. Past fallen soldiers and around corners, those swinging their blades become captured by our entrance through the streets. Slowly, each step we take quiets the chaos. Together, the dragon and I are medicine through the infected veins of war.

The center theater in the Row opens to a broad battleground. I spot my lovers. My friends. They are there, holding their own and cleansing the unjust space around them. Hellano's arms are sleeved in black clouds as he controls many ropes of shadow. Kysi, who isn't Kysi, stands between a mortal and a feral. Agony is a vixen with Luther's lovestruck heart; he practically dances amidst enemy bodies. And Harlynn has picked up a fallen sword ...

She fights for us.

One by one, individuals swing focus to the beast. To me.

The dragon's breath is a hot gust against my backside. Appearing broken and beaten, I continue through the destruction.

Swallowing pains my throat, and bruises have likely formed over the mark of the wed. My outfit is burned and disorderly, but the crown remains intact.

I rise upon the very stage that divided my kingdom. Talons crack an alabaster pillar as the dragon uses it to step on the top of the structure. It groans against her weight. Then, it is silent save for the whispering wind that spirals specks of ash.

All gape in wonder.

Hundreds of eyes do not frighten me now. Not like before, when the genuineness of my reign was clouded by secrets. Now, I stand before them as I am. Mother Nature. The goddess of Beginnings. Guardian of the New World.

It was *my* power that forged the beast looming above my head, staring them down. And it is *my* glare that freezes them in place.

Cato splits the forefront ... The trapped Imperial commander. He glances back at the soldiers who fight for the wrong side. Priscilla's death must have forced the god of Wisdom to reveal himself, because the looks on their faces tells me they recognize him. They remember his endless eyes.

My friend sees them and ponders. What is there to say? How would one shorten a grand explanation into a speech for those who have just lost friends and comrades? To be loyal to someone ... only to learn they were never truly on your side.

Pulling his gaze from the motionless army, two white voids magnetize to me. Then ... the god of Wisdom kneels.

Harlynn breaks free from the crowd. Blood and dirt are matted into her tight ponytail, but she appears unharmed. Her sword hits the frosted field ... and she bends a knee as well.

Shadows shrink into Hellano's palms. His crown remains atop tangled red strands, and it points toward me when he lowers his head.

Ivan disappears to reveal my beloved Heartian King, and Kysi in his true form follows suit with the others.

A wave ensues. Clashing metal meets snow as opposing troops drop their weapons. Heartians. Celestians. Imperials and ferals. One by one, all armies stop and sink to the ground.

The war is over ...

All bow to the Ultimate Queen.

Epilogue

"A new treaty was forged between feral clans and the surrounding lands: no civilians shall set foot on tribal territory unless in search of death, and none shall descend from the peaks to feed upon innocent lives.

Groveheart's aid in the reconstruction of Revelry Row solidified their alliance with Celestia, and the two kingdoms happily coincide near the Capital where their kings reign aside one another. In the throne room of the grand palace, all royal seats have an occupant.

The dawn of the Dragon Age has emerged. The sun conquers the sky once more and shines down upon the lands with a smile. The New World is blanketed in its warmth and peace.

In place of snow ... is beautiful spring."

Cato closes the bundle of pages in the annex of the Ancient Library and feels the cover. On a shelf above the hammock in which he lay, a flexible wing takes the book from his gentle hand and places it amongst his collection of happy endings.

ACKNOWLEDGEMENTS

Thank you to the following people who have supported me throughout the creation of this book:

To my daughter, Scarlet: If it were not for your love of reading, I would never have found my passion for storytelling. Because of you, I did not just start reading and writing again; I found my own taste in music, fashion, and art. Through you, I found myself.

To my husband, Jack: You were the first person to support this book. Thank you for all the extra shifts you took with Scarlet, the meals you brought to my desk, the dishes you cleaned, and all the times you listened to me ramble about these characters when it was surely getting repetitive. One of the biggest things I admire about you is that you are a man of your word. So, when you told me my writing moved you, I took it to heart and kept going. I love you more than words can describe.

To my sister, Nina: If I were to explain the depths of my appreciation in full, it would likely be longer than this novel. I will do my best to condense my thanks but just know that there are not enough words in the world, nor time in the universe, to fully express them.

Writing this book was like running a marathon with obstacle courses. In a storm. Barefoot. I wanted to give up on many occasions, but every time I looked over, you were there. On every street and corner, you cheered the loudest. The moment I finished writing a chapter, your video responses would flood my notifications. Sometimes, they were the only motivation I had to keep going. As I cross the finish line you are the first person I see, already asking for chapter one of my next book. It is impossible to truly grasp the weight of your kind words and the impressions they made. Thank you for reading my book when I did not want to show it. Thank you for telling me that I have what it takes to become an author. Thank you for being my support. Thank you for being my big sister.

To my mom, Jennifer: Never once did you doubt me, even when I doubted myself. I love to see how proud you are to be the mother of a writer. You support me in all caps. Literally. Like, every message I get from you about my book is sent entirely with capitalizations. It is a jump scare every time, but it never fails to make my day. I love you, mom.

To my dad, Gary: If not for the days you babysit Scarlet so I can go to work, I would not be able to afford an editor, a cover artist, beta readers, and all that goes into becoming an indie author. I love you more than infinity plus infinity.

To the first person who read my work, Ruchi: You are the one and *only* person to have read my first draft. I am currently printing it off just to burn it. If not for your kind eyes on the pages, helpful feedback, and positive reinforcement, I may have shelved the project entirely. You helped me turn this book into a real novel. You are good at what you do, and I will always seek you out as one of my beta-readers.

To a fellow author friend, Molly Macabre: Thank you for referring me to your editor and supporting me through my writing journey. Me, a total stranger that happened to come across your social media page, was lucky enough to find a sweet soul like yourself to help me along my way. I will never forget your kindness.

To my editor, William J. Burkhardt: From you I did not just find a kickass editor, but a mentor and friend. Thank you for not just fixing all my incessant contractions, but the consistent positive reinforcement and motivations, the silly email sign-offs, and bringing me into the indie community. You're the man.

In no particular order, more friends and family: Sam, Callie, Kasey, Cory, Katelyn, Alanna, Layla, Cheyenne, David, Roshi, Max, Kayla, Jada, Autumn, Jodi, Jordy, Brennan, Anjelika, Bela—whether it was getting me out of my head for a night of video games, proofreading my work, or simply being cheerleaders, you all have helped me along the way. Nothing compares to the community I have with you all. I love you guys.

And lastly, to the reader: Wherever you are in the world, whatever path you walk in life, thank you for putting precious time into my book. Whether it was a pleasant distraction from your everyday struggles or a relaxing way to spend your afternoon, I hope you got something positive from my story. Until our next adventure, new friend.

Scene break icon: Icon Home, Flaticon.com